Lord of  t

Sooty Feathers
Book II

Also by David Craig

Sooty Feathers

1: Resurrection Men

The Bone King

Thorns of a Black Rose

Lord of the Hunt

Sooty Feathers
Book II

David Craig

Elsewhen Press

Lord of the Hunt
First published in Great Britain by Elsewhen Press, 2020
An imprint of Alnpete Limited

Elsewhen Press, PO Box 757, Dartford, Kent DA2 7TQ
www.elsewhen.press
British Library Cataloguing in Publication Data.
A catalogue record for this book is available from the British Library.
ISBN 978-1-911409-76-2 Print edition
ISBN 978-1-911409-66-3 eBook edition

Printed and bound by CPI Group (UK) Ltd, Croydon, CR0 4YY

Dedicated with love to my Mum, Christine Thomas.
In thanks for forty years of love and support.

Glossary

Grigori: One of two hundred rebel angels, Lucifer among them, who survived his failed insurrection. Exiled to Earth a long time ago, they manifested as the first vampires. Unknown if there are any *Grigori* still in existence.

Ghoul: The first stage of undeath. A ghoul is Made when a human dies within a day and night of drinking a vampire's blood.

Nephilim: A vampire. What a ghoul transitions into, either within three years, or after eating the heart of a *Nephilim*.

Elder Nephilim: An old and powerful vampire. A status either transitioned to after centuries, or attained by eating the heart of an *Elder Nephilim*.

Dominus Nephilim: What an *Elder Nephilim* becomes should they eat the heart of a *Grigori* or *Dominus Nephilim*. Very old, very strong and very rare. Perhaps only a score in existence.

Demon: A fallen angel. One of a hundred million angels who sided with Lucifer but fell during his failed insurrection. Exiled to Hell. A slain *Grigori* becomes a demon. Can only return to Earth if Summoned by a Demonist, Possessing a human vessel.

Demonist:	A magician who can Summon demons from Hell, placing them into a human vessel.
Necromancer:	A magician who can commune with the dead and control corpses.
Diviner:	A magician who can track certain objects, i.e find a person if in possession of some of their blood.
Scribe:	A magician who can tattoo spells onto customers.

Prologue

London 1556

"He burns tomorrow," the guard said with relish as he unlocked the cell. The prisoner's trial was also tomorrow, but that would be a mere formality before the public spectacle.

"I know," George Rannoch said, the long years since his death having smoothed the burr from his accent. Seoras of Rannoch Moor had been a son of northern Scotland; George Rannoch was a son of wherever he chose. A son of sorts to Erik Keel, the man beside him.

"Our testimony saw the prisoner arrested," Rannoch's companion added, his voice a rich drawl. Dark-haired and grey-skinned, he stood a few inches taller than most men, with a regal bearing any king would envy: Erik Keel, fallen angel and *Grigori*, an original vampyre. *My Lord and Master.*

The guard, a broad-faced brute of a man cursed with a pock-marked face, hesitated, suddenly wary. Rannoch could see him thinking, trying to recall everything he had said to the two men he had escorted into the dungeon. God knew, he had said a lot, inflicting a constant diatribe on them as he led them through the narrow stone corridors of the gaol. Had he said anything to suggest that he too was a heretic, a follower of the Reformation empowered by Queen Mary's mercurial father?

Rannoch honestly couldn't say, having ignored most of his rambling. Nor did he care. Lord Keel and his expedition were ultimately bound for Bucharest where an undead war raged, an opportunity to increase the House of Keel's foreign holdings.

The solid wooden door swung open, fouling the already pungent air. Rannoch ceased the breathing that he habitually continued to disguise his true nature.

The guard took a step forward to enter the cell. "I can–"

"Remain outside," Keel said, his tone brooking no argument. "Father George and I will question the prisoner, and his heresies are not for your ears." He cocked his head. "Are they?"

"No, yer Eminence," the guard muttered, hurrying several feet away from the cell door.

Rannoch suppressed a smile, knowing they need not fear the guard eavesdropping on their conversation with the prisoner. Rannoch wore a priest's robes, not that he had any right to them. He *had* been a monk, once. A century past. Keel wore the red robes of a cardinal.

Rannoch raised his lantern as he entered the cell, chasing back the night. The prisoner, a gaunt man in his middle-years with a thick mop of muddy-brown hair regarded them as he stood. Rannoch recognised a keen intellect in the green-flecked eyes that looked them up and down, showing curiosity rather than fear.

"Greetings," Rannoch said, speaking for his master.

"Two *Nephilim*. I'm honoured," the prisoner said with heavy irony. "Are you two the reason I'm here and not finishing my commissioned portrait of Lord Sussex?"

"You recognise us?" Keel asked.

"I've met many in my time."

"A pity they did not recognise what *you* are, necromancer." Rannoch didn't bother hiding his distaste for the warlock.

"Some did. Is that what I've been arrested for? Witchcraft?"

"No. They don't burn witches here. So, we accused you of heresy," Keel said.

The prisoner laughed. "You told them I'm a Protestant. Clever."

"You seem untroubled by your imminent burning," Keel observed.

The necromancer looked at Keel. "You're familiar … yes, I remember you now. A *Grigori*. Cannot recall your name though it may come to me."

"You know me? What I am?" Keel pressed. It was rare to see him taken by surprise. "Who are you?"

"Here and now, I'm Henry Norman, painter of some

renown. Honoured, even, to paint a portrait of Queen Mary. But my parents named me Khotep." Knowing eyes met Keel's. "A very long time ago in a land far from here."

"I remember you," Keel said after a long moment. Shaken, though Rannoch knew not why. He glanced briefly at Rannoch and spoke hesitantly in a foreign tongue beyond Rannoch's ken.

The necromancer replied in the same language. For a minute or two they talked, the words alien to Rannoch but their postures suggesting they negotiated.

"Agreed," Keel said in English. "I ensure a worthy candidate receives your phylactery, and should I require it, you will repay me with one year's service in the future."

"Agreed. I can depend on you?"

Keel looked insulted. "I gave you my word."

Rannoch was lost. They had gone to some effort to arrange the necromancer's execution, only for Keel to instead strike a bargain with him. *Why?*

Keel perhaps sensed Rannoch's confusion. "I will explain later, Rannoch. For now, we should leave."

"Try not to enjoy the spectacle too much, tomorrow," the necromancer said wryly.

"Spectacle?" Rannoch asked.

"I burn tomorrow. I hope it doesn't rain. That never helps," he said knowledgeably.

Chapter One

Glasgow June 1893

Jack Davies followed the lady through the streets of Glasgow, abandoning his pursuit of an inebriated gentleman. Why risk a fight when easier prey presented itself? The unsteadiness to her gait suggested that she too had partaken of drink earlier in the evening. It would explain her foolishness in walking the post-midnight streets alone.

A gas streetlight briefly illuminated her as she passed beneath it, revealing a full-length dark-red skirt, that flared out at the bottom, and a matching bodice. A blue woollen shawl hung from her shoulders, the late June heat making it an unneeded accessory.

The Thirst tightened its hold on Davies, so he decreased the distance between them lest the woman reach her destination or wave down a cabriolet. Anticipation gripped him; the summer months were always a trial for his kind this far north, the height of the season almost a famine if the Sooty Feathers proved inefficient in supplying their masters with victims. And this was not a good time for the secret society ruling Glasgow, fractured by death and treachery.

Midsummer. With the evening sun still lingering on the horizon until eleven o'clock, and rising sharply at four in the morning, he dared not hunt for more than four hours, despite using a nearby shop cellar as his Crypt. Twenty hours a day trapped in the concrete foundations of Bothwell Street. For the past few months he had sustained himself on the diseased blood of the homeless living on the streets, or the prostitutes forced to work them.

But here was a woman of means walking alone unchaperoned. A young woman, Davies noted as he closed the distance, with chestnut-coloured hair worn high beneath a small-brimmed hat. He fantasised about where she had been, about the fine foods and wines she may have consumed, a rich diet he would taste in her blood.

A veritable treat after a mean summer feeding from malnourished whores and vagrants, most soaked in bootlegged gin. Low in Regent Guillam's favour, Davies was used to summers lean in blood, and this summer had been lean indeed.

But not tonight. The young woman ignored a passing cabriolet, perhaps too miserly to pay the fare for a ride home. *Foolish lassie.*

She approached a lane and Davies quickened his pace, his leather soles scraping off the dry cobbles, sun-baked dung filling the gaps. *Now!*

He lunged, grabbing her collar with his left hand and pulling her sharply into the lane, throwing her roughly against a sandstone wall before she could cry out.

Jack Davies had been undead for almost fifty years and had seen every kind of fear reflected in the eyes of those he killed. There was fear in this young lassie's eyes, sure enough, but an expectant fear rather than that of surprise.

He Unveiled, opening his mouth to reveal incisor teeth lengthening to fangs, and saw her eyes widen. Something within whispered that there was recognition within those eyes as well as fear, but the Thirst was riding him hard, too hard to stop now. He ducked his head down towards her throat, eyes fixed on the rapidly beating carotid pulse, already tasting the thickly flowing blood within...

Something burned his mouth before his fangs could fasten on her throat, and he saw the glint of silver around her neck. *Bitch!*

He pulled a handkerchief from his pocket, reaching up to snatch the offending metal from her throat when a flash and thunder roared through his gut. Davies backed off a step, uncomprehending at first as agony roared deep within him. He looked down to see a small gun in the girl's left hand, a derringer.

Any belief Davies harboured of the girl being a random victim disappeared as the bullet burned within him, suggesting it was silver. A lone woman of means might carry a derringer for protection, but silver ammunition told him belatedly that tonight he was the hunted, not the hunter.

I'm not done yet! He lunged forwards, ready to tear the insolent bitch apart for causing him such pain, for *daring* to hunt a *Nephilim*. But she side-stepped and whipped fire across his face. Too late he saw the silver knife in her right hand. There was still fear in her eyes, but it was tempered to serve rather than hinder.

The blade flashed again, this time into his upper chest. Davies felt himself sink to the ground as his heart was cleaved in two…

I was promised eternity. Promised…

*

Kerry took a steadying breath and stared down at the undead lying before her, slain by the silver knife in her hand. She was all too aware that one misstep in the fight would have seen the vampyre tear her throat open and drain her dry, one more bloodless corpse for the Sooty Feather-ruled authorities to declare the result of an accident or dog mutilation. *But not tonight, you bastards.*

"Well done, Miss Knox," a voice said from the shadows. Kerry looked round to see her mentor step into the lane, wearing a long black dress.

"Thank you, Lady Delaney," Kerry said.

"Not the neatest kill, sloppy in places, but satisfactory none-the-less. *Successful* none-the-less." The sun and moon would rise and set together the day Lady Delaney passed a compliment unqualified by criticism.

"I'll do better with my *next* undead," Kerry said dryly, exaggerating her Irish drawl.

Lady Delaney gave her an amused look. "That would be well-advised. Next time ensure the bullet strikes the heart. Giving an undead time to respond will see you dead. They're stronger and more resilient."

"So you've told me."

"So remember." Lady Delaney gave her a tap on the head. "But to kill a vampyre is an impressive achievement, my dear, so take pride in it. Tempered with humility, of course."

"Aye." She had been staying in Lady Delaney's West End townhouse for the past few months, exchanging a life as a struggling actress for that of apprentice undead killer. Once, they had fought alongside the remnants of a Templar gang sent to Glasgow to end the undead threat, and three others like herself dragged into the age-old struggle.

The surviving two Templars had travelled to Edinburgh and never returned, a letter from Knight-Inquisitor Wolfgang Steiner confirming that he and the black American marksman Gray had been given duties elsewhere. A second letter from Steiner, post-marked London, advised that he had been thus far unsuccessful in persuading his superiors to give him more men and send him back to Glasgow to finish what he had started. Nine Templars had died under Steiner's command, not a loss to be ignored regardless of the victories achieved.

Their other three companions, Wilton Hunt, Tam Foley and Professor Sirk had remained estranged from the others since Steiner's shooting of Amy Newfield, a newly Made ghoul briefly aiding them in their fight against George Rannoch. That fight had been won, but the group had fractured. Now Kerry and Lady Delaney fought the undead alone, using rumours of disappearances and deaths to locate likely undead hunting grounds. The long summer days and short nights forced the undead to remain mostly hidden, relying on their human servants to provide them with blood. Lady Delaney had proposed that they take advantage of the season to thwart Sooty Feather activity where possible.

At night they walked the streets and slew any undead foolish enough to think a woman alone was easy bait. Lady Delaney had effortlessly dispatched the first three undead to fall into their trap. Tonight was Kerry's first time as bait and executioner.

By day Lady Delaney trained her to fight with guns, knives and her bare hands. And the intricate rules of etiquette governing high society. The Sooty Feather Society counted many powerful men and women among its members, and Kerry would need to play the part of young socialite if she were to infiltrate that circle. *Learning manners and murder, so I am.*

"I suggest we leave, in case your late stalker has friends," Lady Delaney said pointedly, ending Kerry's introspection. She filled a small glass vial with some of the vampyre's blood.

Kerry smiled brightly. "As you say, Lady Delaney. The streets aren't safe for two women without a gentlemanly escort."

*

Kerry opened her eyes, a restless night leaving her tired. She had slept in this bedroom ever since Wolfgang Steiner had brought her to Lady Delaney's townhouse, delivering her into a world of undead and demons. A worn tartan carpet of green and brown covered the floor, the wallpaper a blend of orange and white flowers. She had gleaned a little of Lady Delaney's history, enough to suspect this room had once hosted one of her late sons.

Twenty years earlier the Sooty Feather Society had recruited Sir Andrew Delaney, intending to make use of his varied business interests. On learning the truth of the secret society's masters, he had tried to get out; the Sooty Feathers possessed him with a demon called *Beliel* to retain control of his businesses.

Beliel had been unstable, killing the Delaney children and torturing Lady Delaney. Lady Delaney had in turn killed her husband's body, sending the demon back to Hell. Since then she had opposed the undead where possible, and Kerry was resolved to join her cause.

For the past few months Lady Delaney had tutored her. Kerry wasn't sure what she offered in return; companionship, maybe? An heir to her forlorn, lonely quest to chase the night?

She dressed, wearing a bright blue day dress, and went downstairs to break her fast. Lady Delany's maid, Ellison, had a bowl of porridge waiting for her. Lady Delaney was already seated at the dining room table eating eggs.

"Morning," Kerry said as she sat at the table.

"Morning, my dear," Lady Delaney said easily. "Recovered from last night?"

"Aye, recovered," Kerry said, with questionable veracity.

"Excellent. I think you've earned a small treat."

Lady Delaney's last 'treat' had left her facing a vampyre alone, so she decided to temper her enthusiasm.

A cabriolet took them to High Street, the oldest part of

Glasgow, now a festering hole of overcrowded misery filled with squalid slums and ramshackle gin shops. Kerry was no stranger to poverty, born and raised in nearby Duke Street, but many of the crumbling tenements here made her childhood home look almost affluent.

They walked swiftly through the narrow sunless wynds that grudgingly separated the maze of buildings, ignoring the feral children that haunted the rookery, gaunt and pale. Hard-faced men sat slumped on the ground, watching them pass through narrowed eyes, drinking bootleg gin that might see them dead or blind.

In other slums, two women travelling unescorted could expect to be accosted, but the footpads here stayed in the shadows and let them pass. They were well aware where Kerry and Lady Delaney were going and knew better than to hinder their passage.

A crumbling arch led Kerry and Lady Delaney down a flight of stone steps that took them beneath the stone railway bridge concealed amidst the slum. Men and women from every class were present, browsing the stalls and tents located within. Tenement houses and dark-windowed shops leaned against the bridge, cracked mossy cobbles running underneath.

"Welcome to the Under-Market," Lady Delaney said.

Kerry recalled what Lady Delaney had told her about the market hidden beneath the bridge, serving as the hub for Glasgow's magician community. The undead and the Sooty Feathers found many of the magical talents useful to them, tolerating the community so long as they caused no trouble. Necromancers were an exception, condemned to burn without exception. Even the undead found some things too much to stomach. Or maybe animating the dead struck too closely to home, and they feared their once-mortal flesh falling under a necromancer's control, turned into a puppet on strings.

One of the houses was a burned-out shell, the handiwork of Steiner and his Templars upon learning the undead used it as a Crypt. The Templars had found a score of ghouls within that house and the cellars below. Newly Made undead began as such, mindless and feral when deprived of blood, so the vampyres kept them off the streets in Crypts like that derelict house. If a ghoul survived, a few years would see it transition into a vampyre, able to extend incisor teeth into fangs, gaining better self-control and the ability to manipulate memories through Mesmerisation.

"Come," Lady Delaney said as she continued deeper into the market. Cages containing dogs, cats, birds and rats were piled up on top of and beside one stall, a roughly scrawled sign stating, 'Familyers'. Lady Delaney hadn't told her much of magic; perhaps she didn't know much.

Kerry spotted a shabby-looking man leaning against a wall, holding a sign identifying himself as a Diviner. She felt a jolt of recognition. "Look, it's Jimmy Keane," she said quietly to Lady Delaney.

"It is indeed." Lady Delaney didn't slow. Evidently her business was elsewhere in the market.

Keane was a man who could find certain things. A sample of Sir Arthur Williamson's blood had allowed him to lead Lady Delaney and her erstwhile allies to a gathering on the Necropolis where the Elder vampyre George Rannoch planned to Summon the demons *Arakiel* and *Beliel*. They had arrived too late to prevent the summoning of *Arakiel*, but they had succeeded in killing Rannoch and rescuing Steiner before he became a Vessel for *Beliel*.

Lady Delaney stopped at a small stall sitting in an out of the way corner. Jars lay on top, some containing different coloured inks, others containing a thick dark-red liquid Kerry took for blood. A man wearing patched trousers and a coat sat on a rickety wooden chair, grey in his hair and beard.

"Morning, ladies," he said, removing his flat cap. "I'm Ben Gould. What can I do for you?"

"Morning, Mr Gould. My young companion is looking for a tattoo ... a special one, the same as the one you did for me some years before."

A look of alarmed recognition passed Gould's face. "You ... I was younger, then, and reckless," he muttered as he ran a hand through his beard. "I've not done one of those in years."

"I'll pay you well, like before," Lady Delaney said in a firm tone. A tone that suggested she would not be taking no for an answer.

"If the Sooty Feathers or the undead learn I'm inscribing *that*, they'll kill me. Anyway, that glyph needs ... an ingredient I don't have," Gould said with a hint of defiance.

But Lady Delaney just nodded. "Vampyre blood." She pulled out the vial containing blood from the undead Kerry had killed last night, as well as several bank notes.

Gould stared at the blood and money, his face a battleground between greed and fear. "I'll do it," he finally muttered, the former winning the day. He stood up and took the vial from Lady Delaney, glancing at Kerry. "You, sit in the chair. I want this to be quick."

"You're getting me a tattoo?" Kerry asked Lady Delaney, confused. Gould was clearly a Scribe, a magician capable of tattooing certain spells onto people with needle, ink and blood.

"Take off your jacket and roll up your left sleeve," Gould said as Kerry sat in the chair. She obliged while Gould poured some ink into a small jar, mixing in the vampyre blood. "I'll need some of your blood, too."

"It will protect you from Mesmerisation," Lady Delaney said.

"I've got that trinket you gave me," Kerry objected, flinching as Gould drew some of her blood with a needle, mixing it with the ink and vampyre blood.

"And if you lose it? One can't lose a tattoo."

"Unless one loses one's arm," Kerry muttered.

"It's a small tattoo, an open eye," Gould said, looking furtively around. "Won't take long. Thank God."

Kerry watched as Gould began his work, dipping the needle into the mix of ink and blood. She tensed as he raised the needle to her upper left bicep and began to tattoo in the glyph. *This'll bloody hurt!*

Chapter Two

Foley blew out a breath as the carriage came to a halt. "Have we arrived? My arse is killing me."

"Sorry, Foley, I'll hire a more comfortable carriage next time," Hunt said with a roll of his eyes. "One with thick cushions for your sensitive posterior." There was a thud as the driver jumped down to the ground, and the door opened a moment later.

"We've arrived, sirs," the driver said. He wore a black jacket, trousers and top hat. Hunt and Foley had taken the train from Glasgow to Crianlarich, hiring a carriage to take them to an inn for the night, planning to return to the railway station in the morning. From there they would travel by train to Oban.

"Thank you." Hunt climbed out of the carriage and took a deep breath, the clean country air evoking ambivalent feelings. The last time he had been in this part of the country, Amelie Gerrard and her family were murdered and he had been kidnapped by George Rannoch. Thinking of Amelie brought back a familiar pang of guilt. She had only died because of her association with him, because she had the misfortune to court a man who caught the eye of the Sooty Feather Society.

Still, that had been on the east side of Loch Lomond, and they were on the west side. Located just north of the loch, the Drover's Inn had been around since the early 1700's, a resting place for Highland drovers moving their herds to the southern cattle markets.

Looking at it, Hunt could well believe its age. Standing three storeys tall, the venerable inn was built from grey stones of every shape and size that issued a dull gleam in the evening sun. A wall of steep hills rose up from the fields behind it, a waterfall near the top spilling over into the valley below.

Foley whistled. "Impressive."

"Yes." Foley had questioned why they were travelling all the way to the Drover's Inn when there were inns and hotels closer to Crianlarich. Hunt trusted that question was now answered.

"Let's hope the ale and whisky are equally impressive."

Hunt smiled as they entered the inn. Foley never changed. After recent events, that was a comfort.

The foyer was painted white to offset the general gloom owing to small windows. An assortment of animal heads hung from the walls, and a musket was nailed over the taproom door. The reception desk occupied a far corner, a young woman waiting expectantly, perhaps the innkeeper's daughter.

"Afternoon, I've got two rooms booked here," Hunt said.

The young woman looked down at the leather-bound ledger. "Under what names, sir?"

"Hunt and Foley."

She flicked back a few pages. "Yes … two rooms. Enjoy your stay."

Dusty old paintings decorated the walls, depicting romanticised Highland scenes of rugged moorland, snow-capped mountains, and cattle and drovers. Their rooms were one floor up, the brittle wooden stairs creaking under their weight as they climbed up. He and Foley carried a small trunk upstairs, containing enough clothes for their overnight stay. Their larger trunks were to be secured in the inn's strong-room.

"After we've eaten, how about we go for a walk?" Hunt suggested. The summer had been a rare one, and he was eager to explore Inverarnan now that he was blessedly away from the city.

"Sounds a grand idea," Foley said to Hunt's pleasant surprise. He had half-expected his friend to want to spend the whole night sitting by the bar. "And afterwards, we can have a drink or two."

Hunt changed into brown tweed trousers, a Norfolk coat and brown leather shoes, content that the Drover's Inn's rustic clientele meant there was no need to dress formally. It saved him from changing after dinner, the clothing suitable for a walk in the country. The sweltering summer heat had led to Hunt favouring a straw boater hat instead of his bowler hat, which Foley disdained in favour of a paisley flat cap.

"Well, if it isn't the Honourable Mr Hunt," Foley observed from the foyer as Hunt descended the stairs. He too wore tweed, albeit a cheaper cut than Hunt's. "Should I bow?"

"Absolutely," Hunt said with a straight face. His great-uncle's recent death had come as no surprise given his age and health, leading to Hunt's father Lewis becoming the 6th Baron Ashwood, and Wilton Hunt the Heir Apparent. The new Lord and Lady Ashwood had travelled up to the family estate a week prior.

Foley had found the whole situation amusing. Not that Hunt expected much change in his circumstances. The 3rd Baron had died childless after losing most of the estate's lands and money, his cousin – Hunt's great-grandfather – inheriting precious little. Hunt's immediate family's wealth was thanks entirely to his mother inheriting the Browning Shipping Company, which she ruled with an iron fist. Hunt's father had defied expectations by maintaining his career in Law while his wife managed the company.

Needless to say, she had been entirely unimpressed with her son's decision to forsake both Law and the family business to study the natural sciences. That decision had seen him rent Foley's spare room and embark upon a nocturnal career as a body snatcher.

Which lasted until not long after one of their exhumed corpses, a newly Made ghoul called Amy Newfield, disappeared on them. Hunt and Foley's investigation had led to revelation and tragedy, and ultimately an uneasy agreement with the Elder *Nephilim* Margot Guillam. In exchange for killing George Rannoch, she had agreed to leave them be.

Still, Hunt had somewhat mended fences with his parents, and Miss Guillam had graciously refrained from having them murdered. A quiet life was all he wanted now. Great-Uncle Thomas's death was sad, but Hunt would be lying if he felt any real grief over it. His parents were now tidying up the late lord's affairs and had invited Hunt to spend the month with them. He had agreed, in turn inviting Tam Foley to accompany him.

Foley had readily accepted, asking Professor Sirk to run the Foley Pharmacy in his absence. Hunt privately suspected the eccentric professor would do a better job than its indifferent owner.

The Drover's Inn's taproom was long but cosy, old Highland broadswords, claymores and tartans hanging from the walls and ceiling. The bar ran about two-thirds the length of the room, supervised by a stout man with curled red hair and a ragged beard. A fireplace waited at the end, swept clean and unlit. Summer had been consistently hot and dry this year, rare in a land infamous for its wet weather.

A wooden bench ran along the front wall, with rough wooden tables placed along it. The floor was stone, slippery in places from spilled drink. There was a pleasant smell in the room; a blend of ale, cooking food, old wood, and tobacco smoke. Hunt and Foley took it all in, then approached the bar.

"Evening, gentlemen," the bartender said with a nod. He had the look of a man well able to handle any drunks who became belligerent. "I'm Owen Dale, the innkeeper."

"Evening," Hunt said. "My friend and I are looking for supper and a drink."

"There's mutton or beef, with potatoes and carrots," Dale said.

Hunt and Foley exchanged looks, breakfast seeming a long time ago. "I'll have the mutton," Hunt said.

"The beef for me," said Foley.

"As you wish, gents. And to wash it down?"

"Two pints of ale," Foley requested.

The taproom was fairly busy, maybe half of those within being guests of the inn, the rest local farmhands visiting for an ale after a hard day's labour in sun-beaten fields. The mood was good-natured, and Hunt soon found himself tucking into a plate of mutton and vegetables. It was filling if unspectacular, but after a day of travelling he found himself devouring it with gusto. The ale tasted strong but not too bitter.

He and Foley relaxed, sipping their drinks and letting the din of conversation wash over them.

"Thanks for inviting me, Hunt," Foley said. A look of concern creased his face. "You're sure your parents won't mind me imposing on them?"

"Of course not." He waited until Foley was taking a sip of ale. "I told them you're my new valet."

"Bastard!" Foley said between coughs as he nearly choked.

Hunt grinned. "Is that any way to address the Honourable Mr Hunt of Ashwood?"

"If you want to see Ashwood, I suggest you mind your attitude, your Lordship," Foley mockingly warned.

"Don't worry, they know you're coming. Still game for a walk?" Hunt asked, knowing if they sat for much longer, they'd be settled for the night.

Foley emptied his mug. "Aye, why not? My legs could use a good stretch."

*

Fresh country smells assailed Foley as he followed Hunt across the field, sheep eyeing them warily. *Don't look at me, I had beef. He's the one who ate mutton.*

The long summer had left the ground dry, long grass swishing as they waded through it. Foley's brief army service had seen him in the Sudan and South Africa, but even the latter had failed to awe him like Scotland's rugged beauty. Steep hills rose up, a blend of greens and browns, the sunlit evening sky alive with birdsong. The chirping of crickets rose from the grass, interrupted by the occasional sheep.

The hills ahead reminded him of those at the back of Largs, but Foley knew better than to say so and dredge up memories of Dunclutha. Hunt had never fully recovered from his captivity, rescued from the home of his family's supposed friend, Sir Arthur Williamson. Physically, aye, but sometimes at night Foley heard muffled shouts coming from Hunt's bedroom.

Sir Arthur had been found dead in a lane several days after the battle in the Necropolis, Foley and Hunt speculating that he had likely been caught by Miss Guillam's people and made an example of, punishment for betraying the Sooty Feathers. But Foley still remembered Hunt's cold-blooded execution of Gerry Walker, the carriage driver who had shot Amelie Gerrard, a girl he'd briefly courted. Maybe Hunt had found Sir Arthur – but Foley doubted it. Regardless, no one would weep for him.

A stream lay ahead, fed from waterfalls in the hills above. They found a shallow rocky ford and used it to get across without wetting their feet, walking further north. Foley was content to let Hunt lead the way, reinvigorated by the clean air, a Godsend after so long in a city stinking of people and industry.

Sirk agreeing to run his pharmacy was a Godsend too, otherwise he would have been forced to decline Hunt's offer to travel north with him. *God, how I hate that damned shop!* He had inherited it from his late parents, finding it a millstone around his neck that threatened to drag him under. Maybe he should just sell it and move away from Glasgow, make a new life elsewhere. *And do what?*

And do what. He had no answer to that question. Fighting the undead had briefly enlivened him, like the action he'd seen in the army, but the melancholy that had haunted him his whole life had found him again, threatening to trap him within that goddamned bloody pharmacy. Maybe he could escape it in the north? Better than the bottle he'd been trying to hide in.

Onwards they walked, clambering over stone dykes and jumping streams, climbing the hills before them. Foley found himself breathing heavily as he followed Hunt up the slope, wondering if the younger man had a destination in mind, or just wanted to lose himself.

He turned, looking behind him to the west where the horizon flushed red and orange from the slowly setting sun. A pang of alarm went through him; if the sun was setting then it must be about ten, and the bar would soon close. Then he remembered where they were and smiled, reassured that the Drover's Inn would serve drinks for as long as it had customers upright at the bar.

A full moon was visible in the still-blue sky. "We should head back," Foley called out. "We don't want to be caught outside if the inn closes." *If the bar closes.*

Hunt turned, giving him a knowing look. "Don't worry, we've circled round. We're not too far."

Foley opened his mouth but before he could answer a howl rose up from nearby woods, long and eerie. "What the *hell* was that?" Hunt asked, squinting at the woods.

"A dog?" Foley suggested. Two more howls answered the first.

"Not wolves, surely?" Hunt asked, staring at the woods with a look of awakened fear on his face.

"The wolves in Britain were all killed off," Foley said. "It might be wild dogs." Not that a pack of wild dogs was an improvement on wolves. He had packed his old service revolver, not that it would do them much good lying within his trunk back at the inn.

"There…" Hunt pointed ahead. "Shit!"

Bile rose up in Foley's throat as he saw dark shapes break free from the woods, running in their direction. In South Africa he'd seen wild dogs chase down an impala and tear it apart.

"Do we run?" Hunt asked.

"No, we have to stand our ground." If they faced down the dogs, then *maybe* they wouldn't attack. One thing Foley knew for sure, running would surely doom them. Nothing attracted a predator like fleeing prey. "Make yourself look big and scary."

"I'm sure we'll terrify them," Hunt muttered as Foley spread his legs and straightened his back, spreading his arms.

Foley drew his pocket folding-knife, for whatever good it would do him. Hunt pulled out a derringer Foley hadn't realised his friend was carrying. "You'll only get one shot with that," he warned, "so be sure of your aim."

"I know," Hunt answered tersely as he extended his arm. The animals were closing. "They're bloody wolves."

"Wolves are extinct," Foley argued, not sounding particularly convincing even to himself. The beasts certainly looked like wolves, with pricked ears and large heads.

"Tell that to them!"

Chapter Three

Foley forced himself to stand his ground as the first wolf reached them, eyes glinting yellow as it bared its teeth. He silently prayed that Hunt's nerve held. If he moved, the wolves would be on them.

The three wolves circled, forcing them to stand back-to-back. *Is this how it ends? We survive the undead, only to be torn apart by bloody beasts?*

A sharp pain burned Foley's right ankle as he lost his balance, his foot falling through a hole in the ground, perhaps a rabbit hole. He pulled his foot free but before he could regain a solid footing, he was aware of a hairy dark blur flying at him.

He hit the ground, winded and stunned from the impact. Desperately he forced the wolf's head up as it went for his throat, feeling its hot breath on his face, drool dripping from snapping jaws.

Maddened yellow eyes glared at him, and it rolled its muzzle beneath his left arm and bit his lower bicep. Pain ripped through him as it dragged him away, his knife fallen and out of sight.

A *bang* echoed out, and the wolf released its hold on his arm and fell on him, thrashing weakly for a few seconds before going still. *Get up! Up!*

Foley pushed the dead beast off him, surprised by its weight. His knife lay a few feet away and he snatched it up before scrambling to his feet, in time to see Hunt desperately load another bullet into his derringer. While the second wolf bared its teeth at Hunt and Foley, the third nuzzled its dead packmate, issuing a low growl of outrage as it sniffed the wound. Foley sensed a change; the wolves had been intent on killing him and Hunt before, but now it seemed personal.

Both wolves hunched low, hate-filled eyes fixed on Hunt as they prepared to leap.

Hunt swung his gun back and forth between the two wolves, his own teeth bared. A chill descended over Foley despite the lingering summer heat, and the wolves backed off a few steps, one whimpering slightly. *A stand-off.* Whatever had spooked the wolves wasn't enough to chase them off, and if the men fled, instinct would drive the wolves to run them down.

A howl rose up the distance, full-throated, angry and commanding. *Oh God, there's more.* Foley looked around for any sign of the other wolves but saw nothing. Instead the surviving two gave Hunt one last baleful look and turned, loping off towards the trees.

"What the *hell* just happened," Foley breathed. Hunt shook his head and slowly lowered his gun. That oppressive chill left, reminding Foley of something, but of more immediate concern was his bitten arm, blood staining the grass. His ankle was tender from twisting it, perhaps the more serious problem if those wolves returned.

Hunt noticed it too. "Jesus! Are you okay? I mean, can you walk?" He tore off Foley's jacket sleeve and tied it above the wound to try and slow the bleeding.

"With some help, aye." He looked Hunt in the eye. "Good shot, you saved my life."

Hunt shrugged it off. "You can thank me later, let's get back to the inn before you bleed to death."

Aye, or before those wolves come back.

Hunt put his left arm under Foley's uninjured right shoulder and supported him as they fled back to the inn. The sky was slowly darkening, the full moon growing bright and silver as they reached a field. Light-headed from blood loss, Foley concentrated on keeping himself moving while Hunt frequently cast fearful looks back, but the wolves did not pursue.

They splashed across a stream, uncaring about soaking their feet, and soon reached the hardened dirt road that would lead them back to the Drover's Inn. Foley's arm felt on fire, and he realised blood loss was not the only risk. He'd seen men die from infected wounds before, burning up in a fever. Not a pleasant end. That a doctor might be able to stop the infection by taking his arm was not reassuring either. *Better to have let the beast rip out my throat.*

*

Hunt sat at the bar, a whisky glass clenched in his right hand. The innkeeper had sent his son to fetch the nearest doctor, but he lived several miles away. Fortunately for Foley, one of the guests was a nurse who cleaned his wound and stitched it. But infection was a risk with any wound, more so when caused by a wild animal's bite.

Foley had been given some broth and ale and was now resting in a room upstairs. *Wolves ... bloody wolves!* Not only had recent times seen them in mortal peril from supposedly mythical creatures such as vampyres and demons, but now beasts supposedly extinct from Britain threatened them. *What will we face next, Satan himself?*

Their brush with death had inspired much heated debate at the bar as other patrons offered their expert opinion on the matter, alcohol only fortifying their positions. Hunt had sipped his whisky (offered on the house for medicinal purposes, God bless Mr Dale), thankful that his hands had finally stopped shaking.

"Dogs," a brawny middle-aged man asserted. He wore a checked suit and waistcoat, evidently a local farmer. A barrelled gut and beefy face suggested he was a man of means, while his livelihood had left his arms and legs solid. He leaned on the bar and spoke with a condescending authority that set Hunt's teeth on edge.

"It was a wolf," Hunt said, his first comment in some time. A few of the other patrons seated at the bar gave him a surprised look. Perhaps they'd forgotten he was there.

"There aren't no wolves anymore, lad," the farmer said.

"I know dogs," said Hunt, ignoring the fact that he didn't, "and they were not dogs."

The farmer opened his mouth, his face reddening. The deference shown to him by the other locals told Hunt he was a man of some position in the area and not used to having his opinions challenged. Still on edge, Hunt suspected that was why he had spoken, to try and goad the arrogant arsehole into a fight.

Footsteps scraped against the stone floor. "Where's my patient?" a man said in a Stirlingshire accent. Hunt turned to see a youngish man with short black hair and a thick moustache, the latter perhaps to off-set his youthful appearance. He carried a brown leather bag Hunt assumed held the tools of his trade.

"Upstairs, Doctor," the innkeeper said, his voice betraying his relief at the doctor's arrival ending the argument before frayed tempers snapped into violence.

"I'll show you which room," Hunt said, slipping off his stool. Foley's wellbeing was more important than venting his frustrations at some loudmouth gentleman farmer.

"The injured man's your friend, aye? Dale's boy told me he was bit. By a dog, like?"

"A big dog," Hunt said, not wanting to distract the issue with the exact nature of the beast. "Thank you for coming out so late."

The doctor looked of an age with Hunt, not yet twenty-five, but he had a quiet confident manner that reassured Hunt. "I often get called out late. Farmers and their hands work all hours and injure themselves." He gave Hunt a cautious glance. "But I don't live off gratitude and fresh air, if you ken my meaning, like."

"I can pay you for your time," Hunt assured him. Barely. His father had given him some travelling money, helpful since Professor Miller's death at the undead Richard Canning's hands had left him an unemployed body snatcher living off his meagre savings. He and Foley had talked of trying to make a similar arrangement with Miller's replacement in the early autumn, but that would require a cautious approach.

Foley was either asleep or unconscious, and the doctor leaned over him and pulled the blanket back to examine his wound. "The wound was cleaned, aye?"

Hunt nodded. "A nurse attended to him on our return."

"Good. She did a fine job with his stitches, too, I'm pleased to say." He placed his hand on Foley's brow and frowned. "He may be burning up."

Cold tendrils of dread slid their way up Hunt's spine. "He has a fever?" That was the news he had feared. Wounds could be stitched, bones splinted, and the body could replace lost blood over time, but infections were a killer. Often slow and agonising.

"We'll see," was the doctor's non-answer. "I'll tend to him, you go back down to the bar."

Hunt was about to say he'd rather stay when he realised that perhaps the doctor would prefer to work without him looking over his shoulder. "Yes, Doctor. Thank you."

The conversation at the bar had moved on from the nature of the beasts to what should be done about them, a more pressing concern to men whose livelihood depended on the livestock grazing in the nearby fields.

"We should arm a few lads with shotguns and send them out to deal with these dogs," the farmer said. Hunt noted he had made no mention of taking part himself, despite much of the livestock no doubt being his property.

Most of the other patrons in the bar voiced their enthusiasm, emboldened by drink.

"Maybe the pack has already moved on," the innkeeper opined. "If they had been here a while, we'd have found sheep carcases."

"Some of my sheep do go missing," the farmer said.

"Aye," a farmhand agreed. "I work at McGeary's farm, and he's aye complaining of sheep going missing now and then."

The innkeeper waved it off. "Sheep will fall into gorges or be rustled by some thief or other, but if it was dogs, they'd leave a mess. Unless you're saying these dogs are burying what's left? Very thoughtful of 'em."

A smattering of laughter went around the bar. "Aye, maybe you're right, Dale," the farmer conceded. "Maybe those taking my sheep have two legs rather than four, but I'll pay a bounty on any dog's head brought to my door. A wild dog, mind."

"Hear, hear," a farmhand said amidst a rumble of throaty approbation.

"An ale," Hunt requested on catching the innkeeper's attention.

"How's your friend?" the innkeeper asked as Hunt left some coins on the bar.

"He's being examined now," Hunt said, making no mention of possible infection. He didn't want to risk the innkeeper fearing it might spread to himself and his guests, throwing Hunt and Foley out. "Thanks for sending your son out for the doctor."

"Glad to hear it, and you're welcome. I was just telling my boy that—"

A howl rose up outside, and then a second, a third, and after that Hunt couldn't tell how many. A silence fell within the bar and no one moved as the howls continued, long and full-throated. Hunt's blood went cold at the sound of it, a savage song of grief and rage. His horror was mirrored on every face, no one daring to move.

"Billy! Make sure the back doors are shut, and lock them," Owen Dale shouted, vaulting over his bar with surprising nimbleness for a man his size, bounding over to the front door at the hall. A moment later there was an iron snap of the padlock being secured.

"What the hell's going on?" someone shouted as everyone scrambled to their feet. That awful howling never ceased, one wolf – these were no dogs, no matter what the others insisted – picking up the dirge as another quietened. Hunt had a good idea why they were here, tracking him and Foley. Damned odd behaviour, though; attacking individuals or small groups in the wild or intruding on territory was one thing, but to surround a building filled with people was something else.

They must really want me and Foley. He kept that suspicion to himself and hoped it didn't occur to the others. If the locals got too frightened, they might decide to just wash their hands of the pair and throw them outside.

Many patrons fled to their rooms and locked the doors. Some of the men in the taproom armed themselves with whatever lay to hand, the innkeeper retrieving and loading a battered old blunderbuss that looked as likely to explode in his face as shoot.

Hunt left the taproom and ran upstairs to Foley's room.

The doctor stared at him, his patient forgotten. "Is that *dogs*?"

"It's whatever bit him," Hunt said. The howling wasn't enough to wake Foley, but he did stir restlessly, perspiration coating his face. Hunt opened Foley's small trunk and found a revolver near the bottom, retrieving it and a small box of bullets.

He handed the doctor his derringer and the last three bullets in his pocket, all of them silver. Expensive, but silver killed undead and footpads both, while lead was less effective against the former. "If they manage inside," he said as the doctor stared at the small gun before giving Hunt an uncertain nod. If the wolves had gone to the trouble of tracking them to the inn which they now surrounded, Hunt and Foley would likely be the first attacked.

He returned to the taproom. If anyone thought to placate the beasts besieging the inn by offering them him and Foley, the revolver in his hand decided them otherwise. There was a thudding noise as one of the wolves threw itself against the door, made from good solid oak.

"Where did you get that?" the farmer asked, showing respect to Hunt for the first time that night.

"It's my friend's old army revolver," he said, placing the spare bullets on the bar.

The howling continued throughout the night, but none of the wolves managed to get inside the inn. Hunt suspected the thuds at the door were more to frighten those inside than a serious attempt to break the door down. Maybe to scare the occupants into trying to flee the building.

Time dragged, Hunt's wits still sharp despite the consumption of another two ales. A few drank themselves insensible, but fear proved stronger than alcohol for most of those in the taproom no matter how much they drank.

Just prior to four in the morning the blackness started to lift outside, and Hunt decided to chance a look. The howling had lessened somewhat but never ceased. Not quite brave enough to look out one of the ground-floor windows, the glass too murky in any case, Hunt walked up the creaking stairs to his room that faced out the back.

He pulled back a curtain and peered out. Dark shapes prowled the perimeter restlessly, occasionally rearing back and howling impotently at the full moon already dipping towards the horizon.

A flicker of orange peeked over the eastern hills, heralding dawn's arrival. Hunt watched as one by one the wolves headed towards the field at the rear of the inn. All save one. A large, grizzled, black-furred wolf released one final howl, yellow eyes finding Hunt. It stared at him balefully for a while before silently following its packmates.

Hunt released a breath he hadn't realised he'd been holding and checked on Foley. Exhaustion had driven the doctor to sleep, Hunt's derringer lying on the bedside table. Hunt pocketed it and the spare bullets, returning Foley's pistol to his trunk. Foley's brow was still hot and clammy to the touch. *Trust him to sleep through a siege by wolves.*

Hunt returned to the taproom, Owen Dale and his other patrons all still awake if bleary-eyed. Despite being sent upstairs to hide, his son had crept down during the night and now curled up on a blanket on one of the benches. No one commented as Hunt retrieved the bullets still lying on the bar. "They've left."

A murmur of relief whispered round the taproom, one or two raising a tired cheer. The innkeeper Dale insisted on serving everyone a dram of whisky on the house in celebration, as if they had won a great victory rather than cowered inside all night, trapped by wild animals.

General opinion was leaning towards the beasts being wolves after all, the gentleman farmer now the loudest proponent of that theory. Hunt suspected the farmer and everyone else present would be regaling others about last night for years to come, and wolves made a better story than dogs.

"Maybe they've been roaming the land for years, killing anyone who crossed their paths, the last of their kind in Britain?" Dale wondered aloud. Hunt suspected the innkeeper would be repeating that line every time he told the story, talking in a hushed whisper over his bar during the long winter nights while a comforting fire blazed in the fireplace.

A brawny farmhand wearing a stained full-length shirt smock frowned. "Maybe. There's also that private estate not far from here, the owner claiming that patch of woods as his own and threatening to shoot trespassers. He's a queer sort, maybe he keeps wolves there?"

"And feeds them what?" the farmer challenged.

"Whatever he wants. Your missing sheep, maybe?" Dale said.

A thoughtful silence fell over the bar.

Footsteps thumped off the stairs, and Hunt turned to see the doctor enter the taproom.

Chapter Four

A whistle screeched out in the night, piercing London's thick greasy fog. Few of those who walked the street even deigned to look up, and those who did looked quickly back down. In a city of millions, the Londoner's creed seemed to be to mind one's own business.

And that suited Richard Canning just fine. Once he would have believed privacy anathema in a city so crowded with people, but he now realised the opposite was true. The hour was eleven at night, and to those still walking London's streets Canning was naught more than a top-hatted silhouette.

The whistle shrieked again from several streets away where Canning had dragged a passing woman into a fog-shrouded alley and drained her dry. A prostitute? A woman in the wrong place at the wrong time? Canning cared not, her blood settling in the pit of his stomach, already invigorating him after many long hours of travel hidden in a box.

Travelling by train no longer held the same appeal that it had before he died, before he was reduced to travelling by freight to avoid the burning sun. But to finally see the fabled streets of London made the inconvenience palatable. Not that he had been given a choice.

No one paid him any mind, their reaction to the police constable's whistle only to hasten their pace, even here. Marylebone was not the overcrowded district of Whitechapel, left infamous by the Ripper murders, but brazen footpads could strike anywhere, emboldened by the fog.

Nicknamed the Glasgow Ripper by the city that hanged him in March, Canning was tempted to visit Whitechapel and make some mischief there, perhaps even stir up panic by killing a woman in a similar fashion to Jack. But time was regretfully not on his side. His master, *Arakiel*, knew his nature well and had been specific; travel to London and visit an address.

Following another's orders was not precisely to Canning's liking, but since the other in question was an angel cast out of Heaven who had once walked the Earth as *Grigori* before dying, only to escape Hell as a demon wearing stolen flesh, Canning felt he could make an exception without losing too much face.

The scale of London excited him, the anonymity and endless victims it offered. He was attracted to the notion of abandoning *Arakiel*, leaving the demon to face Glasgow's undead and its puppet-master secret society alone. Eating a *Nephilim*'s heart had Transitioned Canning from ghoul to full *Nephilim* months – likely years – ahead of his time, but he harboured no illusions about his chances against Margot Guillam, let alone Glasgow's elusive ruler, Niall Fisher. Fisher had betrayed and killed *Arakiel* two centuries prior, eating the *Grigori*'s heart to become *Dominus* and master of *Arakiel*'s House.

Arakiel desired to return the favour, but in his current body he was not much stronger than the Vessel he possessed, a body soft and unused to violence.

Perhaps anticipating Canning's head might be turned by the opportunities of London, *Arakiel* had warned him to keep his visit brief and quiet. Unlike Glasgow, no single undead House held sway in London, the capital carved into territories by *Nephilim*, magicians, demons and Templars. A lone *Nephilim* killing without sanction would be quickly hunted down by whoever claimed that particular district.

That made sense, Canning had to admit. And so, he would complete his task, limit his play and return to Glasgow. Besides, he had some scores to settle there.

Wilton Hunt. Edith Hunt. Lewis Hunt.

Lucifer.

If *Arakiel* let him. For now, the demon had warned him to stay clear of the Hunts.

Canning turned into Harley Street, number 15 his destination. Instead of the sandstone tenements common in Glasgow, the architecture was plain and uniform, a long row of brown-bricked Georgian terraces lining both sides of the street. Variety might be absent, but Harley Street did have the virtue of being in central London, near several railway stations.

He used the silver knocker attached to the grey-painted door of number 15 and waited. The door was answered shortly after by a middle-aged man dressed in a starched black servant's livery. Canning assumed him to be either a butler or valet.

"Good evening," Canning said, managing a polite smile. "I'm here to see Dr Essex."

The servant's dour expression soured on hearing Canning's accent. *Not a great admirer of his Scottish neighbours, then.* "Do you have an appointment?"

Canning shook his head cheerfully, wondering if it would be too great a *faux pas* to rip the man's throat out. "I'm afraid not. I'm here on a Mr Keel's business." Erik Keel was the name by which *Arakiel* had become known centuries past, until his demon name had become all but forgotten.

"If you've no appointment, I regret Dr Essex cannot receive you," the servant said, not bothering to keep the spite from his voice. "He is a very busy man."

The servant stumbled back, pain and panic crossing that fleshy, clean-shaven face, blood turning that starched white shirt red. In Canning's mind, anyway. But his hands twitched to translate fantasy into reality. Consoling himself by Unveiling and taking pleasure in the shiver of fear that crossed the servant's face, Canning spoke again. "*Kindly* tell Dr Essex that Mr Keel – Erik Keel – has sent a Mr Canning to advise it is time to settle an old debt. A *very* old debt. It concerns a *burning* issue, one might say." Whatever that meant. *Arakiel* hadn't bothered to explain.

The servant hesitated. "I'll relay your message to Dr Essex."

"That would be grand of-," Canning started to say as the servant shut the door on him, perhaps fearing the Scottish rogue would help himself to the house silver.

A few minutes later the door re-opened. "Dr Essex will see you," the servant said, his manner somewhat improved. He stepped aside to let Canning in.

"That's good of him," Canning said enthusiastically, flavouring his accent with a hint of Hibernia. A spasm crossed the servant's face at the possibility Canning might actually be Irish. His mother was, so close enough.

Canning removed his top hat and handed it to the servant who grudgingly hung it from a hat-rack. The hall floor was covered in red and black tiles, the walls decorated with beige wallpaper depicting birds in flight. A large oil painting of a lake hung on the wall.

He expected the servant to lead him into the parlour, but the man instead walked into the kitchen and down a set of creaking wooden stairs to the basement. Canning eyed the servant's back and amused himself with thoughts of pushing him down the stairs and claiming he fell.

The servant led him into a large, open basement, white tiles covering the floor and bottom half of the walls. Two spartan wooden tables sat next to the left wall, a clothed corpse lying on each, male and female. A metal table sat in the middle of room, a naked man lying thereon. A smaller metal table sat next to it, bearing the bloody tools of a surgeon – scalpels, saws and drills. Several wall-mounted gaslights lit up the room.

None of the faces were covered, telling Canning that Essex was not a man troubled by sentiment towards the dead. Breathing was something Canning need only bother with when he was required to speak, and on inhaling to introduce himself, he smelled death. Not even the formaldehyde and bleach could completely mask the smells of shit, blood and necrotic flesh.

"Dr Essex, a Mr Canning to see you," the servant said in his funereal tone, bowing slightly. He ignored the dead bodies, paying them no more mind than he would the furniture.

"Thank you, Yates. You may go."

Canning stepped aside to let the servant pass, wondering if the good doctor would appreciate a fourth corpse for his collection. The doctor was in his forties, tall and almost skeletally thin, his long face gaunt and hollow-cheeked. A pair of small spectacles sat atop a beaked nose that loomed over a neat moustache and goatee beard. His grey-flecked black hair was kept short, ending in a widow's peak. His sleeves were rolled up, and he wore a long, gore-stained apron over his shirt and charcoal-coloured trousers. He stood next to the naked corpse, having already removed several organs, his forearms red with blood.

Canning was glad he had indulged his Thirst on the way to Harley Street, or the smell of blood would have tested his self-control. "Evening, Doctor. I'm Richard Canning, an emissary from Mr Keel."

"Dr Theodore Essex. You'll forgive me if I don't offer my hand." The doctor's voice was oddly unaccented, as if he had travelled too much for any one place to settle on him. "So, Mr Keel sent you. Yates said you brought a message?"

Canning pulled out an envelope from his inside jacket pocket and waited until Essex had wiped his hands on a cloth.

"I recall Mr Keel had another associate, a Mr Rannoch. I understood that it would be he who would call on me should Mr Keel choose to call in this particular debt?" Essex used a clean scalpel to rip open the envelope and removed the letter. "That is why I have kept Rannoch updated with news of my current … location."

"George Rannoch was killed a few months ago," Canning said easily. The Elder *Nephilim* had Made Canning undead, feeding him his blood the night before he was hanged, but Canning was not a man shackled by sentimentality towards his Maker.

"That was careless of him," Essex said as he held the letter. He glanced at Canning over his spectacles. "You *Nephilim* seem to believe you have cheated Death, but He finds most of you sooner rather than later."

"You know what I am?" Canning asked.

"I felt you Unveil earlier, and Yates confirmed it. I'll read this in the parlour."

"Your servant seems to hold a low opinion of me," Canning observed. "Would you be overly inconvenienced if he were to serve you in another capacity?" He gave the three corpses a significant look.

"He is a fine valet, I'd prefer to avoid the inconvenience of trying to hire another untroubled by blood and the knowledge that this world extends beyond the natural order," Essex said mildly as they left the basement.

Meaning Yates was aware of the undead, and Essex preferred him living. Pity.

The parlour wallpaper had a yellow background broken up with red flowers, and the carpet was mostly green interwoven with red. A large gilded mirror hung over the black marble fireplace while landscapes and portraits painted in oils decorated the walls. A beige couch and two matching armchairs upholstered in white sat around a polished table. There was a piano in one corner and a ticking grandfather clock in another.

Neither sat as Essex read the letter. "It appears that Death caught up with your master, too. That he was betrayed and usurped by his subordinates who killed him and most of his loyalists two centuries past. That he's currently Possessing a man positioned close to this … Sooty Feather Society, and he requires my help to retake his House." He sounded mildly interested.

Canning studied the oil paintings. They seemed to span several centuries, depicting London, Rome, Paris and other cities Canning couldn't identify. Portraits, too, including one of a severe-looking lady.

"Queen Mary," Essex said, following Canning's gaze. "Before the artist, Henry Norman, fell from favour. Falsely accused of heresy and burned."

One elderly-looking man wore Papal robes, another a nobleman's coronet. The same scene of the Thames had been painted three times but depicting different eras; the oldest was from the Tudor period, the second was of soldiers from what might be Cromwell's time, and the last showed signs of industrialisation in the background.

From what Canning gathered, Essex was a respected London doctor, having mastered his trade remarkably quickly, his services engaged by many of London's prominent citizens. Quite why *Arakiel* wanted him was beyond Canning's ken.

The doctor frowned. "Moving to Glasgow is a nuisance. At the least I require a week or two to put my affairs here in order."

"You're to accompany me on the morning train," Canning said, the threat in his voice sharp and bare to let Essex know in no uncertain terms that he was without choice in this matter.

If Essex was intimidated, he didn't show it. "I owe Mr Keel a debt, one year's service. But I'm displeased by the manner of him collecting it, and the messenger sent to me. Inform your master I'll arrive in Glasgow in two weeks. Ten days at the earliest."

"You'll be on the morning train, or you'll be joining your subjects in the basement," Canning said brightly. He Unveiled to leave Essex in no doubt who was in charge.

Essex looked at him but said nothing, as if his mind was elsewhere.

Canning frowned. When he threatened someone, he expected their *undivided* attention. *Perhaps Dr Essex will be remaining in London after all.*

He took two steps towards Essex and was about to take a third when the parlour door slowly swung open. *His valet, Yates. Perhaps his death alone will convince the good doctor to pack tonight. Let no one say I'm not averse to reasonable compromise.*

Two men and a woman staggered into the parlour, Yates not among them. That was Canning's first observation. His second was that the three arrivals were dead, the corpses from the basement. From their glassy stares he realised all three were truly dead, not an undead among them. Prior to his demise in the Necropolis, Rannoch had spoken to Canning of such abominations; *zombis*, corpses raised and controlled by a necromancer.

Few undead suffered a necromancer to live, and so they were rare and discreet. The mystery of why *Arakiel* wished Essex brought to Glasgow was at least solved. With Canning his only undead servant, the demon wished Essex to off-set his lack of ghouls and *Nephilim* with dead minions animated by necromancy.

A mystery Canning would have done well to solve before threatening Essex. The three *zombis* spread out and closed in on him. He drew his knife and slashed out at the three corpses, driving the blade into the heart of the nearest one.

It ignored a wound that would have killed any ghoul or *Nephilim*, dead unblinking eyes showing no response to the hole in its chest. If there was a way to defeat a *zombi* beyond dismemberment, it eluded Canning as he backed into a wall and they closed in on him.

His undead strength was greater than theirs, but they were untiring, and as the struggle continued, Canning feared his strength would be exhausted before the magic animating his opponents was.

The necromancer ... kill him and the zombis will fall. Unfortunately, that revelation came to him too late. He was dragged down to the ground and held firmly on his back.

Essex stood over him, hands behind his back palm-to-palm as he looked down at Canning. "Two weeks, Mr Canning. Maybe ten days."

Canning was in no position to argue. "You're a necromancer."

"Indeed." A look of distaste crossed his face as he looked around the parlour. "You've caused rather a mess." He straightened one of his pictures hanging askew. "Do you like my oil paintings?"

Canning was surprised at the change in topic. One moment Essex was having his subjects subdue Canning, the next he wanted to discuss art. "They look very fine. Of course, I could make a more detailed study if your friends allowed me to stand." If the *zombis* released him, there would quickly be four corpses in the parlour.

"It's hard for me to be objective," Essex said, evidently still discussing his paintings. "I suppose all artists feel that way about their work."

"They're all yours?" Canning tried to keep his tone conversational in the hopes Essex would foolishly release him. *You can't keep me like this all night.*

He hoped. Maybe the necromancer could. Animating more than one corpse at a time spoke of some skill with death magic, from the little Canning knew of it. Fear crept into his dead heart. Even if Essex had no wish to stab the helpless Canning in the heart, all he need do was hold him there until dawn and pull open the curtains to let in the sun's lethal light.

"Yes, Mr Canning. All mine. I like to believe my brushwork and colouring has become more refined over the years."

"Again, if you allowed me to stand, I could..." He frowned. "They're *all* yours?" Some of the paintings were centuries old.

Essex glanced at the portrait of Bloody Mary and smiled down at him, eyes lit by the wall-mounted gaslights. "*All*, Mr Canning."

"You're not just any necromancer, you're a..." The word escaped him, but Rannoch had spoken briefly and with loathing of what necromancers at the height of their power could accomplish.

"A lich," Essex said. Few necromancers attained such a state, death – natural or otherwise – catching most before they perfected their sorcery, but a few succeeded. Succeeded in creating a ... phylactery, a repository for their soul. When they died, the soul fled to their phylactery until some unfortunate came into contact with it, and found their own soul evicted while the lich's took up residence instead.

It sounded like demon possession, except liches were entirely human. Their soul never left the mortal world unless their phylactery was destroyed. And since the phylactery could be anything, identifying the unholy artefact was difficult.

Essex glanced at the *zombis* who released their hold on Canning, standing motionless. Canning got to his feet but made no move to attack Essex. Why bother? The necromancer would simply return in another body and report Canning's indiscretion to *Arakiel*.

"You are several hundred years old?" Canning asked, recalling the oldest painting.

"Older than that, Mr Canning," Essex said, though he did not elaborate. "Painting is a relatively recent hobby of mine. I made a living from it around the time I met Messrs Keel and Rannoch."

Canning felt a fool; as *Nephilim* he looked forward to years many and red, but twice now in the months since his hanging he had underestimated a foe and owed his continued existence solely to their mercy. This lich, Essex (or whatever name his original body had borne). And Lucifer. *I've developed an unwholesome habit of picking my foes poorly.*

"Are you really a doctor?" Canning asked.

"Oh, yes. Dr Theodore Essex's reputation is owed entirely to me. I took up residence in this body when he was a young man, greatly impressing my professors as I 'learned' skills and knowledge attained long ago. True, the medical arts have advanced greatly, but I long ago learned the human body."

Canning nodded to the three corpses guarding the doctor. "Yet still you study?"

"Mastered is not perfected. And it pleases me to see the subtle changes time has wrought on humanity."

"Will you repay your debt to Mr Keel?" Canning asked in a polite tone.

"Yes." A millennia-old soul looked at him through the eyes of a man aged half a century. "In two weeks."

Canning executed a stiff bow, unpractised in such courtesy. "I'll let Mr Keel know."

Chapter Five

Hunt leaned against the railing of the small steamboat chugging across the Sound of Mull, Loch Aline its destination. Sunlight glittered off the bright blue waters, a clear sky overhead. They had remained in the Drover's Inn for a week to let Foley's infection pass and his wound heal, the wolves having vanished with the dawn. The locals had scoured the woods and hills, finding no trace of the beasts and were keen to believe the pack had left the area.

The Ashwood estate sat north of Kirkaline, a village lying on the western shore of Loch Aline, where it met the sea. The people made their living mostly from crofting and fishing, isolated by hills, mountains and untamed woodland. Rough paths allowed the clannish drovers to move their herds north and east through Glendorcha and the Lewswood to the markets of civilisation, routes too rough for wagon or carriage.

As such, the most reliable route to Kirkaline was by sea. A steam train had taken Hunt and Foley from Crianlarich to Oban, from where they sailed by paddle-steamer to the Isle of Mull. Kirkaline saw few visitors, so the steamboat taking them there from Mull was a small craft mostly bringing in supplies that the village couldn't produce.

Fragarach dominated the sky, the largest of three mountains forming a wall to the north-east of Kirkaline; rising above a forest carpeting the land, the Lewswood, ancient and forbidding, older than memory. Glendorcha separated the mountains, a small river feeding the loch.

Between loch and forest lay stretches of white golden sands, moorland and green fields, and the whitewashed houses of Kirkaline. A granite lighthouse stood sentinel east of the loch at the southern edge of the land, built to ward off ships straying too close to the rocky shore.

The steamboat entered the small seawater loch and approached the stone pier, shouts hollered back and forth as the crew and villagers worked to tie up the boat.

"Couldn't your family have inherited an estate somewhere easier to get to?" Foley complained as he and Hunt left the boat, the crew waiting to unload their trunks.

Hunt ignored him, spotting a dark-skinned man standing at the end of the pier. Most of the men present wore flat caps, but the man in the suit wore a black turban. Hunt had never seen him before, but he held a piece of paper with *Hunt* written thereon.

"Afternoon, I'm Mr Hunt, this is Mr Foley," Hunt said on approaching the man. He looked maybe forty and just shy of six feet, his black beard neatly trimmed; Indian most likely. His black leather shoes gleamed like mirrors, his dark-grey trousers sharply creased. Hunt vaguely recalled his father writing some years past of a new Sikh valet called Dash Singh, looking after his flat in London.

The man bowed slightly. "Good afternoon, Mr Hunt," the man said in a melodious voice, every syllable carefully enunciated. "Mr Foley," he greeted with a polite nod before turning back to Hunt. "I'm Singh, Lord Ashwood's valet."

"Good to finally meet you," Hunt said.

"Lord Ashwood's carriage is nearby," Singh said as he motioned for crewmen to follow with Hunt and Foley's trunks, ignoring the stares he attracted from the insular locals. He was probably the only foreigner they had seen or ever would. Hell, they probably considered anyone born more than fifty miles away foreign.

'Carriage' was a generous term for the wheeled contraption that waited for them. The tradesmen of Kirkaline had done their best, but even the fresh coat of black paint failed to hide what was clearly a converted wagon.

"Lord Ashwood has ordered a new carriage to be brought by boat, but this will need to suffice until then," Singh said with a note of embarrassed apology.

"I remember this old thing from my visits here as a boy," Hunt said cheerfully as Singh opened the door. It had been both a mark of the Hunts' noble station and a sign of their fragile finances before Father married Mother. Hunt entered, followed by Foley. Once the trunks were loaded onto the back of the wagon – which creaked alarmingly – the valet paid the crewmen and joined Hunt and Foley inside. He wrapped his knuckles against the roof and the wagon moved forwards with a jolt.

"I'm surprised to see you here," Hunt said. Singh had been his father's valet in London for the past several years, doubling as butler and always remaining in Lewis Hunt's London flat when his master returned to Glasgow. The Hunts' butler, Smith, had looked after Lewis Hunt when he stayed in the family home, and he never bothered with one when travelling.

"Now that your father is the Baron of Ashwood and retired from Law, he has put his London flat on the market," Singh said. "Mr Smith is too old to act as valet so I was asked to continue in that position, contingent on relocating to Scotland."

"I see," Hunt said. "You'll find Kirkaline and Ashwood greatly different from London."

"It is certainly cleaner and quieter," was the valet's diplomatic response.

Hunt wondered just how much time his father intended to spend up here. He didn't strike him as the sort to play the country lord in the middle of nowhere, and certainly Hunt's mother would want to be near Glasgow to manage the Browning Shipping Company.

*

Foley said little, discomforted at the unfamiliar if starkly beautiful surroundings. He'd travelled extensively with the army but at least then he had been surrounded by hundreds of others equally out of place. The carriage drew stares from the locals, working men and women going about their daily business. No one bowed or scraped, for which he was grateful. He suspected the people of Kirkaline managed just fine without any help from the Hunts of Ashwood.

The drought had left the dirt roads hard, the carriage shuddering over exposed rocks and old wheel ruts. Foley grimaced as the more violent jolts set his wounded arm afire, but he supposed it would be churlish to complain. He was fortunate to have recovered from his infection.

The village passed quickly out of sight as the wagon headed inland, farms and small crofts the only sign of inhabitation. A few fields were visible but much of the land was too rugged for crops, used instead to graze sheep. The rest was the vast forest of Lewswood, separating the peninsula from the rest of the mainland. Foley was surprised it hadn't been cut down for lumber. He was vague on the details but understood Hunt's family had once owned most of the land. No longer.

"We've arrived," Hunt said with a wry smile as the carriage passed through an arched double gate. The estate was surrounded by an old stone wall that had perhaps once stood eight feet tall, albeit long since turned decrepit. He wondered why someone had felt the need for such a wall in this small isolated place. *Maybe a previous lord kept having his flowerbeds trampled by wandering sheep?*

A man wearing servant's livery exited the house, aged about sixty. Foley stayed out of the way while he helped Singh unload the luggage and carry it into the house. He felt awkward watching them work but knew offering to help would only embarrass everyone.

Decades of neglect had taken their toll on Ashwood Lodge, a two-storey house with single-storey outbuildings attached. Slates were missing from the main roof, and that covering the furthest outbuilding appeared to have collapsed completely. The attic windows were boarded up and much of the white paint had peeled off from the walls, revealing cracks in the stonework.

Hunt joined him. "It's stood for almost two hundred years, give or take. I don't think it'll collapse while we're here. Come on."

A middle-aged couple stood at the door, the man dressed in a brown tweed suit, streaks of grey in his dark hair. Even if Foley hadn't met him before, he would have recognised him as Hunt's father. That made the sharp-faced woman by his side in a dark blue dress Hunt's mother, shrewd eyes appraising Foley as he approached.

"Wilton, you've arrived at last, safe and sound," Lady Ashwood said, greeting her son with a kiss on the cheek. "We received your telegram, brief though it was."

"We were delayed near Inverarnan," Hunt said with vast understatement. "Good to see you both."

"You're here now, Wilton," his father said, shaking his hand.

"Father, Mother, this is Mr Foley. Foley, Lord and Lady Ashwood."

Foley awkwardly greeted Hunt's parents, the Baron and Baroness of Ashwood. Not that there looked to be much left of the estate. "Thank you for your hospitality."

"You're welcome, Mr Foley," Lord Ashwood said. "I only hope that our hospitality won't prove too disappointing. As you can see, the house is in a poor state."

*

Hunt sat in the parlour with his parents and Foley, a fish pie cooked with Mrs McCrae's customary skill slowly digesting in his belly. Tarnished cutlery and cracked crockery had adorned the dining room table, the least of what ailed the old house. The interior walls were dirty-white, the plaster cracking in several places, and threadbare carpets covered uneven floorboards that creaked alarmingly under foot. There was no gas or electric lighting, illumination coming from several lit candles placed on tables and the mantelpiece.

Father sat next to Mother on an old couch positioned across from the one Hunt and Foley occupied. As bad as the couches were, neither was in as poor a condition as Uncle Thomas' old armchair, a wrecked old thing exiled outside on Father's orders. *The Baron is dead; long live the Baron.*

"'Hunt' doesn't sound a local name," Foley said. "How did your family come to land and title here?"

Father smiled wryly. "The same way most families did; by taking the land from someone else. Has Wilton not told you the family history?"

"He has not, Lord Ashwood," Foley said, glancing at Hunt.

"We had more pressing matters to discuss," Hunt said dryly. "Just as I never enquired as to why Foley's parents chose to buy a shop and flat on Paisley Road West."

"I rather suspect our family history is more ... eventful than Mr Foley's," Father said with a wry expression.

"I'm sure it is, and I'd like to hear it," Foley said.

"Cigars, gentlemen?" Father offered. "They're Singer's."

Hunt and Foley accepted, the parlour quickly thickening with the rich tang of premium tobacco. Foley nodded his approbation. "Very fine, Lord Ashwood."

Father exhaled a gout of smoke. "A history of the Hunts in Loch Aline … very well.

"The sept Kail'an of the Clan Mackail once ruled these lands, pagans one and all, mostly cut off from the rest of the mainland. Kail'an means 'little Kail', the sept an offshoot of the clan. After the failed Jacobite uprising in 1719 which the Kail'ans supported, Sir Geoffrey Hunt learned of the paganism rumoured to persist in these remote lands. He led four companies of soldiers through the vast forests to the north-east and captured the land, taking Dunlew Castle and bringing Christianity to the remaining natives."

"Whether they wanted it or not," Hunt said.

"Sir Geoffrey's soldiers took Dunlew Castle by surprise and put the garrison to the sword. The castle was significantly damaged in the battle." Father gestured around. "Rather than repair or rebuild it, Sir Geoffrey instead built this house and called the surrounding estate Ashwood. The village was renamed Kirkaline."

"New settlers were brought in to replace the decimated clansmen," Hunt said.

"What happened to the surviving locals?" Foley asked.

Father answered. "Those who did not convert to Christianity fled or were driven out, but some hid in the forest, occasionally raiding their former lands. The wall surrounding this house was not built on a whim. But the King was grateful, and Sir Geoffrey became the 1st Baron Ashwood. I believe many of the original inhabitants sought out their inland kin for sanctuary, but by then word of their pagan practices – doubtless exaggerated by the new Lord Ashwood to justify his landgrab – had spread, and even the sept's clan wanted little to do with them."

"Our ancestor was a ruthless man, by all accounts," Hunt said.

"His grandson, Harold Hunt, the 3rd Lord Ashwood, was a very different creature," Mother said.

Father nodded. "He gambled away most of the lands here as well as his English estate before dying in a duel. Robert

Hunt, his baby cousin and my grandfather, became the 4th Baron and inherited this house and what little land remained. Robert's father had died shortly before his birth, leaving the family with little money and a baby heir to what remained of Ashwood. He did what he could over the years, saving what little could be saved and passed on to future heirs."

"Which wasn't much," Hunt said. "The 2nd Baron had begun efforts to restore Dunlew Castle and make it the family Seat, but the 3rd Baron gambled it away, leaving the Hunts Ashwood Lodge. The castle has since been restored by the McKellen family while the 4th and 5th barons struggled to hold on to what remained of Ashwood."

"Your family has a colourful history," Foley observed.

Much of it red, Hunt thought.

"Oh, yes," Father said. "Tragedy has been ever near the Hunts. My father was the youngest of three brothers, yet the title and estate have fallen to me. But with luck, Wilton will live a much quieter life."

Hunt recalled the events of the past spring and prayed silently that would prove to be the case.

"How do you and Mr Foley plan to spend your time here?" Mother asked. *Before she tells us how we'll be spending our time.*

"We hope to explore the local area, swim in the loch, trek through the woods and climb the mountain. I also want to study local plants and animals to aid my studies," Hunt said quickly before Foley asked about the local pub. If Mother believed they intended to take their ease, she would waste no time drawing up a list of chores to occupy them until autumn. "Tomorrow I'll show Mr Foley around."

"Good. The house and estate also need a lot of work, as you saw, which shouldn't trouble a pair of fit young men like yourselves," Father said with a faintly malicious smile.

Chapter Six

Birdsong woke Foley, a cacophony of high-pitched shrills and hoots. Dawn came early to Ashwood, sunlight piercing Foley's half-closed curtains. Not that he minded, enjoying the novelty of awakening with a clear head unfogged by drink or laudanum. His wounds were still stiff and sore, even after seven days of convalescence in the Drover's Inn, his recovery not aided by the lack of anything to do there but drink.

The room's blue paper was faded and peeling, mildew staining the wall near the window. Sparsely furnished, Foley suspected this spare room was rarely occupied, its floor bare unvarnished wood that creaked underfoot. The window frame was rotting, its paint having mostly peeled away, and spiderweb cracks spread across the ceiling. In winter, he had little doubt that the wind whistled through gaps between the window frame and brickwork, chilling the room and blowing the curtains askew. He was glad he had come in a rare summer untroubled by wind or rain.

Foley rose from bed, splashing tepid water from an enamel basin over his face, bathing quickly before dressing. Hunt had warned him his parents were early risers and that the family broke their fast accordingly. Self-conscious at being a guest of nobility – even if the house was more appropriate for a gentleman farmer fallen on hard times – Foley had resolved to moderate his drinking. He had even left his laudanum at home (save for an emergency medicinal supply at the bottom of his trunk). In truth, he found himself using it less often these days, an abundance of enemies triggering a soldier's instincts against dulling his senses too much.

In the aftermath of Amelie Gerrard's murder and Hunt's captivity at the hands of the Sooty Feathers, Hunt had come close to disappearing into a bottle himself but had thankfully tempered his drinking of late, more like his old self.

Not that the pair still didn't join Professor Sirk for a drink, but it felt less driven by need; three friends united by shared experience enjoying a single malt rather than three victims harrowed by horror trying to drown their fear in whisky.

Suitably dressed, Foley descended the stairs, lured by the mouth-watering smells of cooked bacon and eggs.

*

After breakfast Hunt had made it quickly clear that he had promised to show Foley around the village and surrounding area, perhaps pre-empting Lord and Lady Ashwood assigning them chores for the day. Foley looked forward to seeing his home for the next several weeks, glad to escape the soot and grime of a city baked and broiled by a long summer that showed no sign of ending. The water level of the Clyde had dropped, the river stinking fiercer than ever of shit, piss, and industrial waste produced by the city's mills and factories. A slurry of foulness now travelled sluggishly down to the coast where it met the Atlantic, and good bloody riddance.

Part of him was tempted to sell his shop and flat, and move here or somewhere equally rural, but he was a city man born and bred. *And besides, what the hell would I do?* He was a pharmacist, not a farmer. And he was sure as hell not a crofter or fisherman.

Foley heard Hunt take a deep breath of air. "This is the life, eh, Foley?"

He glanced at his friend. "Aye, I wouldn't cast stones at it." The road was an earthen trail created by years of wagon-travel, grooves worn into the ground. Trees lined both sides of the road, giving the men a welcome respite from the sun. Too hot for wool, Hunt had dressed accordingly, Foley envying him his white linen suit. A straw hat sat atop Hunt's head, though Foley privately found it slightly ridiculous, preferring his own flat cap.

Cats, rats and dogs were the main animals habitually found in the city, but here Foley caught sight of red squirrels darting up trees, rabbits playing nearby, and sheep in the fields. The birdsong he heard was new, too; shrill tweets and the deep hooting of grouse and pheasants. A change from being shat on by pigeons and seagulls.

Shards of sunlight pierced gaps in the canopy overhead, and the warm air was heavy with the perfume of wildflowers. Mushrooms grew in a shaded patch nearby, or maybe toadstools. He couldn't tell without a closer look.

"What are you thinking?" Hunt asked, breaking the companionable silence.

"I was wondering where we can get a tram into town," Foley lied. Both men had slung their jackets over their shoulders, baring their shirtsleeves. In truth Foley was tempted to tug off his tweed waistcoat, too, propriety be damned.

Hunt laughed, a welcome sound. Coming here seemed to shake off the last vestiges of the guilt and anger that had weighed him down since the spring. Since the murder of Amelie Gerrard and her family.

Not that Foley was fooled. He still caught his friend brooding quietly at times, a darkness to his mood. But it was a start. For his own part, Foley found himself less shackled by the chronic melancholia that had clung to his back his entire life, trying to weigh him down with despair and smother him with misery.

Death had stalked him, drawing ever closer, Foley once accepting that he himself would likely be the architect of his demise, curing his malaise with a bullet from his own gun. Assuming the drink didn't kill him first, and God knew no one could accuse him of shirking in that regard.

Instead, he had turned that gun on the undead and those who served it, somehow surviving a night of carnage in the city's Necropolis while two of his Templar allies had died. Better; living had been no fluke, he had *fought* to live, *wanted* to. With his finger on the trigger, there had been no suicidal hesitation to give any of the bastards he faced the chance to kill him instead.

The trees ended and the sun beat down on them once again. Heather-clad hills and peaty moorland stretched on for miles, sheep grazing on the wild grass. There were long-horned Highland cattle too, their thick brown hides the cause for them seeking shade beneath a grove of trees, breaking the silence with an occasional despondent bellow. Foley pitied the poor shaggy beasts, wondering how they didn't just keel over from the heat.

"There," Hunt said, pointing to his right.

Foley squinted, seeing only a hill. "What am I looking at?"

"That's Ash Hill, once called Dunkail'an, an ancient hillfort and original seat of the Kail'ans."

"Aye? Doesn't look like much." Foley had reckoned it just another hill.

"The earliest chiefs of Sept Kail'an held it over a thousand years ago," Hunt said. "When this land was part of the Kingdom of Dalriata."

"You said the original?"

Hunt smiled wryly. "I'll show you the newer castle, Dunlew." He led them off the road and through the narrow treeline to where land met water. Loch Aline glimmered bright and blue ahead, water lapping against the stony shore. Foley looked forward to swimming in the loch, maybe even swimming to the rugged land across the water.

"There," Hunt said, pointing to the north-east.

Foley obliged, looking to the end of the loch. A grey-stoned castle perched on a ridge above a beach of white sand. "Dunlew Castle?"

"Yes. That's the Dunlew estate. The castle belonged to my family – well, after my ancestor killed the previous owner, the Kail'an chief and laird of this area. For a few generations we held it."

Foley recalled Lord Ashwood's story the night before, of the family being laid low by the 3rd Baron's gambling. "A bad hand at cards?"

Hunt stared at the castle that might have one day been his. "Yes. Sir Geoffrey Hunt – later the 1st Baron – didn't take the castle gently, breaching its walls with his cannon. The 2nd Baron died before he could repair it, and his son lost it. I believe it sat derelict for a decade until the McKellen family repaired the damage and extended it. The surrounding estate has been revitalised."

"A family with a lot of money, these McKellens," Foley observed.

"More than us, certainly." Hunt clapped Foley on the back. "Come on, I'll show you Kirkaline."

The road led them to the village of Kirkaline, seen only

briefly on their arrival. Acres of thick untamed forest meant the peninsula was easier accessed by sea than by land, and so it had mostly been left to fend for itself. Foley now understood how paganism had lingered here for so long.

"That's Ardtornish Point Lighthouse," Hunt said, pointing across the blue waters of the loch to the south-east. Small fishing boats sailed the loch, fishermen casting their nets into the water for trout and salmon, keeping a polite distance from one another. The larger fishing boats were doubtless trawling the waters between the mainland and the Isle of Mull.

"I wouldn't want to have to be a lighthouse keeper, I'd get dizzy going up and down," Foley said. Not to mention the isolation. He'd drink himself to death within a year.

"There are dark tales about it," Hunt said.

"Aye? Like what?"

"Well, it's whispered that sometimes the lighthouse would go dark and another light would be lit further inland, drawing unwary ships to their doom so the pagan locals could sacrifice the survivors to their old gods and scavenge whatever goods the ship carried," Hunt revealed.

Foley squinted at the lighthouse, such grim tales having little impact by light of day. "Any truth to the story, or is it just the new Christian mob badmouthing the heathen lot who lived here before?"

"Good question."

The village of Kirkaline was spread along the mouth of the western bank of Loch Aline, consisting mostly of sandstone cottages, almost all whitewashed, built between trees and uneven land. Maybe half were thatched, the rest tiled with slate.

"What's that?" Foley asked, pointing to a ruin sitting atop the cliff.

"An old keep used by the Kail'ans to look out for invaders from the sea, a first line of defence. It ended up being the site of the Kail'an chief's last stand."

"Aye?"

"Dunlew Castle as it was back then was not built to endure an assault by cannon; that coupled with Sir Geoffrey's surprise attack saw the castle fall quickly.

"The Kail'an and his surviving fighters fled to that keep, hoping to hold it long enough for reinforcements to arrive or for Sir Geoffrey to get bored and leave." Foley followed Hunt's gaze to the tumbledown keep, its walls still fire-blackened despite almost two hundred years of rain. What had survived the fire now faced a slow erosion from wind, rain and frost, besieged by every winter.

"It looks too high for your ancestor to turn his cannons against it," Foley observed, surveying the land with a soldier's eyes.

Hunt nodded. "Yes. Sir Geoffrey besieged it. By that time the keep was half-derelict and poorly provisioned. When it became clear no reinforcements were coming, the defenders set fire to the keep as a final act of defiance, most perishing in the flames."

"Aye? I'd have sallied forth and attacked. Better to die in battle and take some of the bastards with me than starve or burn," Foley said.

"Oh, there's more," Hunt said grimly. "Legend says the Kail'an lit the fire himself on the advice of his surviving druids, a sacrifice to the gods they worshipped." He looked Foley in the eye. "Payment for a curse on the Hunts."

Standing as they did in a bright summer's day, it was hard to take such a tale seriously. "You've done not bad despite this curse," Foley observed. "Those old gods weren't up to much."

Hunt managed a smile that failed to reach his eyes. "You think not? The 3rd Baron died in a duel after gambling almost everything away. The 4th Baron's heir and his children died in a storm as their ship tried to reach Loch Aline. The heir's youngest brother – my grandfather – drowned in the loch while my father was young. The middle brother, my great-uncle, died recently a childless bachelor."

He gazed back at the ruin, the site of an ancient curse. "My father and I are the last of the Hunts." He paused as if about to say more but didn't.

He didn't need to. Foley recalled well what had befallen Hunt that spring. The day no longer felt quite so warm, nor the village so welcoming.

They continued into Kirkaline in silence, passing a small church built from neatly carved stones, its slated roof looking new. "Its construction was paid for by the 2nd Baron," Hunt said.

"Not the 1st?"

"The first Lord Ashwood was more interested in forcing out the old gods' worshippers, encouraging Christianity with fire and steel rather than hymns and sermons. He renamed the village Kirkaline and gave some money for the new settlers to build a temporary church while having to protect his new lands from Kail'an partisans. His son was a more pious sort."

"Looks well-kept," Foley said.

"You can thank my parents for that. After years of a leaking roof the timbers inside were beginning to rot, but neither my great-grandfather nor my great-uncle had the money to fund repairs. On the death of my maternal grandfather, my parents made a sizeable donation for the church's restoration."

They walked through the churchyard, Foley reading the epitaphs as they passed the gravestones. None predated the 1700s. "What did Sept Kail'an do with their dead?"

"Ate them," Hunt deadpanned.

"Aye, if you say so."

"They buried their dead in mounds. Some of those hills we passed are old barrows."

That explained why some appeared to have just sprouted up from nowhere, looking unexpectedly symmetrical. "Still, this is new."

"Us walking through a cemetery is hardly new," Hunt said.

"In daylight without shovels, crowbars and a wheelbarrow?"

Hunt managed a smile. "Good point. Fancy digging someone up tonight for old time's sake?"

Their bodysnatching days were at an end. Billy Nugent had been their last exhumation, though their last nocturnal visit to a cemetery had been to re-bury the undead Amy Newfield, shot by Wolfgang Steiner. *Until she disappeared on us again.*

"I wonder where she went to," Hunt said, betraying that his thoughts had run the same course as Foley's.

"Back to Margot Guillam, probably. So long as she keeps away from us." Her first disappearance after her exhumation had been the catalyst for Hunt and Foley learning about the undead; Foley was determined that her second disappearance not drag them back into that dangerous underworld. Her surviving the silver bullet Steiner had shot into her chest had been put down to Hunt failing to tell the Templar that Lady Delaney's spare derringer tended to fire to the left.

At least she and Guillam had left them in peace. Foley was also relieved to note that Guillam had so far not told Roddy McBride their identities. That it was the Templars who had killed his brother Eddie meant little; Roddy's last words to his brother were to kill Foley and Sirk. Instead Eddie and several of his men had died bloodily, and the word on the streets of Glasgow was that McBride was leaving no stone unturned in his search for the two unknown men last seen with Eddie.

One word from Guillam to McBride, and the feared patriarch of the criminal family would know the names of the two men he sought.

Hunt led Foley to a small cemetery partitioned from the main churchyard, separated by an iron gate that squealed as he opened it. A pillared mausoleum sat within, rough marble, and sealed by a grilled iron gate. Gravestones surrounded it, the oldest weather-faded, the newest maybe a couple of decades old.

Foley studied one of the more recent gravestones, noting it memorialised Henry, Iona, William and Aine Hunt, all of whom died twenty-eight years ago. Henry and William Hunt had been set to become the 4th and 5th Barons of Ashwood. "The family tomb?"

"Yes." Hunt pointed to the mausoleum. "The barons and their wives are buried within, the rest of the family have to make do with a common grave. It was opened recently to inter my Great-Uncle Thomas."

They both eyed the marble tomb, gleaming in the sunlight. "So, you've got that to look forward to," Foley said finally. The thought of a stone sarcophagus buried below waiting patiently for Hunt made his skin crawl.

"Yes." A roll call of the Lords and Ladies Ashwood was engraved in the marble, with room optimistically left for plenty more.

"When you invited me up here to see the family estate, this wasn't what I had in mind," Foley said tartly.

"The Horned Lord might be more to your liking."

"What's that?" Foley asked cautiously.

A ghost of the old Hunt appeared as he smiled amidst the

graves of his ancestors. "The inn. Oldest building in the village."

"So long as the ale's fresh." They left the cemetery, the earthen road turning to cobbled stone as they entered the heart of Kirkaline. "That name sounds a bit too pagan," Foley observed.

"It's properly called the Ashwood Arms, but the old name stuck. Even my ancestor's soldiers had the good sense not to burn it to the ground."

"A good pub is an irreplaceable treasure," Foley opined, ignoring stares from the few locals they passed. A row of shops ran along the main street: a butcher's, a general store and tobacconist, and the post office. Stocky men with salt-roughened skin unloaded freshly caught fish from a cart into the fishmongers, the aproned proprietor casting a critical eye over the catch.

They continued down the street, the smells of meat and fish soon replaced by that of fresh bread, and sure enough Foley saw a baker's shop ahead. Next to it sat a weaver's shop, where looms were worked within to process wool into material suitable for sale.

Foley recognised the harbour from yesterday, two fishing boats tied up. There was no sign of the ferry. Two old men sat on the edge of the pier, casting into the loch with their rods.

The clanging of metal striking metal drew louder as they approached the inn. Some heavier industry was clustered round it, requiring to be near the stable to make easier the movement of goods and materials. A stonemason ignored Hunt and Foley as they walked by, engrossed in the piece of marble he was working on.

The clash of metal continued from within the smithy, smoke from the forge exiting a stone chimney. The clanging subsided, and a moment later Foley heard a violent hiss as red-hot metal was quenched in water. Horseshoes hung from the smithy's exterior walls. A master blacksmith could make a good living in a remote place like this, making and repairing tools needed for working the land, and shoeing the draughthorses used to pull the ploughs that tilled it.

A dark-haired youth aged maybe twelve left the smithy, his sooty face drenched with sweat, scorch-marks staining his sturdy leather apron. The blacksmith's apprentice, certainly, maybe a son following in his father's trade. He caught sight of Hunt and Foley, watching them for a moment.

"Do these people know who you are, or is it just the novelty of seeing someone who isn't a cousin?" Foley asked.

Hunt chuckled. "I doubt they know who I am, they certainly don't know or care who *you* are, and strangers are uncommon enough to attract attention."

The stable sat next to the smithy, smaller than Foley expected. On reflection, he decided the inn saw most of its passing trade come by sea rather than by land.

The inn itself was a large three-storeyed building, recently whitewashed and still retaining its thatched roof which looked well-maintained. Its sign named it the Ashwood Arms, but a pair of stag antlers jutted out from the sign, a wink to its original name, the Horned Lord.

"Who is this 'Horned Lord'?" Foley asked, disturbed by a suggestion of devil worship.

"Cernunnos, a god of fertility, animals and the underworld. A hunter." Hunt spoke slowly, perhaps recalling old myths told to him as a child. "Said to be the son of the god Lugh."

"Lugh?"

"A warrior god. Also reckoned the sun god," Hunt said.

"When did you become an expert on pagan gods?"

"I'm no expert, but my father hired a gamekeeper from Dunlew to teach me hunting with a rifle. He would tell me stories of some of the old gods, Cernunnos in particular. Apt, as the Horned God is Lord of the Hunt."

The inn had small dark windows, keeping the interior a mystery. A thick wooden door lay open, either to encourage people inside or maybe just to cool the interior. There was a strong smell of cooking food, and that as much as the prospect of a cooling pint of ale drew Hunt and Foley through the Horned Lord's portal.

Chapter Seven

The midday sky was a clear blue canvas, untainted by clouds as Kerry and Lady Delaney strolled through Glasgow's Botanic Gardens. Long sleeves and a wide-brimmed straw hat sitting atop her curled hair protected Kerry's fair skin from the blazing sun, aided by a clumsily wielded small white parasol.

Lady Delaney was similarly attired, her summer dress pale-blue to Kerry's white. She held her parasol with practised ease to keep her own complexion pale. Tanned skin was considered uncouth among women of status, a mark of those who laboured outside. Kerry was 'fortunate' her skin tended to burn in the summer before peeling pale again, a sprinkling of freckles across her face the only sign of a time when pale skin had not been a consideration.

As an actress, she had spent the previous several summers performing in Glasgow Green's penny geggies – booth theatres made from wood and canvas – her dream one day to perform in the city's grander theatres. Violence was no stranger to the Glasgow Green, and Kerry knew from experience that the sweltering summer days and brief nights would see the working-class families reluctantly sharing the East End park with the rougher denizens of the city.

But the Botanic Gardens and nearby Kelvingrove Park, cocooned in the more prosperous West End, were untroubled by belligerent drunks intoxicated on cheap ale and bootleg gin. Merchant families relaxed on rugs laid on the grass and enjoyed picnics, feasting on sandwiches filled with roasted meat and salads, finishing with cheesecakes and puddings, all washed down with wine or fresh lemonade. Many sheltered beneath the trees, the late arrivals forced to rely on parasols for shade.

Even the University of Glasgow had fled the poverty of the High Street slums, relocating from its mediaeval campus to a relatively new site atop Gilmorehill. The university's sandstone tower was visible above the trees.

Couples of all ages walked through the park while children ran and played. Kerry wondered how many of those here had made their fortunes on the backs of the poor, though she accepted some wealthy philanthropists strove to see the destitute educated and housed in less crowded, appalling conditions. The late Sir Andrew Delaney had apparently seen to the education of those working in his mills, until his untimely death.

Lady Delaney had been forced to sell most of the family's businesses to affiliates of the Sooty Feathers, but she continued to support several charities in the city. Her attention was focused, however, on bringing down the Sooty Feathers and their undead masters.

"A splendid day," Lady Delaney remarked.

"Yes, Lady Delaney. But rather too hot for my tastes." In truth she loved the sun despite its insistence on burning her skin, but Lady Delaney was teaching her to play a young woman from a family of means. To not just play a role on the stage but to live it daily was a challenge few thespians could refuse. And should her performance ring false, she might be unmasked by the Sooty Feathers and killed. Or worse.

Becoming undead, killing the innocent and feasting on their blood held no appeal for Kerry.

"As one grows older, Miss Knox, one discovers it is the cold one feels more in one's bones."

"As you say, Lady Delaney." A young lady did not contradict men or her elders. The formality was something she had struggled with at first; even in private, unrelated women would only address one another by their first name if they were close friends. The working-class residents of Duke Street, where Kerry had grown up, had been far less formal, as were the thespians she had worked with during the previous summers.

A cleared path led them downhill to the riverbank, sounds of laughter and splashing water growing louder. Kerry spied a group of children playing in the River Kelvin, part of her wishing she could join them in the cool water. The North

Woodside Flint Mill lay further down the bank on the other side of the river, and if the children dared play too close to its waterwheel, they could expect to be chased off by the mill workers.

"How are you finding your apprenticeship?" Lady Delaney asked with a crispness in her tone that Kerry had come to recognise as her 'work' voice. On their own for now, the conversation could turn to matters of greater significance than the weather and other insipid topics considered suitable for ladies to discuss.

"I think it's going well," Kerry said hesitantly, suddenly concerned that Lady Delany held a contrary opinion and intended to dismiss her. "I've still much to learn."

"We're in agreement on both counts. You've sufficiently learned etiquette to a degree that I am confident to introduce you to society as my companion without–"

"–sounding like I've just left the bogs of Ireland?" Kerry asked, wincing at the bite in her voice. She had been born and raised in Glasgow, but her parents had emigrated from Ireland like many others and had passed on their accent.

"A fair if harsh way of putting it," Lady Delaney said in mild remonstrance. "Your Irish roots are a benefit, since we can introduce Miss Knox as the daughter of a Dublin merchant family formerly acquainted with my late husband.

"Your mastery of skills that are … shall we say, of an unladylike nature, is progressing well. A lot of room for improvement, naturally, but such skills require frequent practice until you perform them without thinking." Lady Delaney's tone turned sharper, and Kerry turned to see coldly serious eyes watching her. "Fear will make you slow and clumsy. But with sufficient practice, your body will act of its own accord."

A room in Lady Delaney's house had been turned into a gymnasium of sorts, with a bare wooden floor. They sparred daily, Lady Delaney teaching her to fight with an eclectic range of weapons, and with no weapons at all. Picking locks, disguising oneself, following a target undetected … defeating a mortal human, defeating an undead opponent.

Daily they practised with firearms too, in Lady Delaney's basement that she had reinforced with concrete blocks to muffle the sound and protect the walls. Revolvers, derringers and shotguns – Kerry was learning to wield them all, and to load, unload, disassemble and reassemble them until her fingers hurt, so that she could do it without thinking.

But those days were still a long time distant. For now, she could hold her own and fire a gun without shooting her foot off or scaring herself with the noise.

"How did you learn such things?" she dared ask.

"Over a very long time, through trial and error," Lady Delaney answered wryly. "Some skills I learned myself, others I learned from the Templars during a summer in London."

"And will we accomplish anything this summer?" Kerry asked. *Or are we wasting our time, killing bottom feeders while those at the top grow rich and fat?*

"I believe by the time the days shorten, the undead will have endured a lean summer and their servants will be greatly diminished. If we can hurt them sufficiently, it will strengthen Steiner's efforts to convince his superiors to send more Templars back to Glasgow." She shrugged. "We shall see."

Kerry took a breath. "And why me? Why train me, let me stay with you?"

"I grow old, Miss Knox. I tire quicker and my joints ache. I hope to train a replacement, someone unwilling to let evil rule this city unchallenged."

"And the list of candidates was small," Kerry said, her feelings conflicted.

Lady Delaney smiled. "True, but had I believed you unsuited, I would not have agreed to train you."

"What of Hunt, Foley and Sirk? Might they not be of aid?"

"Perhaps." Lady Delaney's voice held a note of caution. "After our contentious parting I've made no effort to contact them, nor they us. And I rather suspect whatever motivated their involvement in the spring was satisfied with Rannoch's death."

Kerry said nothing.

"And one apprentice is enough for me," Lady Delaney said with a smile. "Another three would drive me to distraction."

"Did they not fight well?"

"Professor Sirk fought competently, but he is even older than me. Mr Foley is an effective brawler, using skills learned from his time as a soldier, but our work relies on a more delicate touch. We are assassins, not soldiers."

"And Mr Hunt? He killed Rannoch."

"A lucky amateur." Lady Delaney held up a cautioning finger. "And luck, Miss Knox, is a fickle ally at best."

They walked back to the open grass of the park, sunlight flashing off the Kibble Palace, a large iron-framed glasshouse. Kerry breathed in deep, enjoying the fragrant smells of plants, flowers and freshly mown grass. The park might seem as close to paradise as could be found on earth, but she was well aware the less fortunate toiled a few miles away in factories and mills, choking on dust and cotton.

A football rolled near them, Kerry thoughtlessly kicking it back to the group of adolescent boys to whom it belonged. She winced as they laughed and waved, troubled less by their boisterous response than by the attention it attracted. Young ladies did not kick footballs.

Lady Delaney thankfully let her slip pass without comment.

"What say we partake of a refreshment, Miss Knox?"

"That would be lovely, Lady Delaney," Kerry simpered.

"I know a delightful tearoom nearby."

Grey squirrels flitted up tree trunks and along branches while birds squabbled over scraps of food. A man in a worn grey tweed suit and bowler hat walked about, handing leaflets to any who would take one. Kerry watched a woman gratefully accept one. After a quick glance to check the man wasn't watching, the woman used the paper to clean jam off her young child's face.

"What cause do you champion, sir?" Lady Delaney asked as they approached the man.

"The welfare of orphans, many being exploited in factories and cotton mills, madam," he said, looking pleased at someone showing interest. "Regulations in place to protect the children and limit their working hours are being ignored, and there's been a real increase in child deaths over the past few months."

"Shocking," Lady Delaney said. "A recent increase, you say?"

The man nodded. "Aye, madam. Since late spring. I'm a member of the National Society for the Prevention of Cruelty to Children, and we believe children are working too long, leading to more accidents."

"What of the laws in place to limit the hours worked?" Lady Delaney asked.

"The Factory Act? Many mills turn a blind eye to it, and there are too few inspectors to enforce it. We've tried to find out who the culprits are, but the town council is disinterested." He sounded passionate about his cause and frustrated that those in power didn't seem to share it.

Lady Delaney took a leaflet. "I hope you are able to expose these foul practices."

"The council don't care, probably bought off." He looked around the park. "That's why I'm here. Many rich industrialists live nearby or have friends who do. The mill owners might be happy to turn a blind eye to what their managers and foremen are up to in the name of profits, but if I can bring it to their attention directly, maybe they'll act." He did not sound optimistic.

"I wish you luck, sir."

They left the park and crossed Great Western Road, passing a church on the corner. Wagons and carriages travelled up and down roads covered in sun-baked dung and puddles of syrupy urine left by a multitude of horses. Both sides of the street were busy with pedestrians, shop doors left open to encourage them inside.

The Mulberry Tea Room offered a pleasant respite from the heat and crowds outside. The walls were papered a deep pink colour, and a large oak crockery stand displayed blue-and-white patterned china. A black fireplace sat against the opposite wall, clean and unneeded for the next few months. Round wooden tables covered in long white tablecloths were spread evenly across the open room, four chairs assigned to each. A varnished wooden floor gleamed, free of crumbs and spillages.

The tearoom was only a third full, its clientele almost entirely female. Ladies in floral summer dresses sipped tea, ate scones and cakes, and chatted to one another, all under the watchful eye of a matronly-looking woman of middle years alert for anyone requiring service.

"A table for two, Lady Delaney?" she asked.

"Yes. At my usual table, if you please, Mrs McNeil."

They were led over to a table near the fireplace, the quietest part of the tearoom. "What that man said about the children caught your interest," Kerry said after Mrs McNeil had served them tea and buttered scones from the cake stand. One particular chocolate cake had intrigued Kerry, but she didn't know its name and hadn't wanted to betray her ignorance.

Lady Delaney added a little milk to her tea and sipped it, nodding her approbation. "The plight of mistreated children is of interest to any right-thinking person."

Kerry had drunk tea for breakfast every morning growing up, brewed sparingly from the cheapest tealeaves her mother could find, and she had stopped drinking it on leaving home at sixteen to live with a widowed aunt and cousin upon her parents return to Ireland. But drinking tea was an essential part of a lady's social life, and Lady Delaney had insisted she resume the habit. Now accustomed to the richer blends used by Lady Delaney and tea rooms such as this, she had acquired a taste for it.

She sipped from her cup. "There was more to your interest than that."

"Indeed." Lady Delaney nodded. "Perceptive of you to notice. As you know, the short nights require the undead to rely upon the Sooty Feather Society to provide them with victims to feed from. An increase in disappearances would suggest to me that the society were kidnapping people, but there has been no such increase this year. But an unexpected increase in deaths would suggest...?"

Horror turned Kerry's stomach. "You mean they're feeding off children?"

"Perhaps. Orphans are often employed by mills and factories, accidents sadly common. The less scrupulous orphanages may very well make their wards work too many hours and feel no compunction about exploiting them in other ways. Or if one or more orphanages are selling their wards to the undead, industrial accidents would be a convenient explanation for deaths caused by unrestrained feeding. Some orphanages may even be operating as Crypts."

"God." Kerry looked in Lady Delaney's hard eyes. "There are a lot of orphanages, where should we start?"

"First, we must satisfy ourselves that the undead are indeed responsible for the increase in deaths, that it is not simply increased carelessness. We should examine some of the more recent bodies."

"Where do we do that?" Kerry hoped Lady Delaney wasn't proposing they dig up graves.

"The mortuary, my dear."

Chapter Eight

The lock yielded to Lady Delaney's expertise with two lockpicks. Kerry had hoped to be allowed to try, but time was of the essence. There would be some difficult questions asked if they were caught entering the hospital mortuary, nocturnal arrivals a very real possibility. Death heeded no clock.

She followed Lady Delaney inside, closing the door behind her. Like the corridor outside, the mortuary was unlit at this time of night. The oil lantern she carried was lit but shuttered to prevent light escaping. Now inside, Kerry opened the shutter enough to let them look around the room.

The mortuary was cool, the floor and walls covered in white tiles. It smelled strongly of bleach and other chemicals, but not enough to mask the stench of rotting flesh. Bodies decomposed quickly in the summer, and at least twenty lay on stretchers, covered by blankets and in some cases piled two high.

"Jock Gow, Tess Brown and Padraig Leary," Lady Delaney said as she approached the bodies. Three children supposedly killed in accidents were in the room. The earliest had happened a week past, but no one had troubled themselves yet to claim Tess's body.

Kerry hardened her heart (and stomach) and hunted for the relevant corpses at one end while Lady Delaney started at the other. Ignoring the larger bodies, Kerry lifted the blanket of a smaller cadaver and read the name scrawled on the toe tag: Paul Fletcher.

She re-covered Paul Fletcher's small, bone-white toe and went to the next likely body. *Yesterday afternoon I was enjoying a summer walk in the park and a cup of Darjeeling tea.* Her watch gave the time as almost eleven, the sun had set and now she was searching a room full of bodies.

"I've found Tess Brown," Lady Delaney said.

"Jock Gow," Kerry said on reading another tag.

"We'll start with him."

"Why not Tess?" Kerry asked.

"She's been here a week. I suspect the Sooty Feathers would want any undead victims removed quickly."

"That makes sense," Kerry said, relieved. She'd rather not see Tess's body after a week of corruption. Lady Delaney joined her and together they lifted the stretcher and carried it over to the wooden table at the other end of the room.

Lady Delaney pulled off the blanket without ceremony, and Kerry's skin crawled as she looked down at the naked, scrawny body of Jock Gow. Mr Dermott, the NSPCC man handing out leaflets in the park the day before, had welcomed their afternoon visit to his building. Their interest (and a generous donation from Lady Delaney) had made him most cooperative. The NSPCC had tenaciously obtained details of recently deceased orphans, and Dermott had made those records available.

"Hold the lantern up," Lady Delaney said as she slipped on a pair of spectacles and bent over to examine the body. Jock Gow was aged thirteen according to Mr Dermott's records, but he looked small for his age.

Kerry did so, watching as Lady Delaney searched for signs that undead had fed from the boy. She straightened up. "Your thoughts, Miss Knox?"

She leaned over the body and fought back her nausea, looking closely at the mottled flesh. The undead preferred to feed from arteries, favouring the throat, wrist or upper arm. She saw several small scars on his wrists, recent but healed. The scar on his throat was larger, fresh and raw, made larger by teeth marks. *The wound that killed him.* She imagined the pain and terror the boy must have felt, being fed from time and again until an undead finally gave in to his or her thirst and bled him dry. *Bastards!*

"Well?"

Kerry gathered her thoughts. "There are scars on both wrists, but caused by a razor, I think. I didn't see any scars caused by fangs, so he was fed from by ghouls, not vampyres. The throat wound is unhealed, so I think it was that what killed him."

"That *which* killed him. But very good. Continue."

She took a breath. "Ghouls cut into his wrists more than once, enough to bleed him but not kill him. Until the throat wound. Maybe he started bleeding too slow for them, or maybe they decided just to kill him." She stared down at the pale corpse. "One of them chewed his throat – human teeth, no fangs, so still a ghoul – and bled him dry." She shuddered, imagining the ghoul losing control and tearing at his throat with its teeth. Human teeth; undead were unable to extend their fangs until transitioning into a full vampyre.

"A fair summation, Miss Knox. No accident killed this child, in a mill or otherwise. But was he moved to a Crypt, or are undead dwelling in the orphanage he resided in?" She frowned at the corpse. "Is the orphanage itself a Crypt?"

"What now?"

Lady Delaney looked at the covered bodies. "Now we examine Tess Brown and Padraig Leary."

*

"Here." Lady Delaney handed Kerry a small glass of brandy.

"Thank you." She accepted it gratefully, a tremble in her hands. They had been steady in the hospital and in the cabriolet returning them to the West End, but the shaking had inexplicably started upon returning to Lady Delaney's home.

Floral maroon wallpaper covered the sitting room walls, the left wall hosting old portraits of a man, woman and two young children; Lady Delaney and her family, all, save her, twenty years dead. A large Persian rug was spread out across the middle of the room, its weaves worn and faded with age.

The weather had rendered the white marble fireplace purely decorative for months, a plain mahogany table separating two small couches. Lady Delaney's maid, Ellison, had retired to bed for the evening. How much the maid knew of her mistress's activities was a mystery to Kerry, Ellison discreet to a fault.

"A productive evening," Lady Delaney noted as she sipped from her own brandy. Kerry noted her mentor's hands were steady.

She took a shaky breath. "Aye." Unpleasant memories of the dead children came unbidden to mind. Thankfully, Lady

Delaney had examined Tess, recognising that decomposition would make it more difficult to identify signs of undead feeding. None had been found, the girl's ghastly head wound verifying the claim that she had been struck by a falling piece of machinery.

Padraig Leary showed some signs of feeding, less than Jock Gow. His arm had been caught in a machine, causing him to bleed to death. The smallest children were regularly sent below the machines and often caught in moving parts, many losing fingers or worse. Kerry wondered if blood loss from regular undead feeding had left Padraig slow and dull-witted, the undead killing him by proxy.

"What is our next step?" Kerry asked.

"Both boys lived in the Barrowfield Orphanage. Tomorrow this institution will have the honour of hosting Lady Delaney and Miss Knox, two philanthropists concerned about the wellbeing of the city's orphaned children."

"Will they make time for us?" Kerry had known a few orphans growing up, victims of abuse, neglect and exploitation. When she imagined those who ran such places, she saw cruel men and women jealously guarding their oppressive domains, fearful of interest from the outside world.

Lady Delaney smiled humourlessly. "The offer of a charitable donation opens many doors, my dear."

"As you say, Lady Delaney."

She leaned back and studied her. "I think … Kerry … that we are sufficiently acquainted with one another that we may dispense with the formalities in private. My name is Caroline."

"Thank you … Caroline." Kerry felt her face warm as she said the name, finding her mentor's first name unwieldy on her tongue.

*

An iron fence surrounded the Barrowfield Orphanage, its once-red bricks blackened from decades of soot and smoke. Glasgow's East End was heavily industrialised with factories and textile mills, Kerry's father having worked in a carpet factory near the Glasgow Green before returning to Ireland with Kerry's mother.

They had wanted her to return with them, no doubt planning to marry her off, but the call of the theatre had still been strong then, and she had moved in with her aunt. Playing Lechery in *Doctor Faustus* was as close as she had come to realising that dream, even if Steiner had bribed the manager for the role as part of his plan to capture a leading Sooty Feather. Still, she had enjoyed her time acting in the Glasgow Green in the booths during the past summers.

On being cast out into the world, Glasgow's orphans would dream of little more than shelter and food in their belly. An unattainable dream for many, facing a short life of hardship, disease and deprivation. The boys faced being crippled young by backbreaking labour, and many of the girls would be forced into prostitution, culled by violence or syphilis. Alcohol would kill most who avoided those fates.

Lady Delaney knocked on the sturdy black door. Despite the heat, their parasols had been left at home and they wore conservative dresses in dark colours. A small wide-brimmed hat sat atop Kerry's head, her straw boater deemed too frivolous. *We're serious-minded ladies on serious business.*

The door opened, a young man with a pockmarked face peering at them suspiciously. "Good day, ladies." His expression betrayed his resentment at having to answer the door, though the sight of two ladies of obvious means caused him to adopt a polite tone until he learned their business.

"Good day. I am Lady Delaney. Miss Knox and I are here to inspect the premises."

He blinked a few times. "Inspect?"

Lady Delaney ignored the sudden fear on his face. "Yes. As I explained in my letter, Miss Knox and I are part of a philanthropic group looking to endow three orphanages with an annual stipend to aid them in their fine work. You did get my letter, yes?"

The young man let them inside and hurried to fetch Mr Green, the manager. He returned minutes later, bobbing his head up and down as he led them through the hall into a small parlour, mumbling something Kerry couldn't quite catch.

The parlour was small, and the green wallpaper old and sun-faded where it faced the window, but the brown carpet looked new as did the three-seater couch and armchair with matching patterned upholstery. A new drinks cabinet sat in the corner, its varnished surface gleaming. Kerry caught a whiff of liquor in the air and noted an unwashed glass sitting on a small table next to the armchair. The orphanage had clearly come into some money.

Green arrived, his face flushed. Aged nearer fifty than forty, he had thin hair above a fleshy face. Judging by his girth, if the children ate half as well as he, they would be fortunate indeed. But Kerry doubted it.

"Good day, ladies," Green said through a forced smile. "I'm Mr Green, the manager."

"A good day, indeed, Mr Green. I am Lady Delaney, and this is my companion, Miss Knox." She exuded a distant charm, like a queen deigning to visit her subjects.

Green fidgeted nervously. "My son James said you were with a … a group. That you had come with money?" Fear and hope warred on the man's face; fear that his illicit activities – whatever they were – might come to light – and hope that some group of rich do-gooders were foolish enough to give him money.

Lady Delaney smiled indulgently. "I fear the young man has slightly misrepresented the reason for our visit. We wish to endow three worthy institutes such as yours with an annual stipend to further benefit the resident children, but we must visit all the residences on our short list to identify the three most worthy." She creased her brow. "All of this, and the date of our visit, was explained in my letter."

They had received no such letter, unsurprising since it was entirely fictional, Lady Delaney wanting to catch the orphanage unprepared.

"But I am confident you will find our humble residence entirely to your liking," Mr Green promised, beads of sweat lining his brow. "Mrs Green and I think of the children as our own."

"Is your wife here?" Kerry asked, diluting her accent.

"She is upstairs, tending to the children," Green said.

Putting the fear of God into them, no doubt, and removing any signs of sloth or mistreatment.

"Perhaps you might show us around?" Lady Delaney prompted.

"Some tea first, maybe?" Mr Green asked.

Kerry assumed an expression of regret. "I fear our time is limited, Mr Green. We must visit another home today."

"Of course, Miss Knox," Green said, spurred to haste by the reminder that there was competition for the fictional stipend.

He showed them around, talking constantly as if hoping to distract them from the orphanage's shortcomings – of which there were many. Money might have been spent refurnishing the parlour, a sanctuary for the Greens, but the rest of the orphanage was in disrepair. Bare floorboards creaked underfoot, and cracks lined the walls and ceilings. The dining room was bare except for a long wooden table lined with stools.

"Where does that lead?" Lady Delaney asked on returning to the main hall. A door beneath the staircase had caught her attention. If undead were using the orphanage as a Crypt, a cellar would offer the best hiding place from daylight.

"The cellar, Lady Delaney," Green answered, a flash of guilt crossing his eyes as he looked down.

"Might we take a look?" Kerry asked.

Lady Delaney flashed her a warning look. "Miss Knox, I really don't think we have any business going down into a dirty cellar."

"Surely not," Green chuckled in relief. "The dormitory would be of greater interest to you ladies."

"I look forward to meeting the children, Mr Green, and your good wife," Lady Delaney said. Kerry followed silently, wondering at Lady Delaney's reaction to her asking about the cellar. *Where else would a pack of ghouls sleep during the day?*

The staircase creaked alarmingly as Green led Lady Delaney and Kerry upstairs, James remaining below. Lady Delaney chattered to Mr Green, doing an excellent impression of a lady with a lot of money but little between her ears but air and good intentions.

The upper floor was in an even poorer state than the floor below. Patches of damp stained the ceilings, and there was a musty odour of rot in the air. The floor was bare wood, the boards damaged in places, but they had been recently scrubbed clean. Likewise, the skirting boards were free of dust. The house's bones might be rotting away, but it was otherwise kept clean. Kerry suspected the Greens tasked their wards with the household chores, withholding food or dolling out punishments for any perceived laxity.

Green led them into the dormitory, in truth two or three large rooms that had been knocked into one. Maybe a dozen iron bedframes lined one side of the room, another dozen sitting across from them, thin blankets neatly folded on each bed. A small trunk sat at the foot of each bed. Unlit oil lamps were hung sparingly from the walls, and there were two fireplaces, one boarded up. The other was probably only lit grudgingly, every lump of coal a prisoner. A boy stood at the end of most of the beds, head down and hands folded at his front. Each wore short dark trousers, worn threadbare shoes and patched brown smocks.

A large woman stood in the centre of the room, hands clutched together, her mouth forced into a welcoming smile that twitched from nerves. She wore a dark skirt and blouse, her mousy-brown hair tied back in a bun.

"Lady Delaney, Miss Knox; may I present Mrs Green, my good wife. Mrs Green, I have the honour to introduce you to Lady Delaney and Miss Knox, from the … the–"

"The Hillhead Ladies' Philanthropic Society," Lady Delaney supplied smoothly.

Mrs Green bobbed her head and offered the suggestion of a curtsey. "Welcome," she managed to gasp out. Kerry noted a few of the boys watching her surreptitiously; Mrs Green doubtless ruled these children with an iron rod, mistress of the house and all within it. Seeing her flustered and deferring to two strangers must be an uncommon and gratifying sight for them. Unless they feared what it boded for them.

"Today being Sunday, the children were excused chores and work," Mr Green said.

"Their spiritual wellbeing is as important to us as their other needs," Mrs Green said. "The Reverend Baker gives them their godly instruction every Sunday at the local parish church."

"Excellent," Lady Delaney said with an approving smile, though Kerry knew she harboured a certain contempt for God and religion. "Perhaps Miss Knox could examine the children? Our report must be thorough, you understand."

The Greens agreed to this, the children having no say in the matter. Lady Delaney went downstairs, ostensibly to use the outhouse, though Kerry suspected that was a ruse to check the cellar. While the Greens spoke unconvincingly about how they considered the children as dear to them as if they were their own, Kerry awkwardly examined the boys in turn. She found no serious injuries, mostly just bruises that could be explained by rough play. More concerning were the persistent coughs some were afflicted with, probably due to the cold and damp conditions of the orphanage in winter. She took her time, hoping to distract the Greens long enough for Lady Delaney to check the cellar for any signs of undead habitation.

"Peter's been living here since he was a babbie," Mr Green said, nervously watching Kerry examine the wrists of a small boy aged maybe twelve. "I almost think of him like my own flesh and blood."

Peter rolled his eyes slightly and coughed back a laugh as Kerry surreptitiously winked at him. She could see no scarring on the necks or wrists to suggest any of the children had been bled or fed directly from by undead, but Lady Delaney's continued absence sent a stab of anxiety through her. God only knew what she had found down in that cellar. Or what found her.

If there was trouble, I'd know about it. If Lady Delaney did go down, Kerry fancied she wouldn't do so quietly.

The stairs creaked loudly as someone climbed them, Kerry praying it was Lady Delaney. Or maybe it was James Green coming up to say he had caught her snooping.

Lady Delaney entered the room, not a hair out of place. "Almost finished, Miss Knox?"

"Yes, Lady Delaney. The children look well cared for." *No undead bastards have been feeding from them.*

The Greens led them back downstairs to the parlour, looking relieved that their orphans appeared to have passed muster.

"I'm impressed, Mr and Mrs Green," Lady Delaney lied convincingly, not bothering to say what in particular had supposedly impressed her. "I was sorry to hear about your recent losses, though."

A look of confusion passed over their faces. "Losses?" Mrs Green asked hesitantly.

"Yes. Did not two of your wards die this week? A Jock Gow and Padraig Leary?"

Plainly, neither Green knew of either death, surprise quickly replaced by a furtive guilt. "Ah, well, Lady Delaney, both lads recently found work with the MacInesker Foundation," Mr Green said. "They've taken on five of our lads since early summer, finding them work at one of their mills."

"The foundation also wants to educate their young workers," Mrs Green said with a painted smile on her face. "So, they house them in a building attached to the mill where they are schooled twice a week." Evidently recalling the deaths of two of those sent to that mill, she lost her smile and assumed a look of sadness. "We had not heard about Jock and Padraig, God rest them."

Mr Green shook his head. "Tragic. Such lively lads, they were."

"Laudable of this foundation, to not only employ and educate orphans, but to put a roof over their heads, too," Kerry said. *Laudable. I like that word, must use it more often.* "Which mill did they send the boys to?"

"I don't know," Mr Green had to admit. "They own a number of mills and factories."

"The foundation hosts regular fundraisers," Mrs Green said, then bit her lip. Maybe she worried that if Lady Delaney's fictional group gave money to the foundation, there would be less to give to the Barrowfield Orphanage.

"Lady MacInesker is the patron of the foundation," Mr Green said, missing the vexed look from his wife, too busy trying to distract Kerry and Lady Delaney from the fact they had sent two of their wards away to their deaths.

Lady Delaney adjusted her hat. "We really must be off. You have our thanks for your time, Mr Green. We will write to you our decision regarding which orphanages are to receive our endowment."

The Greens looked happy to see them off, showing them to the door.

"What did you find in the cellar?" Kerry asked as they walked out the gate back onto the pavement.

"Damp, and a lot of it," Lady Delaney said. "I rather suspect any misbehaving children are sent down there in punishment. But there was nothing to suggest the undead use it as a Crypt. The children showed no signs of having been fed from or Mesmered?"

"No, Lady Delaney."

"Caroline when we're alone." Lady Delaney glanced at Kerry. "Your thoughts?"

Kerry took a moment to compose them in her head. "This MacInesker Foundation sounds like something we should look into. I think they're buying children from orphanages around the city and putting them to work in their mills. At least one mill is maybe being used as a Crypt. By housing the children, they can work them during the day and let the undead feed from them at night. Bastards." She coloured. "Sorry."

"Bastards indeed, Kerry. I reached the same conclusion. This MacInesker Foundation warrants investigation." They walked on several steps. "The Greens seemed particularly uncomfortable regarding it."

"The foundation is bribing them to take children off their hands but not off their books," Kerry explained. "As far as anyone's concerned, Jock and Padraig were still living at the orphanage when they died, meaning the orphanage was still getting paid to feed, clothe and look after five boys who were living and working at a MacInesker mill."

Some of the money had been used to improve the parlour, the rest undoubtedly falling into the Greens' pockets. The Greens hadn't even known at least two of the boys were dead. Anger quickened Kerry's heart. They had sold five boys off like slaves and forgotten about them. Were the other three even still alive? If they were, they were likely trapped in a hell, worked into exhaustion all day before being bled for sustenance at night.

"I think it high time you earned your keep, Miss Knox," Caroline said after a thoughtful silence. "Have you ever considered working in a mill?"

"We'll need to find out which mill. I'm not *bloody* working in them *all*."

Caroline smiled. "Perhaps we should call upon this Lady MacInesker and see if we can shorten the list."

"Where can we find her?" Kerry asked.

"The MacIneskers own the Dunkellen estate to the south of

Glasgow. It covers a lot of land, with the city looking to expand there in the coming decades. Sir Neil died last winter of a fever."

"I'm thinking we can't just turn up on her doorstep." Kerry said. "How do we get an invitation – offer her foundation money?"

"Yes. It appears the Hillhead Ladies Philanthropic Society is not yet done with goodly works."

Chapter Nine

"Arakiel," a man said, breaking the silence.

"Erik Keel," the demon corrected, not looking away from the tropical forest before him, millions of years old. Trapped in this fragile vessel, he refused to consider himself deserving of his true name until he was once more *Grigori*. It rankled that his remains were in the possession of Niall Fisher, but at least that meant he might one day fully return. "You're looking better than when last we met, Khotep."

"It's Theodore Essex now, and thank you," the lich said as he joined Keel at the railing overlooking the fossil grove. "A pity I cannot say the same for you, Mr Keel, though at least you can now enjoy the splendid weather outside."

Keel ignored the barb in Essex's tone. As pleasant as it was to feel the sun on his face and smell the flowers populating the park, he would trade it all to restore to his own flesh, confined to the night though he would be. "You took your time in answering my summons."

"I had commitments in London I could not quickly abandon. And I disliked the manner of your man, Canning. An uncouth fellow. Rannoch, at least, had some manners."

Keel was none too fond of the newly Made *Nephilim* either, but he did not have the luxury to pick and choose his followers. Yet. "A pity you didn't warm to him. You'll both be working together in the coming days and weeks."

"An interesting place you chose to meet," Essex said, evidently done discussing Canning.

Keel looked back at what had once been a swamp. The fossilised roots and stumps of eleven trees, believed extinct, had been discovered six years earlier as this part of the Scotstoun estate was turned into the Victoria Park. A decision had been made to preserve the find, the building they now stood in being built around the fossil grove.

Whitewashed walls and a wooden roof protected this fragment of the ancient world from the elements, a frozen remnant of a time when this land was tropical, located near the equator. Keel considered it. *Ancient ... I was old when the stone forest before me was young, when these trees were saplings.*

Or was he. He had been in Heaven then. As always when in the material realm, his memories of Heaven were vague and elusive beyond the purity of the place, a realm of distilled creation. Likewise, he would struggle to describe Hell, struggle to understand what it was like now he had escaped it, but he remembered enough to be thankful for that ignorance.

A shiver ran through him at the thought of Hell. He had spent two hundred of this world's years there. Most of his kindred had spent more than five-times-five that there; no wonder some went insane once Summoned, euphoric at being free from the prison they had been exiled to, the price of losing the war against *Mikiel.*

Lucifer, damn your pride. It was some comfort at least that the former archangel was likewise condemned to a human Vessel, even if he had accomplished the impossible and bred a human child. Lucifer's motive in doing so had initially escaped Keel, an ignorance that had made him uneasy until he realised what Lucifer intended. A letter had been sent, and until it was answered, Keel intended to honour his truce with the fallen archangel. *You don't get to cheat our fate, Lightbringer.*

"Yes, interesting," he said, breaking free from his reverie and responding to Essex's comment.

"Am I to assume a reason for our visit here beyond curiosity? A reminder that as old as I am, you are older by far?"

"You can assume all the reasons you wish, Essex," Keel replied, tired of their game. "I've a job tonight for you and Canning." He looked the necromancer hard in the eye, resisting the impulse to Unveil. Essex was too old to be intimidated by it. "Do you consider yourself ready to repay your debt to me?"

Essex smiled and put his top hat back on. "Consider me

your servant, Mr Keel. For the next twelve months."

"For the next twelve months," Keel said, per their agreement the night before the necromancer's 16th century execution. "Do be careful; Glasgow's *Nephilim* deal with necromancers the same way Queen Mary dealt with Protestants."

Essex's lips thinned slightly at the reminder of how his Vessel during that time had died (arranged by Keel and Rannoch). "I'll be careful. In any event, should this Vessel suffer a mishap, my man Yates knows what to do. Have no fear that death will prevent me fulfilling my oath to you."

Keel nodded, knowing Essex's comment was less to reassure him and more to remind him that so long as the lich's soul was linked to his phylactery, death was little more than an inconvenience to him. "I have your address. Expect Canning to call upon you tonight."

Essex grimaced. "A delight, I'm sure."

*

Silas Thatcher rubbed tired eyes. "What is it?" He had been told to expect a messenger after sunset which, while not unusual, was damned inconvenient in summer. His subordinates sensed his mood and were walking on eggshells, doubtless wishing the police superintendent would just leave. He wished he could just leave, too, but instead he was stuck in his office, waiting.

Standing at the doorway, Sergeant John Grant cleared his throat. "Sir, you've a visitor."

At last. The hour was late, two hours after midnight. Part of him noted an odd set to the sergeant's expression. "Send them in."

A minute later his visitor entered, and Thatcher bit back a curse. The young woman looked maybe fifteen, certainly no older than sixteen, petite and dark-haired. No wonder Sergeant Grant had reacted so. Half the bloody station would probably believe he had a taste for young whores and was brazen enough to bring them here. Margot Guillam, at least, was an adult, and had a bearing about her that one might call almost aristocratic.

The young woman before him had no such bearing. "Who

are you?" he asked.

"Amy Newfield. Miss Guillam sent me."

"Could she not attend herself?" Thatcher asked waspishly, stung by the unfounded gossip the girl's unthinking arrival might spawn.

The girl seemed more interested in the contents of his desk, assorted paperwork he had little appetite to deal with.

"Look at me! Do you not know who I am?"

Marble eyes studied him before answering. Eyes that didn't blink, telling him belatedly the nature of the girl before him. "Miss Guillam sent me," she repeated, the bored hint of a threat in her voice. "And I know who you are, Police Superintendent Thatcher. *Tertius.*"

Fear stole Thatcher's anger. He was a senior officer in the Glasgow Constabulary, third ranking member of the Council of Eight that ruled the Sooty Feather Society, and through it, Glasgow. Among the most powerful men in the city. And yet subservient to the undead who ruled the society in turn. Amy Newfield – he recognised the name now, Made undead in the spring – might be a mere ghoul, but she was still *undead*, and she sheltered under the wing of Margot Guillam, Elder *Nephilim*, Regent of the city, *Prima* of the Council, and second only to the reclusive *Dominus Nephilim*, Fisher.

"You have a message for me?" he asked in a milder tone.

A hint of amusement glinted in Amy Newfield's dead eyes. A hint of amusement and a lot of hunger. Ghouls were unpredictable until they Transitioned to *Nephilim*. "Miss Guillam bids you attend a meeting of the Council in two days."

Confusion overrode the hold on Thatcher's tongue. "She sent *you* to tell me of a Council meeting? A human messenger could have done so." *Done so during daylight, permitting me to leave here hours ago.*

Amy Newfield cocked her head slightly. "Miss Guillam has a list of properties she wishes searched at dawn. Properties she has identified as belonging to the late Sir Arthur Williamson under different names. If so, Erik Keel or his associates may be using them."

The late Sir Arthur, once of the Council until his treachery was discovered, had been found dead in an alley days after Rannoch's death. No one had taken credit for the traitor's death. "I'll need a warrant to–"

Amy Newfield handed him a folder. "This contains the necessary warrants. Miss Guillam had the procurator fiscal attend her earlier this evening."

"I'll have my men execute these warrants," Thatcher promised. Or rather he would hand them to Sergeant Grant and leave the arrangements to him. He doubted Keel would be stupid enough to continue using Sir Arthur's old addresses, but it would keep the Regent happy to know that progress was being made. His own enquiries were yet to yield results.

Satisfied Guillam's orders would be carried out, Thatcher left the police station almost three hours later than originally planned. A cabriolet took him home to his townhouse across the Clyde, overlooking the river. Ordinarily beyond a superintendent's salary, Thatcher enjoyed additional incomes that allowed him to enjoy the finer things in life. Tired and suffering a headache, he promised himself a night of indulgence, treating himself to a few drams from a bottle of-

He slowed, an old copper's instinct warning something was not right. His rise to superintendent had been hastened by his Sooty Feather membership, but he had still done his time patrolling Glasgow's pitiless streets.

Thatcher looked around but saw nothing untoward. The air was warm, almost humid, the cobbles slow to lose the day's heat. Nevertheless, he drew out his gun and cocked it. Silver bullets nestled in its six chambers, a precaution should the undead ever decide his usefulness had expired, or one attacked him ignorant of his identity.

Still nothing, but he hastened his pace, his front door seconds away. Thatcher transferred his gun to his left hand and retrieved his front door key. He climbed the steps leading up to the door quickly, unlocking the door and pocketing his gun, though he kept hold of it. *Just tired, that's all. That damned ghoul has me jumping at shadows.*

Too late he heard something scrape off the path behind him, and he had only half-turned, his gun not quite cleared the pocket when he was shoved forwards, sent sprawling into the house.

A booted foot kicked the gun from his hand as he lay on the floor, a dark silhouette bearing down on him. *Must get up!*

"A *pleasure* to meet you, Mr Thatcher," a cheerful voice said inches from his face. "I've always wanted to kill a policeman. Erik Keel sends his regards."

Pain ripped through his throat.

*

"I thought we agreed that you would break his neck," Canning heard Essex say as he fed from the dying Thatcher's blood. As the man's heart slowed, the flow of blood spurting from his neck artery lessened.

Canning got to his feet, invigorated by the policeman's blood. Feeding from the privileged was always a delight, their blood rich from a diet of plentiful food and generally good health. "No, *you* said it would be better if I broke his neck, and *I* said I understood. I never said I would do it."

"I was going to hang him here, an apparent suicide. But the puncture wounds in his throat might arouse suspicions, no?" the necromancer complained.

"A good point," Canning agreed easily, sated by Thatcher's blood and untroubled by Essex's problem. He was tempted to leave Essex to sort it out, but *Arakiel*'s likely disapproval gave him pause. "He has a gun, why not make him shoot himself?"

Essex didn't greet this suggestion with much enthusiasm. "Is he dead yet?"

"Aye, he's dead."

The corpse twitched, seemingly contradicting this, but Canning knew it was the result of the necromancer's magic. With jerky movements Thatcher got to his feet, red staining his throat and uniform tunic. Blank eyes stared ahead, the corpse reduced to a puppet. Canning didn't like it, unsettled at his suspicion Essex's necromancy might be employed against him. He thought it unlikely, reassured that whatever fell power had brought him back from death left him immune. The necromancer's need for *Nephilim* blood was another bone of contention between them, particularly since *Arakiel* had ordered Canning to supply it.

Canning did not like giving. "What now?"

The corpse staggered across the floor. "I have an idea," Essex said, satisfaction in his raspy voice.

Chapter Ten

What a difference a few months make. Bishop Redfort sat on the sixth seat at the Council table, his face damp with perspiration. He was grateful Regent Guillam had dispensed with the half-masks the Council had been obliged to wear at all meetings under the late Regent Edwards, decreeing they were only to be worn during formal occasions. The Council chamber was poorly ventilated, stuffy in the summer and cold in the winter. The windows had been bricked up, ostensibly to reduce the building's Window Tax, but in truth ordered by the undead in case meetings lasted past sunrise.

For years Redfort had dreamed of sitting on the Council, gazing down at the lesser Sooty Feathers seated at the tables running down the left and right side of the High Table. That dream had been achieved, but the air of dominance, the assurance of control that had permeated the room before spring, was gone, shattered by death and betrayal. The Sooty Feather Moot at Dunclutha in early April had been intended as a celebration of the society's power, a time to bring in new blood and new money.

Instead old blood had been shed. Regent Edwards, Elder *Nephilim* and the Council's Primus, had been slain, along with many members. His successor George Rannoch, ostensibly the society's saviour, had turned out to be the architect of that slaughter, part of his plot to bring back the House's previous Master, Erik Keel.

Rannoch was dead, but the Sooty Feather Society still reeled from that springtime calamity. The new regent, Guillam, had refreshed the fading décor of the Council chamber, replacing the worn carpets, repapering the walls and repainting the woodwork and plaster coving. But it would take more than a coat of paint to restore the society's confidence, to erase the battered faith and fearful mistrust festering between its members.

The polished double doors at the end of the room opened and Margot Guillam swept into the room, *Prima*, head of the Council. She was also Regent, ruling on behalf of the reclusive *Dominus Nephilim*, Niall Fisher. Redfort had never met the vampyre lord who ruled Glasgow and much of the south-west of Scotland, and he was happy for this to continue.

Guillam sat in the middle seat of the table. Seven of the eight chairs were now filled, the Third conspicuously absent. Was *Tertius* delayed, or was he carrying out duties elsewhere? *Or is he floating face-down in the river?*

Even those ruling the society – and through it the city – were not immune from peril. Half the Council, including Redfort, were new to their seats, replacing those who died on both sides of Rannoch's coup. But still death stalked them. Lord McKellen, Lord Commissioner of Justiciary in the High Court, had been killed six weeks earlier, butchered in his bed. *And so the Council had another seat in need of filling.*

Luckily Lord Smith, a fellow High Court judge and Sooty Feather, had been on hand, the obvious choice to become the next *Octavius.* Redfort had ascended from *Septimus* to *Sextus.* Moving up a seat on the Council so soon had been a pleasant surprise, one poisoned by a sliver of fear when another Councillor, the new *Septimus*, had disappeared. Just disappeared. His seat was quickly filled, there being no immediate shortage of Sooty Feathers occupying useful positions in society. *Yet.*

But that didn't change the fact that sitting on the Council no longer boded well for one's continuing good health.

The twelve men and women of the society's inner circle sat in respectful silence at the top of the two tables running down either side of the High Table. Other Sooty Feathers summoned to the meeting sat on the vacant seats, the tardy forced to stand.

Margot Guillam's pale face shone like polished ivory in the candlelight as she surveyed the gathered members. "Thank you all for coming," she said, maintaining the polite pretence that they had a choice.

There was an elephant in the room. Erik Keel. No one

knew if the demon was still in Glasgow or if he had fled with the Carpathian Circus after Rannoch's death. But his name was rarely mentioned at these meetings. Regent Guillam motioned for *Secundus* to make any announcements.

The white-haired man with the trembling hands shook his head. In times like these the Regent should have someone strong and experienced sitting in the Second Chair. Instead the Council's secondmost senior member was old and decades past his prime, overwhelmed and broken. *He's not even worth the trouble of killing.*

Tertius was still absent. *Quarta* cleared her throat, the last to have sat on the Council before Rannoch's coup. A few months prior she had been *Octavia*, the juniormost member. Now she was the fourth of eight. "I can report success in our scheme to establish a supply of blood for our Glasgow Crypts."

"Excellent," said the Regent, though she had doubtless been kept fully informed. "This damnable summer has been the bane of undead. Even *Nephilim* have struggled to control their Thirst, some going rogue." Her tone hardened. "And some have paid the price for that, slain in the street by an unknown party."

A tense quiet fell over the room. Redfort knew what most were thinking: Was Erik Keel behind the killings? Had Steiner returned to Glasgow with a fresh company of Templars? Or had a feud broken out between the city's undead, old grudges exhumed by Rannoch's actions? The latter worried Redfort the most. An undead civil war would catch the Sooty Feathers in the middle, crushing many, to say nothing of what it would do to the city.

Guillam made no further comment regarding the slain *Nephilim*. Redfort knew she would make no declarations of vengeance. Instead those assigned to find the responsible party would be met with individually and quietly given their orders. Was this just the new Regent's style, or did she suspect more traitors in their midst?

A female voice spoke up from near the doorway. "The *Nephilim* looking after newly Made ghouls complain that the rations are small and of poor quality."

Redfort peered down the room, recognising the speaker as Amy Newfield, Regent Guillam's pet ghoul. Slender and aged sixteen (now perpetually), Newfield had been Made by Rannoch, making her a third generation undead. Second generation if one discounted the originals, the *Grigori*. Had it not been for Wilton Hunt's bodysnatching, Newfield would have been one of Rannoch's followers, instead of falling into Regent Guillam's hands and patronage.

"It is the best we can manage," *Quarta* said defensively. "We must be discreet, after all."

"Expand your operation," Regent Guillam instructed *Quarta*. "Outside of Glasgow, if need be."

Quarta bowed her head. "Yes, Regent." Between the Templars and George bloody Rannoch, the city's undead population had been culled, and Guillam was evidently keen to replace those lost, lest another undead House decide Glasgow was ripe for the picking.

Quintus spoke next. "Four members of the Black Wing Club have been granted Initiate status as Sooty Feathers. The Black Wing Club has also extended invitations to eight potential members who may be suitable for the Society."

"Good," Regent Guillam said. "We must replace our losses."

Considered one of Glasgow's most exclusive clubs, the Black Wing Club recruited men and women of wealth, position or potential. Those members identified as being potential Sooty Feathers (as in, they possessed a certain moral flexibility) were initiated into the Sooty Feather Society hiding at the heart of the Black Wing Club. Kept ignorant of the true masters of the society – of Glasgow itself – the initiates were watched for several months before being inducted as full members.

Then they learned the full truth of things. Those who baulked at the supernatural world would be quietly dealt with, just as the late spring and summer had seen a dozen new members suffering mishaps. A high number, but unavoidable given that the events at Dunclutha had prematurely exposed every initiate to the existence of the undead. That coupled with the loss of so many members forced the Council to grant every initiate full membership, some inevitably proving unsuitable for such heavy knowledge.

That did unfortunately leave the Society scrambling to

recruit a new pool of initiates from the Black Wing Club, balancing the need to increase numbers while ensuring they were the *right* numbers. *Quintus* had been given that task.

"*Sextus?*"

Redfort started, Regent Guillam's voice returning his attention to the meeting. "Apologies, Regent. A few malcontents in the magician community have felt emboldened by our recent … misfortunes … to propose resisting the Council."

Someone snorted. "The Council yoke has always sat heavily on some magicians. For years malcontents have talked of rebellion, and for years they've done naught but talk. It's just been words borne of too much gin."

Redfort noted the speaker, a Puppeteer called Bartholomew Ridley. Able to manipulate magically prepared objects such as puppets and stuffed animals, it was unsurprising that magician unrest would be a sore point for him. To say nothing of the lack of a magician on the Council. *A known magician on the Council*, Redfort corrected himself privately. He himself was a dabbler, but his chosen magic was prohibited by the Council on pain of death, and so was one he rarely indulged in.

"Talk and nothing else," Ridley reiterated.

"Some of these malcontents have been emboldened enough to vacate the taverns and voice their opinions publicly in the Under-Market," Redfort said, smiling thinly as Ridley flinched. A whisper rustled round the room.

"The Council's rule is being questioned in public?" Regent Guillam asked in the quiet careful tone of someone wishing confirmation they heard correctly before ordering a dreadful response.

"Yes, Regent. By a few malcontents, I've no doubt, but they do attract small crowds." Redfort couldn't resist needling Ridley. "I'm surprised Mr Ridley is unaware of this."

Ridley went red as many in the room looked at him, scenting blood in the water. Either he was unaware of the goings-on in his own community, or he was aware and had kept silent. Neither cast him in a good light. "I've not been in the Under-Market in some weeks," he defended himself.

"Have your agents mark those paying too much attention to

these malcontents," Regent Guillam instructed Redfort, her unblinking gaze on him. "You already have the names of those denouncing us, of course?"

"Of course, Regent," Redfort assured her. There would be a few magicians found beaten or dead in the coming days, he knew.

Neither the new *Septimus* or *Octavia* had anything to report.

"You all know what must be done," Regent Guillam told the room. "Dismissed. *Sextus*, remain behind, if you please." *Remain behind, whether it pleases me or not.* Redfort sat while his fellow Sooty Feathers filed out of the room.

*

Amy Newfield was waiting in the study with Bishop Redfort's secretary, Henderson, when Regent Guillam entered with Redfort. An old, frayed Persian rug covered most of the wooden floor, oak-wooded bookcases holding ancient tomes with brittle pages bound in cracked leather. A desk and chair sat at the end of the room, the desk bare except for an inkwell, pen and oil lamp.

As pre-arranged, Amy handed Redfort a glass of Speyside whisky, said to be the bishop's favourite.

The grey-haired man smiled. "My thanks, Miss Newfield." He hid his dislike for her well, but she knew it was there. All the living feared the undead, which meant they hated the undead. Henderson, oddly, seemed indifferent to her.

"You're welcome, your Grace." A ghoul scant months old, the Councillors were unsure how to treat her. On one hand she was still a year or three from Transitioning to *Nephilim*, but on the other she was the Regent's right hand, entrusted with many duties. Odd, considering she had been Made by George Rannoch, but then she had never served her Maker.

Thinking about the body snatchers Hunt and Foley recalled her to Steiner, the Templar who had repaid her help in rescuing him with a silver bullet to the chest. The bullet had missed her heart but, being silver, it had rendered her unconscious. She was lucky to have regained her wits as Hunt and Foley re-dug her grave, believing her dead in truth. Hunger had goaded her to silently attack them from behind and gorge on their blood, but enough sense remained to her to know her weakened state would see them prevail. Instead she had slunk off and returned to Margot Guillam.

Once recovered, she had watched Lady Delaney's townhouse, hoping to deal with Steiner, but he was gone from Glasgow, and Regent Guillam had forbidden any action against his associates. For now.

Amy had been Made by Rannoch, but she suspected she knew why Guillam mentored the prodigy of her enemy; trust. Or rather, a lack of trust towards the city's undead and Sooty Feathers. Were more of Rannoch's supporters still in their ranks, secretly serving the demon Keel? Perhaps Possessed by the demon himself? No one knew, least of all the Regent, and so she had taken Amy Newfield under her wing. Amy was newly Made, with no hidden loyalties, and she had proven herself in helping defeat Rannoch at the Necropolis.

Redfort, on the other hand, was trusted only by necessity. Regent Guillam had told Amy that the bishop was ruthless in pursing his ambitions, becoming bishop after the leading contender for the position fell unexpectedly ill. She also confided her suspicions that Redfort was responsible to some degree for the assassination of the previous bishop, casting blame on the Templars.

"How goes your search for Erik Keel?" the Regent asked as Redfort took a sip from his whisky.

"Not well," Redfort was forced to admit. "We do not know if he is still in Glasgow or if he fled with the Carpathian Circus. For all we know, he was killed during the Templar assault on the Necropolis." He glanced at Amy, knowing of her presence during that battle.

"We know he was Summoned. Rannoch boasted as much to Hunt and Steiner before his death," Regent Guillam said, her tone conveying her dissatisfaction with Redfort's answer.

"But without knowing who he Possessed, we've no way of identifying him. Or her," Redfort said, frustration in his voice. "Regent."

"We know Sir Arthur Williamson escaped, perhaps with Keel," Amy said. "Before Steiner shot me, Lady Delaney said she saw him and a few others fleeing the Necropolis."

"Sir Arthur's dead, so we can't ask him," Henderson said.

Everyone looked at the secretary, even Redfort taken aback

at his presumption to speak. A look from the bishop quelled any further comment from Henderson.

"The circus is our best lead," Redfort said. "I've written to churches across Scotland enquiring about it, but no such circus has been reported in any town or village in Scotland."

"Still lying low," Amy said.

"Or maybe slipped across the border to England," Henderson said quietly, an anger in his eyes. He seemed to realise he had spoken again. "Forgive me, my Lady; your Grace. Sir Arthur and the circus undead nearly killed me at Dunclutha. It's a sore topic for me."

"I wanted to speak to you regarding another matter," Regent Guillam said to Redfort before he could chastise his secretary. Light from candle-holders hanging from the ceiling and walls lit up her face, emphasising her chalky pallor. She was still to feed, as was Amy. Thinking of blood caused Amy to glance speculatively at the secretary. He was short and thin, with reddish hair and freckles, aged maybe thirty. Prominent blue veins ran across his hands.

Redfort bowed his head. "I am, of course, your servant, Regent."

"Silas Thatcher has disappeared."

A flicker of pleasure at the news danced across the Bishop's eyes before he assumed a look of concern. "Ill news, indeed. Not only is he the Council's *Tertius*, he is our hand directing the Glasgow Constabulary. Who was the last to see him?"

"I was among the last," Amy admitted, drawing looks. "I passed him several warrants to search properties belonging to Sir Arthur Williamson under different names, properties unknown to the Heron Crowe Bank. He is known to have left the police station just after my visit, a cabriolet taking him to his house. No one has seen him since."

Redfort stroked his chin. "His contingency?"

Regent Guillam took a moment to answer. "Missing."

Everyone save Henderson recognised the significance of that news, the secretary failing to hide his irritation at his ignorance.

"Contingency?" he asked softly, risking either the Regent or the bishop's displeasure.

"Every Councillor must donate some blood upon their

ascension to the Council," Redfort answered absently. "Should they go missing, a Diviner can use the donated blood to find the donor."

Henderson rocked backwards on his heels at the news, his expression oddly opaque. "How was Sir Arthur not tracked, then? After Rannoch's fall."

"His contingency was given by me to a Diviner to find him when we knew he was with Rannoch," Amy said. "After the jar was unsealed, the blood quickly dried and was of no further use."

"I see," was all Henderson said. Redfort shot him a look of irritation, perhaps at his presumption in speaking uninvited.

"Was it taken, do you think, to track Thatcher?" Redfort asked.

Regent Guillam shook her head. "No. Why wait until he was home? And it would mean our enemy – Keel, if not another – has access to the Council vault in this building."

Redfort eyed her shrewdly. "Do you think Thatcher took it himself? With it gone, he could flee if matters turned sour, with no fear of being tracked by magical means."

"The thought occurred." The Regent clearly preferred it to the alternative of an enemy having unfettered access to the Black Wing Club building's restricted upper floor and vault.

"You wish me to search for him?" Redfort asked.

"I *wish* you to *find* him, Bishop," Margot Guillam answered coldly.

Redfort bowed again. "As you *wish*. Regent. Come, Henderson." The bishop strode out of the study, followed by his secretary.

Amy turned to Guillam. "Do you trust him, Mistress?"

"I trust him to act in his own best interest. If someone is killing Councillors, he knows he may be next."

Chapter Eleven

"Slainte," Foley said as he and Hunt raised their pint glasses in mutual salute. A week had passed since their arrival in Loch Aline, the weather glorious. A heavy rainfall a few days prior had refreshed grass and vegetation in danger of wilting, but the sky had cleared of clouds and the sun had returned once again.

The Ashwood Arms had become a favourite of Hunt and Foley's whenever time permitted. As expected, Hunt's mother had compiled a long list of chores to occupy them on the Ashwood estate, tasks too many for the diminished estate staff to complete. The pair had mended fences, restored a barn, and carried water from the well up to troughs in the fields owned by the estate, relied on by the cattle grazing there.

They had whitewashed walls and cleared debris clogging the cobbled courtyard, but Foley had been relieved that Lord and Lady Ashwood had not expected them to repair the ailing house. A building firm had been contracted to restore it once the Hunts and Foley had returned to Glasgow.

Working outside had not been unpleasant, Foley finding himself falling fast asleep each night without the aid of alcohol or laudanum. His wounds had mostly healed, and days in the sun were bronzing his face, neck and arms. He likewise saw a change in Hunt, the younger man building up muscle lost during his captivity.

Not that they were teetotal. Lord Ashwood was generous with his whisky, but Foley was learning the difference between a dram in the evening and drinking himself into a stupor.

After days of hard work in the estate, and a couple of days of rain, the pair had finally returned to the village of

Kirkaline, revisiting the Horned Lord for luncheon and a drink. They had yet to spend much time inside the darkened taproom, instead sitting outside in the rear courtyard, kitted out with rough-wooden benches and tables.

"Slainte," echoed Hunt as he drank from his glass. "We've earned these," he said.

"Aye," said Foley wholeheartedly. The cellar-cooled ale tasted pleasantly bitter and would taste even better when washing down the fish and potatoes being cooked in the inn's kitchen. Work in the adjacent smithy continued, a steady clanging of metal on metal; Foley did not envy the blacksmith and his apprentice having to work indoors next to a hot forge, pounding metal, not in this heat.

"So," Hunt said slowly, wiping foam from his upper lip. "What now?"

"After lunch? We could visit the old keep," Foley said.

"I mean, what about when we return to Glasgow," Hunt said. "What now for us?"

Foley considered. In truth, he had been trying not to think about the future, feeling stabs of panic at the thought of being shackled to his pharmacy for the rest of his life. "Well, Professor Miller's dead, so unless his successor is amenable, our bodysnatching days are done."

"We can make some discreet enquiries when we return," Hunt said.

"Aye," Foley said. In truth, he wondered how genuine Hunt's enthusiasm for resuming their nocturnal work on the side really was. When Hunt was estranged from his parents, aye, he needed the money, but he had patched up his relationship with them, more or less, as evidenced by this stay at the Ashwood estate.

Neither Lord nor Lady Ashwood had questioned Hunt regarding his plans for the future, which led Foley to suspect they were assuming Hunt's return to the fold was imminent. Studying Law, no, but finding a position in the family business? Maybe.

Foley didn't begrudge his friend finding a good job and life, but he doubted their friendship would survive the re-emergence of the Honourable Wilton Hunt, Heir Apparent to Ashwood and the Browning Shipping Company, a man who would soon find himself among the more eligible bachelors of Glasgow. Hell, aged twenty-four, the unmarried status of such a man would soon raise eyebrows. Foley was still unmarried, but no one gave a bent ha'penny about a pharmacist.

"What are you thinking?"

Foley started. "Oh, just about recent events."

"I try not to," Hunt said with a grimace. "Some days, I wonder how we're still alive."

"We were lucky." He forced a smile, troubled by the shadow that still darkened Hunt's moods. "Lucky and good enough to hold our own."

"Barely good enough." Hunt exhaled. "I still wake up in a sweat most nights, dreaming about…"

"About the night Miss Gerrard was killed and you were taken?" Foley guessed.

"Not that night," Hunt admitted with a guilt-twisted smile. "About the nights after, the nights I was locked in a cell. I don't dream about Amelie at all, that I can remember." He looked away. "I wonder why?"

Because she was a passing fancy, a spring dalliance. Something new and exciting. Foley said nothing as he guessed Hunt's thoughts. His friend felt guilty that not only had the Gerrards died because of him, but that his feelings for the girl might have been fleeting. That may have been true, or he may have convinced himself that was the case to protect himself from grief. Foley suspected the former, though love may have grown between Hunt and Amelie Gerrard in time.

"We should discuss our plans for when we return to Glasgow," Foley said to bring Hunt back to the present.

"We just did. We'll see if the new senior medical professor is happy to continue Miller's arrangement, us exhuming bodies that pique his interest," Hunt said.

Foley shook his head, leaning closer. "Not that. I'm talking about the undead and where we stand with them. What we should do about it."

Hunt ran fingers through his unruly reddish hair, elbow leaning on the table. "Margot Guillam's been content so far to leave us be. And the McBrides haven't come calling either. Maybe it's over?"

Aye, keep hoping. It was easy to do that, basking in the sun in a sleepy village far from Glasgow's soot-stained buildings and dung-caked streets, away from the monsters who hid beneath them. "Meaning keep our heads down and our noses clean, and hope they let us be? … Aye." Foley pointedly regarded his empty glass.

Hunt took the hint. "Same again, I assume?" he asked dryly as he rose.

"Well, if you're going to the bar anyway," Foley said innocently.

*

Hunt crossed the cobbled courtyard to the inn's back entrance, two empty pint glasses in hand, sweat beading his brow. The Horned Lord's walls were thick and misshapen, the village's biggest building, and its heart. Its thick-oaked door lay open, and he immediately felt cooler on passing through the darkened portal. Sunlight struggled to penetrate the thick, misted glass windows, the only light coming from a handful of grudgingly lit candles.

He liked the darkened interior, disapproving of public houses that insisted on killing the cosy atmosphere with too much light. Most of the patrons sat outside, but a few were perched on barstools at the bar or sat on benches lining the tables. As his eyes adjusted to the darkness, Hunt identified them as fishermen or labourers, recovering from a hard night's fishing or a morning's work in the heat with a well-earned ale.

Thick-wooded beams crossed the low ceiling, forcing Hunt to duck his head on occasion. The walls were bare stone, uncovered by plaster or wooden panels, decorated by old swords and muskets, and a few stuffed animal heads that looked decades old. A fire-blackened stag's skull boasting twelve-point antlers hung above the bar, a cheeky nod to the village's pagan past, and the name by which the inn was known locally. Its eye sockets were dark holes gazing down on the taproom in a baleful silence. As a child it had always scared Hunt.

Hunt's passage across the flint-hued flagstones drew little attention, the locals more interested in their ale and conversations. The air smelled of cooked fish and tobacco smoke, and the ripe odour of unwashed bodies fresh from the harbour, fields or fishing boats.

Mr Kyle, the innkeeper, had gained weight and lost hair, the remnant now turning grey. Hunt approached the long, oak bar, reputedly the inn's original. Deep in conversation with two farmers, Kyle didn't seem to notice his arrival.

"What can I get you, sir?" a young woman called out brightly as she stepped behind the bar and stood before Hunt. There was enough of the innkeeper in her features to identify her as Kyle's daughter, aged maybe twenty with dark hair.

"Two ales, please," Hunt replied.

"I've seen you and your friend in here a time or two," the barmaid observed as she operated the beer pump, drawing ale from the cellar casks.

"Yes, we're visiting for a few weeks," Hunt said.

"Aye? We don't usually get visitors for so long. Where are you staying?"

"The Ashwood estate," Hunt said reluctantly.

Miss Kyle – or so Hunt assumed – looked at him in surprise. "You're the new laird's son?"

"I am," he admitted, feeling himself flush.

"Lord and Lady Ashwood have been in for dinner. You're almost the spit of your father. How are you liking Loch Aline, Mr Hunt?"

"It's nice. I've been here before, but not in some years," Hunt said.

"There's a lot to see, in the summer, anyway," she said with local pride. "Just stay away in winter. I'm Kayleigh Kyle – everyone calls me Kay."

"A pleasure to meet you, Kay. The winters are bad?"

"Aye, Mr Hunt. When the wind's bad, boats stay away, cutting us off for days or weeks at a time."

He didn't doubt it, hard as it was to envision right now given there was barely a breeze to trouble the loch's placid waters. "Can you recommend anywhere worth visiting off the beaten track? I want to show my friend the best of the area."

Kay frowned in thought. "The view from the top of Fragarach is worth the climb. The heart of the forest to the north is ancient, the deepest parts of it said to have been forbidden to any save the druids."

"No one's explored them since the druids...?" *Since the druids were killed by my ancestor.*

"They say not." She leaned on the bar, lowering her voice conspiratorially. "They say the Black Hunt sent soldiers into the forest in search of any remaining druids, and to destroy the sacred groves, but none who ventured deep into the forest returned." She seemed to recall she was talking to the 'Black Hunt's' descendant and coloured.

"Maybe I'll have better luck," Hunt said lightly.

"The village fair is on Saturday," Kay said. "There will be food, drink and games."

"Games?" Hunt asked, more to move the conversation on from the awkward topic of his family's bloody history than from any great interest.

Kay nodded. "A tug of war, tossing the caber. A traditional game, like rugby, only with fewer rules." She smiled. "It can get rough." *Too rough for you*, her expression suggested.

"Maybe we'll wander by," Hunt said casually. Another patron attended at the bar, and Hunt carried both pints back outside, rejoining Foley.

"You took your time," Foley observed. "Did you have to brew that ale, or were you trying to seduce the barmaid?"

Hunt hoped his newly tanned complexion hid any blushes. "I was asking her about local attractions." He winced at his choice of words.

"Oh, aye?" Foley said with a leer.

"Shut up and drink your ale."

Chapter Twelve

"Inspector Kenmure is here to see you, your Grace," Henderson said, standing at the study door.

"Show him in, Henderson." Redfort paused. "And then be so good as to prepare a report on the household accounts before you finish today. A thorough report, mind." His secretary's sullenness in recent months was grating on Redfort. Whether it was a result of his unpleasant encounter at Dunclutha, or if his head was getting swollen due to his position as bishop's secretary rather than a mere reverend's, Redfort didn't know. He cared less about the cause than the cure.

"Yes, your Grace," Henderson said on withdrawing. The accounts would take him some time, Redfort knew, having purposely mixed up the receipts.

He listened in case his secretary saw fit to mutter under his breath on leaving the study, but he had the good sense not to.

Police Inspector Edwin Kenmure entered, tall and square-jawed. "Good afternoon, Bishop Redfort. You wished to see me?"

"Afternoon, Kenmure. Be seated."

Kenmure sat across from Redfort. A competent if unexceptional policeman, his Sooty Feather membership was in no small way to thank for his current rank, and he was young enough to expect more promotions to come. *So long as he makes himself useful.*

"Family well?" Redfort asked out of habit rather than genuine concern.

"Very well, your Grace, thank you."

Redfort nodded, done with the usual courtesies. "Superintendent Thatcher went missing in the early hours of yesterday morning." He watched Kenmure for any reaction, feigned or otherwise.

Kenmure's surprise looked genuine. "Has his home been checked?"

No, we lacked the wits to search his house. That's why I called you here, to suggest the blindingly obvious. Dolt! "There was no sign of Thatcher there," he said, managing a civil tone.

"I've not seen the superintendent in several days," Kenmure said, but there was a hesitance that caught Redfort's attention. *You're hiding something.*

"And what was the purpose of your last meeting with Thatcher?" Redfort asked.

"He had tasked me to help him with an investigation," Kenmure said reluctantly, not meeting Redfort's eyes.

Now a bishop and Sooty Feather Councillor, there were very few people in Glasgow Redfort felt obliged to hold his temper with. "Need I remind you who I represent, Kenmure? Who I *am?* Lose the coyness, or I'll scourge the truth from you."

Kenmure reddened, unused to be spoken to so. "Mr Thatcher was working with me to hunt Erik Keel. He didn't know who to trust on … in the Society, so it was just the two of us. So far as I know."

On the Council, you mean. Redfort leaned back in his chair, hearing the wood creak. "Did you succeed in learning Keel's whereabouts, or current identity?"

Kenmure shook his head. "No. We conceded it could be almost anyone, so we were concentrating on hunting for any sign Richard Canning was still in the city, perhaps with Keel."

"Canning may have fled with the Carpathian Circus."

"We think he's still in the city," Kenmure said. "A number of bodies have been found, many drained of blood."

"It's been a hard summer on the city's undead. With limited time to hunt, the Thirst has driven some to take too much blood, killing rather than feeding moderately and Mesmering their victims," Redfort said dismissively.

"Undoubtedly, aye, Bishop, but not all of them." Kenmure met Redfort's eyes. "Some of the victims had been tortured, the mutilation matching that suffered by some of Canning's old victims. Before his hanging. Thatcher believed Canning responsible."

"That would not be very subtle of him," Redfort pointed out.

Kenmure nodded. "I said as much to Mr Thatcher. He said Canning was maybe doing it deliberately, that if the undead were threatened with exposure, the Council would be too distracted trying to cover it up to hunt Keel. He has – had – been tasking a few of his officers to clean up as much of the mess as possible."

"I see," Redfort said slowly. It made sense. His respect for Thatcher was growing. A shame the Council's *Tertius* was likely dead, perhaps the result of his pursuit of Canning. "I'll discuss this with the rest of the Council. In the meantime, continue cleaning up Canning's indiscretions. I'll mention your good work to Regent Guillam."

"Thank you, your Grace," Kenmure said, sounding pleased as he stood.

"Hmm." Redfort watched him leave, his thoughts turning to Kenmure's revelations. He rang a bell, and ten minutes later Henderson entered his study.

Five minutes later than Redfort could in good conscience tolerate.

"Ah, Henderson. I'm to attend a dinner tonight. Be so good as to bull my best shoes."

"I'll have the boy attend to it, your Grace," Henderson said.

Redfort made a face. "I've sent him on an errand. Be so good as to attend to it yourself. I want them shining like mirrors, mind. Good man!"

*

It seemed Regent Guillam's people had been thorough in their search of Thatcher's townhouse. Ordinarily the Council could find any of its own via the Councillor's blood contingency, but Thatcher's was still missing. Kenmure's claim that Thatcher had been hunting Canning on the quiet due to mistrust of his fellow Sooty Feathers strengthened Redfort's suspicion that Thatcher himself was responsible for his contingency's disappearance. *Has he really been taken, or has he just seen fit to leave Glasgow?* Redfort suspected not.

Thatcher's contingency was not something he would leave

lying in the open. The cupboards had all been searched and the locked ones jemmied open.

Redfort sat on Thatcher's bed and listened to Jones' noisy search of the study. Thatcher's hairbrush sat on a vanity table, but the hairs on it were insufficient for a Diviner to–

A possibility occurred. Urine *might* suffice. He knelt on the floor and pulled the chamber pot out from under the bed. The housemaid had been annoyingly diligent, however; it had already been emptied.

Redfort poked around the contents of the vanity table, more from curiosity than any expectation of finding a clue. He spilled the contents of a trinket box over the table, finding mostly brooches, buttons, and a key. Nothing of value. The key was made from black iron and had a distinct appearance, familiar even.

His fingers rested on it. The key *was* familiar. But from where? He turned it over and saw the number 47 carved into the handle.

Heron Crowe. Of course the key was familiar. He possessed one of its siblings. The keys unlocked safety deposit boxes in the Heron Crowe Bank, and where safer for Thatcher to hide his blood?

"Jones, attend me," Redfort shouted as he left the room.

Jones met him in the downstairs hall. "Bishop?"

Redfort handed him the key and his Council card. "The driver will take me to the Under-Market and you to the Heron Crowe Bank. This key opens a deposit box rented by Thatcher, and his contingency should be inside. Insist on seeing William Heron. If he is obstructive, show him this card. It identifies you as being on Council business."

"Yes, Bishop." He hesitated. "And then?"

"Then find me in the market. And don't lose that card," he warned.

*

William Heron sat in his office checking over the books with a well-practised eye as was his morning habit. Some claimed that banking was in his blood, and he conceded that wasn't without truth. His family had been the Heron in Heron Crowe for generations and oversaw the bank's day-to-day duties.

The oak desk was over a hundred years old and worth a small fortune, but the rest of the office was spartanly decorated.

A rapping sounded at the door. "Come in," he commanded.

Brian Gorry, one of the banking clerks, diffidently entered. "Excuse me, sir, a Mr Jones is here on behalf of Bishop Redfort."

Heron felt a prick of unease. "Show him in."

Jones entered, a man Heron had seen maybe twice previously. Heron motioned towards the chair on the opposite side of his desk. "Take a seat, Mr Jones. Bishop Redfort's business brings you here?

Jones sat. "Aye, sir." He placed a card on the desk, a black-inked feather and the Roman numeral six engraved thereon. Heron knew without asking that this visit involved the Sooty Feather Society.

"What can I do for his Grace?"

Jones showed him a deposit box key. "I'm here for the contents of this box."

Heron took it, recognising the number engraved thereon. "This key isn't Bishop Redfort's."

"No, it unlocks Silas Thatcher's box."

Heron was disquietened by the irregularity of the request. The impropriety, even. "This is highly irregular. I cannot give just give you access to Mr Thatcher's property."

Jones rested his hand on the feather-engraved card and Heron surrendered.

Damnable Council business. "I see. Very well, on your master's head be it. I wash my hands of this matter." Heron left the office with Jones following. He led Redfort's man underground where two men sat at the entrance to the vault, shotguns resting on their laps.

"Afternoon, Mr Heron," they said.

"Afternoon." Heron nodded to Kenley who stood, ready to follow Heron and Jones inside. The vault door was circular and made from reinforced steel. Heron turned each of the five brass dials in turn to enter the vault door combination, the muffled sound of bolts snapping back an acknowledgement of his success. Kenley pulled the heavy door open, its well-oiled hinges turning without complaint.

Rows of iron deposit boxes waited inside, embedded into the concrete walls. The bank's money was secured in a separate room of the vault, but there were secrets contained within these boxes that men would kill for.

Heron stopped at Box 47. "This is Mr Thatcher's box." Habit compelled him to back away a few paces to give Jones some privacy. Kenley watched from just inside the doorway.

Jones inserted the key and unlocked the box. He looked inside and removed a glass bottle from within.

Heron stared at the dark liquid trapped in the bottle. "Is that what I think it is?"

"Aye." Jones shut the deposit box and relocked it. He handed the key to Heron. "I don't think Mr Thatcher'll have any further need of this."

Chapter Thirteen

The barman placed another pint on the bar in front of Jimmy Keane. It was Wednesday afternoon, little different from most other afternoons. He snatched up his pint and drank deeply, finishing with a belch. No one paid him any heed; the other patrons were ignorant of the finer points of etiquette. A far cry from the more reputable public houses in the city, the Thistledown served bad ale and worse spirits. Its only window had been boarded up for ten years, and there was a perpetual odour of vomit and piss. Its redeeming virtue was its prices, cheap enough for the dregs of the city to drink themselves into an early grave.

It was a short walk from the Under-Market to the Thistledown, allowing Keane to hawk his services in the morning before retiring for an afternoon libation. In years past he had limited himself to two pints and a meat pie of questionable origin before returning to the Under-Market to tout for more work. These days he skipped the pie and bought more ale, drinking himself insensible when he could afford it. On the days he couldn't, he would stagger home in forlorn destitution. When his pocket was heavier with coin, the following morning would find him awaken in a gutter near the Thistledown. A small tattoo on his neck warned *that sort* to leave him be. He preferred his blood inside him.

He was blearily aware of a change in the tavern's atmosphere, provoked by the arrival of two strangers. Even through the smoky gloom it was plain they did not belong in the Thistledown. The patrons watched the two men through bloodshot eyes, calculating how much money they carried and the value of their fine clothes. If the pair were lucky, they'd escape robbed but alive. Unlucky, and they'd be dumped in the street with their throats cut.

The younger said something to the other, and they approached the bar. The elder stepped around a puddle of piss with obvious distaste. There was something familiar about the younger man, though Keane didn't place him as a regular. The patrons watched and waited to see who among them would challenge the strangers.

Two of the more belligerent drunks blocked their passage to the bar. Scarred faces and broken noses marked them as experienced in violence and intimidation. Keane had seen what they could do to a man.

"We don't have time for this, Jones," The older man sounded impatient.

The man called Jones pulled out a revolver and made sure everyone saw it. The two drunks lost their enthusiasm for robbery and returned to their drinks.

Jones. Sid Jones. Keane knew now why the man was familiar. He'd seen him in the Under-Market on occasion, even done a bit of work for him.

The older man stopped in front of Keane while Jones kept an eye on the other drinkers. "Mr Keane," the older said, "might we speak somewhere private?"

Knowing he had no choice, Keane looked to the bartender. "Jack, can we use the room?"

"Aye," was the disinterested reply. "For a penny."

Keane looked at the older man who took the hint and placed a coin on the bar with a disgruntled look. Jack passed Keane the key to the backroom.

The backroom was hired out to whoever wanted it, no questions asked. "I paid a penny to spend time in this squalor?" The man held a handkerchief to his face as he surveyed the filth. It was littered with broken furniture, and the floor was stained with old blood, shit and piss. Moneylenders used the room to administer beatings and worse. In a rare display of business acumen, Jack had thrown a mattress inside and hired the room out to a local pimp for his whores to use. Jones almost gagged at the stewed smells of violence and vice that only fire could cleanse from the place.

Keane tried to keep the fear from his voice. "Who are you and what do you want?"

"I am Bishop Redfort, and I hear you have a particular

Talent." He looked Keane up and down, doubt plain in his voice. Keane's clothes were shabby and layered with stains that spoke of dissolution.

The name Redfort was familiar; not only the city's new bishop but also a member of the Council. That so eminent a gentleman would seek him out personally gave Keane a feeling he hadn't experienced in months; pride. "What talent?"

"You're a Diviner, correct?"

Keane nodded. "Aye, sir. Among the best in the city."

"Once, maybe."

Keane's pride, freshly awoken and tender, was stung by that. "Still," he insisted. Margot Guillam had hired him a few months prior to use Sir Arthur Williamson's blood contingency to lead a band of Templars to the man, and thusly to George Rannoch.

"That confidence will be put to the test," Redfort warned. "You will be paid well, and I expect your discretion. This is Council business."

Keane nodded, not needing to ask which council. "What do you want me to find?"

"A man, probably dead."

"Divining a man's whereabouts is almost impossible, without–"

Redfort produced a bottle containing dark liquid. "Will his blood suffice?"

The man's blood made success far more likely. "That'll do, sir. Has he been missing long?" Keane could still find a corpse through its blood, but the connection weakened as time passed and the corpse decayed.

"A few days," Redfort said. He handed him the bottled blood.

How his Talent worked, Keane couldn't say. All magicians in the city fell under the gaze of the Council, some forbidden, others tolerated. Diviners like Keane were allowed to practise their Talent, such forbearance purchased by their usefulness. He opened the bottle and focused his concentration on the blood inside. He poured a little on his hand and sought out the blood's owner.

*

Jimmy Keane led Redfort and Jones through the streets of the city on foot, his brow furled in concentration. Redfort's carriage had taken them from High Street to the river, where it would wait until their return. Keane seemed confident they were on the right track.

Redfort didn't understand how so dissolute a wretch could acquire such a Talent, but that Talent was Redfort's best hope to find Thatcher, dead or alive. His own was of no help and forbidden besides. "Are we close?"

"I think so, it's weak." Redfort's deteriorating mood wasn't lost on him. "I'm trying."

Yes, trying my patience. When Keane had led them to the river, Redfort was sure the Diviner would announce Thatcher had been dumped into its filthy depths, buried in the silt at the bottom. But instead they had crossed the bridge, Keane's attention focused on the far bank.

"He's near," Keane said, slowing his pace.

"Where?"

"Over there, I think," Keane said. "I'm sure," he amended on seeing Redfort's expression.

"Thatcher's house is in that direction," Jones said.

"I'm aware." Redfort had spent a day searching for the missing Councillor. If Thatcher had simply been stuffed into a cupboard no one had bothered to check, or if he had been away visiting family and was now returned, there would be hell to pay.

Sure enough, Keane led them to Thatcher's house, overlooking the Clyde.

"Jones, tell me someone had the wit to thoroughly search the garden," Redfort said quietly.

"Yes, your Grace," Jones assured him. "There was no sign of recent digging."

"Looking at the ground for signs of digging does not fit my definition of a 'thorough search', Jones." Redfort's temper hung from a fraying thread. If Keane pointed to a patch of earth and announced Thatcher was buried beneath it, Redfort would make Jones dig it up. *With his bare hands.*

"He's in the house," Keane said, standing before the steps leading to the front door.

Redfort handed Jones the key to the house and watched him unlock the door. The three entered.

Keane ignored the exposed floorboards, the disarray caused by the initial search for Thatcher before Regent Guillam assigned it to Redfort. He entered the sitting room and pointed to the fireplace. "He's in there."

"What?" Redfort frowned at the Diviner.

"He's up the bloody chimney. Your Grace," he added quickly.

Redfort stared at the wall above the fireplace. It looked solid and showed no signs of recent damage or repair. While the wall could have been broken and then bricked back up, he doubted it would be possible for the culprits to replace the wallpaper so exactly, even down to old ripples caused by the heat. "Jones, take a look."

He didn't look happy at the prospect. "Your Grace, ain't no way someone stuffed a corpse up that chimney."

"I dislike repeating myself." Redfort gave Jones a look.

His man pulled a box of matches from his pocket and struck one, lighting a candle on the fireplace. He crouched down and peered up the chimney, sticking the hand that held the candle up. A muffled curse echoed up the chimney, and Jones wasted no time in extricating his head and returning to his feet.

He looked at Redfort, soot staining his face. "He's up there. I don't know how they did it, but someone managed to squeeze that body a few feet up the chimney. No one would have found him until winter, when the fireplace was lit." He frowned. "I think it's him, unless he keeps a corpse up his chimney."

Perhaps it's Saint Nicholas. Redfort ignored the smug look on Keane's face. "The work of a *Nephilim*?"

Jones looked doubtful. "I don't see how, your Grace. It's not just a question of strength, it's getting a full-grown man up that tight squeeze and keeping him up there until rigor mortis sets in. But he didn't climb up there himself."

A mystery, and Redfort hated those. "We need to get him out of there. Confirm it is indeed Thatcher."

Jones nodded. "Whoever has to get through that wall will need some bloody big hammers." He shook his head. "With all the soot in there, won't be fun when the wall comes down."

"No, Jones. Best get to it, then, hadn't you? Sooner you

start, sooner you'll finish." He noted Keane trying to edge away. "Mr Keane can assist, after which you'll attend to his payment. I must let the Council know we've found Thatcher."

"We'll need a wagon to get the body to the mortuary," Jones said, not looking happy at the task of bringing down the wall.

"I'll have one sent here." He paused, remembering Jones' words. *He didn't climb up there himself.* "Bring the body to my cellar, first."

Jones frowned. "Not the mortuary?"

Must my every instruction be questioned? "Has my cellar relocated itself to the mortuary, Jones?"

"No, your Grace," Jones muttered.

"Then not the mortuary." He glanced at the fireplace with a sense of disquiet.

*

Shadows danced across the cellar walls as candles flickered. Silas Thatcher lay on the wooden table in the centre of the room, soot staining his hands, face and clothes. He wore no jacket or waistcoat, either removed by himself or by the killer, and his shirt was torn in places and almost entirely blackened. Thatcher's cause of death was no mystery, his throat pierced by a *Nephilim*'s fangs, most of his blood drained. No effort had been made to disguise the cause of death, the killer – Canning? – either believing the body would not be found for months, or just not caring.

It was widely said that dead men told no tales, but that was not always true for those who had developed a certain Talent. A Talent forbidden on pain of (a very painful) death, but one Redfort had cultivated anyway.

Necromancy.

His preparations complete, Redfort placed his right hand on Thatcher's sooty forehead and concentrated. He incanted the required alien-sounding words and pierced the veil between life and death, questing out for the soul of Silas Thatcher. Wherever it dwelled, be it Heaven or Hell. *The latter, I suspect.*

His strength fled, and he knew he had succeeded when he

sensed a presence in the corpse lying before him. "Thatcher?"

The dead man's chest spasmed, its lungs drawing in air for the first time in days. "… Yes …" he rasped.

Excellent. "Tell me who killed you and I'll see you avenged."

"… waiting for me … attacked on … doorstep."

"Yes," said Redfort, impatiently, "but *who* was waiting for you?" *I'm cajoling a corpse.*

Thatcher's blueish lips moved as if to speak, but then he spasmed again. "Who are you?" He sounded different.

Caution stayed Redfort's tongue from answering. Something was wrong. "I'll tell you once you've told me who killed you, Thatcher."

A hiss escaped from Thatcher's lips, a laugh, and a chill fell over Redfort. *Another speaks through Thatcher's lips.*

"Who are you?" Redfort asked, his mouth dry.

"I just asked *you* that," the voice said. "But I suspect you won't answer. I'd expect nothing less than the utmost caution from a kindred practitioner who has escaped detection in this city. My employer will be most interested."

A necromancer. Redfort had believed himself alone in Glasgow, at least since his mentor's discovery and execution years before. "You speak of Erik Keel," he guessed. So, the demon was served not only by a *Nephilim* but by a necromancer, too. At least Redfort knew now how Thatcher had ended up his own chimney; the necromancer had manipulated the corpse like a puppet and made it climb the chimney itself.

"How are you here?" Redfort asked.

"I felt your magic touch the residue of my own in Thatcher's body. Curious, I decided to possess it."

"And Thatcher?"

"Cast back out. I can't permit him to tell tales, after all."

Redfort felt a stab of panic as the dead man's head turned to face him, the eyes opening. *They can see me!* That turned out to be the least of his problems as the corpse shudderingly sat up and rolled off the table.

Redfort stumbled backwards, slamming into the cellar wall as the corpse pursued. Cold sooty hands reached up for his throat…

And stopped. Thatcher's dead lips curled up into a toothy smile. "Until our next meeting." The body collapsed to the ground as the unknown necromancer released his hold over it.

Heart pounding in his chest, Redfort struggled to calm himself, alone in the cellar as shadows danced on the walls. *He – or she – has seen my face.* He'd never felt so vulnerable. If his unknown opponent learned his identity, one word to the wrong person would see Redfort burn. *Still, now I know what happened to Thatcher.* A pity he must keep that knowledge to himself. He had but one choice; find the necromancer and kill them.

A daunting task, to be sure. The necromancer's command of their shared Talent clearly exceeded Redfort's own, knowing when Redfort had turned his magic on Thatcher, and able to sever the connection between the corpse and Thatcher's soul, resuming control of the body.

If he recognised me, he'll surely tell Keel. Which meant Keel had to be found, too, and killed. And Richard Canning was still the best chance to identify and find the fugitive demon. To prevail, he must kill a murderous *Nephilim*, a demon and a necromancer. *Tasks to daunt the stoutest heart, and I was never that.*

He returned upstairs to his study and poured himself a large brandy.

Chapter Fourteen

Lady Mary MacInesker waited to greet her guest, one of a number due to attend Dunkellen House tonight with a view to donating money to the MacInesker Foundation. She watched her footmen assist a lady and her maid from their carriage and assumed a welcoming smile.

The arriving lady was in mid-forties, her hair tied back in a bun beneath a small hat. She wore a dark blue dress and bonnet. A younger woman exited the carriage behind her.

"Welcome, I'm Lady MacInesker." As the other lady was maybe five years older, Mary let a slight note of deference into her tone, but not much as she was the lady of the house. And the list of people to whom she was accustomed to deferring, was very short.

"I'm Lady Delaney, thank you for inviting me, Lady MacInesker."

The name was familiar, and Mary vaguely recalled Lady Delaney and her husband from Glasgow society when Sir Neil MacInesker first introduced Mary to the city upon their marriage. The Delaneys had been a popular couple, until the husband went mad and killed their children, killed in turn by Lady Delaney. Mary seemed to remember a cloud had lingered over Lady Delaney for a while until she was officially cleared of all suspicion. She had become something of a recluse, disappearing from society and never remarrying.

"You're most welcome. Your interest in the MacInesker Foundation is appreciated." And unexpected. Mary had been surprised to receive a letter from Lady Delaney offering her support for the foundation, and her wish to endow it with a legacy.

Lady Delaney glanced back at the young woman. "I trust your staff will take my maid in hand?"

"Of course. Peel, place Lady Delaney's maid into Mrs McKeen's care."

"Thank you, Lady MacInesker. Ellison," Lady Delaney called back, "attend this fellow."

"Yes, Lady Delaney," the lady's maid said. She was young, aged between twenty and twenty-five, and her dark hair had been pulled back. Thin spectacles perched atop her nose.

*

Lady MacInesker's butler led Kerry through the basement corridor that ran the length of the servants' quarters, passing the pantry, store and linen room. The top half of the walls were white plaster while the lower half were glazed bricks, useful in that they reflected what little light made its way into the corridor. Peel the butler was in his forties, tall and running to fat. His waxed short dark hair was parted to one side and his moustache was perfectly groomed. He also had the florid face and veined eyes of a drinker.

"You let me know if any of the lads give you any bother," he said to Kerry, "and I'll sort them out." His words said one thing, but his tone perhaps held another meaning, a suggestion that if she surrendered to his affections, she needn't worry about the footmen bothering her.

Caroline had warned her that female servants were often at the mercy of the family men and male staff; Kerry managed a polite if cold smile. "Thank you, Mr Peel. Lady Delaney is most particular about proper behaviour, and she would take it ill if her lady's maid was exposed to anything lewd. Why, one of her previous maids was caught with Sir Willard Smith's valet, and she not only dismissed her, but did not rest until Sir Willard had dismissed his own man without a reference!"

She hoped that would be enough to convince the butler to keep his hands to himself, lest he share the fate of the fictional valet of the equally fictional Sir Willard Smith.

He said nothing further, stopping outside the housekeeper's still room. No reply answered his three knocks, and so he continued to the kitchen at the end of the corridor.

The kitchen was large and high-ceilinged; the cook and her assistants busy preparing the evening meal, sweating from heat produced by the black iron range running along the left wall.

"Mrs Howe, where is Mrs McKeen?" Peel asked. Senior female servants such as the housekeeper and cook were called 'Mrs' regardless of their marital status. Kerry suspected neither woman was married, the demands of their positions leaving little time for a personal life.

"Outside, Mr Peel," the eldest of the women present said, evidently the cook. She pointed to a door leading out the back, left open in a vain attempt to cool the room, doomed to failure as it was almost equally hot outside.

Kerry followed Peel out into the courtyard where a grey-haired woman with a severe expression on her narrow face supervised a delivery.

"Ah, Mr Peel. As you can see, her ladyship's wine has arrived."

"Thank you, Mrs McKeen. I'll take over. This is Miss Delaney, Lady Delaney's maid, and Lady MacInesker wishes you to take her in hand." Kerry had been told that it was customary for visiting lady's maids and valets to be referred to by the name of their mistress or master.

"Very good, Mr Peel." Mrs McKeen gave Kerry a sharp appraising look while Peel left them to direct the wine's conveyance from the courtyard to the wine cellar. Like the pantry and silver vault, the wine cellar was the domain of the butler, and Kerry wondered how much of Lady MacInesker's wine failed to reach her table.

"I'm Mrs McKeen, the housekeeper." Mrs McKeen led Kerry back into the kitchen, ignoring a kitchen assistant's tears as the cook chastised her over some mistake or other.

Mrs McKeen set a brisk pace as she led Kerry back down the corridor. "That is my sitting room. Mr Peel, Mrs Howe and Miss Carlisle – Lady MacInesker's maid – and I dine in there most evenings." She pointed to her right. "That's the servants' hall."

Kerry peeked inside, surprised by its size. "It's big."

"Lady MacInesker employs forty staff," the housekeeper said proudly.

"That's a lot." Lady Delaney made do with a lady's maid, a housemaid and a cook.

"Most live in the nearby village, the rest in the house." Mrs

McKean gave Kerry a sharp look. "The male staff bedrooms are at the other end of this corridor, and the female staff have rooms in the attic. You'll share a room with Miss Carlisle."

"Very good, Mrs McKean."

"Nell," Mrs McKean called out on seeing a housemaid exit the linen room.

"Mrs McKean?" Nell was of an age with Kerry, fair-haired and weary-eyed.

"This is Lady Delaney's maid. She'll be staying in Miss Carlisle's room and can leave her case there. Do you know which room Lady Delaney will be staying in? … Good, show her where it is."

"Please follow me, Miss," Nell said.

"How long have you worked here?" Kerry asked. Back stairs and servants' corridors allowed the staff to navigate the house largely unseen by the family and guests, and Kerry did her best to memorise the route as they made their way up to the attic. The back passages would come in useful later, the reason she was masquerading as Lady Delaney's maid rather than lady's companion.

"Two years, Miss." She hesitated. "How long have you been lady's maid to Lady Delaney?"

Kerry detected envy in Nell's voice. A lady's maid enjoyed a much greater status than a housemaid. "Not long. My cousin is Lady Delaney's maid, but I'm carrying out her duties while she visits family." That was their story, should any acquaintance of Lady Delaney's attend who might know Jane Ellison by sight.

She wore spectacles and had dyed her hair dark, losing her Irish accent. Cosmetics had added a few years to her age, all a precaution against the day she entered society as Kerry Knox, companion to Lady Delaney. Caroline had assured her there was little chance of anyone recognising her as the dark-haired, be-spectacled lady's maid. Few paid any mind to the servants.

The attic was cramped and poorly lit, occupied entirely by the female staff, a whole house away from the men. Kerry doubted the distance was successful in preventing clandestine liaisons between the staff.

Nell knocked on a door and waited a moment, opening it after no one replied. "This is Miss Carlisle's room, where you'll be staying," she explained.

The room was spartanly decorated, the white walls absent any decoration. Two iron-framed beds lay on the bare floorboards, the only other furniture being two small wooden dressers. A small candle sat on top each dresser, and nightwear sat neatly folded on one of the beds.

Despite the room's cramped size, Kerry knew Miss Carlisle was fortunate among the staff to have it to herself, a privilege of her position as lady's maid. The housemaids would be two to a room. Kerry placed her small case next to the spare bed, unsure what to do next.

Nell hovered at the door. "I can show you to Lady Delaney's room, Miss."

Kerry smiled in gratitude at the maid. "Thank you, Nell."

*

Kerry watched Caroline sip from a glass of lemonade with no little envy. Caroline sat out on the rear terraced garden, observing a few of the younger guests playing croquet on the lawn below, Kerry standing nearby to attend to her needs.

"The best tonic for this heat," Caroline proclaimed as she sat her glass down on the small round table. "My compliments, Lady MacInesker."

"You're welcome, Lady Delaney." Both women were protected from the sun by parasols, Kerry enjoying no such protection. The dinner gong would be sounding soon, butterflies taking flight in her gut at the thought of what she must do afterwards.

They had earlier explored the gardens, some filled with flowers of every colour and description, others set aside for vegetables. A stroll through the woodland garden had been very pleasant, the trees offering shade from the sun.

Kerry and Caroline had visited the stables, though the horses were grazing in a nearby field. The MacIneskers held hunts on occasion, the stables big enough to see to the needs of so many horses.

Much as Kerry enjoyed herself, part of her was appalled at the decadence. The family here lived in spacious luxury surrounded by beautiful gardens maintained by an army of servants and gardeners while not so many miles away people lived in damp, crumbling tenements so crammed together that the narrow wynds and closes were overflowing with shit, never seeing sunlight. Entire families were forced to endure damp, vermin-infested rooms riddled with disease and vice.

Meanwhile forty servants slaved from dusk to dawn serving a widow and her currently absent son in a house big enough for dozens, marble adorning the floors and stairs. A cold anger settled over her.

The gong rang, the guests going inside to the dining room, giving Kerry the opportunity to slip away on entering the house. She climbed briskly up to the next floor and paused. Should she meet anyone, she was heading up to the female servant quarters in the attic, a reasonable explanation for her being in the stairwell.

Kerry took a steadying breath, listening until satisfied she could hear no one else going up or down the stairs. She slipped out into the hall, ready to walk towards the back stairs leading up to the attic should anyone appear. A shivery thrill of excitement went through her as she walked past the discreet entrance to the servants' passage, knowing if she was caught now, she would face some hard questions. The other servants should all be occupied either attending to the guests or their chores, but there was always the risk of a lady's maid or valet being sent upstairs to fetch something from a bedroom, or even a guest deciding to have an early night.

She risked a peek down the main staircase but saw and heard no one. *Good.* Swallowing down her fear, Kerry headed to the wing where the family bedrooms were located. If she was caught here, at best she risked arrest for theft. If Lady MacInesker *was* fully involved in her foundation providing children to the undead, her life itself might be in peril…

Concentrate! Caroline had advised Kerry that Lady MacInesker likely attended to her correspondence in a private sitting room adjacent to the main bedroom. *I hope so – I don't have all bloody night to poke through the house in the hopes of finding where the foundation sends the children it buys!*

The door was unsurprisingly locked, but Kerry had come prepared, pulling out two delicate lockpicks. An internal door was unlikely to be fitted with too difficult a lock, but Kerry's initial efforts to unlock the door failed.

Finally, after what felt like an hour, the lock relented, Kerry flinching at the click. *No one heard it, calm yourself.* She opened the door and squeezed inside, closing it behind her.

With its floral Chinese wallpaper and chaise longue upholstered in salmon-pink, the sitting room looked an unlikely place to find cold-hearted plans relating to the sacrifice of orphaned children, but Kerry knew better than to be fooled by first impressions. An oak writing bureau sat near the window, the likeliest place to find documents.

Kerry stepped lightly on the floor, grateful for the beige-and-brown flower-patterned carpet that softened her footsteps. The last thing she needed was creaking floorboards betraying her presence. She reached for the bureau lid, sighing in relief when it opened without resistance. Gently lowering it, Kerry ran her eyes over the gathered documents.

Lady MacInesker didn't stint for documents requiring her attention, or correspondence in need of answering, but Caroline had opined that their host would want papers relating to her foundation near to hand, to ensure she could provide the would-be donors with any requested information. Near the top was an unfinished letter addressed to a Miss Guillam, advising that a review of local shipping companies suggested that Lord Ashwood's Browning Shipping Company would be a profitable acquisition. Kerry wondered if this Lord Ashwood would be given any choice in the matter.

A folder marked 'MacInesker Foundation' sat on top of other documents at the bottom of the bureau, probably dropped there before the guests arrived. Kerry made a mental note of where it lay and picked it up, careful not to disturb anything else.

Having noted down anything that might prove useful, Kerry replaced the folder back in the bureau and, she hoped, left the room exactly as she had found it.

By the time she reached the kitchen, those servants not attending to the guests were eating simple but good fare provided by the cook. Kerry ate, pretending to ignore the gossip. Attending to Lady MacInesker and her guests had left the staff weary, thankfully too engrossed to pay her any mind (though she noted all took care not to mention Lady Delaney in her presence).

Her belly filled, she decided to return upstairs to Lady Delaney's room, ostensibly to help her mistress to bed. The back stairs were in near darkness, so she had to mind her footing as she climbed up.

"Going somewhere?"

Kerry started, a thrill of guilt going through her even though she was doing nothing wrong. Peel the butler stood at the end of the small passage. "To attend Lady Delaney, Mr Peel."

"I'm sure she can wait a few more minutes for you. No need for you to go rushing after her just yet." There was something in his voice Kerry misliked, an ugly possessive edge. He was also slurring his words.

"She is most particular, Mr Peel," Kerry said forcefully as he moved towards her. "I really must–"

He lunged at her, as she knew he would, fear stabbing at her.

Fear she was expecting, and managed, forcing herself to remain loose and untensed. She had fought undead; this butler should prove little challenge. *Should.* Caroline had also warned her not to underestimate an opponent.

Peel's right hand grabbed her right shoulder, his rank breath blowing over her as he tried to overwhelm her with his bulk. Weeks of training paid off as her body reacted of its own accord, her right hand sweeping up to grab his, her thumb jamming hard into the back of his hand as her left hand hooked his elbow.

Kerry turned slightly to her right, her right hand twisting his as her left pushed his elbow up, followed after by her pulling his hand down. His grunt of surprise turned to pain as she pulled hard, forcing him to unbalance. His strength was greater than hers, but his arm was in such a position that those muscles were unable to work together to break her grip.

She pushed forwards, Peel forced to go down to the ground or suffer a broken wrist. There was a bulge in his trousers betraying his intent towards Kerry. How many women had suffered at his hands? Enduring such assaults was a sad fact of life for female servants in many households.

She had intended to walk off and leave him there lying on

his back, counting on him being too embarrassed to mention the incident to anyone, but the thought of Peel forcing himself on the likes of the housemaid Nell threatened to turn her cold rage hot. Kerry dropped to one knee and revealed the silver stiletto hidden up her sleeve to the stunned butler.

"Attack me again, and I'll kill you," she promised quietly. "If I see you look at any woman here in a way I don't like, I'll kill you. Understand?"

Peel jerked a nod, fear in his eyes.

"I can't hear you," she said softly.

"I understand," he whispered.

"Good." She stood, slipping the blade back up her sleeve. Anger flared once more, and she slammed her foot down hard on his groin. *Bastard. Fucking bastard!*

Kerry left him curled up in agony, walking down the back corridor towards the main hall. Would tonight see him correct his behaviour, or would humiliation make him crueller to his next victim? Kerry suspected the latter, but Caroline wouldn't thank her for leaving a corpse near her room.

"Ah, Ellison, finally," Lady Delaney said as Kerry entered the bedroom.

"Sorry, Lady Delaney, but I was otherwise occupied," Kerry said as she closed the door.

"Doing what, pray tell. Sneaking and skulking, I have no doubt."

Kerry smiled. "Exactly." *And teaching that bastard Peel a lesson he won't soon forget.*

Caroline returned her smile. "And what did you find?"

Taking a breath, Kerry pulled out her notes and went over them with Caroline. When she was more experienced, she knew she would be expected to memorise anything of note; should she be searched, she would have a difficult time explaining the notes scribbled in her little book.

"The Imperial Mill," Caroline said quietly.

"You're sure?" Kerry saw nothing to differentiate it from the other mills linked to the foundation.

"More or less; it's the only mill Lady MacInesker made no mention of tonight. Yet according to these papers, not only does it employ orphans supplied by the foundation, but it is the most productive. Were I Lady MacInesker, this mill would be the jewel in my crown, the proof in my pudding."

"So, what now?"

"I fear you've made a poor lady's maid, and I must dismiss you."

"Oh no, mistress. What will become of me?" Kerry mock-wailed.

"It's the streets for you, I fear, my girl. Maybe you can find work at the Imperial Mill?"

Chapter Fifteen

Their arrival garnered attention from many in the crowd, either those who recognised Lewis Hunt as the new Lord Ashwood, or others simply curious at the presence of strangers at the Kirkaline Fair. The turban and dark features of Father's valet, Singh, drew the most stares. Hunt hadn't expected the village green to be so busy, but the fair had attracted outlying crofters, farmers and the inhabitants of nearby hamlets, all eager to partake in the festivities.

Stalls circled the green, selling everything from fish to wool to carved trinkets, to toffee apples and fresh lemonade. The Ashwood Arms had even set up a stall, serving ale from casks and whisky from bottles. Children were led on small ponies a short distance across the green in exchange for a ha'penny. Large white tents had been set up, providing tea and shade from the sun.

Men had been wrestling earlier, local fishermen and farmhands grappling for dominance under the watchful eye of a referee taking care that no match got out of hand. Even still, no few participants ended their match with bruises, black eyes and torn clothing, cheered on by their friends and family. Musicians played jaunty tunes on flutes and fiddles on one side of the green, a mournful dirge of piped music keening out from the other side. The centre of the green had been left clear of stalls and tents, several burly men loitering there, one holding a long rope. Hunt hoped it was for the traditional tug-of-war and not an imminent hanging.

Men began to congregate near the rope. The organiser noticed Hunt's attention and waved them over. "Come on, the three of you! Four of you," he amended, eyeing Singh.

Hunt, Father and Foley exchanged looks. Foley grinned, signifying his assent. Father's smile was almost as predatory.

"Shall we? You too, Singh."

"As you say, my Lord." Singh said in a neutral tone.

The four of them walked over to the rope while Hunt's mother watched on, holding their jackets. In the end a total of twelve men agreed to take part, Hunt, Father, Singh and Foley joining one side. The others were a mix of age and size, burly farmhands alongside young lads either taking part for pride or to impress a girl in the crowd.

The Hunts, Foley and Singh took their place in the middle of their group, the largest man on their side at the front with the second biggest anchoring them at the back. Hunt eyed the competition and had a feeling his side would be the ones ending up face-down in the dirt.

The organiser – evidently the referee – waited until they had all taken their positions, a second rope lying between the two groups acting as the line. The crowd shouted insults and encouragement. Hunt gripped the rope tightly. Slender and unburdened with an excess of muscle, he held no illusions about just how effective he would be.

His father calmly looked ahead, faintly amused. Singh assumed a stoic expression. Foley, on the other hand, bared his teeth in a grin that challenged the other side to do their worst.

A stout man dressed in a tweed suit and red-faced from the heat, cleared his throat as he joined the referee. "Ladies and gentlemen, as Mayor of Kirkaline it is my pleasure and my privilege – as always – to preside over the tug-o'-war."

He ran his eyes over the crowd, ignoring the cheers and jeers. "As is our tradition, this contest represents the eternal war between summer and winter, sun and moon, and between light and dark. In recognition that the solstice has passed and summer wanes, the winning side will be proclaimed the champions of the sun, a symbol that winter may fall, but the days will warm and lengthen again." There was a smattering of laughter, no doubt due to the hot sun overhead that made summer's waning a joke, and winter seem very far away.

The mayor signalled for them to begin, and Hunt found himself almost pulled off his feet as the struggle started in earnest. He gritted his teeth and tensed his muscles, arching his back as he tried to gain purchase on the ground, the earth too hard for him to dig his feet in.

There was a lot of grunting and swearing as Hunt's team battled to keep to their side of the line, edging towards it despite their best efforts. In contrast to Father and Singh's silence, a low growl issued from Foley's throat as he gave his all. Hunt grimaced as the rope burned his skin, knowing the locals had the advantage of callused skin from years of manual labour.

A roar came from the crowd, equal parts celebration and disappointment as the first man on Hunt's side crossed the line. Foley turned to face Hunt, a look of bitter disappointment on his face that took Hunt by surprise. It was just a game, after all, and Hunt was content that the other side hadn't yanked them off their feet. He opened and clenched his fists, the palms of his hands scraped raw from holding the rope. Foley's hands were bleeding, but he didn't seem to notice.

"A good match," Father said as all contestants shook each other's hands. Several were hesitant to take Singh's, and Hunt caught one man rub his hand on his trousers afterwards, as if fearing the valet's dark skin might be tainted. If Singh noticed, he kept any offence to himself.

"Yes, Father." Lewis Hunt's participation drew a few appreciative cheers, the crowd pleased that the new Lord Ashwood had deigned to roll his sleeves up and take part in the local tradition.

They found Mother seated at a table within the tent, three ales thoughtfully waiting for them. "A fine effort, gentlemen."

"Thank you, Mother." Hunt almost reached for one of the ales, but after a look from Mother he reached instead for his jacket, putting it on. They were all sweating, and Hunt felt that the weather perhaps justified a relaxing of dress standards. Certainly, almost all the gathered menfolk were down to their shirtsleeves. Small chance of his mother agreeing, though, not with the entire village and most of the local farmers present. *The lord's son must look the part. Even if he's sweating like a pig.* Wearing his straw boater had earned him a look of thin-lipped disapproval but sweat still soaked his brow. His arms ached, muscles already tender from the work he'd been doing around the estate.

He took a drink of ale, enjoying the bitter taste but finding it did little to cool him down, though the tent's shade offered a welcome respite. Foley had taken one look at Hunt and likewise put on his jacket. Marching in Africa in full army uniform had given him the stoicism to endure the heat, an advantage Hunt lacked. Father likewise put on his jacket, but the heat, like so much else, did little to visibly trouble the man. The Hunts at least wore linen jackets, Foley tweed, but Singh had come in his black woollen jacket, looking every inch Lord Ashwood's valet. He showed little distress from the heat, either accustomed to it from his homeland, or too disciplined to betray his discomfort.

The mayor joined them diffidently beneath the tent. "Good day, Lord and Lady Ashwood … gentlemen. I hope Charlie calling you over to join the tug-of-war caused no offence, Lord Ashwood? He didn't know who you were."

"I took no offence, Mayor Mulhearn," Father assured him. "Lady Ashwood told you our son was coming, yes?" He nodded to Hunt. "This is my son, Mr Hunt, and his friend, Mr Foley."

Hunt and Foley shook hands with the mayor.

Mulhearn looked over at the field. "The annual rugby match will begin soon, if it's of any interest, gentlemen?"

Foley looked at Hunt. "I'm game, Hunt."

"I'll join in, too," Hunt said, though he recalled the barmaid's comment that this local game followed few rules. He rather suspected it gave men from the village and local area an outlet to settle past grievances. "Father?"

Hunt's father smiled. "I'll sit this one out, Wilton."

The mayor nodded, looking pleased that the two younger men were taking part, and perhaps relieved that Lord Ashwood was risking no injury on the field.

One half of the green was roped off, ensuring no one accidently blundered into the game. Hunt was glad to take off his hat and jacket once again, even if he knew he'd end the game drenched in sweat. The ground was hard and dry, sure to result in some injuries.

Hunt and Foley joined the same team, noting that the rivalry between the fishermen and farmhands had led to each group congregating on opposing teams. Men from the village and outlying hamlets spread themselves out between both teams, perhaps intent on settling their own differences.

Hunt's team wore a strip of green cloth around their arms, the opposition wearing brown. Mayor Mulhearn was to referee the match, a few in the crowd provoking laughter by offering goods or services in exchange for favourable decisions for their supported team.

A whistle blew and the game began. Hunt had played both football and rugby in his younger days, and whatever they played here more resembled a brawl. Curses and insults from the crowd flew as fast as fists and feet from the players, skill and teamwork taking a distant second and third place to brute force.

Foley was in his element, accepting every challenge, and coming close to scoring a few times. Scoring was simple in theory; reach the far end. In practice the player carrying the ball found himself the target of every opposing player, none of whom were shy about throwing fists or elbows in a bid to take the runner down.

Hunt's single brief attempt to score had seen him quickly hurled off his feet, and he found himself almost run over by his teammates in their zeal to attack the opposition. Retrieving the ball was regarded as something of an afterthought. Four players started fighting, too far from the ball to even assume the pretence of playing. The referee and several spectators separated them.

A lithe man a few years younger than Hunt managed to evade the opposing team and score, the first try of the game, putting Hunt's side ahead. Three men had already left the field through injury, a spectator from the crowd joining Hunt's side to even the numbers. *At this rate, it'll finish with no original players.*

Hunt returned his attention to the game. His scoring teammate had tried to replicate his previous success, only to trip and find himself buried under three vengeful opponents who delivered some hard punches. He too was removed from the field, substituted by another man not dissuaded by the risk of injury.

Tempers flared. Four players from each team formed a scrum, and play resumed. After a frantic melee, the ball was knocked free…

And lay forgotten as the players brawled amongst themselves.

The new man on the pitch, fresh and unbloodied, seized the ball and made a bold effort to score, and Hunt followed. Three burly farmhands moved to intercept, and the runner lost his nerve, flinging the ball back to Hunt.

He caught it and cut to his left, leaping aside to dodge the nearest man, alarmed to find himself the focus of every other player on the field. Half wanted to take him down, and the other half would probably trample him by accident to get to the opposition.

A third of the field separated him from the freshly chalked try line, and he clutched the ball as he sprinted towards it, knowing a few more seconds would see him running too fast to-

Someone tackled him from behind, pain screaming through both knees and his right elbow as he struck the ground. The full weight of his tackler pressed down on him and he was aware from the shouts and footfalls that players from both sides were closing in.

Hunt covered the ball with his body, trying to draw himself up on his knees to pass the ball back to a teammate, men from both sides reaching down to try and get the ball. He struggled to breathe, his body aching from the fall and subsequent blows falling on him. There were people all around him, on top of him, pushing and shoving each other.

Panic flared as memories of his imprisonment came vividly to mind, trapped in a dark cell with scant food or water. He remembered the ever-present stink of his own piss and shit, first in the cell in Glasgow, then the one in Dunclutha.

He realised he was shouting but what he said he didn't know, and he doubted anyone else could hear him either over the chaotic melee raging around and on top of him. A last desperate surge of strength let him raise his knees enough to shove the ball back blindly, uncaring which side caught it.

The press of brawling men blessedly moved back as everyone fought over the ball rather than Hunt, leaving him alone. Almost alone.

"Bastard!" someone said, a fist hammering into his side. His attacker struck him with words as well as fists, calling him everything from murderer to thief. The assault seemed personal, beyond even the contentious rivalry of this game, and part of Hunt suspected his attacker knew who he was.

Certainly; he referred to him by name.

Then there was respite, a shadow passing over Hunt to send his attacker sprawling to the ground, followed by the sounds of someone – not Hunt, thankfully – being repeatedly struck.

He managed to roll onto his side, a stab of pain telling him he had bruised ribs at the least, and he saw Foley raining blows down on the bastard. The man wore a farmhand's full-length shirt smock. *What the hell did I do to vex him?* Was the farmhand just taking advantage of the opportunity to beat the hell out of the baron's son, or did he nurse a very old grievance? The Hunts hadn't taken this land gently, and some had very long memories. If the farmhand was descended from a Kail'an, then that would explain his animosity.

Shouts of encouragement from the crowd quietened, turning to consternation as Foley continued his assault and showed no sign of stopping. The farmhand managed to get in a few blows, but Foley shrugged them off, maintaining the upper hand. *He'll kill him if he's not careful.* The rest of the players had been too occupied with their own skirmishes to see what was going on at first, the realisation that there was a danger of the fight escalating from mere fisticuffs to something more serious restoring their senses.

Several men from both sides moved to separate the two men, but a sudden chill went through Hunt, fear crossing the faces of everyone present as if Death's shadow had just crossed them. Foley in particular seemed to feel it, drawing back and looking around like a cornered beast.

An uneasy quiet fell over the green, soft murmurs growing louder as it passed. *Someone Unveiled ... an undead?* No, an undead would perish in the sun. A demon hid among them. There was a familiarity about that Unveiling that Hunt couldn't place, like almost remembering a forgotten dream.

Foley returned to Hunt, reaching out a hand. "Can you stand?"

"Yes." He gratefully let Foley help him up, bruised and sore. But his injuries were the least of his concerns. "Someone Unveiled."

"I felt it. Damn me, but did I feel it!" Foley shook his head. "Are you okay?"

"I'll survive." Hunt grimaced as a shard of pain ripped through him, but he didn't think anything was broken. "Not that I'm ungrateful, but you looked ready to kill that arsehole."

"I wouldn't have gone that far." He didn't sound too sure but forced an unconvincing smile. "But he's a big lad and I didn't want him getting back up and coming after me."

Hunt watched the object of Foley's ire being carried off by three farmhands, one of whom gave Foley an unfriendly look. "I don't think he'll be doing that for a day or two."

"Get yourself a drink and rest," Foley said.

"Where are you going?" His parents looked on stoically, showing neither relief that Hunt was on his feet, nor anger at their heir's rough treatment. Hunt was glad, embarrassed at the thought of being given undue deference. Singh on the other hand looked angry, looking between Hunt and Father. Father seemed to catch his valet's eye, and an unspoken communication seemed to pass between them. Father looked away first. Did Singh expect the locals to give the family special treatment due to their position? To an extent, they did, but this was an insular community with its own rules, and it respected those who respected it.

Foley gave a bloody grin. "Back to the game."

Chapter Sixteen

Wooden tables and benches were placed on the grass once the game was finished, the feast a popular tradition in the village. Meat, vegetables, bread and ale were donated by local farmers and merchants, and Hunt knew few in the area would eat so well the rest of the year as they did tonight.

The Hunts and Foley had been invited to dine at the mayor's table along with other notable locals. Mayor Mulhearn seemed pleased by the attendance of Lord and Lady Ashwood. Evidently Great-Uncle Thomas had not attended in some years. Singh was also seated with them, servants rare in this remote corner, and the mayor not knowing what else to do with the valet. Singh showed neither pleasure nor disappointment at the seating arrangements, keeping his own counsel. He had looked Hunt over after he had left the game, decreeing no serious injury.

Mother had been displeased at the future baron being treated so roughly, though Father had said little. Hunt had noticed a tension between master and valet, and he wondered at its cause. Unfamiliar with Indian culture, he decided to keep his nose out of it.

Other guests at the mayor's table included the Yorks, owners of the largest farming estate in the area. Hunt suspected from their name that the family originated down south, having come to the area with Sir Geoffrey Hunt and been granted lands as reward for services given. The Yorks not only owned the largest farm and many acres of prime land, but they also rented out a few smaller farms and crofts to tenants.

Mr York was approaching his middle years, having the look of a man who worked the land but with the means to dress well when required. His younger wife wore what Hunt suspected was her best dress, their four children ranging from eight to eighteen dressed smartly in dresses or tweed. Mr York kept eyeing Father; he was perhaps used to being the man most feted by the mayor at occasions such as this and was unused to being in another's shadow.

"Will you be joining the congregation tomorrow, Lord Ashwood?" Reverend Harcourt asked. Perhaps he wanted to remind everyone the Sabbath was tomorrow, and to temper today's indulgences. Judging by the loud merrymaking from the other tables, Hunt suspected the local kirk would have a much diminished and subdued congregation tomorrow morning.

"We shall be there," Father said. Hunt knew from experience his father enjoyed a robust tolerance of alcohol, and Mother rarely indulged, so they would be clear-headed tomorrow. *Maybe the only ones.*

Reverend Harcourt looked pleased. "And the young gentlemen?" he asked.

"I'm Catholic," Foley answered cheerfully, saving Hunt from having to commit himself or think of an excuse. "I'll be elsewhere, praying for your heretic souls." *Sleeping off tonight, you mean.*

Mr Mulhearn laughed. A few of the others smiled briefly, gauging the reverend's reaction. Father looked amused but said nothing.

"There's no Catholic Church in Kirkaline," Harcourt said tightly. His reaction suggested he felt the Reformation to be unfinished business, a job half-done and needing finished.

"I'll attend Mass twice my first Sunday back home," Foley lied. Hunt had never known him to attend chapel.

"The local kirk has served the people of Kirkaline well," Harcourt said rather smugly.

"But briefly," Foley said.

"Briefly?" Harcourt asked coldly. Hunt sensed a tension around the table and wished Foley had kept his mouth shut. *Small chance of that.*

"Aye, Reverend," Foley said innocently. "Did the locals not use to worship trees and spirits until the first Lord Ashwood came along?"

"The pagans are long gone from Loch Aline," Mr York said angrily. "The people who settled the land afterwards and rebuilt the village were good Godfearing folk. As are their descendants today."

Harcourt nodded vigorously. "Indeed. Godfearing folk served well by your host's family, Mr Foley."

"Glad to hear it, Reverend," Foley said. "Bastard," he mouthed too quietly for anyone but Hunt to hear. Although Father's mouth twitched.

Some of the others at the table traded unreadable looks. "Loch Aline has a colourful past," Mr Stuart said. He was the head gamekeeper at the Dunlew estate, grey-haired and well-respected in the area.

"I was sorry to hear about Lord McKellen's recent death in Glasgow," said Mr Teague, the postmaster. Kirkaline's remote location made him a very important man, not just in the village but in the wider area.

An awkward silence fell, Harcourt giving Teague an unpleasant look. Lord Hamish McKellen was the late owner of Dunlew, and his ancestor had won the estate from the 3rd Baron of Ashwood. His title came from his position as judge on the High Court rather than any family title. Mentioning that family in the presence of the Hunts was perhaps not politic, but Father showed no reaction or offence. The feud between the Hunts and the McKellens was old business, honour satisfied a century past. Besides, Hunt thought, had the 3rd Baron not been such a poor gambler and duellist, his own great grandfather might not have inherited the title and remaining estate.

"A tragic loss," Stuart said in his rough burr. "His son and heir is dealing with Lord McKellen's affairs in Glasgow and Edinburgh. Otherwise he would have been most delighted to attend, I'm sure."

"Will Mr McKellen not be visiting this summer at all, Mr Stuart?" asked Constable Fowler, responsible for keeping the peace in Kirkaline.

Stuart looked at Fowler. "Mr McKellen will attend before the end of July." The two men shared a significant look.

"I understand Ashwood Lodge requires a lot of work, Lord Ashwood," Mr Mulhearn said, perhaps keen to move the conversation on. Hunt felt it only highlighted that the Hunts were reduced to a crumbling house while the castle they had owned for a handful of generations was in another's hands, but Father betrayed no bitterness.

"Indeed, Mr Mulhearn. I've directed a reputable firm to oversee the repairs and renovation next spring," Father said. "Carson & Sons."

"I've not heard of that firm," Mulhearn said.

"They're based in Glasgow," Father said.

Mulhearn frowned. "Surely a local company would be better suited, Lord Ashwood." The mayor seemed to regard the Hunts bringing in outsiders as a slight against the area.

"One of the local firms I wrote to declined the job," Father said blandly. Busy, or perhaps the builders' family dated back to before the Hunts came to Loch Aline. Grudges died slowly up here.

"All the same, Lord Ashwood, the cost of bringing a firm all the way up here from Glasgow will not be small. And your Glasgow lads will find themselves paying above the odds for materials, if the local lumbermen and masons feel they're taking work that should have gone to local people," Mulhearn said.

"We will bring the builders up here and are well able to transport the necessary materials should the local suppliers prove unreasonable," Mother said coolly.

"Boats are not cheap, Lady Ashwood," Reverend Harcourt said with a condescending air.

Mother's sharp eyes found the reverend. "I'm well aware, Reverend, having managed a shipping company for many years."

Thus routed, Reverend Harcourt averted his eyes.

There was a dawning realisation in Constable Fowler's eyes. "Which company, Lady Ashwood?"

Her eyes found his. "The Browning Shipping Company. I was Miss Browning before I became Mrs Hunt."

Fowler looked at her as if seeing her for the first time. "I see. Lady Ashwood." Perhaps he was troubled by the thought of a woman managing a company.

"How did you and Lord Ashwood meet?" Mrs York asked.

"I had the misfortune to be sailing through the Sound of Mull during a storm twenty-eight years ago, and the ship struck the rocks," Mother answered. Hunt listened, having never heard this story before.

Mr York frowned. "But surely the lighthouse would have

guided the ship to safety."

Reverend Harcourt tried to defuse the tense silence that followed. "Perhaps God was guiding Lady Ashwood to her future husband."

Mother looked at him. "He guided many poor souls to a watery grave, Lord Ashwood's uncle, aunt and cousins among them. My brother Ryan and I were among the few rescued."

Hunt's chest tightened. He had known his father's eldest uncle and family had died at sea, but no one had told him his mother and maternal uncle had been on board the same ship. His paternal great-grandfather, the 4th Baron, had died shortly after, Great-uncle Thomas inheriting Ashwood and its title.

"And so Lady Ashwood and I met here, later marrying," Father said, his tone suggesting it was time to lay the topic to rest.

Hunt was curious to hear more of this family history that had been kept from him but sensed now was not the time. *Later.* He was particularly curious about his Uncle Ryan's death. Mother said he survived the sea, but Hunt knew he had died around the time his parents met.

Roasted beef, mutton and chicken arrived at the tables, the meat a rare luxury for most of the villagers. Carrots, turnips, peas and potatoes were also served, along with flagons of ale donated by the local brewery. The fair was a celebration of the village and the surrounding land, and the bounty of the land was offered up for all to share.

Villagers and visitors alike began to eat, the sun still high above the blue waters and heathered hills of Loch Aline. Hunt's troubles seemed long past and far away as he carved up a slice of mutton.

*

Dusk settled gently over Kirkaline, the sun a blaze of orange on the horizon, the loch like molten gold. The air was warm and tinged with salt from the sea and heather from the hills, alive with the sounds of birds, crickets and the occasional barking dog.

Hunt took one last look and followed Foley into the taproom of the Horned Lord. His parents had returned by carriage to Ashwood Lodge, and children claimed the village green as families living in the outlying farms or hamlets returned home before darkness fell, knowing they must rise with the dawn. Some villagers had returned to their cottages after the feast, but for many the day was not yet done. The Reverend Harcourt had left, doubtless praying for the souls of his wayward flock and that intoxication would not empty his pews too much in the morning.

A few lanterns and candles kept the inn's taproom illuminated just enough to see by, the stone walls and floors alive with writhing shadows. Kay Kyle served ale from behind the bar, looking weary after a day serving ale from casks on the green, with no end in sight.

She gave Hunt a tired smile. "I see you came, Mr Hunt. I hope the local lads weren't too rough with you during the game. I don't know what got into Pat Slater."

One would think I'm made from porcelain. "I survived, Miss Kyle. Kay. But some ale would help my recovery. Two pints, if you please. How fares Mr Slater?"

"Of course." She worked the beer tap, filling two glasses with ale. "A broken nose – not his first – and if he rests tonight and tomorrow, he should be fit to work the fields on Monday. Your friend doesn't serve half-measures, does he?"

"No, he does not." Hunt found he had very little sympathy for Slater, certainly not while his own body ached, but he was relieved Foley hadn't injured the man too badly. "What time do you shut tonight?"

Kay sighed. "By tradition, the Horned Lord stays open on the night of the fair until dawn." She managed a bright brittle smile. "So a wee while yet!"

That was maybe six hours away. "I assume you'll shut early if everyone leaves?"

She gave a snort. "That's never happened. Every year my father has to drag a few lads out. But we're closed tomorrow except for guests."

Hunt doubted he and Foley would stay until dawn, but it was nice to be able to sit and drink without having to keep an eye on the time.

"Are you brewing that ale yourself, Hunt?" Foley called over.

He rolled his eyes. "I've kept him waiting long enough. I

hope the night passes quickly for you."

Hunt paid for the ales and made his way to the table Foley had claimed. The inn's doors had been left open, but the taproom was still hot and smelling strongly of sweat. Most of the men were already drunk, talking loudly over one another. The taproom wasn't too crowded, most standing or sitting in the rear courtyard.

"Flirt with the barmaid in your own time, Hunt," Foley mock-warned him. "Not when you're fetching my ale. Slainte."

"Slainte." Neither lingered as they drank from the glasses. "I was making polite conversation, not flirting." He fought back a burp, a *faux pas* leading to social ostracisation in certain circles. Here many of the patrons showed no reticence over belching, but years of habit still held Hunt.

"It's been a good day," Foley said.

"Yes, though one I'll be feeling for the next few days. As will Pat Slater."

"Who?"

"The man you almost broke your knuckles on," Hunt said. "He missed the feast."

"Ah, that prick. Serves him right." All the same, Hunt caught an uncertainty in Foley's voice, a slight hunch to his shoulders.

"You lost control," Hunt said quietly. "Why?"

Foley took another drink of ale, wiping his hand across his mouth. "I don't know," he said finally. "I felt a … a rage when he attacked you. Not sure how to explain it." He shrugged. "Maybe I just got carried away with the game."

"Maybe." It was hardly a satisfactory explanation. Even when they had fought for their lives, first in Dunclutha and then in the Necropolis, Foley had maintained a soldier's discipline. The Foley who lost control on the rugby field would perhaps not have survived.

"Did your new lady friend tell you when they're closing this place up?" Foley asked.

"At first light," Hunt answered. "But I don't think we should stay that long."

"No, you've got a Sunday Service to attend," Foley said with a grin.

Hunt rather suspected he would have little choice in the

matter, his parents keen to make a good impression with the locals. "Perhaps, but a couple of pints won't hurt."

"And the walk home will sober us up," Foley agreed.

*

They were halfway through their second pints when a slurred voice was heard over the general din of conversation. "There's the bastards!"

All talk in the taproom ended as everyone turned, first to see who had spoken, and then to identify the 'bastards' in question, though Foley had a fair inkling. Three burly men strode into the middle of the room, accusatory eyes fixed on the table occupied by Hunt and Foley. *Ahh. This'll be for us, then. Perfect.*

"Can we help you lads?" Foley asked, finding the rugby match had not entirely exorcised the belligerence from him. Three of them would be a problem, though, and he wasn't sure Hunt was up for it.

"You think you can sit here and drink ale after what you did to my brother Pat?" the lead man asked. Like Pat Slater, they had the look of farm labourers, hardy men used to working the land from dawn until dusk.

"And I'll not see a Hunt sit in the Horned Lord on tonight of all nights. Not after what his family did here," a second man said, his voice quiet but filled with venom. He was the one Foley marked as the more dangerous of the three. The third had a look of vicious joy in his eyes, the sort of man who enjoyed trouble for trouble's sake regardless of whether he had a personal stake in it.

The other patrons looked between the two groups, perhaps enjoying the drama. Certainly, none looked ready to intervene.

"If you leave, you'll not have to see me here," Hunt said slowly.

"You think you're better than us," the first man sneered. "Bloody *Lord Ashwood's* son. Pity Pat didn't knock your damned head off."

"I don't think I'm better than you, but I also don't blame a man for the crimes of his ancestors," Hunt said. Foley was heartened by the controlled anger he heard in Hunt's voice, disguised by his seeming calm. He recalled Hunt's cold-blooded execution of the man who had shot Amelie Gerrard. That Hunt might be needed here tonight.

"Outside! I'll see no trouble in here," said the innkeeper.

"Shall we?" Hunt asked Foley as he started to stand, a slight tremble to his limbs. Fear and anger was purging the alcohol from him.

"Why not," Foley agreed, taking one last drink of ale before standing.

The five of them stepped outside and walked to a patch of grass nearby, followed by almost everyone from the inn, Mr Kyle included, though his daughter remained behind the bar.

"A fair fight, mind, Luke," Kyle said to Pat Slater's brother. "Two against two."

The crowd echoed their agreement, and the third man reluctantly stepped aside. Hunt and Foley found a villager willing to hold their jackets.

"I'll take the bigger lad," Foley said quietly to Hunt. "But watch yours. He may be smaller but he's not as drunk as mine."

Hunt nodded silently, trying to hide his fear.

Everyone looked to Kyle to act as a referee of sorts, a role he perhaps accepted as the price of keeping trouble outside his inn.

"Begin," Kyle said without ceremony, and the fight started.

The larger man went straight for Foley who waited until the last moment before stepping aside and ramming his knee into his opponent's meaty thigh. Luke Slater grunted in pain, and Foley followed up with two rapid punches to his face and a third to his kidneys.

Slater was staggered but far from done, his retaliatory punch knocking Foley back a couple of steps. It lacked the man's full power, but it still hurt Foley's ribs. He couldn't risk looking to see how Hunt fared, but hoped his friend remembered a few tips taught to him before they rescued Steiner.

Rage drove Slater towards Foley in a mad bull rush, the drunk's fighting strategy appearing to be little more than hoping to overwhelm Foley through weight and brute strength. Foley hopped aside again and kicked out at Slater's knee, sending him down to the ground. Aware that the crowd might not look kindly on him hitting a man down on the ground, Foley sportingly waited until Slater struggled back to his feet before swinging his fist up into the man's jaw.

Slater's teeth clacked hard and he fell back down, this time staying on the ground. There were a few cheers from the crowd, either acknowledging the winner or maybe a sign that Slater was not a popular man. Confident Slater was out of the fight, Foley turned to see if Hunt was still on his feet.

He was. Fresh abrasions were visible on his face in the lantern light, but he looked calm and focused. The man he fought had a swelling eye, a sign perhaps that he had mistaken Hunt for a soft easy opponent and tried to toy with him. Certainly, Hunt had not distinguished himself in the rough melee the locals called rugby, but Foley recalled that Hunt was the one who had killed the Elder *Nephilim* Rannoch. He possessed what the late Templar James Burton had called 'frozen hatred', an ability to focus his anger inwards rather than outwards, making him capable of a ruthlessness belied by his usual easy demeanour.

"Get him, Gregor!" someone shouted.

After a few feints, Gregor lashed out again, striking Hunt in the face. He was aiming for Hunt's eyes, trying to impair his vision. A shrewd move, one that separated Gregor from Luke Slater's brutal but unfocused punches.

Hunt managed to partially deflect the fist so that it struck his temple, but its follow-up almost took him in the throat. Encouragement from the crowd lessened as their rough enjoyment of the fight diminished, the more sober or astute realising that Gregor might have just tried to kill Hunt.

Foley stepped forwards to intervene, the fight no longer a simple bout of fisticuffs to avenge blows struck during a rugby game. Hunt cried out as a further punch struck his kidneys. But the punch left Gregor unbalanced, and he found himself too close to Hunt and unable to step back.

Hunt's forehead found the centre of Gregor's face, Gregor's greater height working against him, blood gouting from his shattered nose. Hunt stepped forwards as Gregor stumbled back a step, Hunt's right elbow swinging up to catch the side of Gregor's jaw, and a patch of uneven ground caused Hunt's opponent to trip and fall backwards.

Hunt's face was expressionless, bloodless, his mouth set in

a thin line, eyes shrouded in shadow. There was no look of anger or satisfaction as he drew back his foot and after a moment's cold deliberation sent it hard into Gregor's head.

He looked up and at the silent crowd, perhaps gauging if anyone else wanted to challenge him. The fallen men's companion hesitantly came forwards with a few others to tend to their friends.

Mr Kyle found his voice. "Anyone else up for more nonsense? No? Good."

"Are you okay?" Foley asked Hunt.

He took a shuddering breath. "Yes. You?"

"Aye, I'll live. That bastard tried to kill you."

Hunt nodded. "I know." A few in the crowd jostled by, patting their shoulders and offering congratulations. Luke and Gregor didn't strike Foley as the most popular men in the area, and whatever residual loyalty the locals felt towards their own had diminished after Gregor had aimed at Hunt's throat.

"Well done, lads," Kyle said as Foley and Hunt pulled on their jackets. "Ordinarily the losers would buy the winners a drink to show there are no hard feelings, but on this occasion I think your next ales will be on me. Jim Norrie might find himself down three hands on Monday instead of just one, but at least no one else will bother you during your time here."

"That's good of you, Mr Kyle," Foley said. All the same, he suspected he and Hunt would do well to keep their eyes and ears open when walking the dark, quiet places of Loch Aline. The Slaters and their friend Gregor might well have siblings and cousins taking the view that family honour demanded retribution. Gregor's anger towards the Hunt family suggested a link to the old sept, Kail'an, perhaps a remnant that returned or was never chased out.

"After that, it might be an idea to return to Ashwood," Hunt said. "I think we've had enough excitement for one day."

"Aye, you might be right," Foley said with a tired grin. So much for a quiet time in the country.

Chapter Seventeen

July 1865

"Miss Browning, you should be in your cabin," said Captain Erskine of the *Eclipse*. But he said it mildly. He might be the schooner's captain, but it was owned by the Browning Shipping Company, and she was Miss Edith Browning, daughter of his employer.

"Soon, Captain," she said, staring into the fog surrounding them. They had been warned of it before Tobermoray, but the captain was confident of navigating through it. It had risen from the sea as they passed through the Sound of Mull, the crew lighting every lantern they could find. The ship was carrying goods from Greenock to Tobermory on the Isle of Mull, but Edith's father, Joshua Browning, had agreed to transport the Hunt family to Kirkaline. The Baron of Ashwood was dying, and his eldest son had requested help in reaching Ashwood before that happened.

The Hunts were paying their way, but even still the fares would not compensate the company for the time lost diverting to Kirkaline rather than sailing directly back to Glasgow. Her father had not built a prosperous shipping company by making bad decisions, and Edith had her suspicions at his motive.

She was seventeen and still unmarried, as was William Hunt, son of Henry and Iona Hunt. Henry Hunt was the eldest son and heir of the old and ailing Lord Ashwood, the 4th Baron. When Ashwood died, Henry would inherit the title and estate, followed in time by William Hunt. It was a poorly kept secret that the Hunts lacked money, the 3rd Baron having squandered land and money before dying in a duel the century before.

The Brownings were rich, however, and Edith suspected

her father had set his sights on marrying her to William Hunt, a generous dowry making her an attractive prospect to the impoverished Hunts. She had to admit, she was not averse to one day becoming Lady Ashwood, but she liked living in a city, enjoying the convenience of shops and malls such as the Argyll Arcade. Sleepy Kirkaline sounded dreadfully dull.

A light flickered regularly ahead. "Ardtornish Point Lighthouse," Captain Erskine said. "It'll keep us clear of the rocks until the fog lifts, and then we'll enter Loch Aline."

"I can't see more than two feet in front of me," Edith heard her brother Ryan say as he joined them on deck.

"I thought you were playing cards with William Hunt," Edith said, not bothering to disguise her disapproval.

"I got bored. He only gambles for pennies, so I left him and his parents below."

"A habit you would do well to emulate," Edith told her brother. Ryan had grown up used to money, though he didn't seem to appreciate that earning it took work. When Father died, if Ryan gambled with the company as recklessly as he did at cards, then the Browning Shipping Company would be in trouble. *Father's problem, not mine.*

He laughed. "You're no fun, Eadie."

Edith opened her mouth to reply when she found herself flung off her feet, the air knocked from her lungs as she landed painfully on the deck. There was a horrible cracking sound, followed by cries of alarm.

"We've hit rocks!" Captain Erskine shouted.

"How the hell did that happen?" Ryan asked wildly as the schooner shook from side to side.

"The lighthouse is still ahead, there shouldn't be any rocks this far out," Erskine replied. "Lower the dinghies!" he shouted to his crew as the ship listed to one side. If the hull was breached, they would be in trouble.

"Is it bad?" Edith asked as she struggled back to her feet.

"We're sinking fast. As soon as the first boat's in the water, you and Mr Browning get on board," Erskine said.

"There are other passengers below," Edith shouted, thinking of the Hunts.

Whatever Erskine shouted back, Edith couldn't hear over the sound of cracking wood, and then everything went black.

When she came to, she was on board one of the dinghies

along with her brother and a few crewmen. "What happened?" Her head ached dreadfully.

"Part of the mast fell on you," Ryan said. "We managed to get you in the boat before…"

"Before what?" Four of the crewmen rowed the boat through the fog. Edith looked back and saw the ship had capsized. "Oh, dear God. Did anyone else get off?"

Ryan looked down. "No, just us."

"The Hunts? Captain Erskine?"

Ryan's silence was answer enough.

"How did this happen?" Edith asked. "The lighthouse should have guided us clear of the rocks." The light was gone.

No one had an answer, and as the fog started to clear she saw the dormant lighthouse, revealing the shoreline to be far closer than the light had suggested. No lights shone from it. *What guided the ship to its doom?*

*

Edith looked up as the two men entered the drawing room. Sir Hector McKellen had been good enough to send a carriage to collect Edith and Ryan on hearing of the shipwreck, giving them a room each in Dunlew Castle. Edith had fallen quickly asleep, exhausted by the tragedy. Fishermen had put out to sea to search for survivors but, on awakening in the morning, she had learned what she feared she might; none had been pulled from the sea, the current dragging the dead away.

"Mr McKellen," Edith said on recognising the first man as Sir Hector's son, Hamish. There was a familiarity about his dark-haired companion. Both looked to be a few years older than her.

"Miss Browning, I hope you've recovered from your ordeal?" Hamish McKellen asked quietly.

She managed a smile. "Yes, thank you, Mr McKellen." She looked out the window, thinking of the less fortunate. She knew none of the crew save for the late Captain Erskine, but doubtless many had worked for her father for some years. Families would be owed reparations. The loss of the *Eclipse* was no small matter, though the insurance should cover much of it.

"This is Mr Lewis Hunt," said Mr McKellen. That explained his sombre tone.

Grief had ravaged Lewis Hunt's face. He managed a nod. "Miss Browning. Henry Hunt was my uncle."

"Mr Hunt. I'm sorry for your losses." Did he blame the Brownings? Edith resolved to mind what she said.

"Thank you. It's a bad day for my family. My grandfather, Lord Ashwood, will die today or tomorrow. We're not telling him about Uncle Henry, Aunt Iona or cousins William and Aine."

No wonder he looked gutted. "I'm sorry to hear that."

"Everyone expected Henry Hunt to become the next baron. His brother Thomas Hunt instead will inherit," Mr McKellen explained. "An unwanted elevation for the gentleman."

"Is Thomas Hunt your father?" Edith asked.

"No. My younger uncle. My father was Henry and William's youngest brother. My parents died when I was a child." Mr Hunt's voice was hoarse. "There are just two Hunts left now. God."

"You are your uncle's heir?" Edith asked.

"Only if he does not marry and have a son," Mr McKellen said. "Hunt and I study Law together in Glasgow."

Mr Hunt looked at her. "I came up expecting to bury a grandfather. Now I'll need to arrange services for…" He was unable to finish. Then he looked up, anger in his eyes. "What happened?"

Edith had expected him to ask that. "There was thick fog but light from the lighthouse was still visible. Or so we thought."

"Thought?" Hunt asked sharply.

"The lighthouse was not operational, and the light came from further inland." She met his eyes. "I would very much like to know how and why."

"As would I," Hunt said.

"If the Sound of Mull gets a reputation as a danger to ships, it'll harm trade," Ryan said, surprisingly perceptive of him. Trade from the sea was the area's lifeblood.

"I'll speak with my father," Mr McKellen promised. "We'll get answers."

Chapter Eighteen

The front door opened in response to Canning rattling the brass knocker. "You've been told to expect my arrival," Canning said before the man answering the door had the chance to speak.

"Yes, do come in," Alexander Fitch said. He was in his forties, looking more athletic than Canning had expected. He had assumed the assistant manager of the Heron Crowe Bank's Glasgow Head Office to be a fleshy overweight man, but Fitch evidently kept himself active.

"Thank you," said Essex. The presence of the necromancer was the one thing souring Canning's enthusiasm for tonight's job. *Arakiel* had ensured that Fitch was expecting a representative from the Council tonight, meaning the banker would let Canning and Essex into his home without argument.

Floorboards creaked upstairs, signifying the presence of Fitch's family. Canning's mood brightened; tonight would be even more satisfying than he had first expected. "His family are here," he murmured to Essex.

"Good, leverage to ensure his cooperation," the necromancer said.

Good. Fun and then a feast, Canning thought.

Fitch led them into his sitting room. The room was large and well appointed, not that Canning had harboured any doubts about banking being a lucrative profession. Thick carpets covered the floor, and new mahogany furniture complemented several older oak pieces. "I thought it best to keep my wife and children upstairs during your visit," he said in a conspiratorial tone.

"Probably for the best," Canning said cheerfully.

"Wise," Essex agreed in his funereal tone.

"How can I assist the Council?" Fitch asked, his face betraying excitement and trepidation in equal parts.

"You can tell us the combination code for your bank's main vault," Canning said brightly.

Confusion flitted across Fitch's face, a hint of fear. "I don't understand. Why do you want the code? Surely Mr Crowe would be better approached regarding access to the bank? Or Mr Heron."

"We want the combination so we can get inside and take a large sum of money that doesn't belong to us," Canning told him, enjoying himself. *Arakiel* had forbidden them from approaching the bank's director, William Heron. And if Fitch believed mentioning Edmund Crowe, the secretive other partner of the bank, would cow Canning and Essex, he was greatly mistaken.

"It will go better for you if you cooperate," Essex said. A floorboard creaked overhead, and he looked pointedly upwards.

"Jesus, no!" Fitch said, not blind to the necromancer's unspoken threat.

"Then you'll tell us what we need to know, so we can be on our way." Canning still planned to kill the Fitch family regardless, but Essex would surely tattle to *Arakiel* if Canning lingered overly with the killing rather than attending to the remainder of the night's business.

"I can't." The fear in Fitch's voice was plain, sweat beading on his forehead.

"Perhaps bring down his wife and children," Essex said, couching it enough as a suggestion that Canning didn't bristle too much. Canning bared his fangs and Unveiled as he ascended the stairs. *Let them feel me coming.*

*

Tears streamed from Fitch's eyes, anguish written on his face as he stared down at his dead daughter. "I can't tell you!"

"You know the combination, Mr Fitch," Essex said implacably, his eyes devoid of sympathy as he watched the banker. "Tell us while you still have something to lose."

"Can't," Fitch sobbed. Canning noted he never claimed to not know the combination, he merely refused to tell them.

"The son, Mr Canning," Essex said.

"Just tell them!" Mrs Fitch screamed. The family – what remained of them – knelt on the floor, limbs bound with rope. The daughter lay dead on the floor, bled white by Canning while her parents and brother serenaded him with their screams.

Fitch just gasped out a sob. Canning had to admit, the banker was one stubborn bastard, his loyalty to Heron Crowe admirable, if inexplicable. Canning made no immediate move to go for the son, under no obligation to follow Essex's instructions. Instead he listened to the husband and wife's futile pleading before hauling the young son up effortlessly and sinking his fangs into the slim throat.

"Stop! Just tell them, Alex!" Mrs Fitch screamed. Fitch's wail was like nothing human, but no words came out, certainly not the information Canning required. Time was moving on, so he ripped out the child's throat and dropped him to the floor to bleed out.

"He's not going to talk," Canning said quietly as the hysterical Vera and Alexander Fitch struggled against their bindings to reach their last dying child.

Essex studied Fitch with a clinical air. "No. I suspect he has been compelled not to speak the combination."

"Mesmered?"

"No, but not dissimilar. A magician has put a spell on him not to divulge the combination of the bank."

"Damned magic," Canning said. "*Arakiel* will not be pleased if we don't return with that money." Not that pleasing the demon was something Canning particularly cared about, but he hated failure. "Can you break it?"

"Only death can break that particular spell," Essex said.

"That's no use to us," Canning grumped. The screams were beginning to grate on his nerves.

Essex looked at him. "An inconvenience, nothing more, Mr Canning." He pulled out a thin knife and stabbed Fitch beneath his armpit, striking the banker's heart with surgical precision.

Well, we've no further need of the wife. Canning leaned over and bit into her neck with needle-sharp fangs. She didn't struggle, death perhaps a mercy given her family's fate.

He gorged himself in time to see Fitch rise jerkily to his

feet, his face paling as his blood sank to his lower torso and legs, dead eyes unblinking. "Will he now be able to tell us the combination?" Canning asked.

Essex watched the *zombi*, his will animating it. "No, the spell is rather thorough. However, the combination is still in his mind, and the spell will not stop him from operating the vault's locking mechanism."

"So, we could just have taken him to the bank with us, and forced him to open it?" Canning asked acidly.

"Perhaps, though I suspect there are other precautions in place … but this way we need not worry about him activating any magical alarms or betraying us in some manner." Essex silently directed the corpse to walk to the front door. "And we now have an extra pair of hands to help remove the money."

*

Foley and Hunt meandered along the dark country road, guided only by lantern and starlight. Drunk enough that the walk was taking twice as long as it should, but sober enough to not just sleep it off in a field, the fresh air was helping to clear Foley's head.

"A fine night," Hunt said with a bit of a slur.

"Aye," Foley agreed. The air was warm, the gentle breeze from the sea fresh and invigorating. He had no idea what the time was (and no inclination to pull out his pocket watch and squint at it by lantern light) but a few hours after midnight was his guess.

"I think we might want to let a few days pass before we next visit the Horned Lord," Hunt said after several minutes of silence, both men concentrating on navigating the rough road ahead. Rocks, branches and hardened wheel ruts were all perils hidden in the darkness, the lantern helping them avoid the worst of them.

"That might be an idea," Foley said, amused. "Maybe let tempers cool before we show our faces again."

"Memories are long here."

Foley knew Hunt was thinking about his ancestor's bloody work and the animosity it still aroused among those descended from the original inhabitants. A bit of drunken brawling was unremarkable, but it was Hunt's ancestry that had led to the violence during the game, and later at the pub. "You're not planning to just sit around Ashwood Lodge, are you?" he asked with some concern. Lord and Lady Ashwood would soon find work for idle hands.

"No," Hunt said. "I've been thinking, it might be an idea to spend several days exploring Glendorcha and the Lewswood."

"Aye? Any reason?" Foley was less than enthusiastic about the prospect of days spent trekking through glens and woods. He'd rather take his chances back in the village, where at least the inn served ale.

"I study natural history, remember? It would be a good opportunity to gather information on local geology, plants, and animals. Very few people have ventured into the heart of the Lewswood."

"I don't think we'd make much progress, having to return home each day," Foley said. *He'll get us lost in some old wood.*

"I don't mean to return home each day. We could camp out. Loch Arienas is on the far edge of the forest, we could visit there."

"So, you not only want us to spend our days stumbling through a forest, you also want us to spend our nights sleeping on the hard dirt?" Foley shook his head.

"We could take supplies. Just us, the fresh air, nature, a nice campfire, and no arseholes nursing grudges almost two hundred years old. And enough whisky to drink ourselves insensible each night," Hunt said, a sly edge in his voice.

"You think you can change my mind with the promise of whisky?" Foley asked, the night hiding his grin. *Bastard knows me too well.*

"I do indeed, Foley."

"We can discuss it further later. We'll need plenty of whisky, mind. And your mother will no doubt expect us to finish mending that wall first."

The steady(ish) tempo of Hunt's footsteps turned discordant, a foot scraping on the dirt as he stopped. "Do you see that light?"

Foley turned and looked around, seeing nothing. "The lighthouse?"

"Wrong direction. Look to our left."

He peered through the branches and caught a glimpse of distant flames flickering between the branches. "A fire?"

"A cottage or farm, maybe," Hunt said.

"Let's have a look." Foley led Hunt through the trees, grimacing as branches cut at his face and roots tried to trip him. Had someone returned home from the fair drunk and knocked a lantern or candle over?

They broke through the treeline and headed towards the fire, though already Foley could see it was no house that burned. The flames were too high, for one thing.

"It's Ash Hill," Hunt said quietly.

"The old hillfort, Dunkail'an?" Foley asked. There was nothing there but some stone ruins. Nothing that would burn.

"Yes." Hunt slowed, perhaps hesitant to go closer. "There are people up there."

Foley saw dark shapes moving beneath the flames. Torches, he decided. "A gathering. But why?"

"Followers of the old religion, maybe?" Hunt said. "Shutter your lantern."

Foley did so, though he was confident none of those on the hill would be able to see it, not in the midst of so much light themselves. "You think they'll come for us?" he scoffed.

"We're going to get closer," Hunt said, sounding sober. And a little afraid.

"Why? If a bunch of pagans want to cavort on top of a hill, that's their business."

"I'd agree, but someone Unveiled earlier. It was too sunny to be a *Nephilim*, which means–"

"A demon." Foley watched the hill. "You think the demon's up there?"

"Let's take a quiet look. If they're following the old religion, they'll bear my family no love, and we're not that far from Ashwood. I'd appreciate some warning if a mob carrying torches intends to visit."

That made sense to Foley. "Fair point but stay close to me and keep quiet."

Bruised, tired, and not a little drunk, creeping up a hill in the dark threatened to turn into farce, but surprisingly neither Foley nor Hunt tripped or betrayed their presence to the group. A murmur of chanting lingered in the still air, but too quiet for Foley to discern what was being said. The odd word he did catch sounded Gaelic in any case.

Onwards Foley and Hunt climbed, moving low through wild grass and jagged thistles. A forest of burning torches crowned the hilltop with flame, and Foley wondered just what they'd find. Old tales of pagan sacrifice came to mind, of victims drowned, burned, stabbed or bludgeoned to find favour with the old gods and spirits of the land.

The chanting grew louder, black silhouettes gathered on the hill's summit, torches raised high. Foley heard a rustle and a thump, followed by a grunt of pain. "Careful," he hissed to Hunt, turning to check his friend was uninjured. *Clumsy-*

He stumbled over something hard, the lantern flying from his hand, followed a moment later by the loud crack of breaking glass and a flare of light as the still-lit lantern's shutter broke off. The light died as the candle inside was extinguished. *Shit!*

Foley froze. The chanting ceased, and darkness fell over Ash Hill. A whooping shriek rose up and echoed across the hill for perhaps a minute before finally ending. Panic drove Foley low to the ground, not moving until it stopped. Thereafter he heard nothing.

"Now what?" Hunt said quietly from his side, sounding shaken.

"We've come this far," Foley decided, facing down his fear. He found the half-broken lantern and pulled a match from his pocket, striking it off a stone to relight the lantern's candle.

They continued up the hill and found the summit deserted. No one was there, nor anything left to hint at their purpose.

"I don't like this," Hunt admitted. "What did that bloody shrieking mean?"

Foley peered down the far slope, seeing nothing. "It was to cover their escape. One or two of them remained behind to make a noise while the others scarpered. Then they too left."

"And none tripped in the darkness?" Hunt was sceptical. Certainly, all the torches had been quickly extinguished.

"I doubt this is the first time they've been up here. Maybe they had a rope lain along a safe route down, and the last to go pulled it after them."

"Like Theseus," Hunt said cryptically.

"Aye, exactly." *Who?*

They stood alone in the dark, the mysterious gathering gone like chaff in the wind.

Chapter Nineteen

Canning watched the Heron Crowe Bank, a three-storey building sitting alone on Ingram Street. Decorative pillars flanked the single-storey banking hall's entrance at the front. He had spied on the building alone the night before to familiarise himself with the external security, and he knew that, assuming it was the same from day-to-day, there would be two guards patrolling the perimeter.

"Stay here," Canning said, handing the reins to Essex before hopping off the wagon. The two guards circled the bank in opposing directions, and Canning knew it would be prudent to deal with them silently one at a time. A powerful spell had been placed on Fitch to protect the vault, and Essex had warned Canning that they might encounter further magical defences securing the bank.

He watched as both guards passed the front of the bank, and as they turned the opposing corners, he ran across the road, turning right. Not wanting the scuff of shoe leather against cobbles or paving slabs to give him away, he ran barefoot, his shoes left in the wagon.

These days he preferred to kill with his teeth, the more personal touch, but speed and stealth were of the essence, so tonight he would kill with a sharply whetted knife. The first guard walked slowly, in no rush to complete yet another circle of the bank, believing he had many more to do this night. Not knowing this was his last.

The guard's lantern chased back the shadows as he walked deeper into the darkness, leaving Ingram Street's gaslights behind him. Not knowing darkness approached him from behind. Canning was irritated to find himself taking an unnecessary breath as he pounced, an old habit from when he lived. The sound alerted the guard who started to turn, jerking several times as Canning's knife plunged into his back, air and blood exploding out of his mouth.

Canning wrapped a hand around the guard's mouth, a precaution in case he managed a shout. He didn't, sinking down to the ground, dying without a fight. *One dead, one to go.* Knowing the second guard was even now circling round and would come across his colleague's body in minutes, Canning hurried back the way he had come, feeling cobbles beneath his cold bare feet.

He passed the front of the bank and turned the corner, seeing nothing ahead and knowing the second guard was at the bank's rear. That guard would soon turn the next corner and find the body, raising the alarm. *Keel will not be pleased if we fail.* Canning increased his pace, still somewhat perturbed at such exertions requiring no breath. But not displeased.

A bobbing light ahead betrayed the second guard's location, and Canning reached him with little effort. Confident there would be no witnesses at the rear of the bank, Canning slowed on reaching the still-unaware guard, and cleared his throat. "A lovely night, aye?"

The guard started, his right hand reaching into his jacket pocket as he turned. Reaching for a gun, Canning knew, so he wasted no time in stabbing his knife into the man's throat. Their eyes locked, the guard's wide as he choked on his blood, sinking to the ground, Canning's smiling face his last sight on earth.

Canning knelt and leaned forwards, his mouth fastening around the guard's torn throat, a sluggish river of still-warm blood spilling into his mouth. That river stilled as the guard's heart beat its last, but Canning had no time to indulge himself further anyway, and too much missing blood would signal a *Nephilim*'s involvement.

He found Essex and Fitch waiting for him at the bank's entrance, the latter's animated corpse pale and dead-eyed. "Time to make a withdrawal, Dr Essex," Canning said cheerfully. "If Mr Fitch is willing to assist?"

"Be assured, Mr Canning, that the flesh is willing even if the spirit was not. Mr Fitch is now most amenable to our needs."

"And they say bankers are an intractable breed."

"A moment, Mr Canning."

The sound of scuffing shoes alerted Canning to the approach of a – no, two – persons. He turned to find the corpse of the first guard sluggishly walk towards them, soon after joined by the second. Scenting treachery, Canning turned to Essex. "What is the meaning of this?"

Essex returned his accusatory stare with an untroubled look of his own. "Assistance, Canning." He unlocked the iron-shod bank doors with Fitch's key.

Essex remained outside while Canning sneaked in after the three shuffling *zombis*, Fitch flanked by the two guards.

"How did you two get in?" a voice echoed from the centre of the bank, doubtless from the guard assigned to the main floor. "Mr Fitch! Sorry, sir, I didn't recognise you at first."

There was a guilty edge to the guard's voice, a lingering hint of whisky in the air suggesting to Canning that the guard had been caught drinking. Doubtless he now feared to lose his job. *I've some good news for you there, my man.*

Unfortunately for the guard, it was his life he was about to lose. He stopped speaking, Canning catching a glimpse of him in the dimmed gas lighting. Fitch and the other two guards walked towards the man, their silence perhaps assumed to be anger on Fitch's part for his misdemeanour. There was enough light to see, but it had been turned down due to the late hour.

"Ah, I can explain this sir, I–" He managed a choked-off scream as the three *zombis* pulled him down to the ground, dead hands wrapping around his throat. A shotgun sat on the nearest table next to a half-empty bottle of whisky that glowed earthy-gold.

*

William Heron awoke sluggishly to find his butler gently but urgently shaking his shoulder. "What is it, Jefferson?" he managed irritably through a dry throat.

Jefferson handed him a glass of water from the bedside table. "Apologies, sir, but there's a visitor at the door. She says it's most urgent." He turned on the wall-mounted gas lamp.

Heron squinted at his clock, wondering what the hell called

a visitor to his door between two and three in the morning. "She?"

"A Miss Quinn, sir."

Sleep and irritation fled, chased away by a sudden trepidation. "Show her to the sitting room. Now! Leave it, I can dress myself," he snapped as Jefferson made to hand him his house robe.

What brings her to my door? Heron dreaded to speculate as he threw on his house robe and slid his feet into his slippers.

He entered his living room to find Miss Quinn waiting for him, a grim set to her face. "What brings you here at this hour?" he asked, foregoing all pleasantries. Her hair had been tied back, her blue dress rumpled. All signs of her haste to reach Heron.

Her gaze flickered to Jefferson.

"He has my full confidence," Heron said impatiently.

"Very well." Her dark eyes met his. "The wards I established within the Heron Crowe Bank have been breached."

Heron's chest tightened, and his next breath proved difficult. "Are you saying…?"

"There are intruders in the bank," she interrupted. "The wards were designed to activate if any of your guards died."

Every guard working a shift at the bank was given an amulet to wear, one warded by Miss Quinn to alert her should they die. "Have you raised the alarm?" He winced at the unintended high pitch his voice reached.

"Yes, reinforcements are on their way to the bank as we speak," Miss Quinn assured him. "But I knew you would want to be informed immediately."

"You acted correctly, of course." Heron was aware that his right hand trembled.

"Should Mr Crowe be made aware, sir?" Jefferson asked quietly.

"Not yet," Heron decided. "I'll visit the bank first and assess the situation."

"Your carriage–" Jefferson began.

"There is no time for that," Heron said. "We'll walk." His townhouse wasn't far from the bank.

"Without an escort?" Jefferson looked fearful. The streets were no longer safe at night even for those aligned with the

Sooty Feather Society.

"I assume Miss Quinn did not travel alone?"

"I did not," she assured them. "My escort waits outside and will assure our safety."

*

Canning and Essex stood in the vault beneath the bank, the necromancer having added the bank's fourth and last guard to his pack of *zombis*. This one had realised something was amiss early on and discharged his shotgun into one of the guards from outside, blasting the animated corpse into bloody ruin. Essex's magic seemed unaffected, the corpse still moving despite his organs being shredded into bloody gore.

"Now what?" Canning asked. This would all be for naught if they were unable to access the vault.

"Mr Fitch, if you would be so good as to let us in?" Essex asked. For dramatic effect, Canning assumed, since the necromancer controlled Fitch completely. The dead banker jerked towards the vault door and slowly turned each of the five brass dials securing the vault door. Evidently whatever spell constrained him in life no longer worked.

The bolts released their grip on the circular steel door protecting the fortunes of the Sooty Feathers and their undead masters, a thrill of excitement going through Canning as Fitch pulled open the door.

Essex led them into the vault, illuminating the large steel-reinforced concrete room with his lantern. Canning peered into one room and saw rows of iron deposit boxes embedded in the walls. A larger room in the vault contained the bank's money, thick iron boxes filled with coins and notes, organised by denomination.

"I've never robbed a bank before." Canning's voice echoed round the vault. It was certainly fun, though less so than killing.

"We should not tarry," Essex warned. The *zombis* under his control moved to the money with large sacks and began filling them with cash.

"Sunset is still a couple of hours away."

Essex sounded somewhat distracted, most of his concentration likely needed to control his dead minions.

"That is not my concern. I sensed something when you killed the guards. Given that the bank is not averse to employing magic to protect its interests, I suspect they had wards in place to detect trouble."

"You're saying the bank's people may know we're inside and be on their way?"

"A very real possibility, Mr Canning."

Canning joined the five *zombis* in filling the sacks with bank notes, irritated that their haul would be less than anticipated. Worse; they must take a mixture of high and low denominations, as to attend other banking institutes to change too many higher notes for lower notes would arouse suspicion. After tonight's work, both the Heron Crowe Bank and the Sooty Feathers would be scouring the city for those responsible.

"The work would go quicker if you deigned to assist," was Canning's acid observation on seeing Essex standing by, watching.

"My concentration is needed to keep your five assistants at work," was Essex's innocent reply.

Perhaps two-thirds of the sacks were filled when Essex said, "Enough. We should leave."

Canning didn't argue. He and the five *zombis* managed to carry all the sacks, Canning aided by his unnatural strength, the *zombis* untroubled by strained muscles or backs. They returned up to the bank's marbled public room, lantern light gleaming off the marble floor and glass dome overhead. Canning let the *zombis* exit the bank first, only leaving himself when there were no shouts or gunshots. The sacks of stolen money were dumped into the back of the wagon.

Essex peered up and down Ingram Street. "That should satisfy Mr Keel, and we would be unwise to risk a second trip into the bank."

"A good night's work," Canning agreed cheerfully as he and Essex climbed onto the wagon. A thought occurred, the chance to work further mischief. "Doctor, why not give your lantern to our friend Mr Fitch and send him back inside to the vault? When his employer and colleagues arrive, let them find the rest of their money burned to ash."

But Essex shook his head. "That would run contrary to our instructions. Mr Keel was most adamant that we were only to take as much of the money as we could and leave the rest. I believe he has further plans for the bank."

Disappointment welled in Canning. "Pity." He was surprised to see Fitch clambering up also. "You're bringing your pets with us?"

"Just Mr Fitch. Mr Keel would prefer a degree of ambiguity to surround the theft. Perhaps let them suspect Fitch betrayed them? Regardless, Mr Keel – and I – would prefer the Sooty Feathers not know there is a necromancer in the city." A private smile crossed his face. "And certainly not two."

Canning was about to ask what Essex meant by his last comment, but he was distracted by the other four *zombis* shuffling back towards the bank. The two guards from outside appeared to be going to either side of the bank, and the last two were returning inside. "You're putting them back where you found them?"

"Yes. Their posthumous involvement will go unnoticed." After a short time, he looked at Canning and nodded.

Canning took the reins. "Time we were leaving, then." The wagon rattled down Ingram Street, carrying away a small fortune.

*

Acid burned Heron's gut as he stood within the violated vault of his bank, dismay leaving him dizzied. A full audit would be needed, but he estimated perhaps a third of the bank's money was missing. Ten armed guards now protected the bank, but that wouldn't return the stolen money. One consolation was that the thieves had left the deposit boxes alone; the bank's reputation would have never recovered had the secrets entrusted to them by the Sooty Feathers been taken. The security breach and loss of money was disaster enough. *The other directors will have my head.* It was surely no coincidence that the robbery took place scant days before the bank's next quarterly meeting.

The gaslights had been turned up to full, even as dawn lit up the street outside. The four dead guards had been removed. But questions remained.

"How did they get inside the bank?" Gorry asked quietly,

the clerk summoned like so many of the bank's employees despite it being Sunday morning. The doors were kept locked, only the guard inside having a key to let anyone in. He and Kenley, the vault guard, had been strangled, while one of the two guards outside had been shot, the other stabbed.

Arthur Wallace, a burly man whose brutish appearance hid a quiet intelligence, walked over, a grim set to his face.

"Wallace, good. Where is Fitch?" Heron asked. He wanted the assistant manager to oversee the audit. *I want to know to the ha'penny just how much money those swine took.*

Wallace kept his voice low. "Sir, Mr Fitch was not at home. I found his family dead inside."

Heron's chest ached again. "Dead? How? Fitch was not there, you say?"

"Fitch was not there. I checked his family, a *Nephilim* killed them."

Oh God. He felt light-headed. Had the recent troubles encouraged a *Nephilim* to go rogue? Or worse, were the murders and robbery sanctioned by Glasgow's ruling undead? A bold prelude before seizing the bank.

Miss Quinn spoke. "Mr Fitch is the only one besides yourself and Mr Crowe to know the combination to the vault, aye?"

Heron rubbed a trembling hand across his clammy forehead. "Yes … yes, he does." A thought occurred. "He also holds a spare key to the bank."

"My spell would prevent Fitch from telling the combination to anyone, or even thinking it without the appropriate amulet," she said.

Heron jerked a nod. Unlike Heron or Crowe, Fitch needed to use an enchanted amulet to 'remember' the combination, an amulet locked within the bank. "The amulet is still here." He had checked.

"Maybe a *Nephilim* tried to torture the combination from Fitch, threatening and killing his family? Or maybe he's working with undead?" Quinn suggested. "But my spells were robust. He could not have told anyone, not even under duress. Only death cancels the spells."

Heron remembered the brief confusion on Fitch's face whenever he handed the amulet to him, on days when the assistant manager was entrusted with access to the vault. "We must find him." He considered the *Nephilim* involvement, fear clamping itself around his chest. "I must make Mr Crowe aware."

Wallace and Quinn exchanged disquieted glances at the mention of the bank's senior partner. But Heron suspected he was out of his depth, and if undead unrest was threatening the bank, then Edmund Crowe's intervention might be the only path for its survival.

Chapter Twenty

"Welcome, Kenmure," Redfort said as the police inspector joined him at a low table in the gas-lit lounge of the Black Wing Club. Oak-panelled walls gleamed, immaculately polished like the small, low-standing table before him. A Wednesday night, the club was quiet, allowing Redfort and Kenmure to discuss Sooty Feather business without fear of being overheard.

Comfortable old leather creaked as Kenmure sank into the chair across from Redfort. He placed a glass containing a large measure of spirit on the table. Normally impeccably attired, Redfort noted the man's pocket handkerchief to be unkempt. These might be trying times for the Society, but there was no excuse for letting standards drop.

"A good evening, your Grace," Kenmure said, taking a long drink from his glass and visibly savouring the flavour.

"Your message said you had news of some import for me," Redfort said. He affected only a mild interest, determined that Kenmure not sense his desperation. Bad times for the Sooty Feathers were getting worse. Fear and money were the twin pillars that kept the Sooty Feathers in power, and one of those pillars was toppling.

Word of what had befallen Heron Crowe had spread across the city and beyond, the panicked rush of investors to withdraw their money forcing the bank to close its doors until their cash reserves were restocked. No, word had not spread. It had *been* spread, deliberately by those responsible. A condition of Sooty Feather membership was that one did one's banking through Heron Crowe, and many of the richest citizens of Glasgow now found themselves unable to access their money. The Society would be paralysed until the matter was resolved, forced to rely on credit or small personal reserves.

Fortunately, the Black Wing Club allowed its members to maintain a tab at both the restaurant and bar. The lounge might be quiet, but Redfort could not recall seeing the club restaurant below so busy during the week.

Kenmure didn't rush to answer, instead taking another drink from his glass. "I've found the Carpathian Circus," he said finally.

Redfort didn't like the barely hidden amusement in Kenmure's eyes, but he was more interested in the news. If true, let him have his little moment. If he was mistaken, Redfort would see him broken. "Where?"

"They're camped near a town in Lanarkshire, the local constabulary is watching them closely. An inspector sent me a telegram yesterday."

At last, some good news! "Are they settling in?"

"For now. A promise of reward has been sent to the inspector, and he has assigned a few men to follow the circus, should they leave, and send word of their travels."

Redfort took a small sip from his port. "Good. Good." It would not be atypical of the Society's recent fortunes if the circus disappeared again, but that was unlikely if the constables following it kept a discreet distance. An entire circus of caravans and wagons were not easy to hide. "I'll convene the Council and let them know." *My moment of triumph.*

"That won't be necessary," said a female voice. Amy Newfield passed Redfort and sat in the empty seat at the table. "Regent Guillam sent me on her behalf."

Redfort gave her and Kenmure a level look. "And how did Regent Guillam know Kenmure and I were meeting tonight?" He deliberately didn't give the inspector the courtesy of his rank, suspecting the answer.

"I sent a message to Regent Guillam as well as yourself, Bishop Redfort," Kenmure said with no apology in his voice. "Too many Councillors have died or disappeared, and I wished no delay or misfortune to delay my news reaching the Council."

You wished to make certain you received credit for finding the circus. "I see," was all Redfort said. There was no point in fighting a battle already lost, but Kenmure going behind his back would not be forgotten.

Kenmure repeated his news to Miss Newfield while Redfort nursed his discontent in silence.

"I'll let the Regent know," Miss Newfield said. There was a hesitance in her voice. She might serve Margot Guillam directly, but she was still a ghoul only a few months Made, and her life before that had not prepared her for the vicious intrigues of the undead and the Sooty Feathers.

"Finding the circus is all well and good," Redfort said. "But we have no way of knowing if Keel accompanies them. Between Dunclutha and the Necropolis, they have lost most of their strength, likely a spent force by now."

"Perhaps, your Grace," Kenmure said, oddly unangered by Redfort's attempt to diminish his news. "But even if he is absent, there may be some among them who know the name of the demon's Vessel."

"Have you anything else to tell us?" Redfort said as if addressing a messenger.

"No, Bishop," Kenmure said, clearly rankled by Redfort's dismissive tone.

Amy Newfield stood. "Regent Guillam is expecting me. I'll tell her what you've learned, Inspector."

"I'm sure we'll hear from her soon," Redfort said. Kenmure's discovery of the Carpathian Circus was progress in the search for Erik Keel, and not before time.

Unblinking eyes briefly locked with his. "You will." The ghoul headed to the exit; those members who had been inducted into the Sooty Feather Society, and thus knew what she was, gave her a wide berth.

Redfort watched Kenmure finish his drink, not appreciating the policeman sending a message to the Regent behind his back. With the death of *Tertius* – Police Superintendent Thatcher – Redfort had been appointed Kenmure's contact with the Council, and any information the policeman gleaned should have been passed solely to him. Redfort had known Kenmure for years, disquieted by his uncharacteristic boldness. Always before, Kenmure had treated Redfort with careful respect.

"I must be off, too, your Grace," Kenmure said. "Good evening."

"Kenmure," Redfort said curtly. The policeman left the table with a visible swagger Redfort found most unbecoming.

William Heron sat at the head of the table, his brandy untouched. Six of the other eight bank directors sat on either side, leaving the chair at the opposite end empty. It was almost eleven, two hours after the start of Heron Crowe's second quarterly meeting of the year. In the best of times the meetings passed quickly, with the six men present well-satisfied with their dividends and praising Heron's perspicacity. In the worst of times the meetings dragged on as he duelled with them across the table. This meeting was one of the latter.

The bank had performed well for the most part, but the robbery in the early hours of Sunday morning had triggered panic, and the directors demanded an accounting.

"Insurance in time will cover our losses ... our *substantial* losses ... but the faith of our clients has been shaken, some finding themselves financially vulnerable," Walter Herriot pointed out. "Our association with the Sooty Feather Society has proven beneficial, I do not dispute that, but if it has drawn us into an internal feud that has nothing to do with us ... nothing to do with us," he repeated, "then we should consider ending that association."

Heron knew Herriot wasn't the only director to hold that opinion, he was merely the one giving it voice. But did he hold the majority view? "Walter, I do not need to remind you that our bank has made many enemies over the years. We know nothing yet save that Alexander Fitch is missing, and at least one *Nephilim* was involved. It may well be an undead opportunist taking advantage of the recent troubles. In which case we would do well to keep the Sooty Feathers and Lord Fisher's undead close to our bosom."

His fingers brushed against his brandy glass as if to take a sip, but instead he continued. "Heron Crowe has been associated with undead since its earliest days. The first incarnation of our bank was formed and funded from the financial carcase of the Knights Templar during its disbandment. It may have been a few centuries until Oliver Heron merged his company with that bank to form Heron Crowe, but let me assure you, the Templars have not forgotten where our capital came from."

"Ancient history," Herriot said dismissively. "We should look to the future, and as directors it is our responsibility to ensure the right man is at the helm."

Charles Saddler broke the awkward silence. "No one is unmindful of your excellent work, William," he said kindly, "but what we must ask ourselves is, are you the man to lead us into the next century?"

"I stand with William," Gavin Timson said gruffly. Morris Campbell nodded in agreement.

Heron swallowed, looking at all six faces, most of them inscrutable. Two for him, two against. If it came to a vote, his future rested on the last two. "I would remind you all, he said forcefully, "that I've led this bank for six years. My father led it before me. This is the Heron Crowe Bank. It is my name on the letterhead, not yours."

"I think we should have a vote. I propose Mr Heron stands down as chairman," said Herriot.

Saddler nodded. "I second it."

So that is that. Heron felt his stomach drop and his heart quicken. There would be a vote, and if it went against him, he would lose control of the bank his family had co-founded in 1653. His throat tasted of bile. He would only get a vote if there was a tie. "Very well. A vote is called to remove me as Chairman. Who is in favour?"

"Aye," said Saddler.

Timson thumped his hand on the table. "Nay."

"Aye," said Herriot.

"Nay," said Campbell.

Carson hesitated. "Abstain." William felt a sharp stab in his chest.

Devlin didn't hasten himself to answer. He knew his vote would decide the issue. Heron's shirt was slick with sweat. Devlin opened his mouth to speak.

Someone stepped through the doorway and walked to the end seat. "Nay." Edmund Crowe sat down.

"Nay," Devlin answered quickly.

Heron let out a breath and wiped a handkerchief across his brow. *I'm saved.* "Good evening, Edmund," he said to Crowe, wondering how long he had listened in on the meeting. His dramatic arrival ensured that even had Devlin voted Aye, it would be a tie, giving Heron the deciding vote.

Knowing this, Devlin voted accordingly. Heron wondered what his original answer would have been.

Everyone muttered a cowed greeting to Edmund Crowe, the deputy chairman of the bank and co-founder. He rarely attended meetings, content to leave the bank's business to Heron and the other directors. Saddler and Herriot had gone pale. *Treacherous shits.*

Crowe curtly acknowledged the others. "Evening, gentlemen," he said, his voice raspy and dry as old parchment. "In light of recent events I thought it prudent to attend, to assure you all," dead eyes turned to Herriot as he spoke, "that William has my complete support. His family have been the soul of this bank since its founding." As Crowe had co-founded the bank with Oliver Heron over two hundred years earlier, no one contradicted him.

He got up and walked past Heron, his old black suit smelling musty as always. "A good evening to you, gentlemen."

The *Nephilim* left, and Heron turned back to the table. "Any other business?" he asked mildly. He drank half his brandy in one shaky gulp, the liquor burning his throat.

There wasn't.

*

Canning knew a momentary fear as he heard the lid being jemmied free from the coffin protecting him from daylight during the journey from Glasgow. He almost screamed on seeing a burning bright light above him, believing his companion was exposing him to a Final Death from sunlight.

But it was just a lantern, he realised, relief relaxing his muscles. *At least I did not cry out.* Essex was hard, a predator in his own way, and weakness invited betrayal.

"We've arrived, Mr Canning," Essex told him.

The journey by train had been long, Canning feeling the Thirst acutely. A wagon had then brought Canning and Essex to the circus, the necromancer ostensibly transporting a coffin for burial. The circus might have fled Glasgow after Rannoch's death, but they had remained loyal enough to eventually send word of their whereabouts by way of a coded advertisement in the *Glasgow Herald* newspaper.

Canning emerged from the narrow wooden coffin, noting that the circus hid in a copse of trees. Why *Arakiel* had chosen now to make contact with the circus, Canning didn't know. Clearly the demon's plans were approaching fruition.

The weather-faded caravans and wagons of the Carpathian Circus were familiar to Canning, having spent a few weeks with the circus immediately after his Making. Much of that time had been spent locked in a trunk as punishment for failing to kill Wilton Hunt and his friend, but memories of that unpleasant time with the *Nephilim*-ruled circus-folk were still vivid. They had suffered his presence on Rannoch's orders, but they had shown him no welcome, merely one of many expendable ghouls newly Made by Rannoch. Now he returned to them as *Arakiel*'s right hand.

Night had fallen, fires lighting up the camp. The Romani, mostly women and children, watched Canning's approach with hard-eyed suspicion. Always an outsider, Canning expected no warmer welcome when they recognised him. He noted with spiteful pleasure that the circus had fallen on hard times, their numbers diminished.

Two of the three *Nephilim* leaders, Marko and Lucia were dead. Bresnik was the surviving leader of the trio who had enslaved and corrupted the circus two centuries prior, after Niall Fisher overthrew Erik Keel in Bucharest. For two hundred years the circus had waited for word from George Rannoch to come to Glasgow, to take revenge against Fisher. The circus had answered Rannoch's call and paid a steep price in blood.

Many of the other circus vampyres had died in the Glasgow Necropolis. Dunclutha and the Necropolis had seen most of the mortal men of the circus dead, leaving it a spent force in Canning's opinion. Canning would have left it to its wounded exile, but *Arakiel* evidently still sought to wring some use from it.

Bresnik and four fellow *Nephilim* waited. "Canning," Bresnik said. "Have you fled Glasgow? Where is *Arakiel*?"

"He lives," Canning said. "It is time to return to the fold."

Chapter Twenty-One

Regent Guillam chaired the Council meeting; the nights when the leader of the Council attended rarely, leaving most of the business to *Secundus*, had died with Guillam's predecessor Edwards. The new *Prima* attended every meeting, holding the Society together through threat and force of will.

"Firstly, I invite you all to join me in congratulating *Quintus* for finding the remains of the late *Tertius*," Regent Guillam said.

The assembled Sooty Feathers interpreted an invitation from the Elder *Nephilim* as a command, and so politely applauded Redfort. Thwarting the attempt to conceal Thatcher's death had been a small victory in a time of setbacks and lack of progress, and Redfort was happy to bask in the approbation.

He bestowed a gracious nod on the assembled Society members, saying nothing. Tonight had seen him and five of the other Councillors ascend a rank, and he was pleased that his first night sitting in the Fifth Seat had seen him receive his due. His satisfaction was marred by the knowledge that by rights he should be telling the Council of the whereabouts of the Carpathian Circus, but Kenmure had stolen that from him by going behind his back.

"Tonight, we welcome the Council's newest member, who will join us as the Eight Seat, *Octavius*," Guillam said. On cue, a man stepped from the shadows and walked towards the head table, sitting at the far end; Edwin Kenmure. *Bastard*.

Redfort understood Guillam's reason for selecting Kenmure. For years Thatcher had linked the police with the Council, an important tool in the Sooty Feathers' rule of Glasgow. Thatcher needed replacing, and Kenmure's success in finding the rogue circus – and perhaps the demon Keel – made him as good as any other Sooty Feather in the constabulary.

"Thank you, Regent," Kenmure said, sitting ramrod straight. Redfort looked away, knowing he must watch his back with the policeman. Few surprised Redfort, but Kenmure's deft politicking certainly had.

He expected Regent Guillam to disclose the discovery of the Carpathian Circus' location, more good news for a Society that sorely needed it. But she too had a talent for surprising Redfort. "By now you all know of the money stolen from the Heron Crowe Bank."

An angry mutter rose up from all gathered. They knew, and many faced ruin if the situation was not soon remedied. Having all Society members use the same bank, a bank aligned with the undead, had doubtless seemed a good idea at the time, another string tied to each member. Now those strings threatened to choke the Society to death.

"I heard that the insurance company are saying it was done by an employee, and they won't pay!" someone shouted from the other end of the room. Outraged enough to raise his voice, but not stupid enough to do so within sight of Margot Guillam. Growls of agreement rose up from around the two tables seating the Sooty Feathers not on the Council, albeit a growl that reduced to a cautious murmur from those seated nearest it.

The Regent's knuckles rapped once off the table, silence falling over the room. Redfort risked giving her a sidewise glance, noting the chilled expression on her bone-white face. She hadn't yet fed, clearly, and Redfort wondered if her eye would fall on some unfortunate in the room a little too loud for their own good.

Regent Guillam handed the new *Tertia* a slip of folded paper which she in turn passed to Redfort. He unfolded it, seeing two words written in Guillam's ancient, elegant script: *Say nothing*.

Regent Guillam looked slowly around the room, from face to face. "Mr Crowe has explained matters to the insurance company, and they will be recompensing the bank without delay. I'm assured Heron Crowe will be fully reopened by early next week."

Relieved applause echoed across the room. Applauding the news that their funds would soon be available to them, certainly, but Redfort suspected many in the room realised just how close they had come to trying Guillam's patience. Reginald Fredds, the Council's *Quartus*, and the only undead besides the Regent who was a Councillor, remained ominously silent, taking a keen unblinking interest in the louder dissenters.

"Is there any further business?" the Regent asked, her tone suggesting anything raised that she did not find pertinent would land the speaker in her bad graces.

A rattled throat clearing from *Secundus* was the only sound in the room, but the longest serving Councillor save for Regent Guillam said nothing. *An empty seat during a time the Society needs strong leadership, a tired old man lacking the decency to just die.*

Lord Smith, the Council's *Sextus*, spoke. "Regent Guillam, if I may?"

She nodded. "Speak."

Candlelight gleamed off Lord Smith's white hair, the Lord Commissioner of Justiciary aged in his sixties, a few dark strands still populating his neatly trimmed beard. "You will recall my predecessor on the Council, Lord McKellen, was brutally murdered in his bed two months ago."

Redfort recalled it all too well. Lord McKellen's business interests abroad and his position as a High Court Judge had seen him appointed to the Council the same time as Redfort, but it had proven a short-lived appointment. Fellow Sooty Feather and High Court Judge Lord Smith had been his obvious replacement.

Lord Smith continued. "I've been helping his son, Mr Alasdair McKellen, attend to his father's estate, Alasdair inheriting the McKellen businesses here and in other countries, as well as the Dunlew estate near Loch Aline."

"Your point, *Sextus*?" Regent Guillam asked.

"In light of our recent financial troubles, Alasdair would make a useful addition to the Society. Investing in his diverse business interests would protect us from a repeat of our Heron Crowe troubles. He is a young man, only twenty-six years old, and able to offer years of useful service to the Society."

"What of his character?" *Secundus* asked. "Membership

requires a robust fortitude." Meaning could he stomach intrigue, murder and learning the supernatural truth.

"I'm surprised that such a promising young fellow wasn't recruited years ago," Redfort said.

"McKellen has spent the past three years living in Argyll, managing one of the family's smaller estates," Lord Smith said. "He completed his probation period in the Black Wing Club shortly before leaving Glasgow."

"Why leave?" Regent Guillam asked. Reading between the lines, it seemed clear the young man had been exiled.

Lord Smith cleared his throat. "He has a young man's appetites and indulged them rather too freely and … enthusiastically. Lord McKellen was concerned his son's lack of discretion risked the family's good name and sent him to the country where there would be fewer … distractions."

Meaning young Alasdair was drinking and whoring too much, and Lord McKellen sent him out of the city to protect the family from scandal. And perhaps his heir from syphilis.

"He is my late husband's distant cousin, a promising addition," *Tertia* said. The Society would lure in Alasdair McKellen with the promise of satisfying his baser desires, until it owned him body and soul. *Like it owns all of us.*

"Continue supporting him through this difficult time, *Sextus*," Regent Guillam said. "Nominate him for the Sooty Feathers."

"I've already put his name forward, and he is most keen to establish himself in Glasgow society," Smith said. "I suspect his father had already educated him as to subjects he will learn of should his Sooty Feather membership be confirmed." Suggesting that the late Lord McKellen had told his son something of demons and the undead.

Tertia spoke hesitantly. "I'm hosting a garden party soon, it would be a good opportunity for the Society to welcome Cousin Alasdair back to Glasgow."

"When?" the Regent asked.

"The first weekend in August."

"Very good," the Regent said. "Make the necessary arrangements. I expect those here invited to attend to show Mr McKellen every consideration. The Society requires fresh blood, and McKellen may be just the sort we need." That McKellen would likely die an early death from a pickled liver or syphilis was of no concern to Margot Guillam, so long as he did her bidding until then. If he possessed an enduring usefulness, he might even be Made undead.

There was no further business, and so the Regent dismissed the Society. "*Quintus, Octavius*; attend me in the study. I have tasks for you," the Regent said.

Redfort's heart quickened. Clearly this pertained to the Carpathian Circus.

*

"Be seated." Redfort and Kenmure each took a seat on the opposite side of the desk from Margot Guillam. Amy Newfield placed two glasses of whisky on the desk in front of them. Neither she nor Guillam took a drink, which only drew attention to what they drank, what they were.

"My thanks, Miss Newfield." Redfort looked at Guillam. "I noticed you made no mention of the circus, Regent."

"And risk word reaching the circus that their whereabouts are known to us?" The Regent shook her head. "No. I want it kept quiet. Tell no one."

"You suspect traitors in our midst?" Kenmure asked.

"Suspect it? Yes," Guillam answered bluntly. "Our interests have suffered too much recently."

"Dealing with the circus will be difficult if none know of it," Redfort observed.

"You both know of it. I'm assembling a force to attack the circus. Led by the both of you."

"Both of us?" Redfort disliked the sound of that. He preferred to work from the shadows. He was no soldier to lead men into battle. They had a tendency to die.

Dead eyes watched him. "The men will not be told who they are fighting until the day they are to attack the circus, but their captains must know. As you two are the only ones beyond Miss Newfield and myself who know the circus has been found, that narrows my choices, no?"

"I am no soldier," Redfort observed.

"I'm sure Superintendent Kenmure will take care of you, Bishop," Miss Newfield said.

So, Regent Guillam arranged for a promotion within the constabulary as well as the Society. "I'm sure he will,"

Redfort said, not meaning it. Kenmure had revealed an ambition Redfort hadn't suspected in the man before, and he didn't relish spending days with him hunting a fallen angel and his vagabond followers.

"The circus won't be expecting us, your Grace," Kenmure said.

"When are we to leave?" Redfort asked, his misgivings unspoken.

"When Kenmure's men confirm the location of the circus."

"Soon," Kenmure promised. "Last telegram I received reported they were on the move."

The wait would give Redfort time to attend to other pressing matters he had been forced to neglect of late. *Such as finding Keel's necromancer.*

Redfort was about to stand when Guillam spoke again. "We have one more thing to discuss, Bishop. Kenmure, you may leave us."

Kenmure did so, giving the two undead a courtly bow.

"How else may I be of service, Regent?" Redfort asked. It was perhaps too much to hope that she was regretting Kenmure's elevation to the Council and wished him quietly taken care of while they were away.

"The Society has suffered financially this year, even before the Heron Crowe disaster. While the bank will recover, I had already tasked someone to advise on ways for us to increase our income, and she has submitted her report," Guillam said.

"How so?"

"We've invested in companies exporting and importing materials, however if we were to handle the shipping ourselves, our profits would increase."

"You want ships," Redfort deduced.

"I want a shipping company. The Browning Shipping Company, to be exact."

The name was somewhat familiar. "Will its owners be willing to sell?" Not that it mattered, since the Society's reserves were depleted. An offer of sorts would be made, one accepted if the owners wished to live.

"They are not to be given a choice in the matter," Guillam said, her voice hard.

"Who owns it?"

"Lord and Lady Ashwood."

"The Hunts? Your instructions were to leave that family alone," Redfort said. Miss Newfield gave a start at the mention of the Hunts.

"Circumstances change. They are staying at their estate near Loch Aline, not far from the Dunlew Castle."

"The home of Alasdair McKellen," Redfort said.

"Yes. Instruct Roderick McBride to accompany Mr McKellen home. While there, McBride is to 'convince' Lord Ashwood to sell the Browning Shipping Company." Unblinking eyes fixed on Redfort. "Make it clear to McBride he is to involve McKellen and defer to him, unless he proves incompetent. I would learn if McKellen has the same steel his father had before we waste our time on him."

"McKellen will be involved in this matter?" Redfort stared at Regent Guillam, wondering if he had heard her correctly. "Alasdair McKellen?" He wasn't even an Initiate yet, and already he was being involved in Society business.

"Are my instructions unclear, Bishop?"

"Not at all, Regent," he assured her.

"Excellent. Ensure they are clear to McBride, too."

Speaking with the infamous crime patriarch was not something Redfort relished. The man was a brute, albeit a useful one. "He'll want payment, or a share in the company."

"Pay him in information. Tell him the Hunts no longer enjoy my protection. Tell him the men last seen in the company of his murdered brother are Thomas Foley and Charles Sirk, both friends of Wilton Hunt. My information is that Foley accompanied Hunt to the family estate and may be found there. McBride may deal with Foley as he sees fit, so long as Lord Ashwood agrees to sell his company."

"McBride can be persuasive. How much is he to offer?" Redfort asked.

Guillam handed him the contract, the sale price looking to be perhaps a third the value of what a profitable shipping company might be worth. McBride would need to be *very* persuasive to get Lord Ashwood to agree to sell. If Wilton Hunt's friend was involved in the death of Edward McBride, then the Hunt family were in for an unpleasant time. Redfort had known the family for years and had even baptised Wilton Hunt. *A shame. I've always rather liked the Hunts. Most generous with their donations.*

Chapter Twenty-Two

On entering Walker's Bar with Jones, Redfort had expected to find an establishment not much better than the Thistledown, the shebeen frequented by Diviner Jimmy Keane, but to his surprise Walker's was no illegal drinking den. Indeed, it looked almost respectable. The bar ran along the left side of the taproom, clean and polished, and the bottles shelved along the wall were labelled. The law said the bar should have shut at nine, but at eleven it was still open with a few patrons either slouched at the bar or seated at one of the small round tables. Redfort doubted the local constables would dare press the issue, not given the bar was owned by an associate of Roderick McBride's.

A thuggish looking man with a thick-browed head looked over at them. "Your business here?"

As agreed, Jones did the talking. "We're here to see Roddy McBride." The less attention Redfort drew, the better. As Bishop of Glasgow, his presence would raise questions.

The man looked them over, his lip curling. "That's Mr McBride to you. And why would he want to see you two?"

Jones took a couple of steps forward, his shoulders squared, his feet apart and his knees not quite straight. "Tell him a Featherman is here to see him." Jones was not an especially clever man, but he had his uses, good with a cosh or knife, or with his finger on a trigger. He had killed a *Nephilim* on Redfort's orders once and captured Templar Inquisitor Wolfgang Steiner. Not a man to be intimidated by a jumped-up street tough.

Redfort had expected the man to find McBride and pass on the message, but he chose to take umbrage at Jones and stood threateningly before him. *How tiresome.*

"If you don't tell me what this is about, I'll–"

A flash of silver interrupted the threat as the tough found a blade at his throat, held by Jones. "Just tell Mr McBride. Or if I don't kill you, he might for pissing us about."

The man left, tugging at his collar.

"Well handled," Redfort said.

"It would have helped, sir, had you sent a message to McBride asking for a meeting," Jones said as the knife disappeared up his sleeve.

"I don't *ask* for meetings, Jones. And given the mortality rate of my peers on the Council, I prefer to make few appointments these days."

Less than a minute later the tough re-appeared, looking pale and not a little chastened. "Mr McBride will see you. Just you," he said to Redfort. At least he had sufficient wit to recognise Redfort as the one in charge.

"Very well," Redfort said.

As he followed the thug to the office behind the bar, he heard Jones asking for an ale.

The office was spartanly decorated, bare wooden floors and brick walls. Stained playing cards, an almost empty bottle of whisky, and three glasses sat on the table in the middle of the room. Two men sat around it. Redfort knew Roddy McBride by sight, a hard man with a broad face and broken nose, wearing a fine set of clothes. Crime paid well.

The other man was old and scarred, his head shaven to reveal a web of scars crossing his scalp. He wore a stained apron, suggesting he worked behind the bar.

Recognition crossed McBride's face. "Bishop Redfort. What brings a man of the cloth here at this hour?" Always a belligerent man, the death of his youngest brother a few months prior had left McBride even quicker to anger. His only lead was that the two men last seen with Eddie were friends of Wilton Hunt, but Regent Guillam had made it clear Hunt was to be left alone, otherwise McBride would doubtless have paid him a visit and not left until his two friends were named.

That prohibition hadn't made life any easier for the denizens of the Gorbals, however, as they bore the brunt of McBride's thwarted rage. There had been a spate of murders, the victims having been tortured first in his frenzy to identify those who had killed his brother.

His companion looked at Redfort in surprise. "Should I be honoured?"

McBride barked a laugh. "Don't bother bowing, Harry. It ain't God who brings him here this hour, is it, Bishop?" The man's tone was verging on disrespect. He wasn't stupid enough to defy Margot Guillam, being well aware what she was, but the Council's interference in his quest to avenge his brother hadn't won them his love, either. *Tonight will see that change.*

Redfort glanced at Harry, presumably the owner of the public house. "Perhaps we should talk alone, Mr McBride?"

"Harry Walker owns this bar and is my friend. You can speak in front of him."

Deciding to be blunt, Redfort asked, "What does he know? He is no Sooty Feather."

"Neither am I, Bishop. He knows enough. His son Gerry died at Dunclutha," McBride said.

Gerry Walker, now I recall. The younger Walker had been a carriage driver for McBride, the man who assisted Rannoch in capturing Wilton Hunt between Loch Lomond and Glasgow. "Very well. If he proves a liability, I'll have him killed."

Walker reddened, getting to his feet, fists clenched. "You think you can come into my bar and threaten me?"

"I can do as I will. I'm here on Council business," Redfort said coldly. "Regent Guillam sent me with a task for McBride." He counted on mention of the Regent to cow the two men, but he had a derringer hidden up his right sleeve just in case. Though that would be only good for one of the men. *I hope your ears aren't stuffed with wax, Jones.*

"Harry," McBride said quietly. "Take a seat."

"As you say, Roddy." Walker sat back down and took a large swig of whisky, giving Redfort a dark look.

"What does Miss Guillam want? I've little time for the Council these days," McBride said.

"*Regent* Guillam is aware of your discontent and seeks to give you satisfaction regarding your late brother," Redfort said, a diplomat when he wanted to be. "She wishes you to go north to Loch Aline and ... persuade ... Lord Ashwood to sell the Browning Shipping Company for well below its value."

"That's quite a trip. What's in it for me?"

Redfort smiled, enjoying himself. "Lord Ashwood is Lewis Hunt. His son Wilton has two friends you're looking for."

A killing rage entered McBride's eyes. "My price is Wilton Hunt and the freedom to question him until he names his associates last seen with Eddie."

"Wilton Hunt is not yours to harm." Redfort held up a calming hand. "I also have the names of the two men you seek, the pair you left with your brother. Thomas Foley and Charles Sirk. Foley is a guest of the Hunts, so you can deal with him as you attend to the Regent's task."

"Tell Miss Guillam I'll see it done," McBride promised.

"Excellent. I have the details for you, and a copy of the contract Regent Guillam wants Lord Ashwood to sign. Do try and not kill the Hunts; it might raise legal issues over the sale."

Bloodshot eyes narrowed. "And this Foley?"

"Deal with him as you please," Redfort said carelessly.

*

A knock on the door interrupted William Heron's pleasant reverie. He put down his scotch with a vexed sigh and waited for his valet to answer the door. Given the late hour, he wondered who it could be.

The whisky was a well-aged Dalmore, a gift of contrition from those bank directors who'd tried and failed to oust him. He was not disposed to be polite to whoever interrupted his enjoyment of it, a well-earned indulgence now that the insurance company had agreed (after some arm-twisting) to make good the bank's losses.

There was a shout and the sound of breaking furniture from the hall. Fear pulled Heron from his armchair. His first instinct was to investigate the commotion, but recent events had instilled caution in him, so he seized a poker from the fireplace and waited.

"What's going on?" he demanded, heart pounding. "Jefferson, answer me."

The door opened, and a ruffian entered the sitting room with a bloodied knife. The man was pale and had unruly brown hair, Heron shivering despite the clammy summer night.

"Who are you? Where's Jefferson?" Heron demanded. There was a dampness around his groin as a serpentine fear squeezed him, releasing his bladder. He knew enough to recognise a *Nephilim*'s Unveiling when he felt it.

The *Nephilim* said something in a foreign tongue, and William Heron's chest tightened as he realised he was going to die. The vampyre sheathed his knife and advanced on Heron, pulling rope and a hood from a small sack. *I'm being kidnapped!*

His would-be abductor turned as a third man entered the room, and Heron felt hope blossom as he recognised Edmund Crowe, his undead colleague. *Unless Crowe is behind this, having decided to remove me from the bank after all.*

"William, move to the other room." Crowe commanded. Heron obeyed with alacrity.

He heard thuds and bangs and the smashing of glass and wood. Then it ended, fear and hope warring in his gut.

"William, it is over," Crowe called out. *Oh, thank God!*

Heron returned to his sitting room to find Edmund Crowe the victor, the other undead lying motionless on the floor with a poker sticking out of his chest. The vampyre banker regarded his bloodstained jacket with distaste before turning his attention to Heron. "Evening, William. You are unharmed?"

"Thank God for you, Edmund, thank God!"

"God had little to do with my arrival," Crowe said with a dry chuckle.

Heron looked at the corpse. "Who was that?"

"I don't know, but a *Nephilim* I've never met before attacked me earlier, underestimating my strength. I suspected they might also strike at you and so hastened here. Too late to save your butler, I fear."

Heron digested that. Due to being largely independent of the Glasgow *Nephilim*, Edmund Crowe was often overlooked when one thought of the Elder *Nephilim* of Glasgow. But an Elder Crowe was, having seen the crusades. "Who do you think is behind this? The Council?" He remembered the thwarted attempt to unseat him from the bank. "Saddler and Herriot?"

Crowe pointed to the body. "He was undead, and his friend who attacked me spoke with an Eastern European accent. I suspect they are survivors from the Carpathian Circus, returned to do Keel's bidding." His glassy frozen eyes met Heron's. "We can assume Keel was behind the bank robbery."

Heron was dismayed to see his whisky glass had been knocked over and the bottle smashed. *A damned waste of a good whisky.* "He had a hood and rope. I *think* he was sent to take me alive."

"So not an assassination. I fear something else is afoot. Wait here."

Crowe left the room, returning after a minute. "There was an old wagon outside when I arrived, but it left on seeing me exit the house."

To take me away and do God knows what to me. "What now, Edmund?"

Crowe regarded him. "I've been meeting with Regent Guillam. She wishes to solidify control over the city through closer alliance with ourselves. The Council has already agreed to grant one of us the next vacant Council seat. An opportunity."

That was a lot to take in. On one hand, either Crowe or Heron sitting on the Council would give the bank greater influence in the city. On the other, the Sooty Feather Society was on increasingly shaky ground, and if it fell, so might the bank. "How long would we have to wait for a Council seat to become vacant, though? Months?"

Crowe smiled thinly. "Given the state of the Society, days or weeks."

"Do you think the promise of a Council seat inspired the attack on us, Edmund?"

"I think it likely, William. Be on your guard."

*

"Here," Essex said as they trudged through a small grove of trees, darkness cloaking the land. A clear black sky hung overhead, pricked by countless silver lights, starlight and moonlight.

"Are you sure?" Canning asked dryly. He had been leading the horse all night, through the fields and rough country roads that made up the Dunkellen estate to the south of Glasgow, owned by a Lady MacInesker. Upon contact being made with the Carpathian Circus, Canning's next mission had been to travel here with Essex.

"Quite sure, Mr Canning," the necromancer said, sarcasm going above his head as usual.

"We've spent half the night sneaking around this estate, walking up and down the riverbank," Canning said. "How does this stretch differ from the rest, apart from being a chore to walk through?" His trousers were torn from the thick, thorny vegetation making up much of the grove, and his shoes were covered in cow shit. *I miss the city.*

"The difficulty in walking through here is one reason I picked it. I do not anticipate anyone wanting to enter without good reason and finding the carcase. Also, it lies between Dunkellen House and the village. Mr Keel was quite clear on that requirement. We must be downstream from the house but upstream from the village."

Canning drew out his knife. "Let's get on with this."

"Wait! You cannot simply kill the horse," Essex said. "I have complicated magic to work first."

"Then get on with it, Doctor." In life Canning had been a butcher by trade, though of late the animals he had turned his knives to walked upright on two legs rather than four.

Essex drank from a flask containing some of Canning's blood and worked his dark sorcery, all of it beyond Canning's comprehension. "Now, Mr Canning. Into its guts, if you will."

"Finally." Canning stabbed his blade into the horse's stomach, listening to it scream in agonised terror. Blood and guts spilled onto the ground as it collapsed.

"Roll it into the water."

Canning obliged, shoving the dying horse into the river, knowing it would quickly drown. "Are we done?"

The necromancer was a dark shadow in the night. "We are indeed done for tonight." The horse's flank was visible above the water, the moonlight gleaming off its ashen-coloured coat.

Behold, a pale horse.

Death would not be riding *this* horse, but He certainly rode its sorcery-tainted blood downstream towards the sleeping village of Kaleshaws.

Chapter Twenty-Three

Occupied by his clerical duties and preparations to deal with the Carpathian Circus, Redfort was forced to wait until Monday afternoon before he could continue his investigation into the rival necromancer. He journeyed by carriage to the Under-Market, gathering place of the city's magicians, still troubled by the presence of another necromancer in Glasgow. Discretion would be required, lest he betray his own use of the forbidden magic.

At least at this time of day there would be few undead loitering around, even with the shelter provided by the railway bridge running over the market. The ghouls who haunted it previously had been slain by the Templars, the Crypt destroyed. Regent Guillam had shown no interest in reclaiming its ruin.

Anonymity seemed the safer course, so Redfort had exchanged his clerical collar and top hat for a worn woollen suit and flat cap. Getting to the Under-Market required passing through some of the worst slums in Glasgow, so Jones accompanied him as a precaution. Jones had been required to display his gun to one gang of young robbers, who had thereafter slunk off back into a shadowed, dung-stained wynd.

The closer one got to the market the less danger there was from the denizens of the rookery; the foolish few who dared trouble the market's patrons soon occupied unmarked pauper graves. No formal warnings had been issued to the slum-dwellers, but most understood the unspoken rule not to underestimate strangers venturing beneath the railway bridge, appearances counting for nothing. Harsh lessons had been taught and heeded.

A few ragged whores displayed themselves beneath the

bridge, but those forced to sell themselves for coin found that a different commodity was required of them by some clients. Undead unfussy about the quality of the blood they imbibed haunted the market at night, paying coin for blood. The better-heeled among the *Nephilim* could be choosy, 'acquiring' healthier donors; others had to settle for syphilitic vagrants and prostitutes, their steady diet of diseased blood leaving them in a state of perpetual decay.

Desperation occasionally led to the bottom-feeding undead attacking those they shouldn't to slake their Thirst, and the ruling *Nephilim* would either deal with them directly or instruct the Society to hunt down the rogue. The last thing the undead or Council wished for was the existence of vampyres to become common knowledge. Even those who fought the undead, like the Templars, shied from opening that Pandora's Box, not knowing the result of such profound revelations.

The market was moderately quiet. Redfort noted a pale-faced woman standing safely within the shade, staring wistfully out at a patch of cobbles caught in sunlight. Whether she was just there to catch a safe glimpse of sunlight or was after blood, he didn't know. Her hair was tied up and her beige dress looked neither dear nor cheap, but desperation this time of year was known to drive even the moderately well-off undead to extreme measures to sate their Thirst. Summer was often hard on the undead, more so this year. It would have been ironically worse had the undead not suffered losses of their own in the spring, lessening the numbers needing blood.

Scribes plied their trade, tattooists who needled glyphs of ink, blood and herbs into the flesh. Some glyphs were passive, others required activation. Redfort had two mystical tattoos, one an eye inked onto his lower back that would protect him from Memerisation from all but the most powerful *Nephilim*, and the other, a more recent acquisition, was a feather tattooed onto his shoulder. The feather told any who saw it and recognised its significance that Redfort sat on the Sooty Feather Council.

But it was more than just ink. The tattoo had been prepared and inscribed onto his flesh by the most skilled Scribe in Glasgow, its ingredients a secret known to few. It protected him from demonic Possession, a precaution to prevent demons from infiltrating the Council. Every new Councillor endured the feather tattoo upon their elevation.

Redfort hadn't come to the market to browse. Another necromancer operating in the city, perhaps working for Erik Keel, was bad enough, but they had seen Redfort through Thatcher's dead eyes. He or she had to be found quickly, quietly, and eliminated. If the necromancer was new to the city, they would perhaps not recognise Redfort by sight, but that was not a chance he was willing to take.

Like many magics, necromancy required reagents, the sort not found in common pharmacies. Redfort's anonymous rival would need these reagents, stocked only by the Under-Market's apothecaries. *But I must be circumspect in my enquiries.*

"Jones, remain here." Redfort visited the largest apothecary stall, making a show of perusing the wares. He used necromancy sparingly himself, but even still he needed supplies on occasion, sending Jones to buy them here. Better not to be seen with Jones in case the apothecary made the connection.

"Can I help you, sir?" the apothecary asked. Miss Gershaw was tall and stick-thin, long-armed and dressed in a dirt-stained brown dress. Her hands were dirt-stained, and Redfort suspected she grew many of the herbs and reagents herself in one of the city's allotments.

"I wish to know if anyone has recently bought the following reagents, Miss Gershaw."

She scowled. "I'm sure my customers would rather I not discuss their business with–"

He showed her his card, a plain piece of white embossed with a black feather. She answered with a sharply indrawn breath.

"What reagents?" she asked quietly.

He handed her a list, preferring to play the part of messenger.

Miss Gershaw squinted at the list in the Under-Market gloom. She wanted him gone, and quickly. And not just because he was here on Council business. He saw her eyes widen; the reagents on the list were used for dark magic indeed. Other customers joined them, so she dabbed a pen in ink and scratched a mark against some of the items on the list.

Redfort took the list back but was unable to make it out clearly. *Old age does not come alone.* Irritably, he snatched out his spectacles and put them on, the words coming into sharper focus. He felt a tingle ripple through him as he saw the reagents Miss Gershaw had marked. "Describe the person who bought these."

Her eyes flickered left and right, and she leaned closer to ensure no one overheard. "Cornelius Josiah. He's a regular customer."

"Josiah?" Not a name he had expected to hear.

"He's…"

"A Demonist. I know." Redfort had thought himself on the cusp of learning the identity of the necromancy, but instead found himself with two unsolved mysteries instead of one solved. "When was he last here?"

"A week past on Thursday," she said. "To pick up a large order."

"When did he place this order?" Redfort asked, thoughts colliding.

"Three weeks ago," Miss Gershaw answered with a shrug. "He's a good customer, always pays," she said with a hint of reproach. Redfort absently supposed she would prefer the Council not chase away or kill her business.

"My thanks to you, Miss Gershaw." He strode away from the stall, trying to order his thoughts and make sense of what he had learned.

Jones rejoined him at the edge of the Under-Market as they walked through the arch and up the worn steps leading to the slums surrounding the railway bridge, and the market beneath it. "Did you learn anything, your Grace?"

"Yes." Redfort was not in the habit of confiding his thoughts to Jones for the sake of it but voicing them out loud might help him make sense of them. "Cornelius Josiah has been buying a lot of reagents."

"Josiah? But he's a Demonist," Jones said.

"I'm well aware." It was rare, very rare, to find a magician capable of mastering two different magics, and Josiah was too young to have done so. He Summoned demons, meaning he was not the necromancer Redfort hunted.

"Might he be working with the … the one you're after?" Jones asked.

Redfort noted Jones' use of the word 'you', suggesting he was none too keen to be the one sent to dispatch a powerful magician. *But I did not buy a dog to bark myself.* "Perhaps, but the reagents he bought are also used by Demonists." To buy so many of them suggested he wished to summon a lot of demons.

Demonists who would Summon the Fallen from Hell only did so on the orders of the Council, and Margot Guillam had said nothing about a desire for more demons. Indeed, to the best of Redfort's knowledge, some time had passed since the Council had last Summoned one. The *Beliel* incident had reflected poorly on them all.

"Josiah has been missing since George Rannoch's fall," Jones said.

"Indeed." The assumption was that the Demonist had been engaged by Rannoch to Summon Erik Keel back from Hell, Josiah not knowing the then-Regent was working to betray *Dominus* Fisher. His body had not been found in the Necropolis, so it was assumed he had fled the city. *But perhaps not. And perhaps he still serves Keel, fearing the Council's wrath after Summoning that demon.*

"How many demons can he summon, though? Not like he can know more than a few names," Jones said. One had to know how to correctly pronounce a demon's name, and Lord Fisher only commanded the loyalty of a few.

"Keel," Redfort said, his gut tightening. A demon himself, Keel would know the names of fallen angels beyond count, malevolent ancient beings trapped in Hell for millennia who would be only too happy to serve Keel's cause for a short time in exchange for respite from damnation.

"Oh." They walked on in silence for a short time. "At least demons can't possess no one on the Council."

"No, they cannot." Another threat uncovered, and Redfort was still no closer to identifying the necromancer who had controlled Thatcher's corpse. Or identifying the body worn by Keel as he continued to plot against the Sooty Feather Society and its undead masters.

*

The noise was constant, the never-ending clacking, rattling

and hissing of the textile mill's steam-powered machinery thundering relentlessly all day every day, except for Sundays. Caroline Delaney had trained Kerry to blend into the highest echelons of society, but there was no call for etiquette or embroidered dresses here in the Imperial Mill in the heart of industrial Glasgow.

They hadn't had to wait long for a position to become vacant at the mill, Kerry finding work as a frame spinner working on a loom. Dust from the yarns got everywhere, covering her and getting in her throat. The mill was kept oppressively warm and damp to keep the cotton strong, the heat leaving Kerry faint, almost unbearable in an already stifling summer. It was like being in Hell.

Men were a minority in the mill, mostly engineers employed to maintain the machines or overseers charged with watching those spinning and weaving. A lot of children worked in the mill, working more hours than was legal, scrawny creatures paid a pittance to clean the still-operating machinery, risking fingers and worse. The smaller ones crawled under looms to repair broken threads.

Kerry arrived at the mill each day dressed in a dirty, drab, shapeless dress, her hair tied back beneath a scarf. Twelve hours later she would leave with a face gritted with dust and soot, returning exhausted to Caroline's home with raw, cramped fingers and a burning thirst. The mill was slowly killing her, she knew, grateful she wouldn't be there long.

The Imperial Mill boasted an enviable productivity, but inexperienced though she was, Kerry failed to find any evidence to account for it. The workers kept their heads down and worked fast enough to avoid a beating but made no great effort.

The orphans employed and housed by the mill were pale and sluggish, quickly exhausted by their long shifts, and more than a few had suffered injuries. Kerry hadn't dared show an interest in them lest she arouse the overseers' attention, but she had her suspicions as to the cause of their lethargy.

Sunlight filtered through gaps in the soot-stained windows, and another shift dragged itself to a weary end. *The sooner I find proof of undead activity here, the sooner I can finish this pretence*, Kerry thought. She had never shied from honest work, but this was soul-crushing misery. Laws had been passed to protect children from the worst of it, but they were openly flouted despite the best efforts of the NSPCC. And if it proved too much of a nuisance, the Sooty Feathers would intervene.

No one paid Kerry any mind as she trudged out of the mill, the other workers wracked by cramp and exhaustion as they headed home. Decades of industrial activity had blackened the streets and buildings, thick columns of smoke pouring up from giant chimneys looming over the tenements. Disease was common here, Kerry knew. *But people need jobs to feed their families.*

Her skin sticky from sweat and grime, Kerry walked towards the centre of town, enough coin hidden on her person to pay for a tram ride to the more prosperous West End. The Woodside area where Caroline lived in her townhouse was like night and day to the soot-stained tenements crammed with people here in the East End, and Kerry felt a stabbing guilt at the good food and soft bed that awaited her across the city. Only a few miles separated Kerry from the mill and Caroline's home, but it was like crossing into a different world.

*

The soft bed would have to wait. Kerry had wearily returned home only to find her mentor's patience equally exhausted. Caroline had announced they were returning to the mill that night, giving Kerry barely enough time for a quick bath to wash off the day's grime, followed by a rushed dinner of cold meat saved from the night before.

A cabriolet had taken the pair back into the East End, dressed in dark, drab dresses made from cheap cotton. Looking like a working-class woman came easy to Kerry after a lifetime of practice, but she was surprised at how well Caroline managed to disguise herself as a middle-aged housewife, tea granules rubbed into her face to weather it, her hair tied back.

This was clearly not Caroline's first time playing the part of someone else, a wardrobe in her cellar filled with different clothing, and a broken-in pair of poorly stitched shoes completed her disguise as she stepped over the sun-hardened shit covering the East End streets. Children ran about the streets, those not too tired from their day's labour. Disreputable men and women hung about the corners and gin shops, drinking from bottles and eyeing Kerry and Caroline with speculative eyes.

Both women walked confidently on, heads high. Looking weak was not healthy in this area, Kerry knew, and invited attack. Caroline and herself were well able to defend themselves, hidden derringers carried as a final precaution, but they were here to spy on the Imperial Mill, not brawl with gin-soaked footpads.

Kerry's stomach turned on seeing the red-bricked textile mill, smoke still belching from its vast chimney. It wasn't nerves from tonight's espionage that affected her, she knew (well, not just that), but rather her hatred for the place. And she'd only worked there for a few days. *How do the others tolerate it? How do they not go mad?* Maybe some did. Maybe others died bit by bit, day by day, drowning their misery in gin, their dreams and spirits crushed.

The short nights that had flirted with Glasgow in the midst of summer had slowly started to lengthen, the sky to the west burning orange behind the silhouetted city. The undead would be emerging from their Crypts beneath the city or behind bricked-up windows, looking to prey on the unwary walking Glasgow's streets.

"The mill still operates," Caroline said as they walked slowly past it.

"Aye, it does," Kerry said in surprise. The smoke billowing from the chimney was as thick as ever, and flickering lights shone behind the mill's many windows, piercing glass coated by dust on the inside and soot on the outside. Even muffled by sandstone walls, she could hear the muted thunder of machinery in full operation. "But the workers have all left."

"Indeed," Caroline said.

Orphaned children lived in a small dormitory attached to the mill, given food and board for their labour, an uneven trade. Though preferable to starvation. "You think they're working the children all day and night?" she asked in horror. That would explain their listlessness and propensity for accidents.

"Worse." Caroline didn't alter her pace, nor make her interest in the mill obvious. "The undead work the mill at night, feeding off the orphans. Afterwards, the children will be Mesmered to forget their nightly ordeal."

Kerry tasted bile in the back of her throat, her stomach threatening to vomit the meat she had eaten earlier. "My God."

"You'll not find Him here, I fear," Caroline said with contempt.

Kerry stared at the mill, wondering at the horrors within, hidden below the ground where she worked each day, unaware of their slumbering presence. "Bastards!"

"Indeed. We know now how the mill is so productive despite much of its workforce being unfit for their duties."

"What do we do about it?" Kerry asked. *Burn the bloody place down and salt the fucking ground it stands on.*

"Further investigation is warranted," Caroline said as they walked briskly away from the mill, heading to a cabriolet stand.

"Investigation? We know they've got undead in there, killing children! Those bastards are murderers, whether the weans die from blood loss, or from accidents caused from blood loss."

"We *suspect* there are undead in there," Caroline corrected. "You will take steps to confirm or deny our suspicions."

That quietened Kerry for a moment. "How?"

"By sneaking into the building's basement – tomorrow, if the opportunity presents itself – and seeing for yourself if there is a Crypt there. If so, count the number of undead. I suspect there will be ghouls, and one or two vampyres to keep them in check and Mesmer their victims."

"Why might they all not be vampyres?"

"They would not tolerate working the mill every night, I suspect. Not when there are houses full of people close by. But take care, all the same."

"I'll do it," Kerry vowed, recalling the pale faces and deadened eyes of the children stumbling about the mill floor every day, some losing fingers in the machines through lack of concentration. "What happens if I find undead down there?"

She heard wry amusement in Caroline's voice. And a

warning. "You'll leave quickly and quietly, taking no action. We'll consider our next step depending on what you find down there."

Kerry recalled the layout of the mill. "I think I know how to get down to the basement."

"Take care," Caroline stressed. "Getting into the basement will be dangerous if you're caught by the overseers. And even if you get in, you risk an undead awakening. Look for your chance, but don't act unless it is a good one."

"I'll be careful," Kerry promised.

"Good. I hope we don't have long to wait for a cabriolet. Tomorrow will be a long day for you."

Won't it, just.

Chapter Twenty-Four

Fear cut through her exhaustion, the enormity of the task before her striking like little bolts of lightning. An overseer, Hardy, had already lashed Kerry with harsh words for her dwindling concentration, and another lapse would be answered with his fists. She had bobbed her head and apologised, silently promising herself that if she and Hardy crossed paths again, he would see a different side of her.

For several hours she continued with her tasks, taking care that the threads not get tangled as machines clacked, rattled and hissed endlessly. The engineers had to be constantly vigilant, kept busy with the frequent breakdowns. Knowing now that the machines were only given a few hours respite, Kerry wasn't surprised they were prone to breaking.

All morning she had waited for a chance to sneak off and investigate the basement below, her skin crawling at what she suspected lurked beneath her feet. Ghouls sated nightly with the blood of children. The same children who carried out their tasks listlessly, left pale from the frequent feeding. Did the undead give the children respite to recover, or did they just remorselessly feed from them until either blood loss or accident put an end to their misery?

A cry issued out, a child's, interrupting the work as heads turned to see its author. "Someone's hand's caught beneath the machine!" a voice called out.

"It's Rab," a young voice wailed. Some went over to help the boy trapped beneath the loom, blood staining the strands of cotton. The machines carried on remorselessly, and most of the workers were forced to continue with their tasks lest more threads tangle up and interrupt the work further. The overseers would not tolerate that.

Kerry knew she'd not find a better chance. A sliver of guilt stabbed her as she sneaked off from her post towards the basement stairwell, knowing everyone else was either carrying out their work or trying to help Rab. The overseers would be busy making sure that their precious machines weren't damaged and that their workers didn't linger overlong in helping the injured boy.

The basement stairs were out of bounds, the overseers making it clear anyone caught trying to go down them would be thrown out beaten and without a job. Finding out what lurked below *was* Kerry's job, and anyone who tried to beat her would regret it.

So she kept telling herself as her guts turned to water. She ran down the stone stairs into the waiting darkness below, not a single lantern lit. Fortunately she had matches, though she dared not light one until she was in the basement.

On reaching the basement floor Kerry slowed, her heart beating like a drum, sweat pouring from every pore. She didn't bother trying to step lightly, knowing the raucous sound of the machines would drown out any sounds she made.

Darkness swallowed Kerry as she walked deeper into the basement, only a glimmer of light following her down the concrete steps. With trembling hands she pulled out a box of matches and a small candle, striking one of the matches and placing it against the wick until it took flame.

Walls and pillars divided the basement into smaller chambers, built to support the factory above and the immense iron weight of its machines and boilers. Spare parts for the machines, boxes filled with bobbins, and some raw cotton ruined in transit lay on the stone floor, but Kerry knew most of the raw materials and finished product were stored in the adjacent warehouses.

Onwards she walked, ignoring the muffled rumbling above. The air was hot and musty, the basement enjoying no ventilation. A door waited at the end of the corridor, thick oak cracked with age, but the iron padlock securing it looked new.

Kerry knelt on the ground and put down the candle, withdrawing two lockpicks from her pocket. The padlock looked simple and cheap, intended to dissuade casual interest in the room beyond. If her and Caroline's suspicions were correct, those slumbering beyond this door were all the security required to take care of thieves.

Not a comforting thought. The lock surrendered to Kerry's persistence, and she laid it quietly on the floor, retrieving her candle before standing. She rested her right hand on the door, knowing the flame would be a beacon in the dark that lay beyond, but knowing also she dared not enter blind.

The door opened to her push, and she entered, acutely aware the injured boy upstairs would soon be dealt with, and the overseers ensuring everyone returned to work. With every breath controlled, Kerry trod lightly, using the candle to light her way. Rows of boxes were lined up on the floor, most against a wall but others in the centre of the room. Long and narrow, large enough to hold a man or woman.

I've found a Crypt. Or had she? Caroline had taught her to be thorough, to assume nothing. She must be sure. A fine fool she would look if she and Caroline returned to wreak vengeance on boxes filled with cotton. She counted maybe twenty boxes within the room, maybe more hidden in the shadows.

The undead usually slept during daylight, conserving strength for their nocturnal existence, but that wasn't always the case. Still, she needed to be sure. Loosening the silver stiletto hidden up her sleeve, she approached the second nearest box and examined it. Nailed shut. The one nearest the door was likely to contain a vampyre tasked with stewarding the ghouls towards their Transition. And ensuring their Thirst did not result in an indiscriminate bloodbath. She would have preferred to open a box containing a ghoul rather than a vampyre, but the nails removed that option.

I'm being careful, not stalling. So she told herself as she approached the box nearest the door, no nails securing its lid. Squatting down and placing the candle on the ground, she gripped the box lid and took a breath. And lifted.

The lid came free, sliding to the ground. As it did so Kerry let her blade drop into her right hand while her left snatched up the candle. The flame flickered as she held the candle over the opened box, wobbling as she held it there.

A dark-haired corpse lay within. Her face was pale, eyes closed, hands clasped on her waist. Pink suffused her lips, colour that would fade as time passed from her last feeding.

Knowing the woman and her fellow undead had fed that night from the orphans residing in the dormitory attached to the mill, as they did every night, Kerry wanted to plunge her blade into the heart of the abomination before her.

But that would alert the others to their discovery, and they would be moved to a new Crypt, the children taken with them or killed outright. *I must leave no trace of my presence. And tell Caroline what I've found.*

One last look at the undead satisfied her the creature was undisturbed by her trespass, and she covered it once more with the box lid before quickly leaving the room. She closed the door and snapped the padlock back into place, dashing back to the steps. She paused on reaching them, blowing out the candle and hiding it in her apron pocket. She took a calming breath and crept back up the steps.

No one had noticed her missing. The overseers were too busy watching one of their own beat the unfortunate Rab who cowered on the floor, one of his fingers a bloody stump. No one interfered. The other children either returned to their tasks or watched through dull eyes.

*

"A succinct report and a job well done," Caroline said as they sat within her living room.

The rest of her day in the mill had passed sluggishly, Kerry wishing she could just up and leave. But to do so might draw suspicion, and so she carried on with her task, trying not to choke on the hot, dust-filled air.

"Thank you," she replied, basking in Caroline's approval.

"Twenty boxes, you say." A slight frown wrinkled Caroline's brow.

"Give or take. I dared not stay long enough to do a proper count." She winced at the defensive note in her voice.

"Of course not. Your task was to confirm the presence of undead, and that you did. Fifteen or twenty makes little difference."

"No?" A further five undead to kill sounded a lot to Kerry.

"No." Caroline sipped from her brandy, Kerry aping her. "Two of us going in there is foolhardy."

"You're saying we do nothing? We just let them murder

children?" Kerry felt her face grow hotter. "I didn't spend bloody *days* in that hell just for us to do nothing!"

Caroline raised a hand. "Calm yourself," she said crisply. "Cool heads prevail, hot heads make mistakes."

"I'm sorry," Kerry said, taking a calming breath. Composed, she asked: "What are your thoughts, Lady Delaney?"

Caroline took another sip of brandy. "We will need help if we're to confront a Crypt full of ghouls, and doubtless at least one vampyre. To say nothing of a factory of Sooty Feather-paid men charged to protect the mill and its secret."

"Templars?" Kerry harboured little love for Steiner, given the circumstances of their acquaintanceship, but his subordinate Templars had held him in great esteem, two dying to rescue him from Rannoch.

"Unavailable, judging by Mr Steiner's correspondence. No, I think we must look further afield."

"Who?"

"Professor Sirk, and Messrs Hunt and Foley," Caroline said, a wry smile playing at her lips.

"Them?" They had heard nothing from the trio following from their acrimonious parting after the Necropolis skirmish and Steiner shooting the Newfield ghoul.

"Them. They may require some persuasion to help us, I admit," Caroline said.

Kerry sighed. "But we won't know until we ask them."

Caroline's lips quirked. "Quite so."

"Tonight?" Kerry paused. "Do you know where to find them?"

"Tomorrow. Mr Foley owns a pharmacy in the South Side, which will be shut by this time."

Kerry felt mixed feelings at that. On one hand she was relieved at not having to leave the house again; on the other, that meant another day working in the mill. "I should go to bed." She covered her mouth to hide a yawn.

"You do look tired. But there is no requirement for you to rise early. The Imperial Mill will have to manage without you."

*

Kerry and Caroline entered the Foley Pharmacy on Paisley
Road West. Caroline had given the peeling sign above the
shop a thin-lipped look but made no comment as they passed
through the door, a bell jangling to alert the proprietor that he
had customers. *Or potential thieves.*

Various bottles and boxed herbal remedies occupied the
wooden shelves attached to the shop walls, the more
expensive remedies such as laudanum stored on shelves
behind the counter. The wooden floor creaked beneath them.

"Good day, good morning, how may I assist ... Lady
Delaney." The man behind the counter was not Tam Foley
but rather Professor Sirk, and he seemed surprised to see
them. "And Miss ... Miss...?"

"Knox. Kerry Knox," Kerry said. The itching at the back of
her throat had lessened, her spirit buoyed by the knowledge
her days as a millworker were behind her. No more watching
young girls and boys being maimed by machinery, weakened
after night after night of horror at the hands of the undead.
No more having to ignore the leers of Overseer Jennings, all
the while wanting to knock his bastard rotting teeth down his
bastard fucking throat.

"Lady Delaney. Miss Knox. Welcome. To the Foley
Pharmacy," Sirk said gravely. "How can I serve you? A
lotion to prevent sunburn? A cream for the skin? Perhaps
something to sooth stomach cramps during that particular
time of the month?"

Neither Kerry nor Caroline dignified any of that with a
response. "Professor Sirk, a pleasure to see you again, if a
surprising one. I was expecting Mr Foley."

"A pleasure that is entirely mine," Sirk said with an
awkwardly forced courtesy. "Alas ... Mr Foley has gone off
with Mr Hunt to visit Mr Hunt's estate near Loch ... Loch
..."

"Loch?" Caroline suggested, a bite of impatience in her
voice.

"I forget. But a delightful place, Hunt assured me."

"I'm sure. When do they return?"

"Mr Hunt has an estate?" Kerry asked, finding that difficult
to believe.

"Mr Hunt's father recently inherited a barony," Sirk said.
"If a rather small one."

A lord's son? Kerry had rather liked Wilton Hunt, an endearing blend of confidence and awkwardness, and his brief run as Lucifer in *Doctor Faustus* had been impressive for an inexperienced actor. Her stomach sank on hearing he was a baron's heir, and she wasn't quite sure why.

Sirk continued. "Mr Foley has gone with him, asking that I run his pharmacy during his absence."

"Very good of you, Professor Sirk," Kerry said, turning her thoughts away from Hunt.

"I've no classes at the university during the summer, and it gave me something to do. Foley also agreed to let me keep any money left after the expenses were paid." He looked around the shop. "I've done rather well, if I say so. It seems Foley's chief accomplishment was to drive away customers who have patronised this shop since his late father established it. Even the ones who still come here have commented that my management has been a great improvement."

"We did not come to discuss the pharmaceutical trade, nor for any remedies," Caroline said pointedly.

Sirk blinked away the abstracted look on his face, suddenly shrewd eyes fixing on them. "You've found some new undead or ungodly menace and desire help in dealing with it?"

"Succinctly put," Caroline said. "Perhaps we could discuss it somewhere more private?"

Sirk snorted. "Prior to my management, you could rest assured that this shop was as private a place as any in Glasgow. But I take your point. I've a shop to manage, but if you return this evening at six o'clock, I promise I will give your matter my fullest attention. Foley owns the flat above this shop."

He's rather full of himself, Kerry thought.

"Until this evening, Professor," Caroline said.

*

Kerry and Caroline returned to the pharmacy as agreed, Sirk escorting them into the common close and up to the flat on the next floor. Like many tenement closes in Glasgow, the floor and stairs were concrete, and the lower half of the walls were tiled. There was a faint smell of the pipe clay used to clean the close, that task falling to the residents of a different flat each Friday. Kerry recalled cleaning her own tenement close when she lived with her parents, her mother judging her efforts with a sharp eye and sharper tongue. Had she failed to be thorough, her family would have never lived down the shame of their neighbours' judgement. And judge they bloody would!

"This is Mr Foley's home," Sirk said as they entered the flat. "Mr Hunt rents the spare room."

"He's the son of a lord but he stays here?" Kerry asked, finding that hard to believe. The flat looked to be untidy and in a state of disrepair with paint and wallpaper starting to peel. Worn carpets covered the floor and the furniture looked old.

"There is, or was, some tension between Mr Hunt and his parents," Sirk said. "Regarding his choice of study."

"I see." Not that she did. She looked around.

Sirk noted her interest. "Mr Foley inherited this flat along with the shop below from his own parents. I'll boil some water for tea, do take a seat."

Kerry and Caroline sat in the sitting room while Sirk clattered around in the kitchen, soon after emerging with three cups and a teapot. "I brewed this in anticipation of your visit."

"Thank you, Professor Sirk," Caroline said as Sirk poured each of them a cup. Kerry quickly muttered her own thanks.

They all took a sip, Kerry almost grimacing. It tasted awful. Caroline assumed a mask to hide whatever her own opinion on the tea was, but Kerry noted she left her cup well alone thereafter. Sirk slurped noisily from his cup, seemingly unaware of how bad it was.

"From what I gleaned during your earlier visit, you're looking for allies in another small crusade. Against Glasgow's undead, I assume, or has another cause captured your attention?"

Anger simmered behind Caroline's eyes. Old and burning ever bright. "Against the undead, Professor. Always demons and the undead, and those who serve them."

"I see. Do tell me more."

Caroline's hand brushed against her teacup from habit

before she evidently thought better of it. "We have discovered a Crypt of undead beneath the Imperial Mill. The mill is owned by the MacInesker Foundation, which we suspect is linked to the Sooty Feather Society."

"Interesting. Why a mill of all places?" Sirk asked.

"The children," Kerry said. "Orphans employed by the mill are housed within a dormitory next to it. By day they work and by night the undead feed from them." She forced herself to take a calming breath.

"A number have died, not unsurprisingly. The foundation is buying replacements from local orphanages," Lady Delaney said, her own anger controlled.

Sirk looked doubtful. "Rather brazen. Has no one taken notice?"

"No one who cares," Kerry said.

"Saving ourselves." Caroline leaned forward. "Tomorrow morning, we will deal with the undead, and make clear our displeasure to those operating the mill."

"Why is Steiner not here with you? Has he still to replace his losses?"

"Mr Steiner is in London. His superiors have not seen fit to return him to finish what he started," Caroline said.

"Just two of you, then?" Sirk looked doubtful.

"You would be a third," Caroline said quietly. They had hoped that Hunt and Foley would have been a fourth and fifth, but there was nothing they could do about that now.

Sirk sat quietly, his teacup nestling forgotten in his hands. "It sounds a rather dangerous and foolhardy venture."

"It is," Caroline agreed, a smile twisting her face. "But we're going anyway."

"They're feeding from children night after night. Killing them bit by bit," Kerry said, emphasising every word. "Children, Professor Sirk."

From what she knew of him, he had fought the undead in Edinburgh decades before with a group of likeminded citizens. That venture ended badly, with Sirk losing a number of friends. He had hidden away in Glasgow for years afterwards until Hunt and Foley convinced him to return to the fight. Had fighting the undead in the spring helped put those old ghosts to rest, or did they haunt Sirk once more?

The professor took a shuddering breath. "Well. It will add

variety to my day. Running a shop is rather repetitive."

Caroline exuded satisfaction. "Excellent. I'll bring the guns and silver ammunition."

"Burning is effective against the undead, if we can set the Crypt alight before they awaken," Sirk said. "There are suitable chemicals stored here."

Caroline looked dubious. "We'll need a means of safely transporting them."

"Foley left his horse and wagon for my use. I'm not sure using them to attack the undead and engage in arson were quite his intentions, but he can voice his disapprobation upon his return." Sirk took another slurp from his tea. "Assuming he has not killed himself drinking Lord Ashwood's cellar dry."

"Lord Ashwood?" Kerry looked up, recognising the name.

"Mr Hunt's lordly father. Why?"

Kerry looked between Sirk and Caroline, "I saw a letter at Dunkellen House. Lady MacInesker was writing to a Miss Guillam about a Lord Ashwood and a shipping company."

Sirk's eyes narrowed. "The Browning Shipping Company?"

"Aye."

"I fear Mr Hunt and his family may be in some danger," Sirk said. "I should write – no, too remote. Safer to visit Loch Aline and warn them in person."

"A good idea, Professor," Caroline said. "But it can wait until after we deal with the Imperial Mill tomorrow, yes?"

He gave a short reluctant nod. "Yes. Tomorrow we destroy the mill."

Breaking the mill was sweet news to Kerry's ears, but fear soured her stomach. *This is real. More dangerous than sneaking around the mill's basement. By this time tomorrow either a score of undead will be destroyed, or we'll be dead.*

Chapter Twenty-Five

Fear and anticipation tied Kerry's guts in knots, her palms sweating within leather gloves as she walked with Lady Delaney and Professor Sirk towards the Imperial Mill. Fear of the inevitable violence waiting, and anticipation at finally confronting those responsible for the exploit and murder of children; the men as well as the undead resting, gorged, beneath the mill.

On leaving the wagon they had covered their lower faces with red cotton scarves, gone the drab pauper's dress Kerry had worn while working in the mill. Today they had come for war and dressed for the occasion. Sirk wore the same worn tweed suit he likely wore teaching his classes at the university, but Caroline and Kerry's outfits had been tailored for battle, allowing an ease of movement not normally enjoyed in ladieswear.

Kerry wore a black riding habit over her dark-red blouse, covering a corset of Caroline's own design. Like all corsets it was ribbed, however the bone ribs were placed to protect the torso, not shape the figure. The habit bodice was double breasted like a man's jacket, liberally decorated with silver buttons to sting any undead trying to grapple with her, and she wore black trousers beneath a riding skirt that opened at the front. Her hair was bobbed at the back like Caroline's, to deny opponents the opportunity to grab it. She strode through the shit-covered street in practical black leather boots, ignoring stares from passers-by.

A small bag hung from her shoulder, holding her revolver and spare ammunition. Her derringer was hidden in a bodice pocket, and a sheathed silver knife hung from her hip. Caroline was similarly attired, red to Kerry's black. They were bringing blood and death to the Imperial Mill and had dressed accordingly.

Caroline and Sirk both looked tense but calm, both veterans of such action. Kerry wondered how she looked to them, her face flushed and not just from the morning heat. The chimney loomed overhead as they entered the mill's walled yard and approached its towering main doors. Already Kerry could hear the muffled cacophony inside.

No one opposed their entry, dull-eyed workers too engrossed with their tasks, a moment's distraction leading to ruined work and a beating, or injury from the machines; either could lead to the loss of their job. Sirk left two large cases by the doors.

Caroline wrinkled her nose. "It's very unpleasant, more so than I expected. I fear I owe you an apology for sending you here, Miss Knox."

"Get us all out of here in one piece, and I'll consider us even," Kerry said, dust already tickling her throat. Two overseers walked towards them, both known to Kerry. *Does Jennings recognise me?* He would soon.

"Can I help you?" Jennings asked. His tone was polite, lest the three be people of importance. He addressed Sirk, but it was Kerry who answered, pulling down her scarf.

"Good morning, Mr Jennings. I've come to hand in my notice."

He squinted at her. "Who are…?" Recognition sparked in his eyes, and he looked her up and down, trying to reconcile the woman before him with the quiet worker from days before. "You!"

Caroline spoke. "Call your fellow overseers over, divide all money kept in the premises between your workers, release them, and stay out of our way while we attend to our business."

Jennings reddened. "Who the hell are you?"

"Concerned citizens," Sirk said. "I suggest you don't test us."

"Test you? I'll f–" He found himself staring at Caroline's derringer. Sirk likewise had freed his rifle from the brown paper wrapping it and aimed it calmly at the other overseer. Kerry fumbled to draw her revolver from her bag and began looking from side to side to identify approaching threats.

More overseers were hurrying over, brandishing knives and

clubs. There was a gunshot, a bullet ricocheting off a nearby machine. Kerry spotted an overseer on a gantry across from them, aiming his gun down at them. "Up there!"

Sirk swung his rifle up and took aim. The overseer fired again, missing. Sirk fired in return and didn't.

Maybe they were emboldened by Sirk's rifle chamber being empty, maybe they didn't think the two women would shoot, or maybe they just feared their Sooty Feather masters more than Kerry and her associates. Regardless, on seeing Sirk's attention occupied shooting their armed colleague, those on the ground attacked. Caroline's derringer fired into the nearest man's face, felling him.

Kerry acted despite fear snaring her thoughts, hours of hours training making her hands work of their own volition, pulling the trigger to shoot Jennings as he lunged at her. She jumped back as he fell at her feet, crying out and clutching his chest. It was almost as if another controlled her body as she aimed the gun at the next overseer and pulled the trigger again.

The gun clicked. Too late she realised she had forgotten to re-cock the hammer. Her second attacker barged into her, knocking her to the ground and sending her gun out of reach. The man was short and stocky, and the part of her mind that recalled Caroline's training told her that she was no match for him toe-to-toe. She recalled the derringer in her bodice pocket but knew the overseer was too close; already he was lifting his foot to kick her.

An explosion sounded nearby, Kerry grimacing in pain from the intensity of the sound. She was dimly aware of bodies falling but was too busy trying to survive to worry about her friends just yet.

Kerry rolled to her right and drew her legs in, kicking both feet out at his left knee. He cried out as he fell, the force of the kick twisting his leg in a direction it wasn't intended to go. *Get up!* Rolling to her feet and freeing the derringer from her pocket, she looked for the next threat.

A wisp of smoke drifted from the left barrel of Caroline's shotgun, its twin barrels sawn off for concealment. Caroline had warned Kerry the shortened shotgun was devastating at close range but ineffective from a distance. Three overseers lay bleeding on the ground, shredded by pellets. One man's face was gone, another's upper chest was a bloody ruin. The third was screaming on the ground, his arm bleeding.

Caroline and Sirk seemed to have everything in hand. Sirk was beating someone with the butt of his rifle while Caroline had cocked the second hammer and levelled the shotgun at the remaining overseers.

"I think that is enough." She spoke loudly and the remaining overseers stepped back, their defiance gone. They stared in shock at their dead or injured friends on the ground. Sirk pulled back the bolt on his rifle to eject the empty shell and load another bullet into the chamber from the magazine. He ignored the overseers before them, running his eyes along the upper levels of the mill, trusting Caroline and Kerry to keep the prisoners in line.

Kerry looked around the mill lest any of the workers side with the overseers but was unsurprised to find that none had. Most watched the confrontation fearfully, making no move to involve themselves. She retrieved her fallen revolver and pocketed the derringer. She didn't pull back the hammer but kept her thumb near it just in case.

"As I was saying," Caroline said, "I require one of you to unlock the safe."

One man reluctantly stepped forwards. Kerry and Sirk used rope and twine to bind the remaining four overseers while Caroline followed the fifth to the office.

"You won't get away with this," Hardy said, kneeling next to his fellows. None of the overseers had been kind, but Hardy had taken a particular pleasure in bullying the workers.

Kerry stood over him and pulled down her scarf. "Who's going to stop us? You?"

He squinted at her. "Who the hell are you lot? Do you have any idea who you're dealing with?"

"We know," Kerry said. "And we'll deal with those below soon enough."

He blinked. "You know about … them?" Kerry had seen fear in his eyes.

"We know. We know why you're buying children from the orphanages, and why so many of them are dying. Bastards!"

Hardy started to proclaim his innocence, but Kerry interrupted him.

"I worked here for only days and I saw you beating the children, the sick pleasure you took in it." She pulled down her scarf.

He squinted up at her, recognition dawning after a few moments. "You."

She nodded, pleased. *Now it's your turn to be afraid.*

Caroline exited the office, escorting the overseer out at gunpoint. He dragged a large sack into the centre of the factory floor.

"May I have your attention, all of you," Caroline said loudly. The workers just stared at her, mutely.

Kerry whistled sharply. "Come here, shut up, and listen, is what she means."

The workers shuffled over, mostly women and children.

"I am here to announce the Imperial Mill will be closing for business today," Caroline said. "However, there are ample funds here to compensate you for the loss of employment." She opened the sack, revealing it was filled with money taken from the mill safe. Caroline seemed perturbed at the lack of enthusiasm to claim it.

Kerry sighed. "We're shutting these bastards down. Help yourself to the money." After a brief hesitation, the bolder of the workers moved forward to claim coins and bank notes from the sack, overseen by Sirk to ensure a roughly even split. Kerry just hoped they spent it frugally, that it lasted until they found more work. Odds were, many of the orphans would later have it taken from them by force, but there was nothing Kerry could do about that. *Better to be robbed than to be bled slowly to death over weeks by undead.*

Caroline watched as the last of the workers took a share of the money and hurried out of the mill. "You know what to do, Professor."

Sirk nodded. There were explosives within the cases he had left by the door.

"I forgot to ask, where did you obtain so much nitro-glycerine?" Caroline asked. "I can always find a use for it, but a woman buying dynamite would draw attention."

"I made it. It's my own recipe, more stable than nitro-glycerine," Sirk said proudly. "Had it been less so, one good bump on the road would have blown us all to hell."

"What a useful man you are," Caroline murmured. Kerry

had a suspicion the Sooty Feathers would soon discover just how combustible their assets were.

Confident the overseers were tied up, Kerry led Caroline down into the basement level of the mill. Kerry emptied the regular bullets from her revolver and reloaded it with silver-crafted ammunition while Caroline broke open her shotgun. She removed the empty shell and the unused one, slotting in two shells filled with silver pellets.

"Let us hope they are not expecting us." She closed the shotgun.

"And if they are?"

"Don't be too stubborn to run. They won't follow us up into the daylight."

Kerry carefully cocked her revolver as they reached the door separating them from the undead inside. She carried a small lantern while Caroline carried a flask of flammable liquid. One of the keys Caroline had taken from the overseers unlocked the door, which creaked open.

Kerry fought to quiet her breathing as she led Caroline inside, the lantern open just enough to let them see. Like her last visit, long boxes were stored in the room. By night the ghouls toiled in the mill overhead, tirelessly making cotton thread before feasting on the blood of unwilling children. By day they slumbered down here, protected from daylight. *But not protected from us, not today.*

"Quietly," Caroline whispered, and they stepped as lightly as they could over to the boxes. There were eighteen of them lying in rows on the basement floor, most nailed shut. A precaution against any ghouls rising early and venturing up to the mill?

Caroline placed her shotgun down on the floor and looked at Kerry, making her hand out like a gun. Kerry took the hint and drew her revolver while Caroline jemmied open the nailed-down box lid. With an intent expression on her face and a silver knife in her hand, she lifted the lid. Kerry pulled back the hammer of her revolver and held her breath.

Enough light filtered through the lantern shutters to let them see. A man's corpse lay inside the box, pale-faced and waxen. Except it wasn't really a corpse, Kerry knew. She watched the undead for any sign of movement. There was likely no more than one full vampyre in the basement, but even a ghoul was a danger to them. And if she had to shoot, there were seventeen more undead in the room with them, albeit trapped in the boxes.

Caroline removed an iron spike from their bag of tools and handed it to Kerry. She waited until Caroline had drawn and cocked her derringer before uncocking her revolver and putting it down next to her foot. She took the spike from Caroline and placed it on top of the undead's chest.

A thick-wooded mallet in hand, Caroline pointed an inch to the left and Kerry moved the spike accordingly. She held her breath while Caroline swung the mallet, her aim good. Bone cracked as the spike was driven deep into the undead's chest and piercing his heart (Kerry hoped).

A nudge from Caroline startled Kerry, and she realised she had been staring at the slain undead. Evidently satisfied his heart was cleaved, Caroline was already surveying the other boxes for signs of undead awakening.

Nothing. They jemmied open the next box. A woman lay inside, dealt with in the same way as the male undead. Kerry had earlier wondered why they didn't just stab the undead with their silver knives; Caroline had said that risked the blade catching on a rib.

They carried out their grim duty box after box, making eight undead dead in truth. Easier work than Kerry anticipated, though she sweated from the heat and excitement. *So long as they don't wake up.* Kerry jemmied open the ninth box and pulled off the lid while Caroline covered it with her derringer. This undead was male, looking gaunt and bow-legged. If the vampyres were being indiscriminate in their Making, it meant they needed numbers quickly, either to replace those lost in the spring, or they were preparing for war and needed expendable soldiers. Maybe both.

Caroline placed the spike over the ghoul's heart with one hand while her other aimed the derringer at his head. Kerry readied the mallet, nerves trembling her hand slightly as she readied for her swing. This was her first time, and she hoped she aimed true. Hitting the ghoul's shoulder wouldn't kill him, it would just wake him up and make him angry. *It. Not him.* It was easier to think of the undead as things, not people.

Caroline nodded slightly, and Kerry eyed the spike, tensing

her arms to swing…

Her periphery caught a slight movement, and she looked at its face to see eyes staring up at her, yellowed and sunken. Her heart jumped a beat and she opened her mouth to warn Caroline when the ghoul lunged up, knocking away the spike placed against his – its – heart.

Kerry struck it on the head with her mallet, but the blow was a glancing one that served only to disorientate it for a moment. But a moment later a *crack* echoed around the basement, the ghoul falling back with a hole in its head. That moment had been time enough for Caroline to aim and fire her derringer.

"Quickly," Caroline whispered as she placed the spike back against the ghoul's heart, perhaps unwilling to assume her bullet had killed it. Keeping her eyes fixed on the spike, Kerry swung the mallet, striking the spike to one side and driving it in at an angle.

"Shit," she swore, looking at Caroline for guidance.

Caroline studied the ghoul. "I believe it's dead," she said slowly.

"Should we not make sure?"

"We should and will, but first we'll deal with those remaining, before–"

There was a hollow thud from one of the boxes, fear clenching Kerry's innards. Then another, and a third, and she snatched her revolver up from the floor before stepping back. "They can't break through those boxes, can they?"

"The ghouls, perhaps not. But the vampyre's lid is not nailed. We should have found and dealt with it first." Caroline's voice was tightly controlled, unlike the shrill threat of hysteria Kerry winced to hear in her own.

"To hell with this." Kerry fired into one of the boxes, re-cocking and firing again until her gun was empty. She broke the gun open and started to reload it with bullets. At least the box bearing six small holes no longer thudded.

"Inefficient," Caroline chided her. There was a sound of splintering wood from the side of a box. More blows followed, and it broke apart while Caroline watched calmly with her shotgun ready.

"Watch!" Kerry cried out as the undead she had made a mess of spiking got back to its feet, not dead after all. It moved like a puppet missing half its strings, a small bullet in its brain and a spike near its heart, but it was still a threat. Caroline's hesitation in choosing between targets was their undoing as a piece of wood flung at her knocked her arm aside, one of the shotgun barrels discharging into a wall.

Kerry closed her reloaded revolver and cocked the gun, firing into its head. It fell on top of the lantern, the basement falling into darkness.

"Greet our guests," a female voice said, and breaking wood sounded all around them. Horror seized Kerry as she realised the vampyre had awoken.

"Recover the lantern!" Caroline shouted as she replaced the spent shell in the shotgun. Long hours of training, of following Caroline's commands by habit, meant Kerry did so despite her growing panic. It didn't provide much light, just enough to see by.

Dark shapes rushed at them, undead monsters, abominations fit only for Hell. But today they faced not children but grown women, armed and determined. Kerry raised her arm, trying to decide which undead to shoot first. There were so many of them, and so close, too close…

Caroline's shotgun fired, flaying the closest undead who screamed as silver scourged the flesh from them. The gunshot echoed painfully around the brick room, and Caroline turned to her right and fired again. Movement on her periphery caught Kerry's eye and she turned, firing wildly at the shadow flying at her. Gripped by panic she pulled back the hammer and fired again, deafened by the thunder and blinded by the muzzle flash.

Not trusting her aim, she fired blindly one more time. When her vision cleared, there was a dark shape lying on the ground. Many of the undead had been caught in the twin shotgun blasts but Kerry had been warned not to assume them done. The silver pellets would cause them great pain, but unless any of the pellets destroyed brains or hearts, they would return to the fight. Sure enough, flesh-torn ghouls were getting back to their feet, howling in pain and outrage.

Kerry turned back to help Caroline who had just shot the third closest undead with her derringer before dropping the empty gun and drawing a revolver from her shoulder bag. Two more undead approached, moments from reaching them.

Caroline hesitated perhaps a heartbeat, and shot the furthest, blackness gouting from its head a heartbeat before the closer undead tackled her to the stone ground.

They struggled, woman and undead, two shadows grappling in the darkness, and Kerry dared not shoot lest she hit Caroline. One of them went still and the survivor rose, Kerry blowing out a breath she hadn't realised she was holding on recognising the victor to be Caroline.

"You'll die," the female voice said from the shadows, all hate and deadly promise. Kerry suspected it was the undead she had seen in the box during her first visit, the vampyre assigned to watch over the resident ghouls. Fighting a vampyre in the dark was an excellent way to end up dead.

Caroline picked up the flask and tipped it upside down, the liquid spilling out fast across the floor. Kerry picked up her fallen lantern and flung it forwards, hearing glass shatter and a *whoosh* as the liquid ignited. Maybe four undead remained, two of them screaming out as they caught fire. Kerry recognised one of the others as the undead she had spied in the box, and took aim, firing. Her first shot missed, but the second struck home. She took half a breath, held it, and aimed at the vampyre's head, adjusting for its movement. One gentle squeeze of the trigger caused the gun to buck in her hand, and blood, brains and bone exploded from the vampyre's skull.

A rifle fired, ending the last undead. Sirk, newly arrived.

Caroline retrieved her revolver, her knife gleaming red and silver by the light of the flames. "Let's leave."

"A fine idea," Sirk said. "I've put my explosives in place."

"Why did I not shoot the closest undead before?" Caroline surprised Kerry by asking as they returned to the mill's main floor.

Kerry recalled the situation. She had thought it odd at the time, as the undead she hadn't shot had been the closest by that time and had wrestled Caroline until she had finished it with her silver knife.

"The closer one was the smaller of the two," she said slowly, trying to recall what she had seen during a chaotic time.

"Yes. And?"

"And you knew that the one behind it was bigger, and that

if it got too close, it would probably overwhelm you?" Kerry guessed. "You shot the greater threat."

"Indeed, Kerry." Caroline sounded pleased. Even in all this death and chaos, still she taught.

"What of the prisoners?" Kerry asked. The surviving overseers were still tied up.

"Leave them," Caroline said. Kerry heard Hardy breathe a sigh of relief, and she was tempted to strike him.

"Now, Professor," Caroline said as they reached the main doors.

"It will be my distinct pleasure, Lady Delaney." Sirk struck a match and knelt next to a trail of gunpowder he had sprinkled earlier while Kerry and Caroline were fighting the undead.

Sirk stood quickly, a flicker of pain passing his face. "I suggest we do not linger."

The three of them hurried out of the mill, exiting the yard when the first explosion came, followed by several others in quick succession.

They turned to admire their handiwork. The mill still stood, smoke issuing from its shattered windows. But the overseers were undoubtedly dead. Whatever small pang of guilt Kerry felt at being party to the killing of helpless prisoners was outweighed by the knowledge that those men had knowingly helped sacrifice innocent children to the undead. It also prevented them from passing a detailed description to the society; today's attack would not be lightly shrugged off. *To hell with them.*

"The mill is out of commission?" Caroline asked.

Sirk regarded the building, a satisfied smile on his face. "Oh, yes, Lady Delaney. The explosives I placed will have destroyed the boiler and several delicate, expensive pieces of machinery. I also arranged for the floor to collapse in on where the undead hid, burying them."

"Excellent, Professor."

Sirk regarded her, sparing Kerry a quick glance. "I'll be leaving for Loch Aline this evening. What now for you ladies?"

Caroline took a breath, wiping her face with a handkerchief. "The architect of this dreadful scheme remains at large."

"So now we call upon Lady MacInesker?" Kerry guessed.

"Not immediately. I received a card in the post from the good lady, inviting me to a garden party at Dunkellen House."

"Courting you for donations," Kerry said. "Will I be playing the part of lady's maid again?"

Caroline studied her. "I think not. I think it time you were introduced to Glasgow society as Miss Knox, my companion."

"That sounds delightful, Lady Delaney." *Another part to play.*

"Do be careful," Sirk said. "The newspapers are reporting that the village of Kaleshaws, near Dunkellen House, is suffering an affliction, with many villagers stricken."

"Deaths?" Kerry asked.

"None as of yesterday, when the paper was printed," Sirk said.

"The cause?" Caroline asked.

"Unknown. There is speculation it was born of the long summer. But bear it in mind, ladies."

"We shall," Caroline promised. "Good luck in Loch Aline."

Chapter Twenty-Six

Foley and Hunt stood on the mountain summit, the whole world seemingly before them. Fragarach was the highest peak in the area, and the air was colder this high up, and refreshing.

"Quite the view," Hunt said, red-faced and sweating.

"Aye," Foley said, mopping his brow. Worth the hours spent climbing the mountain. His flat cap was tucked into his pocket. Hunt still wore his straw boater despite gusts of wind threatening to snatch it. *Ridiculous bloody excuse for a hat.*

Loch Aline lay to the south, sparkling blue waters that connected with the Sound of Mull. Fishing boats ploughed the loch with their nets, so small as to look like toys. The Ardtornish Point lighthouse was visible next to the sea, its services little required this summer, but its keepers earned their pay during the ferocious winters.

Dunlew Castle sat at the inland end of the loch near a beach of brilliant white sand, grey-stoned and misshapen, more recent extensions added to the original mediaeval keep. The white-washed walls of Ashwood Lodge were visible to the south-west. To its west lay Ash Hill, the ancient hillfort once called Dunkail'an. The village of Kirkaline was further south, wisps of smoke rising from what Foley guessed to be the inn and smithy. Fields of grass and heather-strewn moorland stretched out from the village and farms dotted across the peninsula, interrupted by small copses of trees and hardened dirt roads.

The land turned wilder as Foley gazed northwards. A road stretched from the loch through the forested Glendorcha, the Dark Glen, running between Fragarach and its smaller western siblings. Loch Arienas was further to the north-west, the easternmost edge of the water just visible across the vast forest separating it from Loch Aline.

As the crow flew, the distance between Fragarach and Loch Arienas was not great, but it was nigh impassable directly. To get there, as Foley and Hunt intended, they would need to travel south again and turn north through the ancient Lewswood separating Ashwood from the northern loch.

The southern edge of the forest had been thinned and tamed over the past century, and a road had been carved through the north-eastern part, but Hunt had warned that few ventured into its heart, that it had been left untouched since the pagan Kail'ans fled. A safer route to Loch Arienas and Lew Abbey on its southern shore would be to travel Glendorcha's road north, and then turn west, but Hunt wanted to explore the forest.

Foley pulled out his silver hipflask and took a large swig of whisky. "Here." He passed it to Hunt, the liquor warming his throat as it slid down his gullet.

"Thanks." Hunt also took a swig but made a face.

"Not to your taste?" Foley wondered if his friend was getting spoiled from their recent good living, his palette too good for cheap whisky.

"For some reason, drinking out of silver leaves an unpleasant taste in my mouth. Don't know why."

"I'll bring my gold-plated hipflask next time."

Hunt smiled at his dry tone but said nothing, handing it back. Bottles of whisky were hidden in their packs near the edge of the forest, enough to see them through the next few days.

A few days had passed since their departure from Ashwood, telling Hunt's parents that they would be spending time exploring the land, Hunt taking notes and drawing sketches of plants, trees and fauna. Foley had believed the trip just an excuse to spend the nights drinking, free from parental disapproval, but Hunt's enthusiasm had been clear to see.

"Are you sure you want to go there?" Foley asked, seeing Hunt stare to the west.

"Yes. Think of it as an adventure."

"Walking through that forest won't be easy," Foley warned. He'd passed through some inhospitable terrain during his time in the army and knew they wouldn't find convenient paths in the forest. "It'll be thick and wild, and easy to get lost in."

"We're in no rush," Hunt said. "And we can wash our clothes and bathe in Loch Arienas."

They were starting to smell, their clothes dirty and sweat-stained. "A swim will be nice," Foley said. Dust from climbing the rocky mountain stained his worn walking boots and the calves of his trousers. He had underestimated just how long it would take them to reach the top of Fragarach, their progress slowed as the incline steepened.

But the view made the effort worthwhile, he couldn't deny.

The walk down the mountain was faster than the ascent, but perhaps more dangerous as loose scree could be perilous, threatening to snatch their feet from under them. Foley led Hunt down the south side of the mountain, giving them a good view of Loch Aline and the Atlantic Ocean beyond it. Halfway down the trail turned west, the Lewswood's western boundary marked by a ragged line of trees.

Their packs still waited for them, hidden in a copse of trees a couple of miles down the road. Putting on his old army pack returned Foley to his time as a junior officer. Dirt from Africa still stained worn leather rendered waterproof by many hours of diligent waxing by Foley. Hunt had purchased a canvas pack in Kirkaline.

The good weather saved them the need to buy a tent, freeing more room in their packs for biscuits, dried meat and fish. And whisky, of course, carefully wrapped in spare clothing. Water canteens hung from Foley's Sam Browne belt, supported by a thin leather strap pulled over his right shoulder. At his insistence both packs contained canteens filled with water, over Hunt's objections. Hunt had pointed out they would be able to refill their canteens from the two lochs, and there were sure to be streams within the forest, but Foley was too seasoned a campaigner to risk getting lost without water. *He'll just need to bear the weight.*

Hunt made as face as he strapped the pack to his back. "Feels like I'm carrying a horse."

"It'll get lighter once we've drunk some of the whisky tonight," Foley said with a grin. In truth his own pack was a heavier burden than expected. *I've grown softer in the years since I left the army.*

The trees of the Lewswood offered a welcome shade as they entered the forest, heading north. Before leaving Ashwood, Foley had found his old compass lying at the bottom of his pack, its silver tarnished. It had been a gift from his father on being commissioned into the army, along with his Webley-Pryse revolver. The compass would keep them from going in circles, and the revolver would keep them from falling afoul of anything that meant them harm. Foley hadn't bothered asking Hunt if he had brought his derringer. *He likely takes it into the outhouse with him.*

Not that Foley blamed him. Hunt had said little about his time in captivity, but every now and then a shadow would fall over his eyes, and Foley knew it had left its mark on him. Even after a few weeks of peace in the family home, muffled screams during the night were not uncommon.

Time passed, and onwards they walked, deeper and deeper into the Lewswood. The day grew darker as less sunlight penetrated the thickening canopy overhead, the trees growing taller and thicker.

"Few venture in this deep," Hunt said quietly. Slight noises sounded around them as small animals scurried through the undergrowth, and there was an occasional flapping of wings. But there was no birdsong.

There were no paths this deep in the forest, branches raking their heads and clawing at their clothing as they trekked deeper into an eerie twilight. The ground turned to earthy, the perpetual lack of sun meaning nothing grew beneath the trees but moss and fungi. "Not an inviting place, is it?"

"The surviving Kail'ans fled here when my ancestor took their land," Hunt said, twigs breaking underfoot. "He sent men in pursuit, but no soldier who passed beyond this part of the forest returned. Beyond here is its heart."

"Let's set up camp here," Foley suggested. He eyed the forest ahead uneasily, a tangle of impenetrable gloom.

Hunt stopped and looked around. "A good idea."

Within an hour they had a small fire started, there being no shortage of kindling, and they even had fresh meat for their dinner. Rabbits had come too close to their camp, their burrow having no memory of Man, and Foley managed to shoot two of them before the rest fled.

Fat crackled in the flames as Hunt turned the rabbits on a

spit over the fire, a bottle of whisky nestled against a tree root.

"What's the plan?" Foley asked. They were in a land of their own, gone from the world. He took a particular comfort in the thought that none of those minded to kill them would ever find them in this forest.

"In the morning I'll take a walk and sketch anything of interest," Hunt said. "God knows what's flourished in this forest, untouched by people."

"And after?"

Hunt took a swig of whisky. "I'm confident we'll exit the forest tomorrow if we continue north, close to Lew Abbey and Loch Arienas. We'll visit the abbey."

"Why the abbey?" Foley was not one for religious places.

"If those people we saw on Ash Hill the night of the fair were pagans, then their ancestors must have returned here in the past century or so, given the number."

"And if so, the names of subsequent births will be in the church records," Foley said, catching on. "But why would they be in the abbey?"

"Reverend Harcourt told me that the records were moved there back when the church roof was leaking, before my family paid to restore it. They were never returned."

"You want to see if and when there was a flood of new surnames, then?"

"Worth checking. Not saying we do anything about it, but I'd like to at least know the names of those who may hold a grudge against me and my family. First, though, I want to explore this forest in the morning."

*

Hunt delved deeper into the Lewswood, fighting through stubborn branches that clawed at his head and clothes, the forest resisting human intrusion. He had left his hat back at the camp where Foley was sleeping off last night's whisky. Hunt was suffering, too, but resolved to keep to his intention of exploring the heart of the Lewswood and sketch whatever took his interest.

The morning passed, the forest floor enduring a perpetual gloom. The further into the forest Hunt got, the older, thicker and taller the trees got. He no longer had to battle branches, there being few descending to his height. Instead, a vast canopy spread out overhead, only the occasional shard of sunlight breaking through.

There was little vegetation, the ground starved of the sunlight needed to sustain it. He found moss-covered rocks and patches of fungi growing wild. Trunks rose like pillars, enough of a gap between them that Hunt could walk freely between them. It felt like walking through a vast hall of endless pillars with a roof of green and brown overhead. A cathedral of wood and leaf.

He had sketched several trees and collected samples of various fungi he didn't recognise in case there were any previously undiscovered. *Maybe I'll have a mushroom named after me.*

The dry brown ground was soft and loamy, the protective embrace of the forest sheltering the topsoil from being washed away by heavy rains. He wondered how long it had been since anyone had stepped foot here, if ever.

How long had it been, he couldn't say, but he soon realised he was not the first to tread this part of the forest. Hairs rose on the back of Hunt's neck as he stood before a circular grove of trees with images and symbols gently carved into the bark, a wide space separating the grove from the surrounding forest. Small stick-figures of people and animals made from tied twigs dangled from the branches, some having fallen to the ground.

He took a breath and dared himself to enter the grove, soon finding himself in a clearing. A large circular space awaited, an inner ring of stones placed within, some standing as high as his knee, others stretching above his head. Symbols of the sun, moon, wolves and horned stags, and wavy lines had been carved into the stones. The carvings were still visible, again largely untouched by wind or rain.

This is where the pagans gathered. Where Sept Kail'an practised its religion, worshipping old gods and spirits of the land. He felt like an interloper, unwelcome. Was that sense of lingering enmity he felt, his imagination, or did these ancient trees know his blood and remember the days of death and fire when his ancestor brought an army here and broke the people of their faith?

I should get back. Foley would have packed up the camp by now and be awaiting his return. The forest looked the same in every direction, but he had Foley's compass, and all he need do was walk south-east.

Twigs broke underfoot as Hunt returned the way he had come, leaving the ancient shrine behind, a testament to a time long gone. *Or is it?* Hunt recalled the rite he and Foley had spied taking place on top of Ash Hill, people gathering for an unknown purpose the night of the village fair. Maybe the old ways weren't as dead as most believed. And those who practised those ways might still visit this grove to pay their respects and would not welcome a scion of the Hunt family desecrating it. He quickened his pace, shadows dancing all around him in the gloom.

*

It was afternoon by the time Hunt and Foley left the forest, walking out onto the shoreline of Loch Arienas. The land was as ruggedly beautiful as that surrounding Loch Aline, the only sign of human habitation being Lew Abbey resting atop a cliff overlooking the loch.

The cold waters of Loch Arienas washed away the last of Hunt's fatigue as he swam, the sun bright overhead. Not a swimmer, Foley seemed content to bathe near the edge of the loch. The loch was fed from freshwater rather than the sea, making it pleasant to swim beneath the surface, not that he could see much.

"Where did you learn to swim?" Foley asked, sounding a little envious as they lay on the grass, letting the sun dry them off. They had washed some clothes and hung them over rocks and branches, drying quickly in the sun. It would feel good to wear clean clothes again, to feel clean again.

"Here, when I visited as a child." Those had been good days. His earliest memories of visiting here were contrasted to his then-life living in London. The difference between the industrial immensity of London and the rural wilderness of the Morvern peninsula…

"Here? This loch? Bit out of the way, I'd have thought."

"No, Loch Aline. This is my first time at Loch Arienas."

Foley stood, putting on his woollen trousers and cotton

shirt. "We should visit the abbey now if we've to be on the other side of the forest by dusk."

"Agreed." After seeing that shrine, Hunt had little wish to spend another night in the Lewswood.

Lew Abbey sat atop a cliff overlooking the loch, a starkly granite contrast against the cloudless sky above and clear waters below. The weathered abbey looked mediaeval, built from misshapen rocks, a forbidding presence amidst the rugged moorland, the only sign of civilisation for miles. Tall, arched oak doors protected entry, and Hunt felt a hesitance to ring the large iron bell nailed to the wall next to them.

*

The library smelled of old paper, musty from a lack of ventilation. Old shelves lined the walls and two misshapen tables sat in the centre of the room. The stools were hard and uncomfortable, Hunt wondering if they were a deliberate choice by the monks as a sign of their austerity. *Maybe they think too much comfort will lead them to Hell.*

The Benedictine monks had been taken aback by the arrival of Hunt and Foley, clearly not used to visitors in their remote locale, but Abbot Lachlan had proved only too happy to accede to Hunt's request to visit their library on learning he was the son of Lord Ashwood. The abbot had thereafter made several comments regarding the state of the monastery, including a leaking roof. Wanting the abbot's help, Hunt had agreed it was disgraceful that the monastery lacked funds for maintenance and promised to speak with his father to rectify it.

After that, the abbot had eagerly directed his monks to aid Hunt's research, assigning him several elderly men in black robes to look out the required tomes from the library shelves.

"You're a hard bastard," Foley said quietly, taking a seat next to Hunt. He had been visiting the steward, arranging to buy some food for their trip home.

"Hmm?" Hunt looked up from the brittle-paged book whose faded writing he was struggling to read, following Foley's gaze. A white-haired monk was ponderously climbing a set of creaking step ladders to return a volume of the Kirkaline Parish records. "You could go help him."

Foley snorted. "I'm fine sitting here, thank you, your Lordship. What have you learned?"

"I've gone through the Kirkaline Parish records, those still legible. After my ancestor killed or exiled the Kail'ans, the newly built kirk started their records, and the same names mostly appear over and over in the births, deaths and marriages. For the first fifty years or so. Then a lot of new names start appearing."

"A new influx of settlers?"

"So it appears. But oddly sudden and in such numbers. Why would a dozen families just appear? It's not like there was a plague or similar causing the baron to seek replacement tenants. And more oddly, none of them bear clan names. Many were named after their trades."

Foley frowned at the old leather-bound book as Hunt carefully closed it. "Any names you recognise?"

"Some, but it's been a century and a half, and the families have mostly intermingled. The Slaters are one family that caught my eye."

Foley leaned back, almost falling over, evidently forgetting he sat on a stool. "You think descendants of the Kail'an sect waited two generations and then returned to the area under new names, bringing back paganism to the area?"

"Yes. If they ever left. I suspect some lived wild in the forest and surrounding hills, raiding cattle and stealing crops."

"What do we do about it?" Foley asked, ever the practical one.

"Nothing." Hunt breathed in deeply, looking at the mildewed stone walls. "So far as I can tell, they're doing no harm. Either the rest of the locals are ignorant or are turning a blind eye. I think the latter."

"They don't like you very much," Foley pointed out.

"I'll try and bear up under my crushing disappointment of failing to make new friends here."

Foley's eyes widened. "Damn me," he breathed.

"What?"

"The family who own Dunlew Castle? The McKellens, aye?"

"Yes. What of them?"

"Think of the name McKellen, but not as you would spell

it," Foley said. "Think of what it means."

Hunt thought. *McKellen ... Son of Kellen...*

Kail'an. Son of Kail'an. "The McKellens are descended from the Kail'ans," he said softly.

"Was it a McKellen who duelled your ancestor?"

"Yes, a Cullen McKellen. His family have owned the Dunlew estate since."

"The Kail'ans got their castle back after all. Maybe your family's misfortunes here owe more to design than fate, eh? Maybe the returned sept decided to give their dead chief's curse a helping hand."

"Gentlemen," a dry voice said. Hunt looked over to see a middle-aged monk had quietly joined them, his once-dark hair peppered white. There was a knowing air of intelligence in his eyes.

"Afternoon, Brother," Hunt said.

"Abbot Lachlan said you've an interest in local history. It's something I've studied during my time here. I'm Brother Justin."

"At the moment I'm interested – academically speaking – in the old pagan settlers of this area, no offence to you or your brethren," Hunt said with a note of apology.

"As it happens, I've studied the old ways, too." A smile wrinkled his face. "'Know thine enemy'". Brother Justin listed a number of the old gods, some Hunt was aware of.

"Cernunnos was popular, I've no doubt, given the large forest," Brother Justin continued. "But Lugh, the sun god, was the one chiefly worshipped in these parts. Some legends say he was the father of Cernunnos. He was also the father of the Irish hero Cu Chalainn. Or perhaps they are both aspects of Lugh. There was no singular religious authority, the legends vary from region to region."

"Lugh?" Foley frowned. "Like Lucifer?"

"Both names come from the Latin for light," Hunt said. "What made Lugh so special?"

"I do not know," the monk admitted. "But remnants of his worship still linger. The festival of Lughnasadh was a popular one back in the day, and if it was still celebrated, this year it would likely fall on Sunday the 30th of July. The largest mountain, Fragarach, is named after Lugh's sword. He was said to have a fearsome hound companion. Local legends even claim Lugh walked this land."

For no reason he could discern, Hunt asked, "The forest, too?"

"Yes." The monk looked pleased at the question. "The forest is named after him. Lewswood is a corruption of Lugh's Wood."

"Lew Abbey?" Foley asked with a grin.

Hunt felt a chill as Justin returned Foley's smile. "Just so. Officially the area is named after St Lewis, but I suspect that was a convenient fiction, the new religion merely a fresh coat of paint hiding the old."

"My father won't be pleased to hear that," Hunt said. "He's named after St Lewis." *I wonder if he knows the Lewis everything's named after here is a pagan god?*

"Ironic indeed. The most sacred grove of the old religion was located near the old hillfort, Dunkail'an." Justin's grey eyes met Hunt's. "That grove was burned down by Sir Geoffrey Hunt, who built his estate on the land."

Ashwood. Hunt grimaced. "Not a man to do things by half, I fear."

An old anger simmered in Justin's eyes. "He was not, Mr Hunt. He crucified many druids first, nailing them to the trees before setting them alight. The family of Chief Kail'an was said to be among them."

"Bloody hell," Foley blasphemed. Hunt felt sick at the thought. *My family's home is built there, where men, women and children were crucified and burned. Jesus Christ...*

"Thank you for your insight," he managed. "Foley, I think we've taken enough of the brother's time."

"Aye," Foley said, rising from the stool, a sick look on face.

"You're welcome," Brother Justin said, a look of faint malice whispering across his face. He seemed a little too knowledgeable of the religion preceding Christianity here. Hunt suspected the village and farms near Loch Aline weren't the only places he would find followers of the old ways.

"What now?" Foley asked as they left Lew Abbey. *Lugh's Abbey.* The God of Light's grove may have been burned, his followers scattered, but maybe he was having the last laugh after all.

"Now we return to … to Ashwood."

"We're done camping?"

"Not quite. I want to speak with my father. Alone, if you're content to camp without me." They had more to discuss than dark family history; there was an enemy in the midst, Kail'ans perhaps still waging a war begun long ago by Sir Geoffrey Hunt.

A look of distaste twisted Foley's mouth. "I'm happy to stay away from the site of a massacre. I knew your ancestor was brutal, but that…"

Hunt nodded. He wanted to know how much his father knew of their family's crimes, how he could bear to live in a house built on the ashes of tortured men, women and children. And warn him of the McKellens.

Chapter Twenty-Seven

"Foley. You look like shit. How long have you been here?"

Foley turned right to see Hunt take the stool next to him at the bar. *How long have I been drinking, you mean.* "An hour, I think." *Maybe two.*

"More like two or three," Hunt said cynically.

"What can I get you?" Kay Kyle asked from behind the bar.

"A pint of ale," Hunt requested. She promptly fetched one.

"Thank you," Hunt said as he passed over some coins.

"You're welcome," she said with a bright smile. She certainly took a greater interest in Hunt than she had Foley, not that he minded. He had been content to sit and drink, alone with his thoughts.

Hunt spoke to Foley once the barmaid had gone to another customer. "You really do look rough, are you coming down with something? Or did you finish all that whisky? There couldn't have been that much, unless you had another bottle or flask hidden away you didn't tell me of?"

Foley assumed a wounded scowl. "I'm offended you would think that of me." He rubbed an unshaven jaw. "I don't know what's wrong with me. I fell asleep, and when I awoke, I felt bloody out of sorts. Aching all over."

"Odd."

"Aye." He'd awoken naked and clammy a short distance from the campsite; maybe the whisky he'd drunk had hit him harder than usual. "It's all this fresh country air," he accused Hunt.

"Yes, I'm sure. Nothing at all to do with you and what remained of our whisky."

Foley decided to change the subject. "How did your talk with your parents go?"

"Could have gone better, could have gone worse," Hunt

said. *Meaning he wasn't disowned, at least.*

"Do tell." Foley took a drink from his ale. His body still ached, his head too. The ale couldn't make it worse, surely. He'd survived dysentery in South Africa, he could survive this, whatever it was.

"Well, I told them what I'd learned about our family's glorious history crucifying women and children before burning them alive." A bitter smile twisted his features. "They knew of it but felt it something best left in the past. So they said. As we stood on the very site of … of it."

"And?" Foley prompted.

Hunt jerked a shrug. "And nothing. My father rather acidly asked what I suggested he do about it now, almost two hundred years later. Burn the house down?"

"What did you suggest?"

Hunt drank some ale, not answering. *Meaning there was nothing to say.* "Did you mention the return of the Kail'ans?"

"I did bring it up," Hunt said a little evasively. "Told them about the settling of so many families a couple of generations after the surviving Kail'ans fled, the similarity between the name Kail'an and McKellen. My father said it was again in the past, even if there was a connection. My mother sarcastically expressed her surprise at my scholarship and said if I wished to spend more time in holy places, I was welcome to attend church with them every Sunday."

Foley grinned. He liked Lady Ashwood's sharp tongue (so long as it wasn't directed at him) and respected her, but by God was he glad she wasn't *his* mother.

Hunt continued. "If the McKellen who killed the 3rd Baron Ashwood in a duel did in fact orchestrate it, did in fact cheat to win, then there's not much to do about it now. The McKellens have owned the castle for over a hundred years, and the one who killed the baron is long dead."

"They weren't overly concerned?"

"Not overly, no." Hunt took another swig of ale. "For one thing, Lord McKellen was an apparently respectable judge. For another, he died recently. We may have an excuse to look around tonight, though. Several sheep were found slaughtered by a wild dog, and foresters are leading a group of locals to hunt for it."

"I heard a few talking about it earlier," Foley said. "Going by the wounds, it sounds like a big bastard," he added dubiously. Their misadventure with the wolves four weeks earlier still preyed on his mind.

"We'll be fine," Hunt said. "There'll be a lot of us, armed with rifles and shotguns. The full moon will help us."

"And helping the local farmers deal with a beast killing their livestock might rehabilitate the Hunt name a little," Foley guessed shrewdly. "So long as we're not killed in a 'hunting accident'."

Hunt's smile was forced. "I need to do *something*. And the pagans have had ample opportunity to deal with us. We'll keep our wits about us." His eyes fell on their ale. "Meaning no more of that."

*

"If you're so keen to make the locals like you, maybe next time buy everyone drinks at the bar?" Foley suggested as he, Hunt, and a few others entered the Lewswood.

"This is cheaper."

The party of hunters had divided into three groups to cover as much of the area as possible, each led by a forester from the Dunlew estate. So far they'd found no trace of the beast, and the foresters who'd tried to track it earlier in the day complained that the tracks were confusing, ending just outside the forest. Foley had gone quiet on seeing where they ended, quietly telling Hunt the tracks were near where he had camped the night before. Hunt suspected that when he returned to Ashwood, he would not be alone, unless of course the beast was killed.

That didn't look likely. If the hound or whatever it was didn't want to be found, it would have little difficulty evading its hunters. The men crashed through dark-shrouded woods, some carrying oil lamps, others carrying either a rifle or shotgun. On hearing Foley was a former soldier, Billy Forrest had handed him a spare rifle. Hunt had to content himself with an oil lamp and Foley's revolver hidden in his coat pocket.

The initial enthusiasm of the group waned as the hours passed and afternoon threatened to turn to dusk. The men armed with guns had grinned at those left to carry the lamps, but Hunt suspected that should darkness fall, they would reconsider who were the lucky ones.

His more immediate concern was with Foley. The man had worsened as the day went on, despite the ale having worn off. Maybe so many days outside had taken their toll on him?

He looked up, seeing the moon slowly emerge in the twilight sky. "A full moon, as I–" he started to say, before hearing a thud.

Foley had collapsed to his knees, his rifle forgotten on the ground. He began to convulse, his face in his hands as he cried out in pain.

"What's wrong?" Hunt cried out as he ran back to his friend. His first thought was that Foley had stepped in a rabbit hole, but that was clearly not the case. Foley's breaths turned ragged and gasping, and Hunt heard bone crack. A low cry escaped from Foley's lips, turning into a wet gurgle as blood poured from his mouth. His hands tore frantically at his waistcoat and shirt, buttons spilling to the earth as he ripped it open, baring his chest.

Hunt had almost reached him when Foley's chest and abdomen tore open, ribs cracking apart like bars on a shattered cage. Foley fell still, dead eyes gazing upwards. And still his destruction continued. *Jesus, no!* His skull cracked apart, an eye dropping from its socket. Hunt could only watch in numbed horror as Foley's skin shrunk tightly around his bones, as if his flesh was being consumed from within. His skin turned pale and dry as papyrus, and his remains seemed to diminish.

Something emerged from his chest, hauling itself from between splayed ribs, small and bloody. As Foley's corpse rotted away, his killer grew apace. Painfully, judging by the cracking of joints, the stretching of bare blood-flecked skin, and its yelping cries.

Hunt was vaguely aware he carried a gun, but he was too stunned to reach for it. *It's a dog*, he thought at first. *No, a wolf*, he amended, seeing its large head and pricked ears. By now it was larger, fur sprouting from skin, its black and grey colouring not unfamiliar to Hunt. He had seen wolves like the one growing amidst the ruin of his friend four weeks earlier at the Drover's Inn.

"The beast, it's here!" someone cried out, followed by the sound of men crashing through the trees. The wolf had stopped growing, and by the time it raised its head, Foley was little more than dessicated skin and bone lying on bloodstained earth.

A rifle bolt was pulled back, and Hunt turned to see one of his companions take aim at the wolf. He was quick, but the wolf was quicker. A blur of black and silver slammed into the forester, a bloodcurdling snarl followed by a brief high-pitched scream as the man's throat disappeared in a spray of blood. The wolf worried him like a dog with a rat. Hunt was stunned by the nearby blast of a shotgun, but when he regained his senses, he saw the shooter had fired too hastily, missing the wolf.

Earth and vegetation were ploughed up as the wolf tore along the ground towards the shooter, a farmhand also called Tam. In seconds he too was knocked down, thrashing in vain as his scream was cut short.

Hunt could still hear his last surviving companion, only now he realised the man was running away from the slaughter, not towards it. *Smart man*. Not that it helped Hunt much. The wolf raised its bloody maw to the sky and howled long and loudly.

And then it turned its yellow eyes on Hunt, baring red fangs and issuing a low throaty growl full of menace. For the second time in four weeks he found himself facing a wolf. They had survived their first encounter, Foley lucky to escape with a bitten arm. He had not been so fortunate this time, this wolf somehow tearing him apart from the inside-out.

A bitten arm ... Hunt recalled stories of lycanthropy, passed on by a werewolf's bite. A full moon shone down on them, same as it had the night they had been attacked at the Drover's Inn. *The wolf, it's Foley.*

Oh, God. Hunt managed to draw Foley's revolver with a shaky hand as what had once been his friend raised its hackles and lowered its head. "I don't want to shoot you," Hunt said. Not that the wolf showed any sign of comprehension. *Or maybe I should. Would you want to live as a beast? You've already killed two men, Foley, you poor bastard.*

No. The change was temporary, Hunt realised. The beast had first appeared the night before, the first full moon. Yet Foley had returned in the morning, with no apparent memory.

Last night all he'd killed were sheep, at least. Now two men lay dead. With Hunt likely to join them. Would Foley realise what he'd become, or would he dismiss his awakening naked as a result of too much drink?

The wolf stalked Hunt, drawing closer, growling. Any moment now, and it would leap, either tearing out Hunt's throat or disembowelling him. *Then he'll feed.*

"Stay back," he pleaded, aiming the gun at the Foley-wolf and pulling back the hammer. *I don't want to shoot, but God help me, I will.* At least these wolves were mortal, he knew that much from killing the one that bit Foley.

Hunt was about to throw up, and he knew he was moments from either killing his friend or dying. Fear turned into red anger for a moment at the injustice of it, and a coldness seeped into – no, seeped *out* of him. He had felt this way once before, the night he shot George Rannoch in the Necropolis. Part of him recognised the wolf; not as Foley but as something old, familiar and connected to him.

The wolf froze, its yellow eyes locked on Hunt's. It growled again, trying to goad Hunt into flight, but Hunt stood his ground, gun aimed at it. He'd fire if he had to. He felt like steel, cold and hard, fear sliding off him. The wolf whimpered and backed away a step, but it didn't run. Confident the tree to his left was solid enough to hold his weight, Hunt uncocked the gun and pocketed it, taking a breath before leaping up and grabbing hold of a lower branch.

That coldness cocooning him from fear and rash action fled, panic flaring in him once more as he scrambled up the tree, expecting to feel teeth and claws ripping into him at any moment. He chanced a look down, and while the wolf had indeed darted at him, he was too high up for it to reach him. The tension gripping his chest muscles loosened on realising he was safe for now. So long as he stayed in the tree.

Had I not returned to Ashwood yesterday but instead camped last night with Foley...

The wolf prowled below, knowing Hunt would have to come down eventually.

*

He awoke with a groan, the ache gripping his limbs bone-deep. As Foley groggily tried to sit up, he realised he'd again passed out naked. He'd already lost one set of clothes the night before, forcing him to put on a dirty pair. The thought of having to skulk around naked, trying to return to Ashwood without anyone seeing him, sent a spike of panic through him.

Wait, I wasn't drinking last night. The last he remembered was hunting some beast with Hunt and a few others in these very woods. Like yesterday morning, his skin and hair were sticky, covered with some residue. He looked around, the morning sun piercing the trees above. Even a little sunlight was enough to sting his eyes, but he spotted his clothes lying nearby, looking bloody. *What the hell happened to me last night? Where's Hunt?*

His second question was quickly answered as Hunt dropped down from a nearby tree, looking tired and pale. "Hunt! What were you doing up there?"

"We need to talk," Hunt said in a strained voice.

"Damn right we do." He was about to speak again when he noticed the two bodies lying in blood-flecked bushes. A cold dread seeped into his marrow on seeing them. "What happened? Was that … me?"

"It wasn't you – I mean, it was the wolf," Hunt said.

"What wolf? The beast is a wolf?" *Wolves here too?*

"You're the wolf this time, Foley," Hunt said quietly. He explained what he'd seen, Foley not wanting to believe him but seeing no reason not to.

Foley's guts clenched as a terrible thought occurred. Even worse than killing. He'd killed men before. "Did I – did the wolf…?" *Did it eat from them? Does human flesh digest in my guts? God help me.*

Comprehension dawned on Hunt's face. "God, no! You – it – probably swallowed some blood, but it was more interested in trying to kill me. Even if the wolf did eat blood or flesh, it burst out of you, and you burst out of it. God knows how."

Foley closed his eyes, relieved. And guilty that he had killed two men. Even if it wasn't quite him.

"I can't rationally explain what this is, but I believe it must be connected to the wolf that bit you." Hunt stepped towards him, but a distance remained between them. Foley sensed his friend had a suspicion as to the cause of … this, but was reluctant to say it.

"It wasn't a wolf, "Foley said, closing his eyes briefly. "At least, no more than I am."

"What do you mean? You know of this?"

"A bit. The Templar Jamie Burton told me and Sirk some of the other unnatural … monsters in the world, beyond demons and the undead." He forced himself to look Hunt in the eye. "I was bitten by a werewolf. The other wolves likely were werewolves, too. And as I lived, I'm … I'm…"

"Now one too," Hunt finished quietly. "I've heard it referred to as lycanthropy. Is there a cure? What does it mean?"

"It means that every full moon, I'll turn into a wolf. It'll rip itself free from my body, and at dawn I'll pull myself free from it. And Burton never spoke of a cure." *Beyond a bullet to the head.*

"After last night, more men will be hunting you. It," Hunt said. "We'll need to keep you safe, there's a full moon tonight. If we keep you in your room and you don't see the moon, you won't … change?"

"I doubt it works like that. To be safe, I'll need you to lock me in a secure cellar."

Hunt grimaced. "What do I tell my parents?"

"To stay away from the cellar?"

"Yes, very good." Hunt sighed. "At least we won't have to worry about you getting shot tonight. It's the last full moon, I think, and you'll be fine afterwards."

"For another four weeks."

"We'll worry about that in four weeks. We can always lock you up in your shop cellar back home." Hunt stepped closer. "I'll do what I can to help."

"Like what?" Foley knew he was being churlish, but he was too far gone in self-pity to really care.

"Well, I can housetrain you for one thing, so you don't piss all over the flat," Hunt said with a straight face.

"Oh, fuck you." Foley barked a laugh despite himself, feeling a surge of affection towards his friend. He might have become half a monster, but Hunt still stood with him.

"And I can take you for a walk in the park. Buy you a nice bone if you behave."

"Very funny."

Chapter Twenty-Eight

Not for the first time, Hunt looked up at the sky, anxiously searching for any sign of the rising moon. Dusk was still some hours away, even with sunset now a little earlier than it had been four weeks before. From what Hunt remembered, the sun had been setting by the time the werewolves attacked them, but did that matter? Was dusk a necessity of the transformation, or just a full moon in the sky? They didn't know and would take no chances.

Securing Foley in the cellar would not be a problem, the door stout enough to confine even the powerful wolf Hunt had barely survived the night before. The problem would be explaining the situation to his parents. He took a breath of the fresh warm air perfumed by nature rather than people and industry, something he'd miss when they returned to the city.

"Well?" They had dined with Hunt's parents, Hunt and Foley loitering outside the front of the house while Mother and Father enjoyed the pleasant evening in the rear courtyard. Hunt had looked forward to seeing the renovations planned by his parents to restore the family seat; now all he could see were innocents nailed or tied to trees before the grove was burned to the ground. *Ashwood indeed.* Sir Geoffrey, later the 1st Baron, had been a hard man with a dark humour.

"I just need to think of something to tell my parents. Any ideas?"

"You could tell them I'm about to turn into a bloodthirsty beast."

Hunt gave him a sour look. "I was hoping for a more plausible explanation." Foley might joke, but Hunt could tell his curse lay heavily on him, as did the two men killed the night before. Their bodies had been found and the band of men tasked to hunt the wolf now did so in greater numbers.

Another reason to keep Foley safely confined. He suspected if the wolf died, the man would die too. Luckily the fleeing survivor hadn't seen Foley become the wolf.

"We've a visitor," Foley said, looking down the road.

Sure enough, a man on horseback was riding towards the house, his seat not the best to Hunt's critical eye.

"It's Sirk," Foley said in surprise. Sure enough, the rider was close enough for Hunt to recognise the professor.

"What's he doing all the way up here?" Hunt asked.

Foley rested his hands on his hips. "Let's ask him. He can also tell me why he's not in Glasgow minding my shop."

Sirk dismounted the horse, almost falling onto his backside. "Gentlemen, excellent, a pleasure seeing you both."

"What brings you here?" Hunt asked.

"You've not burned my bloody shop to the ground, have you?" Foley wanted to know. Hunt suspected part of his friend would shed few tears if Sirk had.

Sirk took a moment to scowl at Foley. "Your shop was in the same condition it was in when you left it, Mr Foley. Dare I say, in *better* condition. Several customers have commented favourably on my management of your affairs. One went so far as to say there was no need for you to hasten your return."

Seeing an argument brewing, Hunt cut in. "We can discuss the pharmaceutical trade later. Why are you here, Professor? Glasgow to Loch Aline is a bit far for a social call."

"I've come to warn you that the Sooty Feathers are taking an interest in your family's company, Mr Hunt. Lady Delaney and Miss Knox – you recall the good ladies, yes? – found a letter being written to Miss Guillam. You recall *her*, I have no doubt."

"You're working with Lady Delaney and Miss Knox?" Foley asked in surprise. "How did that come about?"

Hunt's mood darkened. "Steiner too?"

Sirk looked between them, deciding to answer Hunt first. "Mr Steiner's Templar duties have to date *not* precipitated a return to Glasgow. However, their absence has not hindered our efforts against the Sooty Feather Society, or their undead masters. As for how I came to be working with Lady Delaney, that is a rather long and eventful tale."

"You can tell us about it while we stable your horse," Foley said.

"Where did you get the horse, anyway?" Hunt asked as he led them round to the stable.

"I hired it from the Ashwood Arms Inn." Sirk glanced at Hunt. "If it is not too much of an imposition, may I stay here tonight?"

"Of course," Hunt said. An alarming memory returned to the fore. "We'll need to lock Foley in the cellar before dusk, though." He could worry about Margot Guillam's intentions towards his family after.

"Pray why?"

Foley gave a heavy sigh. "That's *our* long story, Professor."

While they groomed and stabled the horse, Sirk regaled them with an accounting of his activities with Delaney and Knox; raiding a mill and killing a score of undead. In turn, Sirk was told of Foley's 'problem'. The professor's curiosity had a clinically callous air about it, being more interested in observing Foley's transformation than in offering any solutions to prevent it, but if anyone could come up with a solution, Hunt suspected it would be Sirk.

Summer still lingered in the air, a lack of breeze keeping the evening pleasantly warm, and so Hunt found his parents still sitting around a small table in the courtyard. "Mother, Father; may I introduce you to Professor Sirk, from the university? He is here doing research and came by to pay his respects. Professor, these are my parents, Lord and Lady Ashwood."

After courtesies were duly exchanged and no objection raised to Hunt's request for Sirk to stay the night, Hunt, and Foley returned to the front of the house to further discuss Sirk's reason for coming to Loch Aline while the professor went into the house with a small case. Hunt's heart quickened on finding himself being drawn back into that bloody world of undead and demons, and not in a good way. *I thought I was done with that world.*

Foley peered down the road. "More visitors."

Sure enough, a wagon rattled up the road towards them, four men sitting in the back. A spike of alarm went through Hunt. Had the locals somehow learned Foley was the wolf?

Concern was etched on Foley's face, but he said nothing. The wagon stopped near them, and three of the four men in the back jumped down, the teamster keeping hold of the reins. There was something familiar about him. A look of shock crossed Foley's face, which paled. "Oh, shit."

"What?" The man remaining in the back of the wagon kept his cap pulled low and his face turned away. The three men approaching Hunt and Foley looked more like city folk than locals. City folk from mean streets.

"It's Roddy McBride."

Hunt instinctively knew which one was Roddy McBride. The patriarch of the infamous family carried himself with a hard confidence, narrowed eyes aimed right at Foley. He barked something, and his two men pulled out revolvers. *You came a day too damned late, Professor.*

"Now would be a good time for you to change," he whispered, fear pitching his voice upwards. A wolf ripping the McBrides limb from limb would be a definite boon, even if it might turn on Hunt afterwards.

"Aye," Foley said. "Where's your derringer?"

"In my jacket pocket." Which was doing him no favours hanging in his room. Memories of the Gerrard murders in that remote farmhouse crashed through his mind, of days locked up knowing he might be killed at any time. He pitched over and retched.

Not much came up, but he still spat to clear the bile from his mouth, and he straightened up to find Roddy McBride watching him pitilessly.

"You must be Wilton Hunt, the son of Lord Ashwood," he said, sounding distinctly unimpressed. "I'm Roddy McBride." He gestured carelessly to his right. "My younger brother, Johnny."

Eyes the colour of granite shifted to Foley. "My *youngest* brother since Eddie died. He was last seen in your company. Mr Foley." He said Foley's name with relish, and Hunt wondered at the lengths the man had gone to learn that name. Had Margot Guillam given them up, or had he simply found them through dogged persistence, terrorising the city until someone talked?

"This is Harry Walker," McBride said, introducing the man to his left.

Anger handed Hunt back his voice. "A relative of Gerry Walker?"

"I was Gerry's da'," Walker answered, giving Hunt a suspicious look, and sure enough Hunt saw the man who had helped kill the Gerrards in the thug before him. He knew better than to admit being the one who had killed Gerry Walker. Not that it mattered, he was unlikely to live beyond the next several minutes.

"What brings you here?" Foley asked, Hunt marvelling at the hard defiance in his friend's voice.

"I'm here to make a business proposition to your friend's father," McBride said. "Avenging Eddie is my payment for coming here."

"You know my father?" Hunt doubted it. They were unlikely acquaintances.

"Not yet. But I look forward to meeting the grand lord." The McBrides and Walker escorted Hunt and Foley round to the back of the house at gunpoint.

Mother and Father were seated in the rear courtyard, a jug of apple juice on the wooden table. Surprise showed on their faces as McBride and his men confronted them with guns drawn. McBride didn't bother sending anyone into the house. *Sirk.* Maybe the professor could avoid detection. Or better yet, save them.

"What is the meaning of this?" Father asked. Outwardly Father looked calm, but Hunt knew him well enough to recognise the tightly bound anger simmering in his eyes. Part of him felt relief on seeing his father, the young boy who believed his father capable of handling anything, of protecting him from any danger. There was outrage on Mother's face.

"I have a business proposal for you, Lord Ashwood," McBride said.

"And you think threatening my son was a wise prelude to making this offer?" Father looked unintimidated. *But he doesn't know who he's dealing with.* He glanced at Hunt. "Are you unharmed?"

"Yes, Father."

He looked imperiously at McBride. "Who are you and what brings you here?"

"I'm Roddy McBride. And I'm here for your company, which you'll sell to me."

McBride sat uninvited across from Father and slid a piece

of paper across the wooden table, along with a pen and ink bottle. "The contract regarding the sale of the Browning Shipping Company."

"My wife deals with company business." Father passed the paper to Mother and clasped his hands.

Mother opened the paper and read it, her hands shaking slightly. "The company is worth thrice this." She looked up at McBride. "Outrageous."

McBride was enjoying himself. *Not every day he gets to bully a lord and lady.* "You'll find that price is generous. It includes your son's life."

Mother continued reading the contract, a frown creasing her brow. "According to this, ownership of the company will pass to a Margot Guillam. Not you."

She did sell us out. Hunt wondered why his mother was dragging this out. Selling would cost them the family company; refusing to sell would cost them their lives. But it was McBride's reaction to that name that caught his eye. A fleeting look of fear. *He knows what Guillam is.*

"I'm here on Miss Guillam's behalf," McBride said. "You would be wise to sell, if you value your life. If you value your son's."

Mother and Father shared a look, a chill going through Hunt. She pushed the paper away. "We will not be selling. I suggest you return to Miss Guillam and tell her our decision."

McBride didn't say anything for a moment. His men were visibly taken aback at Mother's defiance. They were used to Roddy McBride breaking men steeped in violence to his will. To see a middle-aged lady defying him despite his men and guns came as a surprise to them. To Hunt, too. He wondered if she knew just what sort of man stood before her.

"You'll sign that, or I'll send your son to fucking Hell." McBride was shaking, and Hunt knew it wasn't from fear.

"I will not." Mother's voice was calm and unmovable.

"Give me five minutes with them, Roddy," Johnny McBride said, cracking his knuckles.

"You think your money and title protects you–" McBride stood, towering over the Hunts.

"Enough." The last two men from the wagon appeared. One was Jock Stewart, the Dunlew estate's head gamekeeper, a shotgun cradled in the crook of his left arm. The one who spoke pulled back his cap, Hunt recognising him as Dunlew's new master, Alasdair McKellen himself. *A Sooty Feather, I'll wager.* Hunt remembered McKellen from the Black Wing Club a couple of years back, making a fool of himself after too much drink.

He seemed to have left the fool behind, McBride surprisingly deferring to him. McKellen continued. "You've made Miss Guillam's offer, McBride, and it's been rejected. We'll convince them another way, one that will increase my standing here."

Anger crossed McBride's face. "Give me ten minutes and it'll be damned well signed."

"You read Miss Guillam's instructions, McBride. If they refused to sell, I'm to have first shot at convincing them." Part of Hunt had to admire McKellen's balls, to talk to McBride like that. Miss Guillam seemed to have put McKellen in charge, but she was many miles to the south, and McBride's temper appeared to be on a frayed leash.

"Fine, we'll do it your way. But I'll take what I was promised tonight, one way or the other."

"By all means," McKellen said with little interest. "We've a long journey ahead. Jock, I saw a wagon round the side. Prepare it, we'll need two."

"We should check the house," McBride said.

"Leave it. The wagons will be full enough as it is without dragging servants with us," McKellen said.

"And if they talk of what they've seen?"

"No one's seen anything. And here, who would they tell?"

Chapter Twenty-Nine

Fear and anger had distracted Hunt from paying too much attention to where they were being taken. At first he had assumed they were travelling to Dunlew Castle, where his parents would be given a choice between spilled blood or spilled ink. The wagons rattled north along roads of mud baked solid by months of summer.

But instead of following the road round the loch to Dunlew, Jock Stewart guided the wagon further north through a field, turning west rather than east. They were too far north to be going to Ash Hill, and there was nothing here but the Lewswood. *They're taking us into the forest.* Hunt felt a pit form in his stomach as he recalled the ancient shrines to the old gods lying deep within, sacred sites that someone had refused to allow the forest to swallow completely.

Sure enough, the wagons were abandoned at the edge of the forest and the prisoners led deep into its unwelcoming depths. Branches had clawed at Hunt's face, old roots grabbing at his feet in the gloom. No one spoke, a panic growing inside Hunt's breast. He felt shame for his ancestor's opportunistic brutality almost two centuries past, but he had no wish to be the Hunt to atone for it.

"We're nearly there, Chief," Stewart said to McKellen in Gaelic, holding a lantern in his spare hand. Hunt had been taught the language, though he understood it better than he spoke it. He thought he could smell wood burning, a flickering light piercing the trees ahead. Dusk was nearly upon them.

"Good."

"You're descended from the last Kail'an chief," Hunt said, certain his and Foley's suspicions were correct.

"He *is* the Kail'an chief. The mac Kail'an until his father died, and now *the* Kail'an," Stewart said, gripping Hunt's arm tightly as he led him through the forest. "Descended from the last chief to openly bear the title. He is Alasdair mac Hamish mac Hector Kail'an, and my line has served his since the sept began."

"Your family could have spared you what is to come, Hunt, had they just sold their company," McKellen said. The others were a short distance behind, being escorted at gunpoint by the McBrides.

"We're here," Stewart said, a look of reverence on his weathered face as the group entered a clearing in the forest. A circle of stones rose up from the loamy ground like fingers, encircled in turn by a series of small fires that lit up the clearing. Hunt and his captors were not the first to arrive, a coven gathered outside the stones, turning to face the new arrivals. Flame and shadow danced together, a contrast to the people who stood still and silent, heads bowed in reverence.

We're fucked, Hunt thought. Half-remembered tales of people being put in wicker baskets and burned in sacrifice to demanding gods and capricious spirits came unbidden to mind. Maybe these pagans were of a more genteel disposition and would let them off with a red smile across their throats.

Most of those gathered wore brown robes, though a few wore white. Priests of the old religion, perhaps?

"Your chief has come," Stewart announced formally, his voice booming across the clearing. "Give homage to the Kail'an, beloved of the gods, on this last full moon before Lughnasadh. We have brought strangers, so tonight we speak in English that they will understand."

A quiet murmur whispered round the coven as McKellen's sept dropped to their knees.

"Rise," McKellen said, his voice carrying around the clearing. "You have come as you always have, as our ancestors have since time forgotten, to the sacred places of Lugh's Wood, where our people once walked with gods and spirits."

McKellen surveyed his followers, there being maybe twenty of them; perhaps a few more concealed in shadows shrouding the edges of the clearing. "Tonight is my first in this wood with you as chief, and I would see it marked with a gift. A gift of vengeance to you and our kin murdered by the Black Hunt, and a gift to the gods. At Lughnasadh I will gather the whole of the sept, but tonight a select few of you have been invited here." He looked to those in white robes. "Long have the druids of Lugh's Wood kept the candle of our faith burning when many sought to extinguish that flame forever." He spoke like a man speaking rehearsed lines.

He strode closer to the stone circle, into the midst of his people. "I present to you Lewis and Wilton Hunt. The last of their cursed line, and tonight we make an offering to the gods."

"A sacrifice!" someone shouted. Hunt was close enough now to see the faces of the Kail'ans, some that he recognised. He was unsurprised to see Pat and Luke Slater, the brothers smiling their hatred at him. Constable Fowler was another familiar face, a surprise, but less of one than seeing the innkeeper and his daughter.

Kayleigh Kyle had smiled and flirted with him, welcoming him into the Horned Lord. Tonight there was no welcome on her face. Brother Justin from the Lew Abbey was also present, giving Hunt a crinkled smile as their eyes met. McKellen might not have known for sure Hunt's parents would refuse to sell the company, but he had evidently taken the precaution of inviting only the more fervent of the Kail'ans, those unlikely to baulk at a little human sacrifice. Particularly if it was a hated Hunt.

McKellen lowered his voice. "Your last chance, Lady Ashwood. Sign over your company and lose a husband. Refuse, and lose your son first and husband second. Had you signed at Ashwood, you could have saved both."

Mother gave him a scornful look, earning a chuckle from McBride. Did she doubt McKellen's resolve? He was committed now, and to back down would see him lose the faith of his people. They had been promised the death of a Hunt.

Two of the white-robed druids helped Stewart drag Hunt into the circle of stones. A massive slab of stone lay dead centre, cleared of moss and debris. His only hope now was for someone to happen by and rescue them. Professor Sirk had escaped detection, but Hunt doubted that he would be able to find this place as night started to fall. *I've more bloody chance of the old gods themselves turning up and demanding my release.*

"Brother Eoin, have you the knife?" To Hunt, McKellen said, "I understand you and your friend have already had dealings with Eoin Slater's sons? Old Eoin, like his father before him, is the High Druid here."

"I have, Laird," an old man rasped from a whisky-scoured voice, his long hair and beard white streaked with grey. He held a thin, ancient-looking knife of bronze. It looked freshly whetted, at least, sharp enough to make Hunt's end a quick one. Foley looked up at the sky, but the canopy hid the moon from sight. Did he need to see it to change, or did it only happen after the sun had set?

McBride laughed coarsely. "What do you think, lads? Will she sign before or after the knife is at her son's throat, eh?"

"Quiet!" Father looked at McBride, his voice cracking like a whip. "I've tolerated your insolence enough."

McBride spoke in a deathly quiet voice. "No one speaks to me like–"

No breeze stirred the warm night air, but a chill fell over the clearing, one that cut to the marrow. Someone had Unveiled, Hunt realised. A *Nephilim* or demon was present. Everyone present flinched as if struck, and a horror fell over Hunt as he realised the *cold* came from his father. *A demon. God, no. My father*.

The demon Possessing Father looked at the Kail'ans and McBrides, their faces reflecting shock and bewilderment. "I am known to some of you as Lugh; Cernunnos; sometimes Bel. To others, Lucifer; Iblis; Lightbringer and Morning Star. The Devil. It has been a long time since I last walked openly among you in these woods your ancestors named after me."

Hunt's world tipped over and fell into the abyss.

Foley muttered an obscenity while Hunt made himself look at what had once been his father. Mother, oddly, showed no surprise. *She must be in shock.*

McBride stared at Father – at the demon in Father's body. "You're the ... Devil?"

"You lie!" High Druid Eoin Slater stepped forward. McKellen had gone pale, and a silence had fallen over his followers. If the Kail'an chief was indeed a Sooty Feather, he knew a demon when it Unveiled.

"I tell the truth, Slater," said Hunt's father, the Devil. "Your father Summoned me years ago atop Dunkail'an to Possess Lewis Hunt. That generation of Kail'ans had thought to summon one of their 'gods' into a Hunt."

"Prove it," Pat Slater shouted. If Hunt was having a difficult time accepting his father was a demon, Lucifer no less, the gathered Kail'ans were having an equally difficult time reconciling that one of their foremost gods had walked the earth for years without revealing himself to them.

A familiar expression of amusement crossed Lucifer's face. "High Druid, come hither and hear the old words. The words I told your ancestors so that you would know me from imposters."

Doubt crossed Eoin Slater's face as he hesitantly approached the man claiming to be the god Lugh, the Devil, the Prince of Lies. Lucifer whispered something into Slater's ear, and the old man shuddered.

"He speaks truly, he is Lord Lugh," Slater managed hoarsely, eyes staring at Lucifer. "Years ago, my father, Chief Hector, and others of the sept were found dead on top of Dunkail'an. Hector's son, Hamish mac Hector Kail'an, forbade we talk of it, saying only it had been dealt with. That was you? Why? Why murder and abandon your people?"

"Perhaps 'my' people rejected me on learning the truth," Lucifer said.

"Let us just say the reality did not match their expectations," Mother said with a cold smile. "Most of you present that night did not survive the disappointment, turning on one another." She spoke as if she had been there.

Hunt felt sick. Was she a demon too?

Alasdair McKellen looked lost. "My grandfather was present when you were summoned? And my father knew? Why did he not tell the sept? Why keep it even from *me*?"

Lucifer looked at him. "He had his reasons at first. And then he had no choice. Hector McKellen was dead, and Hamish McKellen preferred to spend his time practicing Law in Glasgow, in time becoming Lord McKellen of the High Court."

McBride found courage from somewhere, raising his gun. "Devil or not, I'm not returning to Miss Guillam without that contract signed."

"Consider well the enemy you choose, McBride," Mother said. "A vampyre, or Lucifer. One can pain you briefly in this life, the other perpetually in the next."

Hunt recalled Sirk telling him that only death could remove a demon from their host. His father's soul had already moved on.

McBride shifted his aim to Hunt. "I can still kill *him*, Lady Ashwood."

"Lower your gun," Lucifer snapped, unleashing an anger Hunt had only seen hinted at before. "Harm my son, and I assure you, McBride, you will have an eternity to regret it."

That dreadful threat stayed McBride's hand. "Why do you care about Lord Ashwood's damned son?" he wanted to know. Hunt was curious too.

"I've been Lewis Hunt for twenty-eight years."

Dizziness spun Hunt's head. "I don't understand," he managed. He was twenty-four. Which meant...

Lucifer glanced at Hunt. "Wilton is *my* son."

Hunt was aware that Foley was staring at him. As if he had never seen his friend before. *He thinks I'm a demon. Or the damned Antichrist.* Worse, he might not be wrong.

McBride seemed shaken too by that revelation, but when he spoke, he had regained some of his confidence. "I can still kill him. I can kill you too, devil or not."

Lucifer looked unimpressed. "Consider your soul's ultimate destination. And who rules there. And that was the last time a threat against my son will pass unanswered tonight." His voice was iron sheathed in ice.

"McBride," McKellen started to say.

"Enough. This is beyond you heathen fools." McBride said nothing further for a moment, considering Hunt's parents. "I see I need to show you I'm serious. This is for Eddie." He pointed his gun at Foley, a gunshot echoing off the trees, the tang of gunpowder lingering in the air.

Hunt's chest squeezed tight as his friend collapsed to the ground, the blood fleeing Foley's face, his eyes and mouth opening in shock. Hunt saw McBride point the gun down at Foley and pull the trigger again before Hunt could protest.

"No!" Hunt struggled in vain to break free as Johnny McBride and Harry Walker grabbed him. Tears burned his eyes as his friend began screaming. McBride regarded his handiwork with a smile of ugly satisfaction. Foley made a keening sound that ripped at Hunt's soul, a sound of agony he knew he would never forget.

"Two in the gut, he'll die slowly and feel every second of it," Walker said with relish. Both Pat and Luke Slater had been bested at fisticuffs by Foley and seemed to enjoy the bloody spectacle.

"Bastards," Hunt raged, red-hot grief and anger seizing his tongue as he spat at Walker and heard himself shout, "I killed your bloody son!"

His reckless admission made the older Walker recoil as if struck. He raised his gun to strike Hunt when McBride intervened.

"Harry! Leave him." McBride's command was absolute, Walker hesitating. "He's lying. That wee bastard's never killed anyone. I've filled my pot with harder shits than him."

"I'm telling the truth," Hunt said, staring into Walker's bloodshot eyes. "I shot Gerry in the leg and the chest. At Dunclutha. In the kitchen. He murdered people I cared about." He took a vicious pleasure in the wounds his words reopened.

"Harry. No." McBride spoke quietly, his words demanding obedience, a demand Walker reluctantly acceded to.

Lucifer's lips were pursed together as he looked down at the dying Foley. "That was a mistake." His voice was cold as the grave, filled with dark promise.

"It was a pleasure," McBride disagreed, but he failed to hide the effect Lucifer's words had on him. He was committed now, and he seemed to know he had crossed a line. The agitated Kail'ans spoke amongst themselves, clearly in disagreement with one another.

"Drag him away," Eoin Slater ordered his druids. "He can die in the wood, where his blood won't further defile this sacred place."

Grief left Hunt sick and disorientated as a crying Foley was dragged from the clearing, his hands clutching his belly while his blood stained the earth. He wouldn't die for a while, but die he would, and alone.

"I suggest no one makes any sudden moves my companion or I might interpret as hostile," a familiar voice called out.

Chapter Thirty

Hunt wiped away hot, salty tears and turned to see Professor Sirk and Dash Singh at the edge of the clearing, shotguns in hand, taken from Ashwood's gun room. *Had they arrived a few minutes earlier, Foley might still...*

"Who the hell are you two?" McBride demanded. His eyes narrowed on seeing Sirk. "You! Coming here saves me the trouble of hunting you down. I've just shot your friend, and Eddie can rest in peace when I kill you too."

"A displeasure seeing you again, Mr McBride. An occasion that won't repeat itself, I hope," Sirk said. He and Singh couldn't hope to win against the pagans and Glasgow thugs, but they looked more than capable of dispatching the first few to move. No one looked eager to make that sacrifice, and so a stalemate seemed likely for the moment.

"I suggest you lower your weapons and let us leave," Lucifer said to the McBrides and Kail'ans. "My patience nears exhaustion."

"He's the Devil. He told us," McBride said, perhaps trying to turn Sirk and Singh to his side. The valet showed no reaction and the shotgun rested comfortably in his hands.

Sirk looked at Lucifer, his eyebrows drawing together when no refutation appeared forthcoming. "An unfortunate revelation. My condolences on the loss of your father," he said to Hunt. "When did the Possession occur?"

"Before I was born," Hunt managed. Sirk's mouth opened, the professor quick to grasp the gravity of that revelation.

"We can discuss it at our leisure once this situation is resolved," Lucifer said.

"Whatever happens, you die," Walker promised Hunt, straightening his gun-arm, fear spiking through Hunt as he saw the vengeful resolve in the man's eyes.

Mother raised her right arm, followed by a *crack*. Walker fell to the ground, and Hunt saw a derringer in his mother's hand, perhaps hidden up her sleeve until she found the right moment to wield it. Jock Stewart and the McBride brothers kept their guns aimed at Lucifer, Sirk and Singh, Mother having shot her single bullet.

"As I said, any further threats against Wilton will be answered." Lucifer looked around impassively as Walker struggled to breath, coughing up blood. He Unveiled himself once again, displaying a contemptuous disregard for the guns around him.

Hunt knew both McBrides were tempted to shoot, he could see it in their eyes, but there was fear there too. How does one shoot the Devil? What if they missed? What if they *didn't* miss? With souls tarnished beyond redemption, vexing the King of Hell was not a wise choice. *Does that make me a Prince of Hell?*

"McBride," Lucifer said softly, his voice a whisper as he stood beneath an apple tree. "Death is coming here. You would be wise to leave."

"Aye," Roddy McBride breathed. He looked around. "I hope you all bloody kill each other. I'm done here." He and his brother picked up their dying friend and disappeared into the dusk-shrouded woods. Night was upon them.

"Enough of this, I say we kill them," Luke Slater shouted.

"Aye!" agreed Pat Slater. "Kill them all."

"A sacrifice to the true gods," McKellen ordered, trying to regain control of his sept. "Kill this spirit sent here to work mischief among us."

The gathered coven's faith in their religion had been shaken, but many seemed to think that killing the newcomers would kill the truth and let them return to the comfortable lies of their forebears. A majority of the Kail'ans called out their support for McKellen and the Slater brothers. Others, like the Kyles, remained silent. Eoin Slater, the High Druid, stood as if in a trance. Instead of overwhelming the Hunts, Singh and Sirk, the gathered pagans turned on one another.

Blood had been shed in this ancient place of worship and more looked imminent. Some of the Kail'ans argued and brawled amongst themselves. Others drew knives and called again for the Hunts to die, though no one looked eager to be the first to attack and be shot down. Neither Sirk nor Singh understood Gaelic, but the tone of the mob was clear enough, and they held their guns ready. Lucifer looked as if his attention was elsewhere, waiting for something.

"Kill this false god!" Pat Slater shouted, maddened by the night's revelations. "Maybe this Lewis Hunt is a trickster using magic to pass himself off as Lugh."

Lucifer stood his ground. "You forget your legends. I am Lugh, and I call my hound, *Failinis*."

A dreadful howl echoed round the woods, fear and hope intertwining in Hunt's breast. *Foley!*

A dark shape flew from the darkness and flung Eoin Slater to the ground, the old man dying before he could cry out for help. He might even have welcomed death, broken as he was by the night's hard truths.

The enraged wolf was not sated with one man's death, bringing slaughter to the clearing with fang and claw. Jock Stewart tried to aim his gun at the wolf, only to be shot by Singh.

Shotguns roared, and Kail'ans once again died in their sacred place, the werewolf running down many who tried to flee. Luke Slater led three men in a wild charge, hoping to overwhelm Singh before he could reload. There was more thunder as Sirk emptied his second barrel into them.

Hunt tripped over an old root, a shadow falling over him. "I'll kill you, at least," Pat Slater growled, his grandfather's ritual knife in hand, poised to bury it deep in Hunt's chest.

Blood sprayed over Hunt's face as the wolf that had been Tam Foley tore out Slater's hamstrings, the man screaming as he fell. Not that he screamed for long, the wolf snatching his throat in its large jaws and breaking it with a savage shake. Hunt feared the wolf would turn on him next, but some of the Kail'ans fled, instinct driving the predator to pursue those running.

Once the wolf had left, Sirk approached and helped Hunt up. "A peaceful holiday in the country you told Foley this would be, if I recall."

Hunt didn't bother responding, his attention drawn to Kay Kyle kneeling over the body of her father, killed by one of his sept as their united purpose was shattered by Lucifer's revelations.

"He died in the presence of his god," she said quietly.

"He died so that bastard McKellen could try and force my parents into selling their company," Hunt said cruelly, finding he had no pity for her. There was no sign of the young chief among the nearest bodies. Maybe he'd fled, or maybe he lay dead or dying outside the shrine.

She looked at him. "A damned Hunt and the son of Lugh. Should we hate you or revere you as one of our legends?"

"Cu Chulainn I'm not." A weariness fell over Hunt, and he found he couldn't hate her. "Maybe settle for indifference and just leave me be?"

Hunt's father approached.

Lucifer.

Kay stared. "You're really Lugh, God of Light? And the Horned Lord?"

"I am, or at least part of the inspiration behind the legends, Miss Kyle."

A discordant laugh swept past her lips. "I used to spit in your ale when you visited our tavern, the grand heir of Ashwood deigning to visit his inferiors. My family is of the line of Kail'an chiefs, descended from a sister of the mac Kail'an who escaped the Black Hunt's soldiers. My great-grandfather took the last name Kyle on returning here and marrying the then-innkeeper's daughter."

The Devil looked down at her. "I think we can assume Alasdair McKellen is done here as chief. You should leave."

"What of your hound?" She looked around fearfully for any sign of the beast Lucifer had rather theatrically claimed to be *Failinis* of legend. Foley.

"He's occupied for now. Go. Tell the others what happened here. Tell them where the search for vengeance led these people. Tell them to look to the future instead of the past."

"As Lugh commands?" she dared to ask.

"As I suggest." Lucifer's voice hardened. "Should any of you come after me or mine again, I will not exercise the same restraint I did here tonight."

Kayleigh Kyle took one look at the scattered bodies, at a 'god's' notion of 'restraint' and nodded quickly, fleeing into the darkness. In truth, Lucifer had done none of the killing tonight, leaving it to Mother, Sirk, Singh and Foley. The old religion had died this night, or at least had been culled of its more fanatical adherents.

Hunt and the others regarded one another. The Devil and his wife, parents Hunt realised he knew not at all. Professor Sirk and Dash Singh. "Thank you," Hunt said, knowing it was inadequate.

"Mr Singh is a fine tracker," Sirk said.

"It is not difficult to track a score of people," the valet said wryly. A noise drew his attention, alarm crossing his face. "It's back."

The wolf returned from hunting down Kail'ans, a growl rumbling in its throat as it regarded Hunt and the others. "Don't shoot!" Hunt said. It drew closer, bearing sharp teeth flecked with saliva.

"What would you suggest?" Sirk asked in a strained voice, his revolver aimed at the wolf, the empty shotgun lying at his feet.

"At the least, do not use silver bullets if your gun is so loaded," Lucifer said.

"What difference?" Sirk asked.

"If the wolf survives a non-silver bullet, the man will emerge with the dawn, none the worse for wear. Same as the wolf ripped free from the dying man tonight. But silver will prevent the transformation and the wolf will die, the man dying with it."

Sirk watched the wolf. "Foley looked to have been fatally wounded by McBride. Will he not still die of his wounds upon changing back?"

"Rest assured that Mr Foley will emerge from the wolf free from injury," Lucifer said. That revelation lifted a weight from Hunt's shoulders, that his friend would not die after all. So long as they didn't kill him now.

"But if you kill the wolf outright, both will die," Hunt warned. He recalled the wolf he had killed four weeks before, the one that bit Foley. *I killed a man or woman that night.* Another cross for him to bear. Or perhaps it was another milestone passed on his road to Hell.

"I've got it covered," Singh assured Sirk, his shotgun aimed at the wolf. The professor quickly broke open his gun and removed three bullets, replacing them with those cast from lead.

Lucifer fixed his gaze on the wolf. "Permit me." The wolf

crouched and snarled as Lucifer stepped towards him.

"Watch!" Hunt shouted from habit, alarm flooding him at the sight of his father facing down a wolf ready to lunge. Then he recalled who his father apparently was and wondered how he'd feel if the wolf killed him.

The wolf moved forwards, muscles taut as it prepared to leap. And then Lucifer Unveiled, the wolf yelping and backing off a few steps. It growled again, snapping its jaws, but Lucifer stood his ground, staring back. After a moment the wolf slunk off, giving them a baleful look before loping away, vanishing silently into the night.

"Should we follow?" Sirk asked. "From a cautious distance, naturally."

"There is no need," Lucifer said. "When dawn arrives, the man will return. We wait."

Sirk glanced at Lucifer. "For the light to come, heralded first by Venus."

The Morning Star.

Hours passed and dawn arrived, sleep having eluded Hunt, though he feigned it to avoid conversation. He looked around, tendrils of light piercing the canopy from the east as the sun finally rose. Bodies lay scattered around the shrine, among them Stewart and the three Slaters. Kyle the innkeeper. Hunt didn't see Constable Fowler among the dead. Perhaps he had escaped the Lewswood, or perhaps the wolf had run him down out there in the darkness. They did find Alasdair McKellen just outside the clearing, killed by a knife wound. Slain by one of his own.

Chapter Thirty-One

They all sat at the dining room table in Ashwood Lodge, joined by a washed and dressed Foley, the tension palpable. They had found Foley lying naked and dazed not far from the shrine and showing no sign of the wounds given to him by McBride. A robe removed from a dead Kail'an preserved his modesty on the journey back.

It had been a long walk from the Lewswood to Ashwood, the fleeing Kail'ans or McBrides having taken the wagons left at the edge of the forest.

Hunt sat at the far end of the table, opposite Lucifer, whose valet Singh stood behind him.

"You have questions," Lucifer said with vast understatement. Hunt refused to think of him as his father. Foley's eyes returning to Hunt, as if he looked at a stranger.

"My most pressing question is why I should not send you back to Hell right now," Sirk said to Lucifer. Foley said nothing, perhaps still dwelling on the previous night. He had been shot in the belly twice and left to die, only to turn into a wolf.

"*Samiel* is not yours to kill," Singh told Sirk. "If he is to be returned to Hell, that privilege is mine."

"*Samiel?*" Sirk asked. Hunt was more curious about the valet's statement than the multitude of names his infamous father wore.

"My true name," Lucifer said. "After the Fall, my fellow *Grigori* called me Lightbringer in ire at the consequences of our defeat and the lethal sun that awaited us here."

Goosebumps rose on Hunt's arms as Lucifer Unveiled. Except it felt different to what he had felt during the earlier confrontation, he realised. Lucifer was not the one Unveiling. "You're a demon, too," he accused Singh. An alien name came to Hunt as he looked on the valet, but he couldn't articulate it. Not yet.

"I am no demon." There was contempt in Singh's voice, anger at Hunt's assumption. "I'm *Seraphim*."

"Is there an explanation forthcoming?" Sirk asked, his hand resting on his revolver.

Lucifer gathered his thoughts. "What do you know of the aftermath of the War in Heaven?"

Sirk answered. "You led a rebellion against the archangel Michael, losing. The two hundred or so rebels who survived, including you, were exiled to Earth to become the first vampyres, the *Grigori*. Progenitors of the *Nephilim*, the first humans turned undead. The rebel angels who died in heaven were exiled to Hell, demons only able to walk the earth by Possessing humans."

"A succinct summary," Lucifer said in approval. "But what of *Mikiel*'s angels who perished?"

"They were not restored?" Hunt asked.

"It does not work that way," Lucifer said. "Approximately 100 million angels died on each side, leaving *Mikiel* with a diminished Heavenly Host of the remaining 100 million. His casualties could not simply be resurrected in Heaven. Instead, they were scattered to various worlds, doomed to reincarnate as mortals over and over. The *Seraphim*."

Hunt was not the only one to look at Singh who stood stiffly.

"I know not the exact numbers, but a few thousand of us were sent to *this* world," Singh explained. "We are born, we live, we die, and then are born again. Sometimes we recover knowledge of who we truly are, other times we live a full life ignorant of our origin. Memories of past lives are sometimes clear, other times less so. Heaven is like an unremembered dream. Thankfully, perhaps," he added softly.

Sirk looked thoughtful. "So, angels are little different from demons. Two sides of the same coin. What of the souls of those you Possess?"

Singh's dark eyes locked with his. "We inhabit our new bodies at the point of conception. No soul is displaced. We are not Summoned."

"And between lives?" Sirk asked. Ever curious, the professor would ask questions until noon if allowed.

"I have no memories of that. We exist in a limbo."

"Purgatory," Foley muttered.

Singh looked at him. "As good a name as any."

"You're an angel. He's the Devil. And you're his valet?" Foley shook his head.

"Lord Ashwood pays my salary, but Lucifer is not my master," Singh said.

"He is most capable. And it allows him to keep an eye on me on behalf of *Mikiel*." Lucifer's gaze flickered to Hunt. "Which was a condition for the *Seraphim* not correcting a certain ... anomaly I created."

"Anomaly?" Sirk asked.

Lucifer started to give Singh a warning look. "*Kariel–*"

Singh pointed at Hunt, ignoring Lucifer. "Him. I do not know if he was permitted by *Mikiel* or how *Samiel* managed to conceive him, but *Mikiel* visited me in a dream years ago, tasking me to keep watch on *Samiel*. And on his offspring."

Hunt found all eyes on him, and he knew they would never look at him the same. *I'm tainted. A demon's spawn. The Devil's son.*

"He is unusual?" Trust Sirk to indulge his curiosity first and foremost.

"He is unique. Possession renders a human body unable to conceive. Even *Seraphim* like myself are infertile." There was an ancient pain in Singh's voice, perhaps the echo of hundreds of lives lived who never had children.

Hunt was aware of Foley watching him, but he wouldn't meet his gaze, afraid of what he'd see there.

"Demons and *Seraphim* sound very much alike," Sirk said, his misgivings towards Singh – *Kariel* – clear.

Singh answered. "When a demon's Vessel dies, it returns to Hell. When a *Seraphim*'s Vessel dies, it is reborn in another. Beyond that, the chief difference between angels and demons is that the demons chose the wrong side. Chose *him*."

Lucifer barked a laugh. "I would contend we chose the *losing* side. Whether we were right or wrong remains to be seen."

Singh gave him a dark look. "Defeat and exile has done little to cure your arrogance, *Samiel*."

"What did you fight over?" Sirk asked. "It is commonly believed it was over God's command to His angels to bow down to Mankind."

Both angel and demon gave Sirk an exasperated look. "I don't quite understand what we fought over," Singh admitted. "In this form our comprehension of existence is … limited. Think of your mind trapped in an ant's, trying to explain your science to other ants."

"But rest assured, your species was not the cause of the rift in Heaven. In a universe vaster than you can comprehend, we were barely aware of such primitives," Lucifer said. He glanced at Singh. "And you accuse me of arrogance."

Hunt tensed as Sirk asked, "And your son, is he demon or human?"

"A hybrid. Just as your body was born of your parents, and your soul was born of theirs, the same is true of Wilton." Lucifer looked at Hunt as he spoke. *My father. The Devil.*

"I'm nothing like you," Hunt said, returning that stare.

Sirk cleared his throat. "Not entirely true, Hunt. Your ability to twice resist a *Nephilim*'s Mesmer was never explained. Until now."

Lucifer gave his son a knowing look. "And you've Unveiled at least twice that I know of. The first was the night of the trouble at the Necropolis."

Hunt's breath caught in his throat. That was the night he killed George Rannoch. He remembered Rannoch Unveiling, and something dark and old within him rising to challenge the *Nephilim*. A look of shock had appeared on Rannoch's face, and Hunt had shot him. *I Unveiled.* "The second time?" he whispered.

"The night before last, when you were hunting the wolf with Mr Foley. If I were to surmise, he turned into the wolf while you were with him, but something happened to keep him at bay?"

Hunt nodded despite himself. That cold feeling had risen inside him, and the wolf had shied back. At the time, he supposed part of the wolf was still Foley and recognised him.

"Every angel and demon Unveils differently. As part of me is part of you, ours is the same. That is how I was able to sense you Unveiling that night at the Necropolis, despite the distance," Lucifer said.

"Unveiling works on werewolves?" Sirk asked.

"For myself – and Wilton – yes. A result of my … participation in their creation long ago. My unwilling participation." Lucifer seemed reluctant to say more.

"You knew I'm a werewolf. How?" Foley asked. He'd mostly just sat there in silence.

"I first suspected when you arrived, telling me of the wolf attack and your injury. There are no natural wolves left in Britain, and their reputation for attacking people was one not wholly justified. As the full moon drew closer, I sensed the taint in you grow stronger."

"You say wolves do not normally attack people. Their recent actions in attacking Hunt and Foley suggests otherwise," Sirk said. "And we all witnessed what Foley … forgive me, the wolf Foley turned into, did to those unfortunates earlier."

"You confuse wolves with werewolves," Lucifer said. "Werewolves are not a natural creation. Perhaps I'll tell you of their origins, one day." He noted Sirk's interest was piqued. "But not today." He looked at Hunt. "Your mother can tell you the circumstances of my Summoning."

Mother opened her mouth to speak but Hunt cut her off. "I don't want to hear it. I don't want to hear how you could marry Satan, bear his child, and still sit in church every Sunday with the damned Enemy by your side." Anger rose within him. "And you have the gall to lecture *me!*"

"There are other concerns we should address," Sirk said before Mother could respond.

"Such as?" Mother asked, her face flushed and eyes narrowed in anger as she stared at her son.

"The McBrides have fled. McKellen is dead and the more fanatical of his sept killed or routed, but we are still in danger," Sirk said.

Lucifer nodded slightly. "Margot Guillam desires the Browning Shipping Company. McBride and McKellen failed, but if McBride learns Foley still lives, he may act again."

Hunt tried to concentrate on the threat to him and his friends (and family, such as it was). "We thought the Sooty Feathers content to leave us be, but that's no longer the case."

Sirk cleared his throat. "Before travelling here to warn you of the Sooty Feather interest in you, I assisted Lady Delaney in the destruction of a Crypt of ghouls hidden beneath the Imperial Mill. This mill – before I blew it up – was owned by

Lady MacInesker through her foundation. It was from Lady MacInesker's private papers that we learned of Lady MacInesker reporting on the Browning Shipping Company to Margot Guillam, and thus anticipated a move against you."

"This Lady MacInesker would seem to be a person of interest to us," Foley said. "Or has Lady Delaney already sent her on to 'Lord Ashwood's' other 'estate'?"

"Not as of yet. Lady Delaney intimated that she has been invited to a garden party at Dunkellen House, the home of Lady MacInesker," Sirk said. "I believe whatever misfortune Lady Delaney intends to befall Lady MacInesker will happen then and there."

"An interesting coincidence," Mother said.

"How so?" asked Sirk, saving Hunt the need to address her.

"Does the similarity in name not strike you? Dunkail'an, the ancient seat of the Kail'ans, and Dunkellen, the estate of the MacIneskers?"

"I assume there is a link?" Sirk asked.

Mother nodded slightly. "Indeed, Professor. In the mid-Eighteenth century Neil MacInesker married June McKellen. The MacIneskers built a new house on the family estate in the south of Glasgow, from the ruins of an old castle. They named it Dunkellen House, in tribute, I expect, to Dunkail'an. By that time, Dunkail'an had been renamed Ash Hill, and Dunlew was a ruin owned by the Hunts."

"So, a son of the last Kail'an chief survived the attack by Sir Geoffrey Hunt. Mac Kail'an – son of Kail'an – was anglicised to McKellen. He had a daughter, June, who married the MacIneskers of Glasgow. A connection between the McKellens and the Sooty Feathers," Hunt said aloud as he fitted the pieces together.

"Yes. The eldest son of Neil and June MacInesker was also called Neil, inheriting the Dunkellen estate. The second son, Cullen, took his mother's maiden name, McKellen, and in time challenged Harold Hunt, the 3rd Baron of Ashwood, to a duel." Mother sipped her tea. "McKellen won, regaining Dunlew Castle."

"What now?" Hunt asked. He had left Glasgow – fled, if he was honest – to escape this otherworld of demons and death, only to find it waiting for him here. To find he was irrevocably a part of it. That there was no escaping it.

"I suggest we travel to Dunkellen House and assure the Sooty Feathers we find there that it would be in their best interests to exclude us from any future intrigue," Lucifer said. "I daresay we'll find a number attending this garden party."

"And if Margot Guillam is there and is 'unconvinced'?" Hunt asked, looking into the cold blue eyes that mirrored his own.

"I made a deal almost thirty years ago with Niall Fisher. Margot Guillam would be wise to honour that agreement, Wilton."

"All well and good," Foley said. "But how will we get into this garden party? Climb a wall and sneak in?"

"You forget who I am," Lucifer said, as if his identity hadn't been a spectre hanging over the room since their return. Lucifer smiled faintly. "The new Lord Ashwood. As such, Lady MacInesker sent us invitations some weeks ago. We had not thought to attend, but the situation now warrants us leaving Ashwood a little earlier than planned."

"Three invitations only, I fear." Mother looked at Foley and Sirk. "Unless you gentlemen wish to pose as carriage driver and valet to Wilton, I fear you'll be unable to attend directly."

"We can stay in the village of Kaleshaws, an ace up your sleeve if required, so to speak," Sirk suggested. "If the pestilence in the area still persists, I can offer my assistance."

"Pestilence?" Lucifer asked.

"A peculiar malady, one that strikes its victims with fever and lethargy, but last I heard, no one yet perished from it. I'm most interested in observing some of the sick." Sirk spoke with an air of detached curiosity.

"Mr Foley can assist you," Lucifer said without bothering to learn Foley's opinion on the matter. Foley didn't look particularly pleased but offered no comment either way.

"A ferry will convey us to Oban in good time." Mother said. "From there, one of my ships can return us to Glasgow."

"Then we're agreed," Lucifer said. "We travel to Dunkellen House to ensure an end to Sooty Feather interference. One way or another."

A chill went through Hunt. *One way or another.*

Chapter Thirty-Two

Foley waved his hands in weary irritation, a swarm of horseflies having plagued him ever since he left the village near Dunkellen House. He and Sirk had arrived in Kaleshaws village that morning, travelling separately from the Hunts. The pestilence Sirk had mentioned had worsened, more villagers and neighbouring farmers becoming sick. And after many days of lingering between life and death, the first of those afflicted had succumbed the night before.

"What are you hoping to find?" Foley asked. He wondered if Sirk was just looking for an excuse to get them out of the village, away from the sick and dying. The professor was a qualified medical doctor, even if he hadn't officially practised in many years, but he seemed confident the facecloths they wore would protect them. Foley had more confidence in Sirk's suggestion that they drink weak ale rather than water from the river.

"The cause of the pestilence, Foley." He led the way with purpose. "Why is the village afflicted but none from Dunkellen House?"

"You think a dead cow or sheep is rotting upstream?"

"If there were some cases of dysentery, that would be a reasonable theory. But I've seen nothing like this sickness before, to linger so long before killing. And for the first to die in the same night? No, there is something else at work here."

"The river is miles long," Foley pointed out.

"If the cause is in the river, I suspect we'll find it between the village and Dunkellen House," Sirk said. "Otherwise the family and staff would have fallen sick."

They forced their way into a grove of trees and thorn-bushes, using sticks to force a way through. Foley wondered what Hunt was up to. Probably preparing for his ball and a night of drinking fine wine and expensive whisky. *He sure as hell isn't beating through jagged bushes looking for ... whatever we're looking for.*

Something in the water caught his eye. "Professor, over here."

"A moment." Sirk was making slower progress through the vegetation. "What do you see?"

Foley pointed at the water's edge. "A dead animal. A horse I think."

"Do not get too close to it," Sirk cautioned as they navigated their way towards the river.

"It's dead, I don't think it can hurt us," Foley said.

"The dead and sick villagers might disagree."

Which made sense. Foley studied the dead animal from a distance, half of it above a river shrunk by too much sun and too little rain. In normal times, the horse would be completely submerged. It was pale, the colour of burned ash, a stench of rot coming from it. "You think it's fouled the river?"

Sirk peered at it over his spectacles. "I think there is more to this pestilence than that. The sickness acts like none I've seen before. How did the horse get here? It would not willingly go through those thorns, I think, and the bushes near the edge are crushed."

Foley noticed that too. "You think it was pushed into the water? Maybe it came down the river and died here."

"Look at its abdomen, Foley. This poor beast did not die naturally."

Sure enough, its guts had been ripped open. *Why do such a thing?* "Why?"

"I do not know. I'm reluctant to wildly speculate, until we learn more."

"We should pull it out of the water," Foley said, not relishing the idea.

"Carefully. I brought gloves, which we will dispose of afterwards."

Dragging the dead horse from the river took all their strength, the animal rotting and bloated. Foley shuddered at the thought of the unsuspecting villagers drinking water from the passing river, bathing in it…

"What now?" Foley asked, resisting the urge to rub the sweat from his brow.

"We return to the village and find something combustible. We return here and burn the corpse," Sirk said. He carefully removed his gloves and dropped them near the corpse.

"And that will end the pestilence?" Foley asked, likewise disposing of his own gloves.

"Unlikely, but I pray it will reduce the number of new cases." There was a grim, almost fearful expression on his face as he looked down at the dead horse.

"What is it?"

Sirk spoke quietly, as if fearing to be overheard. "'And behold a pale horse, and he that sat upon him, his name was Death, and hell followed him.'"

*

Redfort looked out of the carriage window as it rattled along the country roads on the outskirts of Glasgow, bumping through the Dunkellen estate. The estate was mostly green fields, pockets of woodland remaining on land too rugged to farm. Most of the people lived in villages of small cottages, the rest tenants renting the scattered farms. There was a weaving and cloth industry in the village of Kaleshaws, still surviving despite competition from Paisley, Lanark and the city factories; and a small coal mine; but Redfort knew the estate's best asset was its proximity to Glasgow, a city desperate for land to expand onto.

Dunkellen House was hidden from view by woods covering much of the surrounding land, perhaps retained as a buffer between the house and the rest of the estate. Onwards the carriage travelled, the trees thinning out to reveal fields on either side of the dirt road, Highland cattle grazing to the right. Redfort looked to his left, seeing a moss-stained stone motte in the distance running along the furthest edge of the field, perhaps a remnant of an older house or castle. The MacIneskers had owned this land a long time.

Henderson sat silently across from him, lost in his own thoughts. Jones was with the rest of the company who were to eliminate the Carpathian Circus, travelling by wagon. Meantime the company was to camp on a field within the estate. A number of Sooty Feathers were to gather at Dunkellen House, and Regent Guillam wanted no repeat of

Dunclutha. They were also to keep away any villagers trying to flee to the house in fear of the sickness still ravaging the area.

Dunkellen House appeared on the left side of the road as the carriage passed through the gates, flanked by trees on either side. It came to a halt, and Redfort waited until a footman opened the door to let him out. He sensed a wrongness in the air, like a shadow just out of sight that never came into view. *My imagination?*

The Georgian house was compact and austere-looking, four floors high and extended to the east and west by newly constructed single-floor pavilions. Redfort stood on the cobbled yard while his luggage was unloaded. The butler and a further two footmen stood at attention next to the entrance, awaiting the arrival of their mistress. Fully unloaded, the driver waited to lead the carriage through the western gatehouse to the lower courtyard.

Lady MacInesker emerged from the house, dressed in a beige dress. "Bishop Redfort, it is an honour to welcome you to my home."

Redfort inclined his head, smiling jovially. "I was humbled by your invitation, Lady MacInesker. Your foundation does godly work, and the Church will aid you however it can." The foundation's latest project was decidedly *ungodly*, but who was Redfort to cast stones? A pity it had suffered such a catastrophic setback with the destruction of the Imperial Mill.

"Greatly appreciated, your Grace, greatly appreciated. Do come inside and freshen up." She looked at the elder of the footmen. "Gareth will attend to you during your stay. Your man may sleep in the visiting valets' bedroom."

"Too generous, Lady MacInesker. Henderson will stay with my men camping in the field you have set aside for them," Redfort said spitefully, denying his secretary the relative comfort of the room provided for guests' valets.

The entrance hall was grand, black and white marble squares covering the floor. It sat between the basement and ground floor levels. White marbled stairs to the left and right of the hall led up to the main floor, a varnished mahogany banister installed on the inner sides. Flanked by the two sets of stairs leading up was a set of stairs leading down to the lower entrance hall and servants' quarters. The mahogany wall panels had been painted white, slightly paler than the cream rococo plasterwork decorating the walls and ceilings.

Silver vases bursting with fresh summer flowers sat atop tall marble pillars, flanking the lower entrance hall archway. Portraits lined the staircase walls, memorials to family members long gone.

Gareth the footman led Redfort up to the ground floor and down the central corridor. A light-grey carpet ran down the centre of the corridor, revealing polished oak flooring to either side. Ionic columns supported part of the floor above, more decorative coving added to where the walls and ceilings met. A gilded mirror sat above a marble fireplace halfway down the corridor, further portraits and landscapes hanging from the walls.

Redfort was impressed by the house and had pondered acquiring such a retreat for himself. But he preferred living in the heart of Glasgow, feeling the beat of the city's pulse. *Perhaps when I retire.*

A winding staircase waited at the end of the hall, taking Redfort up to the first floor. Gareth opened a bedroom door and stood aside for Redfort to enter, thereafter following him inside. He was to act as Redfort's valet during his stay. A private man, Redfort was content to let his butler Hendry perform that role while at home, and for his hosts to provide him a footman while visiting. Other than a cook and housekeeper, he employed Henderson as secretary, and Jones to attend to more ... practical tasks.

The bedroom was sparse but comfortable, floral cream wallpaper decorating the walls, a mahogany dressing table, wardrobe and chest of drawers proving more than ample for the two nights he was to stay. The four-poster bed looked old and worn, but Redfort was satisfied the bedding was clean.

*

Lady MacInesker's cook had prepared a fine meal, in Heron's opinion, either a late lunch or an early dinner. He was no dancer himself, lacking the natural grace, but he knew those present who intended to attend Lady MacInesker's ball in the village hall would appreciate having the time to digest their food.

"My compliments to your cook, Lady MacInesker," Bishop Redfort said. "I have an excellent cook of my own, or I would be tempted to steal yours."

"Mrs Howe will be gratified to hear her efforts appreciated, your Grace," Lady MacInesker said. There were eight at the table, Lady MacInesker deftly managing to arrange an equal split of gender. She had been escorted into the dining room by the elderly Lord Provost, Sir Wilbur Poole. Bishop Redfort had escorted Mrs Carlton, a lady of means in Glasgow whose husband had been bedridden for some time. Lady Delaney had been escorted by a Doctor Essex, a London physician of some renown. A lowly banker in such refined social company, Heron had been coupled with Lady Delaney's young Irish companion, Miss Knox.

"Your invitation for tonight's ball and tomorrow's garden party was a pleasant surprise, Lady MacInesker," Lady Delaney said. "As is your hospitality tonight and tomorrow night. I fear my old bones would protest overmuch had I to travel here from the city both days."

Lady Delaney looked anything but frail in Heron's opinion. Those gathered were among the minority privileged enough to stay in Dunkellen House for the garden party. Most of the other guests who lived too far to return home were to lodge in the better of the local inns, those away from the afflicted village.

"Do you look forward to the ball, Miss Knox?" Lady MacInesker asked. "I had a passion for them when I was your age."

"Yes, Lady MacInesker," the young woman answered.

"Will you be dancing, Mr Heron?" Lady Delaney asked. Her name tickled Heron's memory for some reason, though he was almost certain she did not have an account with the bank.

"It is not for me," he said deprecatingly. "I'll remain here with Sir Wilbur and Bishop Redfort."

"Speak for yourself, Mr Heron. I enjoy a good waltz," the bishop said, causing a few expressions of surprise around the table. A dancing bishop risked becoming a figure of ridicule, though Heron held no illusions about the sort of man Redfort was. He hadn't become a bishop or a Sooty Feather Councillor through charitable works.

"You may count on my company, Mr Heron," Sir Wilbur

said with a cough. "My dancing days are many years behind me."

"I shall also be staying behind. With Lady MacInesker's permission, I should like to peruse her library," Dr Essex said. He had said little, as if his mind were elsewhere. The renowned London physician had offered his services to the afflicted villagers, though to date had yet to diagnose a cause or cure. Lady MacInesker's gratitude had extended to giving him a room in the house and an invitation to her ball and party.

"Of course, Doctor."

Heron knew why his own invitation had been extended from the garden party tomorrow to include not only his attendance at tonight's ball, but a guest room within Dunkellen House itself. Money. The MacInesker Foundation had borrowed extensively to renovate and upgrade the Imperial Mill, a loan that the foundation had been comfortably repaying thanks to the mill's enviable productivity.

Until it suffered catastrophic damage. The official story cited an explosion caused by a leak from an unknown gas pipe running nearby, but Heron suspected sabotage, perhaps ordered by the demon Erik Keel. Regardless, while insurance would cover the cost to restore the mill, the foundation still owed Heron Crowe a lot of money.

If Lady MacInesker believed special treatment would win her a reprieve from Heron, she was in for a disappointment. The bank was in a precarious position itself, having lost investor confidence. Only Regent Guillam's influence kept the Sooty Feather members from closing their accounts. Heron might be convinced to reduce some of the repayments until the mill was operational again, but that was as far as he would go.

*

"An excellent luncheon," Redfort congratulated his host. While the other guests decamped from the dining room to the music room, Redfort took the opportunity to meet Lady MacInesker in private.

"Thank you, your Grace," she said. She handed him a small glass of brandy, retaining one for herself.

Redfort looked around the library, similar in design to the main corridor, partitioned by Ionic columns. The library extended into the eastern pavilion, the house's expansion overseen by the late Sir Neil MacInesker. The *latest* late Sir Neil MacInesker, rather, it being a common name in the family. Bookcases had been built into the walls, filled with several thousand books. He wondered idly how many were for reading and how many were for show. A piano sat at the eastern end of the library next to a large window.

Lively music sounded from next door, the music room. A local organist had been hired by Lady MacInesker to entertain the guests prior to their leaving for the ball.

"A successful day for the foundation, I hope," Lady MacInesker said. Seven guests were a small number, but most were persons of means and position. One of those guests was the reason Redfort was keen to speak with the lady of the house.

"Yes, I'm sure you – I mean the foundation – will benefit from some generous donations as a result of tonight. You spoke most passionately at dinner about its goals and aspirations. Let us hope they will be enough to restore the Imperial Mill." Redfort's presence had been requested to show that the foundation had the Church's support.

She looked at him sharply. "Spare me your sly tone, Bishop. Did you wish to speak with me about something important? If it can wait, I've guests to entertain."

"You can play the hostess in a few minutes, *Tertia*," Redfort said.

The use of Lady MacInesker's Council title quietened her ire. "If this is Council business, you should have raised it earlier. *Quintus*." Her use of his own title was deliberate, a reminder that her third seat on the Council was senior to his fifth.

Redfort was unimpressed. Aside from the *Primus* or *Prima*, seniority on the Council was rarely observed, the hierarchy truly determined by the grit of the individuals. "In the spring you were *Octavia* and today you are *Tertia*. Impressive. Except that it surely cannot have escaped your notice that we are dropping like flies?"

A troubled look crossed her face. "Is that what you wish to discuss? Our fragile mortality?"

Redfort sipped his brandy. "In a manner of speaking. What do you know of Lady Delaney?"

Lady MacInesker pursed her lips. "Little. A wealthy widow with too much time and money on her hands, perhaps increasingly aware that she has fewer years ahead than behind, and eager to assure that when her time comes, St Peter will not find her good works wanting."

"She is the widow of Sir Andrew Delaney." He saw recognition spark in her eyes at the mention of that name.

"He went mad, did he not? Killed his children and was killed in turn by Lady Delaney in self-defence?"

"I forget, this was before your time in the Society." She had joined the Sooty Feathers ten years ago, replacing her husband on the Council after his death over the winter. Odd, but from what Redfort had gathered, the MacIneskers enjoyed a long association with the Sooty Feathers, there always being one of the family sitting on the Council.

"Lady Delaney was connected to the Society?" Lady MacInesker asked.

"No, but her husband briefly was. He was fully initiated into the Sooty Feathers, only to have a crisis of conscience. He tried to leave. Rather than just kill him, the Council had him Possessed by *Beliel* in order to seize control of his business interests." Redfort had only been an initiate himself in the Society at that time, a lowly clergyman still unaware of the undead.

Lady MacInesker's eyes widened. "Now I recall. *Beliel* lost control and killed his Vessel's children. Regent Edwards forbade the Society from Summoning him again." She exhaled. "I had not connected that tale with Lady Delaney. Why is she here? A coincidence?"

"I think not." Redfort peered down into his brandy glass for a moment. "I spotted Lady Delaney on a paddle steamer departing Largs the morning after the Dunclutha incident. In the company of Templars and the newly rescued Wilton Hunt."

Chagrin crossed Lady MacInesker's face. "She is a Templar?"

He tapped his glass. "Aligned with them, certainly." He recalled Steiner had been in the company of a woman the night Benjamin Howard had been abducted from the theatre by the Templars, a woman not dissimilar in build from Lady Delaney. "A coincidence that the Imperial Mill is attacked by two women and a man shortly after a Templar ally takes an interest in the foundation that owns it? I think not." The mill workers' account of the raid had been broadly consistent, some even claiming the younger woman had worked at the mill for some days.

"We must deal with her." Her hands shook, and no wonder. She had invited a possible enemy into her home.

Redfort snorted. "How? Surely you don't intend to just kill her? I rather suspect your other guests will take it ill if you murder her in front of them."

"Then what do you suggest?" she snapped. Her face was pale; someone had been killing Councillors, and *Tertia* perhaps feared Lady Delaney was the killer and had come to empty yet another council seat. Redfort rather doubted Lady Delaney was behind the killings – certainly not the late *Tertius*, Silas Thatcher. The Templars had even less tolerance for necromancers than the Council. *Enemies are gathering, and we are weak when we should be strong.*

"I'll speak with her, subtly let her know that we know whom she is friends with." Redfort smiled thinly. "I rather think she will *shit* herself."

*

Not a fan of organ music (it reminded him of work), Redfort was pleased when the organist finally finished 'entertaining' everyone in the music room. The room itself was tastefully appointed, the floor carpeted red, its walls painted red in contrast to the white ceiling. A white marble fireplace sat cold and clean, the offending organ installed on the east wall. Large and small Old Master paintings hung from the walls, an oak table placed in the centre of the room.

Two couches and a pair of chairs provided seating for those guests wishing to sit, others standing. Redfort had been too distracted by Lady Delaney's offending presence to pay the other guests much mind.

The lady in question stood in a corner of the room, ostensibly admiring a painted depiction of a ship braving a wild sea. Noting she stood apart from the other guests, Redfort seized the opportunity to have a word with her.

"Lady Delaney, a pleasure seeing you again."

She glanced at him. "It has been many years, your Grace."

He smiled. "More recently than that, Lady Delaney."

She looked at him enquiringly.

"We were on the same paddle steamer sailing from Largs to Glasgow in the spring," he explained, looking her in the eye. *And we both know who you were with.*

Lady Delaney smiled, her grey eyes betraying no evident alarm at her unmasking. "I recall now. You were Bishop-elect then, were you not? After Bishop Mann was so awfully murdered. It's fortunate you were available to take his place, your Grace."

"Fortunate, yes." He tried to shift the conversation back to their brief meeting. If Delaney did indeed know Steiner, then she likely knew of Redfort's role in the previous bishop's assassination. "What took you to Largs?"

"I was hoping to meet some friends," she said easily.

"I trust you found them in good health?" He had expected alarm, but her eyes reflected only amusement.

"One of them, yes." She smiled. "I met up with the other several days later, a mutual acquaintance, finding him in good health. A state which continues."

She's talking about Steiner. "How delightful. Perhaps one day I'll meet him again." *On my terms. He can grant me the very great favour of dying.*

"He'd like that very much," Lady Delaney assured him. "Did you enjoy your own time in Largs? I understand there was an unfortunate accident in Dunclutha House, with a number of fatalities."

"A lowly clergyman like myself was not invited to Dunclutha," he lied.

"But lofty enough to be invited here by Lady MacInesker," Lady Delaney remarked. "How fortunate for you, on both counts."

Redfort felt a grudging admiration for Lady Delaney. Unlike Steiner, she took time to play the game; the Templar inquisitor had been all threats and scowls, showing no aptitude for subtlety or intrigue. *Two decades have passed since the death of her husband. I wonder how much of that time she has spent working against us from the shadows, the Society never suspecting.*

"Laudable of you to support Lady MacInesker's

foundation. Donations will be essential to the restoration of the Imperial Mill," Redfort said. *More of your handiwork?*

"A terrible accident, what befell the mill," Lady Delaney said. "I hope the foundation has learned not to make the same mistakes this time around."

"I'm sure they took the accident to heart. I'll leave you to admire the paintings and bid you a good afternoon." He smiled thinly. "Until the ball, at least."

"Good afternoon, Bishop Redfort." She bared her teeth in a smile. "I understand it is to take place in the village hall. Let us hope you do not catch this sickness."

"Lady MacInesker has ensured that the village hall remain closed since the illness began," Redfort assured her. "And besides, I enjoy a robust health."

He rejoined Lady MacInesker, who looked at him enquiringly, a glass of wine in her hand. "Did you frighten her off?"

"Not noticeably," he admitted. "But she knows I know who she is and whom she is acquainted with. I doubt she'll try any mischief here." He paused. "All the same, have your people keep an eye on her." He was tempted to arrange a more permanent solution to the Delaney problem, but prudence stayed his hand. Neither Lady MacInesker nor Regent Guillam would thank him for bringing undue attention down on Dunkellen House.

"An ancestor of your late husband's?" Lady Delaney had joined them unnoticed, looking at a faded old portrait on the wall of a man wearing a white ruff and a decorative black breastplate.

"Yes," Lady MacInesker said after a shocked pause at Lady Delaney so brazenly joining them. "Sir Neil MacInesker, who lived and died in the 16th century."

"Your son and late husband are called Neil. A family name, I assume?"

Lady MacInesker nodded. "Yes. We know it goes back at least to the mid-13th century, records showing a Sir Neil MacInesker owned a castle near here. The name has passed down the family." There was something in her tone, as if she was enjoying a secret, but also reluctant to say too much about her husband's ancestry. She gave Redfort an oddly furtive look, as if her reticence was more to do with him than Delaney.

Chapter Thirty-Three

The carriage took Kerry and Caroline to the village hall where a small orchestra played music, the centre of the wooden floor set aside for dancing. Maybe thirty guests were present, so far, less than a third staying at Dunkellen House. The rest either lived close enough to travel by carriage or had hired rooms at the local inns. Kerry had seen no signs of the pestilence, Lady MacInesker taking pains to ensure none of her guests were upset by the distressing sight of sick villagers.

So far, Caroline's etiquette lessons were paying off, Kerry not having embarrassed herself. A few of the older guests remembered Lady Delaney and accepted Kerry as her companion without question. She knew she should participate in conversations, but not too brightly. She should speak in a clear but subdued tone. And she must *never* discuss politics or contradict a man.

The voice of Peel, Lady MacInesker's butler, rose over the din of conversation and music. "Ladies and gentlemen, I have the honour to present Lord and Lady Ashwood, and their son, the Honourable Mr Hunt."

Kerry turned in surprise, and sure enough Wilton Hunt followed a middle-aged couple into the hall. He looked very fine in his formal tails, a different man to the one she remembered from the theatre or at the Necropolis.

"Ah, I'm delighted you could come," Lady MacInesker said in greeting.

Bishop Redfort looked surprised on seeing them, but he quickly assumed a more welcoming expression. "Lord and Lady Ashwood. Mr Hunt. A pleasure seeing you all again. I trust the journey from Ashwood was not overtiring?"

"It was tolerable, your Grace," Lord Ashwood said. Kerry saw a similarity between the two Hunt men. She also sensed a tension between parents and son, the latter looking uncomfortable in their company.

*

"Lady Delaney, Miss Knox, this is Lord and Lady Ashwood, and their son Mr Hunt," Lady MacInesker said. Hunt found himself staring at Kerry Knox, the actress he recalled from the theatre and Lady Delaney's house now looking every inch the socialite.

She wore a dark blue evening dress tailored to her figure, its upper sleeves puffed out. Her chestnut hair was arranged in tight curls atop her head, freckles sprayed across her pale face. They had first met at the theatre, Miss Knox playing Lechery to Hunt's Lucifer in *Doctor Faustus*. *Lucifer ... Fate enjoys a joke.* Both had infiltrated the production under false pretences, searching for the Sooty Feather Benjamin Howard.

"Lord and Lady Ashwood, Mr Hunt, this is Lady Delaney and her companion, Miss Knox," Lady MacInesker said, finishing the introductions. After courtesies were exchanged, she left them to speak with other guests.

Mother and Lady Delaney made a little small talk, all the while trying to get the other's measure. Hunt was amused to see his mother had met her equal, for once. *Both were married to demons, for one thing.* Though Lady Delaney had killed her Possessed husband; Mother had borne hers a son.

"…and my son, Mr Wilton Hunt," Mother was saying. Hunt found himself under scrutiny from both ladies, not a comfortable sensation.

"Miss Knox and I are already acquainted with Mr Hunt," Lady Delaney said. "As well as Professor Sirk and Mr Foley. I trust they are in good health?"

"Excellent health," Hunt said. "Professor Sirk heard of the illness here and has offered his services. Mr Foley is helping him." If the Hunts found more trouble than they could handle in Dunkellen House, Foley and Sirk were to assist.

"I'm pleased to hear Professor Sirk found you. He had a matter of some urgency to discuss with you," Lady Delaney said.

"That matter was resolved," Hunt assured her. *Damn me, but was it resolved!*

"Did you enjoy your journey, Miss Knox?" Lucifer asked.

"The view from the carriage was lovely, Lord Ashwood," Miss Knox said. She had refined her accent, her time with Lady Delaney having smoothed her rougher edges. Had Hunt not known her previously, he would have accepted her as a well-bred young lady without question.

Miss Knox's acting skills and Lady Delaney's tutorage had paid off; she played the part of Lady Delaney's companion well. The Sooty Feathers gathered would smile at the pretty young woman, never suspecting she and her mentor worked against them. Even having heard Sirk's account of their raid on the mill, Hunt found it difficult to envisage Miss Knox firing a gun. *Which is the point, I suppose.*

"Mr Hunt?"

Hunt felt himself blush, realising he had been staring at her. Embarrassed at his lapse, and angered by the amusement in his father's – *Lucifer's* – eyes, he asked, "Would you care to dance, Miss Knox?"

"I would love to," she said after a brief pause.

A waltz was playing as Hunt and Miss Knox stepped onto the dancefloor, Hunt taking her hand and waist as they joined the other couples.

"You look like your father," Miss Knox said as they danced to the 'Blue Danube'.

No, I look like the man my father Possessed. "Yes," he said, thinking of nothing else to say. Lady Delaney would not take well to the revelation that Lord Ashwood was really Lucifer in the flesh. *Or that I'm his son. I must mind my tongue.* He would do well not to be fooled by a pretty dress, a charming smile, or her pleasant Dublin drawl.

"Have you and Lady Delaney identified any Sooty Feathers?" he asked bluntly, taking care to keep his voice low.

The real Kerry Knox answered. "Give us a bloody minute! We only arrived today." She realised her lapse and reddened. "Dunkellen House is a lovely place. Lady MacInesker is very fortunate," Miss Knox said.

"Yes, she is. My parents and I will be staying there, too. We didn't arrive until after the rest of you had left for the ball." Hunt slowed slightly, ensuring they didn't get too close to the next couple. "My family once owned a castle larger than Dunkellen House." *Built near the hillfort that Dunkellen House was named in memory of.*

"Really? What happened?"

"An ancestor lost it in a game of cards."

A perplexed look crossed Kerry Knox's face, a woman who had grown up with next to nothing perhaps trying to comprehend the stupidity of someone carelessly wagering a castle in a game. A moment later it was replaced by one of polite commiseration, Miss Knox bound by etiquette to have no opinion on a gentleman's actions. "I'm sorry to hear that, Mr Hunt."

*

"Lord and Lady Ashwood, my condolences on the loss of your uncle, and my congratulations on your elevation," Redfort said as he joined the three, still perturbed at the attendance of the Hunts. *Should they not be mourning the loss of their shipping company?* "And Lady Delaney, I was unaware you were all acquainted."

"Thank you, your Grace," Lord Ashwood said. "It has been many years since we've had the pleasure of Lady Delaney's company."

"Twenty-four years, in fact, since the four of us were last together," Lady Delaney said, her gaze including Redfort.

"Oh? I confess I don't recall," he admitted.

But there was remembrance in Lady Ashwood's eyes. "Yes, Wilton's Christening. You did the honours, your Grace. Sir Andrew and Lady Delaney attended both the cathedral and the celebration afterwards in our home."

"We brought along our children, Andrew and Christopher. Andrew was almost three, Christopher one. I remember Andrew wanting to hold the baby, almost crying when I told him he was too young." There was a sheen of moisture on Lady Delaney's eyes, a window giving her a view into the past.

Lady Ashwood gently took her hand. "You held Wilton instead, sitting on the couch with him on your lap and your children to either side. They were all very good, sitting still long enough for the photographer to take the picture. I still have it."

"I would like to see it one day, if that would not be too much of an imposition."

"No imposition at all," Lord Ashwood assured her. "You may call upon us at your convenience."

Redfort found himself remembering that long-ago day, watching the happy young lady dandle baby Wilton on her knee with her two children flanking her in their Sunday best. Both dead now at their father's hands, Possessed by *Beliel.* Benjamin Howard had attended too, a friend of Sir Andrew Delaney, and the man who would lure him into the Black Wing Club and thereafter the Sooty Feathers. *The ties that bind us together.*

And occasionally tighten to choke. Sir Andrew was many years dead, his Possessed body slain by his wife. Mr Howard had been murdered by Steiner in the spring, and the Hunts would likely soon join him in death if Margot Guillam so commanded. Lady Delaney too, now that she had been marked as an enemy of the Sooty Feathers.

Her eyelids flickered, and the tears were gone, the window closed. "A kind offer, Lord Ashwood. One I shall take you up on once I've attended to more urgent matters." Her granite eyes rested on Redfort.

He turned his attention to Lord Ashwood. Given Redfort's suspicions regarding Lady Delaney's affiliation with the Templars, the Hunts would bear closer scrutiny. Neither Lord nor Lady Ashwood showed any sign of injury or distress from Roddy McBride's visit; had they left Ashwood prior to his arrival?

"I hope our son has remembered his manners, Lady Delaney," Lady Ashwood said. "I'm surprised to learn he is more recently acquainted with you. I had feared he was learning bad habits and keeping low company."

"Mr Hunt is a credit to your family, Lady Ashwood," Lady Delaney assured her. She looked over to the dance floor where he danced with her young companion. "He dances well."

"As does Miss Knox," Lady Ashwood said. "As a boy Wilton was reluctant to learn, but I insisted. Speaking of which, you promised me a dance, husband."

Lord Ashwood smiled. "Of course, my dear." He took her by the hand and led her to the floor.

"They make a handsome couple," Redfort said.

"Which couple?" Lady Delaney asked, looking between Hunt and Knox, and Hunt's parents.

"Lord and Lady Ashwood, of course. Mr Hunt and Miss Knox are still learning one another's movements. Lord and Lady Ashwood, on the other hand, move as one."

"I see what you mean," Lady Delaney said. "But youth has a charm all of its own."

"A charm balanced by age and experience." Redfort reached out his hand. "Would you do me the honour, Lady Delaney?"

*

"There are familiar faces here," Hunt said. Many eminent ladies and gentlemen were in attendance, the occasion recalling him to the balls he had attended prior to falling out with his parents. He didn't remember ever visiting Dunkellen House before, but until recently his father had been Mr Hunt, London lawyer, not the Baron of Ashwood.

"All Sooty Feathers?"

"How would I know? Many of them are in the Black Wing Club, certainly."

"As good as, then," she said.

"I'm a member," he said, stung by the contempt in her voice.

*

She looked at him in surprise, almost tripping. "Really?"

"I think most in the club have no knowledge of the society, let alone undead."

"I'd have thought you'd have quit, now you know." She tried to keep her voice neutral; she had no right to judge him.

"I thought about it," Hunt said. "But until McBride and McKellen, no one connected to the Sooty Feathers had taken any action against us. I don't know if that was on Margot Guillam's instructions, or whether they just forgot about us while recovering from George Rannoch and the circus. Regardless, I thought it better not to remind them I'm still around."

"You never thought of fighting back? You killed Rannoch." *A powerful vampyre.*

Blue eyes that had aged since she had first seen them in the Royal Princess's Theatre met her own. "Rannoch killed people I cared about. Murdered them because they were with me, because I poked my nose into the affairs of the Sooty Feather Society. You might think this is all a grand adventure but there can be a dreadful price to be paid."

Kerry wasn't overly worried about retribution, her close family far away in Ireland. She conceded it would be different for Hunt with his parents living in Glasgow. "You're worried they would kill your parents?"

He shocked her by laughing quietly. "I did. Until recently."

"When they attacked your family anyway," she said, thinking she understood. He had told her briefly of the attack on his family up north.

He just shook his head.

*

Lady Delaney was a stiff dancer. Possibly she was out of practice, her husband cold in his grave for twenty years. Redfort always enjoyed dancing, ignoring the surprised and almost scandalised looks he got. As a bishop and member of the Sooty Feather Council, he could do whatever he damned well pleased.

"Lady MacInesker must be gratified by the number of guests who attended despite the threat of infection," she said.

"Her gatherings are always among the highlights of the social season. She has kindly taken steps to ensure we are untroubled by the sick."

"Very kind," she said dryly. "Let us hope this week ends with fewer fatalities than Sir Arthur Williamson's party at Dunclutha."

That was uncalled for. "Let us hope so. A most unfortunate accident." He disliked the knowing amusement on Lady Delaney's face.

"There have been many accidents recently. You mentioned the Imperial Mill earlier?"

"A gas pipe situated too close to the mill, I hear, that leaked into the basement and blew up due to a spark." Redfort repeated the official explanation. "An accident unlikely to be repeated."

Lady Delaney smiled back at him. "There are many gas pipes and many mills in Glasgow. Who can say what other accidents are waiting to happen? Or illnesses."

Despite himself, Redfort admired the woman. A formidable adversary.

*

"Your parents dance well together," Kerry said to Hunt, watching the older Hunts move almost as one.

"Lady Delaney and Bishop Redfort rather less so," Hunt replied. He seemed to be trying to avoid his parents.

"What?" She turned, seeing her mentor dance with the bishop, the pair looking more interested in conversation than in their waltz. The music slowed, signalling that the dance was coming to an end, many of the couples returning to the side.

Kerry and Hunt joined Caroline, alone now that her surprising choice of dance partner had moved on to another small group of people. She wondered how tempted Caroline had been to just pull out her derringer and shoot the bishop.

"What are your plans for tomorrow before the garden party?" Hunt asked.

"Lady Delaney and I will walk the gardens, take tea with the other ladies, and perhaps do some embroidery," Kerry answered brightly. "A delightful day!"

He gave her a look. "Of course, Miss Knox. What will you really be doing?"

She lowered her voice slightly. "We'll be exploring the estate, identifying Sooty Feathers, and ensuring that Lady MacInesker answers for the children she sacrificed to the undead."

"That sounds equally delightful."

"Will you be assisting us, Mr Hunt? Or do you have more pressing demands on your time?" Kerry caught the sarcasm in Caroline's voice, and so did Hunt, judging by the flush that reddened his cheeks.

"I would be honoured to accompany you, Lady Delaney," he said with cold courtesy. "What time should I attend you?"

"After breakfast, I think. You should know we break our fast early. I understand some of you young gentlemen have a rather flexible definition of morning."

"What do you expect to find?" Hunt asked.

Lady Delaney spoke quietly. "Knowing the local area to establish routes of ambush or escape will be of benefit should things awry." Kerry was glad those piercing grey eyes weren't fixed on her. "Or does a lack of planning and preparation embody all your activities, Mr Hunt?"

"Did you not tell us the MacIneskers are related to the McKellens of Dunlew?" Kerry asked before words between him and Caroline became heated.

"Yes. The families branched off last century, but they're still tied. Dunkellen's cattle is from Dunlew stock," Hunt said. "Not that it matters, Alasdair McKellen is dead. I'm not sure if there are any others of that branch."

Lady Ashwood rejoined them. "I'm pleased to see you still remember how to dance, Wilton. You look very pretty, Miss Knox, most graceful."

"Thank you, Lady Ashwood," Kerry said. "You and Lord Ashwood made a handsome couple, if I may say so."

"You wish to speak with me, Mother?" Hunt asked, almost rudely.

The look Lady Ashwood gave him suggested she did not consider him too old to have his ears boxed, but all she said was, "Your father and I wish a word. If you can excuse my son for a time, Lady Delaney?"

"Of course, Lady Ashwood."

His reluctance to speak with his parents was clear to Kerry, but there was no graceful way for him to avoid it. "Very well, Mother. Lady Delaney, Miss Knox; it was a pleasure."

Kerry watched Hunt follow Lady Ashwood out of the hall. "Not a happy family, it seems."

"Indeed not. But I will not see our mission's success put in doubt by a young man's parental estrangement. If we cannot rely on Mr Hunt, we will keep our own counsel. Professor Sirk is not far and has proven himself a reliable ally."

Kerry sipped her white wine, finding it rather too sweet. "We've done well enough ourselves so far."

*

Lucifer stood with his back to the hall, gazing out across the silhouetted village. "Wilton," he said, his back to him. "I'm pleased you came. We need to clear the air."

"What do you want to discuss with me?" Hunt asked. Several responses had come to mind, but an ingrained deference to his parents as well as a whisper of self-preservation against instructing the King of Hell to go fuck himself ensured he remained civil.

Lucifer turned, looking through Lewis Hunt's eyes. "I appreciate, Wilton, that the recent revelation came as a shock to you. That my identity, and thusly your own heritage, has caused you some disquiet. However, these are dangerous times, and I insist that we be reconciled. Discord does us no favours while we are here, in the presence of enemies."

"Or what, you'll send me to Hell without supper? I'm bound there anyway, am I not?" That inevitability twisted his guts, the injustice of a fate predetermined by birth.

Amusement shone briefly in Lucifer's eyes. "I did not go to considerable effort to ensure your creation just for company in Hell, Wilton. Rest assured that Ashwood is the only domain you'll inherit from *me*."

Hunt was about to ask just why Lucifer *had* gone to considerable effort to conceive him when his mother interrupted. "We called you out here to answer your questions, to clear up any misapprehensions regarding your heritage."

"How?" Hunt asked. The question that he had burned to ask since learning the awful truth, the question whose answer he feared the answer to. "How did you come to Possess Lewis Hunt and marry my mother?"

Mother and Father looked at one another. "A question best answered by your mother, Wilton." Lucifer clasped his hands behind his back. "I was only present at the end. She was there for the beginning."

Mother looked at Hunt. "Twenty-eight years ago, I was on board one of your grandfather's schooners with your Uncle Ryan. The then-Lord Ashwood was dying, and his eldest son and family were returning to Ashwood with us. The ship was lured onto the rocks and sunk, only Ryan, myself and some of the crew survived..."

Chapter Thirty-Four

Saturday 28th July 1865

A few days had passed since the *Eclipse* sank. Ryan had sent a telegram to their father whose terse reply relayed his relief and an instruction to await his arrival on board another company ship. The surviving crewmen had been taken in by local villagers, Ryan having promised suitable recompense upon Father's arrival. He and Edith had been made welcome by the McKellens at Dunlew Castle.

Another time, Edith would have enjoyed guesting in a remote Highland castle overlooking a loch, surrounded by starkly beautiful moorland and hills. But she was too scarred by grief and shock to be moved much by the local beauty, her mind's eye constantly gazing back to that tragic night.

Hamish McKellen had been looking into the lighthouse mystery with an increasingly frustrated Lewis Hunt, making little progress. He was away on an errand for his father, Sir Hector, when Hunt arrived at Dunlew late in the afternoon to tell the Brownings that someone wanted to meet them to pass on information. He refused to tell them where they were going, beyond advising them to dress robustly.

Edith had been given some clothing belonging to Hamish McKellen's mother, choosing to wear an old riding dress and some well-worn leather walking shoes that pinched her feet a little. Ryan had an easier time of it, a seamstress having adjusted one of Hamish McKellen's tweed suits to fit. Mr Hunt had not exaggerated the need for outdoor clothing, leading them west past the northern shore of Loch Aline as they skirted the edge of the Ashwood estate, turning south.

"There," Hunt said as he pointed to a solitary hill. "Ash Hill. "That's where we've to meet our man." Dark clouds crowded the sky but thus far there had been no rain. August was a week away, the indifferent summer looking to continue with grey skies and occasional showers before turning to autumn, not that anyone would notice much difference.

"Rather out of the way," Edith said doubtfully. Surely there were better places to meet?

"He doesn't want to be seen talking to us," Hunt said impatiently. Edith had never met the man prior to the shipwreck and could not speak to his normal demeanour, but he seemed perpetually angry, driven to learn why the schooner carrying his family (and the Brownings) had ended up on the rocks. Edith suspected he was also a touch paranoid; the only reason he seemed to trust them, beyond them having no local connection, was that their family had lost a ship and men.

They climbed the hill, Edith wondering whether Hunt and the man they were to meet had thought this through. Secret meetings on top of a large hill did not strike Edith as being conducive to maintaining secrecy. Rocks were piled near the top, so perhaps they provided cover?

Hunt seemed to manage the climb better than Ryan, Edith's brother being more interested in late nights carding and drinking than in active pursuits such as tennis, swimming or bicycling. Edith had always enjoyed long walks, her only complaint today being the pinch of her borrowed shoes.

Dusk was not far off, a tinge of red to the west. Edith took the opportunity to admire the view, though it was somewhat ruined by the sight of wreckage from the *Eclipse* strewn on the distant shore.

"Some of these rocks look to have been placed deliberately," Edith said, turning her attention to the top of the hill. They stepped down into a large hollow near the summit, surrounded by large rocks. At the top she had seen a long stone lying flat on the ground, mostly buried.

"Ash Hill was an old hillfort once, in pagan days," Lewis Hunt said, already looking around for the man they were to meet. A man, they all hoped, with answers to why so many had died. Why the lighthouse had been dimmed, a siren light lit, and a ship murdered on treacherous rocks.

"Mr Hunt." Edith turned to see a tall man in a frayed coat step out from behind some rocks. He looked about fifty with mousy-brown hair going grey and a thick beard. A farm labourer, by the look of him. He was smoking from a pipe.

"Mr Slater," Hunt said, the relief in his voice telling Edith he was the man they were to meet. She let out a breath, deciding her earlier misgivings were unfounded. "This is Mr and Miss Browning. They owned the schooner my uncle, aunt and cousin were passengers on."

Slater nodded. "I'm glad you brought them."

"Mr Hunt says you have information explaining what happened," Ryan said. He was not known for his patience.

"Aye, Mr Browning." Slater puffed from his pipe. "The lads in the lighthouse stopped the light while others inland lit a similar one, opening and shuttering it to make it look like the coast was further away. Your ship was lured onto the rocks."

"Why?" Ryan's face turned crimson beneath his unruly reddish hair.

"To kill the Hunts. A sacrifice to the god of the sea, Lir. In times past the villagers used to lure ships onto the rocks and salvage the cargo as it washed ashore, the doomed crew an offering to Lir."

"Why kill my family?" Hunt wanted to know.

"Your ancestor committed atrocities on this land. A debt of blood some here have waited a long time to repay."

"How do you know all this? Why tell us?" Edith asked. There was an anger in Slater's voice and a knowing look in his eye she didn't care for.

"I know it all because I was one of the men with the light. Because I'm the High Druid of these lands, quietly returning the old ways, the religion of the original people. And why not tell you? You won't be telling anyone else." There was a hint of regret on his face when he looked at the Brownings. "I'm sorry you two were caught up in this, but sacrifices are necessary. The innocents murdered by Geoffrey Hunt must be avenged. The old gods will walk Lugh's Wood once again."

Hunt's face had gone pale. "You bastard! I'll kill you for this!" He looked about to attack Slater when more men and women appeared, a few armed with hunting guns. "I'll see you all hanged!"

Fear made Edith dizzy though she took some comfort from Ryan standing protectively near her. Maybe eight surrounded

Hunt and the Brownings, Sir Hector McKellen among them.

"Talk sense into these people, Sir Hector." There was desperation in Hunt's voice as it seemed to dawn on him that they had walked into a trap. Judging by the expressions of those gathered, they had no friends present. Every face looked at Hunt with naked hatred.

"My family have long awaited this moment, Hunt," Sir Hector said. "In Glasgow and beyond I am known as Sir Hector McKellen, but here I am Hector mac Duncan Kail'an. I am *the* Kail'an. Laird of Dun Lugh and Chief of the Sept, descended from the Kail'an who made his stand in the keep by the sea, sacrificing himself and the last of his men to curse your damned line."

"This is madness!"

"This is justice. For a century and a half my sept has worked quietly against your family. Your uncle and cousins were not the first to die by our will. One of my ancestors goaded the 3rd baron into betting Dunlew, and then months later killed him in a duel. Dunlew ... or as it was called when my people first built it, Dun Lugh. Only two Hunts now remain, and at dawn we bring back Lugh Himself. Fitting, as tomorrow is Lughnasadh."

"You're mad!" Hunt was shaking. "Does your son know you intend my murder?"

"My son has not fully embraced his heritage, more interested in southern city ways," Sir Hector said with regret. "And who said we're going to kill you? You'll walk away from here, I assure you." Laughter ringed the hill as Sir Hector's followers shared in his mirth, enjoying a secret.

"Before dawn, the druids will attempt what has not been done in centuries. One was born to us possessing the power to summon the gods." Sir Hector looked at Slater. "High Druid."

Slater turned to the other pagans gathered. He spoke in Gaelic, a language Edith had been taught from childhood by her mother, hailing from the Highlands. "The power to speak to the gods was always a rare one, and rarer still was possession of the blood needed. But mac Kail'an's time in Glasgow has been well-spent, winning the favour of the *fae* there to acquire blood from a *baobhan sith*."

"A plan almost half a century in the making. Aisla, come

forward," Sir Hector said in English. "It's time for the reunion."

A nervous anticipation suffused those gathered as a woman approached Sir Hector. She looked to be almost fifty, unremarkable, grey-haired. She wore a white robe.

Lewis Hunt gasped like he'd seen a ghost. "Mother!"

The woman glanced at Hunt but made no reply.

"Will you be ready to begin just prior to dawn?" Slater asked. He might be a humble farmhand as far as most of Kirkaline were concerned, but it was clear he was a leader of the pagans festering in its heart, second only to Sir Hector.

She stood straight and confident. "Yes. The gods have granted me the power to call them forth. Ancient scrolls preserved by the druids of old contain the names we must speak to summon the gods and what must be done. Your son's associates in Glasgow have provided the blood we need. I am ready."

"Do we have the blood with us?" Slater asked formally.

"It will be brought here before dawn," Sir Hector assured him.

"Mother! I was told you died," Hunt shouted. "Mother!"

Aisla walked up to her son. "We'll speak soon, Lewis."

Edith, Ryan and Lewis Hunt were tied up while torches were planted into the ground, lighting up the hilltop as dusk fell, followed by night. The pagans chanted and danced around a large fire, celebrating as the hours passed, some drinking heavily. A Christian, the whole thing turned Edith's stomach. *Will they cut out our hearts?* She knew little of pagan ways, but the Glasgow Cathedral's new minister, Reverend Redfort, claimed they had been a godless people given to great evil and human sacrifice. Worse, even, than Catholics, and *they* claimed to eat God's flesh and blood.

Slater called for quiet, the High Druid's authority absolute. Silence fell over the hill. A glimmer of fiery orange appeared on the eastern horizon, dawn minutes away.

Four men dragged the prisoners to the hill summit where Sir Hector McKellen – Hector mac Duncan Kail'an – waited, standing on the flat stone Edith remembered from the day before. They had been given a little water, but Edith was tired, scared and hungry. Ryan had shouted insults at the pagans until one of them had struck him, after which he kept silent. Hunt had said nothing, his spirit bewildered and broken.

The pagans formed a circle around the stone, surrounding Edith, Ryan, Lewis Hunt, Sir Hector, Aisla and Slater. On Slater's nod, a woman and man pushed Lewis Hunt down onto the stone. Every face Edith saw illuminated by torchlight looked ambivalent, a mix of anticipation and apprehension.

Aisla approached. "As a child the druids discovered I have the power to summon the gods. I'm not the first with the Gift to be born into the sept in recent centuries, but those few who came before in recent times did not have the blood of the *baobhan sith* needed to complete the rite. We learned that such immortal creatures of the night could be found in the cities, and so two actions were agreed. First, that when the Kail'an had a child, it would be sent to Glasgow to join those who serve the *fae* there, the dead brought back by blood of the gods.

"Second, that if I was willing, I would marry into the cursed family that wronged our people. That I would wed a Hunt and bear him a child. That child was you, Lewis, named after the god you will become."

Hunt stared at her. "I don't understand. I was told you and Father died."

"I was willing to wed a Hunt, bear him a child, but I would not live out my days with that damned family. When you were a child, I went sailing with your father in the loch. Two druids drowned him as an offering to Lir, and the boat was overturned. So far as anyone knew, I died with him."

"Why?" It was almost a whisper.

Eyes without pity looked at Lewis Hunt. Eyes of his mother. "Because it is fitting that the last Hunt becomes the Vessel of Lugh. The God of Light will live among His people as Lord Ashwood, a fitting revenge on the Black Hunt, Geoffrey."

"Who are you?" Hunt asked, staring at the woman who bore him.

"I'm a cousin to the Kail'an."

"Your sacrifice brings much honour to your people, Aisla," Sir Hector said. "In one night, you'll end the Hunts, save for your son's uncle who will be dealt with soon, and bring back

Lugh. Most of our kin may have lost the will for revenge, but Lugh will show them the way."

"Ryan!" Edith shouted as her brother was dragged next to Hunt. Aisla began a chant in a language neither English nor Gaelic, a tongue that raised the hairs on the back of Edith's neck. The others quietly chanted, "Lugh," over and over. *Do they really believe a god will appear before them?* Judging by their expressions, doubts still lingered. Having been taught that there was only God, Edith was sceptical to say the least, but those inhuman words uttered by Aisla left a worm of doubt burrowing through Edith's piety. And regardless, if this Lugh failed to appear, the pagans were unlikely to cut their prisoners free and send them on their way with an embarrassed apology.

Hamish McKellen appeared atop the hill, breathing heavily and in the company of two of his father's foresters. One carried a glass flask containing a dark liquid. "What is this, Father?" he asked on seeing the Brownings and Hunt. "I tolerate your old rituals, but you go too far! The Brownings are not part of this."

"Be silent," Sir Hector commanded his son. "You are the mac Kail'an, one day this will all be yours."

Hamish McKellen unhappily held his tongue. Venus was visible in the sky. The Morning Star.

Aisla accepted the flask from a forester and let dark blood fall on Hunt's face. When he opened his mouth to let out an angry cry, she poured some inside, causing him to choke on it.

He thrashed futilely against the bonds securing him. Sir Hector held up a scarred bronze knife. "This is the ceremonial knife used in our rites from centuries past." He handed the knife back to Slater as Aisla said, "*Samiel,*" repeatedly, the others taking up the chant.

"*Samiel.*"

Sir Hector might be a lord to these people, but as dawn slowly crept over the horizon, he was a spectator, content to watch his druids conduct their vile rite.

"*Samiel.*" He was joining in now. The name, first said as a whisper, was now spoken louder, more confidently. His son stood quietly by his side, face ashen as he watched the ritual.

Slater stood next to Ryan, and on Aisla's nod he slashed

Edith's brother's throat, blood spurting over the helpless Hunt. "*Samiel.*"

"Ryan!" Edith screamed as her brother bled violently to death, his blood staining the grass. Part of her saw Hamish McKellen watching the murder in disgust. But he did naught more than watch.

"*Samiel.*"

Edith sobbed as the chanting continued, knowing she would be next. But no one seemed in any rush to drag her over and mingle her blood with her poor brother's. Hunt was convulsing, as if some otherworldly power had seized him. A wave of sunlight lit up the moorland to the east across the water, the loch itself gleaming gold.

"*Samiel.*"

Ryan stopped moving, bled to death. *Brother!* Hunt thrashed around as much as his bonds allowed him.

Aisla threw her head back and raised her arms. "*Samiel!*"

The torches flickered, going dark for a heartbeat before flaring back to life, and a chill cut through Edith to her marrow, an overwhelming *wrongness* assailing her. As if a door to somewhere awful had cracked open. *God save me!*

Lewis Hunt went still, watched by an apprehensive Slater. Aisla broke the silence, sounding exhausted. "It is done. Our god is here."

"I know the words He told us long ago, that we know it is Him and not an imposter," Slater said. He cut Hunt free and helped him to his feet. Waves of cold dread washed over Edith, some lasting several moments before fading. The druid spoke quietly with Hunt, treating him with an almost worshipful deference.

Slater dropped to his knees. "Lugh, Lord of Light, has returned to us, walking this sacred land in the body of Lewis Hunt, descended from the man who drove out our kin all those years ago!"

A murmur rippled across those gathered, some smiling, others reining in their enthusiasm until they saw confirmation that their High Druid spoke truly. Lewis Hunt looked at them, a confused look on his face as he studied them. Through her grief and fear, Edith realised it was their clothing that confused him.

"Lord Lugh, we have brought you back to us," Sir Hector

said, kneeling before his god. "I am Hector, the Kail'an. I swear to serve you as my ancestors did."

"With you leading us, we'll drive the Christians into the sea. The old religion will be practised openly, and with you walking among us, none will dare oppose us," Aisla said, her eyes alight. The son she had hated was now the god she worshipped.

"You're all fools!" Hamish McKellen strode from the small crowd. "You think you've summoned a god?"

"Be quiet, boy!" Sir Hector rounded on his son. "You doubt what your own eyes have seen, what you have *felt?*"

The younger McKellen stood his ground, contempt on his face. "You've summoned a demon, not a god. *Samiel* is a demon's name. What you call *Baobhan sith* call themselves *Nephilim*. Vampyres!"

Denials and consternation rose up from the gathered druids.

"You've gone mad," Ailsa cried out.

"Have I? I've learned much in Glasgow. I wanted to believe you were right, that we were bringing back a god, that we were bringing back Lugh, but I've met a demon before. I pleaded my case before the Sooty Feather Council for the *Nephilim* blood you just used, blood needed for the Summoning. Regent Edwards laughed as I told them of the rite, told me we what we really summoning. I didn't want to believe him. He told me when I was done with this nonsense, I might rise to high station in Glasgow."

Edith stared at the demon. She attended Church but her heart had never really been in it, her belief lukewarm at best. Until now. A fallen angel stood before her, cloaked in the flesh of Man.

Hamish McKellen faced the demon within Lewis Hunt. "Was there ever a Lugh, and you just usurped his identity, or were you Him all along, playing our ancestors for fools? Sniggering as they worshipped you and your kind, bowing and scraping."

"Strike him down, Lord Lugh!" a druid called out. Edith heard desperation in his voice.

The demon finally answered, struggling to form the words. "I am the kernel of truth at the heart of the myth of Lugh, the string tying different legends together. Some of your people called me Lugh. Or Cernunnos, the Hunter and Horned Lord.

When I died in one body and was brought back in another, some argued I was my own son, calling me Cu Chulainn. But always I was *Samiel*. Lucifer, cursed as the Bringer of Light by my kind. I aided your ancestors, shared knowledge with them. If in time stories turned to legends and you thought of me as a god, so be it."

The Devil ... They opened the Gates of Hell with the blood of my brother and let loose the Devil. But despite her horror, Edith felt a cold, hard satisfaction as she witnessed the death of Sir Hector's dream. He and the druids had murdered Ryan to summon Lugh, only to find Satan before them. *Kill them all!*

"No!" Aisla looked stricken as she looked at what she had bought with the life of her son.

"He lies," one of the druids said in desperation. "It is a test by Lugh. If we kill this spirit, Lugh will come back to us."

"Our ancestors were tricked by the Devil," another argued. "We've worshipped a lie. A damned lie!"

The druids argued amongst themselves, angry words turning to blows. Hamish McKellen untied Edith.

"Go," he said heavily. "I'm sorry about your brother." He turned and walked down the hill, washing his hands of the religious turmoil tearing his sept apart.

A gun fired, High Druid Slater falling dead to the ground. Sir Hector stabbed the shooter with the bronze knife still stained with Ryan's blood. Today was supposed to be the day he brought back one of his gods. Today was to be the day his pagan religion left the shadows. Instead, his son's revelations had destroyed that dream, and Edith felt no pity for him.

Sir Hector picked up the fallen gun and advanced on the demon he had believed a god. "I'll send you back to Hell!" He reloaded the gun while the others fought amongst themselves.

Edith found herself walking towards the stabbed druid, no one moving to stop her. She pulled free the knife that had killed her brother, surprised at the resistance she felt as flesh reluctantly yielded bronze. Light-headed, she walked towards Sir Hector McKellen who was too busy ranting at an impassive Lucifer to notice her.

She looked at her brother's body, hot hatred burning her as she rammed the knife into Sir Hector's back. Again and again she stabbed him, blood staining her hands and forearms as the Chief of the Kail'ans sank to the ground, the gun falling from his grip.

Someone pulled her away, and she looked up into the blue eyes of Lewis Hunt. A thrill of fear went through her. *Lucifer.*

"Thank you, I assume that thing he held would have killed this body?"

"You don't know what a gun is?" she heard herself ask.

"I've not walked this world in many years. A great many years, I suspect."

Part of Edith wondered if she should stab him, should send the Devil back to Hell. But the bronze knife was still stuck in Sir Hector's body. She wondered why none of the druids attacked them, but on looking around she saw only the dead remained, Aisla among them.

Edith knelt next to Ryan, holding her brother's cold hand.

"What now?" Lucifer asked after several minutes.

Edith looked up at him. "I was staying at Dunlew."

"Dun Lugh?" His pronunciation differed from her own.

She realised the castle must have been built after his last time here. "A castle owned by the McKellens." That castle's laird lay dead by her hand. "I may no longer be welcome."

"Ah. I recall it now. Memories from Lewis Hunt, my Vessel. When I was last Summoned, the Kail'ans lived here on Dunkail'an." He looked around the hill. "Time has not been kind to it."

"You have Mr Hunt's memories?"

"Some, of varying clarity. As time passes, I should be able to pass for him."

"And what will you do?" Edith forced herself to ask. The Devil was loose in the world. She found herself uncaring.

He gazed down at the loch, looking lost. "I don't know. I'm free from Hell but find myself in a world I don't know. In times past I guided the people who lived here, content my enemies would not find me in so remote a place." He smiled wryly. "It appears I'm no longer welcome here, their descendants having wrapped stories and legends around me. What of you?"

"I must make arrangements for my brother's body to be recovered." Tears slid down her cheeks. "As I said, we were staying at Dunlew, but…"

"Do you know how to operate this … gun?" Lucifer asked.

"Yes," Edith answered, wondering if she should have lied.

"Excellent. I think we should make our way to Dunlew and impose upon the new Kail'an." Lucifer smiled.

"We?"

"That family has wronged yours, killing your brother. It is only fitting that they make restitution, recovering the body for you until you are ready to return home … wherever that is. And as they Summoned me here, I shall impose upon them too."

There was something about the Devil that Edith warmed to, an attitude that seemed to mock convention. "You'll stay here, then?"

"No. I remember a … a city of towering grey stone, of many people. This Vessel … lived there. Studied there." A frown creased Lucifer's brow as he seemed to remember more of poor Lewis Hunt's life. "He studied laws."

"The Law. You really intend to live his life?"

"What choice do I have? Once I'm satisfied the new Kail'an will cause no trouble for us, I will go to Ashwood, the home of Hunt's uncle, Thomas." Lucifer's speech was improving, sounding more and more like Lewis Hunt. "In time, I will travel to this … Glasgow, and continue his … my … studies. Where will you go?"

"To Glasgow, also. My family are sending a ship to collect me. And my brother."

"Perhaps we can travel together. You can show me the city."

The Devil wants me to show him around Glasgow. She felt tired and grief-stricken, dazed by the night and morning's events. "Perhaps, but we must be chaperoned."

Lucifer tilted his head. "A custom?"

She nodded. "Yes. I am now heir to my father's company. He will expect me to make a good marriage, now, to a man who can operate the company when I inherit. To walk with a man not my husband would incite gossip." She had been resistant to wed, valuing her independence. With Ryan now dead, she knew her father would press the matter after an appropriate time. A pang of resentment struck her; why should she not run the company? Why surrender it to a man?

"I will respect these … customs," Lucifer said dryly. "But I suspect you are not someone who bends to custom for custom's sake."

She managed a small smile. "I am not."

"Good, for I fear you must risk great scandal walking alone with me to this Dunlew."

The Devil jokes? "I'll take that risk, sir."

Lucifer grinned. "A relief, since I must confess that I do not know the way."

Edith and Lucifer walked down Ash Hill towards the road leading to Dunlew Castle, where Hamish McKellen had likely fled. In deference to Edith's knowledge of this age's technology, Lucifer suggested she carry the gun.

Chapter Thirty-Five

Hunt listened silently as his mother recounted how Lucifer had come to Possess Lewis Hunt. He was relieved to learn that his mother had played no part in the Summoning, that indeed she had been a victim of the whole thing. Her actions afterwards were where comprehension failed him. "And then you *married* him?"

"We met several times in Glasgow," Mother said. "By then my father was insisting I marry, but most of the men who courted me had their eyes on the company I had become heir to after Ryan's death. I decided then that I wanted a partner, not a master. By that time your father had decided he wanted a child, and so in time we wed. And conceived you."

"A circumstance you've given me occasion to regret, Wilton," Father added with a dry edge.

"But Lord McKellen knew who you are. If he was a Sooty Feather, would he not have told them so when they captured me?"

"Lord McKellen was Mesmered by Niall Fisher, *Dominus* of Glasgow's *Nephilim*. I requested it of him when we met."

"You've met Fisher? I understood he was a recluse, that even few among the Sooty Feathers have met him," Hunt said.

"It seemed only polite to introduce myself to him, given I was moving into his city. I requested he Mesmer McKellen to not speak of my identity, to not even think of it. Fisher did this in return for a promise that I not interfere in his business, a condition I was happy to agree to. I've little interest in undead intrigue."

"So, McKellen forgot?"

"Part of him remembered but chose not to speak of it, or even dwell on it."

"And the Kail'ans just let you go?" Hunt asked.

Mother spoke. "None know what happened that night. Lord McKellen succeeded in quelling the ambitions of the more fanatical followers, and likely arranged accidents for those druids who survived the Summoning. Aside from those we had the displeasure of dealing with recently, the majority practise the religion and perform their festivals peacefully, the local people content to turn a blind eye to it."

"I'm pleased we cleared the air, Wilton," Lucifer said after a long silence. "There is danger here, a wrongness. I sense it but know not its source. Be on your guard."

Hunt walked away, making no reply. Was he just supposed to accept the Devil was his father and act as if nothing had changed?

*

"Fold." Hunt laid his cards down on the table, seeing no point in trying to bluff with such a mediocre hand. His heart wasn't really in the game, anyway, realising he had absently emptied a glass of its whisky. Carriages had conveyed Lady MacInesker's guests back to Dunkellen House for drinks and entertainment once the ball had ended.

A footman poured more whisky into his glass. Hunt was among the youngest of the men around the poker table. The only one he knew well was Lord Smith, a family friend whom he had last met at Sir Arthur Williamson's party, the night he had met Amelie Gerrard. Thinking of the young Frenchwoman drove Hunt to take another deep drink of whisky, letting it burn his throat.

The others he mostly knew of, at least by name or reputation. Bishop Redfort was a surprise to find at the gambling table. He had left his cloak of piety at home, proving himself a canny player. Glasgow's Lord Provost, the Right Honourable Sir Wilbur Poole, had graced Dunkellen with his presence, a coup for Lady MacInesker. Aged seventy, Sir Wilbur looked frail, his hands shaky. His concentration was also suspect, though the others present had refrained from taking advantage of the old man.

One of Glasgow's most quietly eminent bankers sat at the table; William Heron of the Heron Crowe Bank. A bank involved with the Sooty Feathers, Hunt knew. The last two players were Dr Theodore Essex, a famous London physician currently visiting Scotland, and Edwin Kenmure, a senior officer of the Glasgow Constabulary.

Redfort won the hand, a smile unbecoming of a bishop on his face as he gathered in the pot. Kenmure had bluffed despite only holding two-sixes, and Lord Smith had folded despite holding a very good hand. The banker Heron had played conservatively, betting aggressively with good hands but folding early when his cards were poor. Not a man to bluff. *Unless he wishes us to think that, waiting until a particularly good pot is at stake.*

Cigar smoke drifted across the table. No one seemed impatient for the next game, and Hunt was happy not to lose any more of his dwindling money. He'd spent little over the past month, owing Foley no rent. A gulf had separated the friends since Lord Ashwood's secret had come to light, and Hunt wondered glumly if he should look for a new abode. *And the means to pay for it.*

"May I join you?" a familiar voice asked, an unwelcome one.

*

"You may have my seat," Dr Essex said as he stood. He looked strained, perhaps fatigued after attending to the sick in the village. He had taken precautions, he had assured everyone, to avoid catching it himself. Redfort certainly hoped Essex's confidence was not misplaced; Death had finally arrived in the village the night before, harvesting a savage crop from the earliest afflicted.

He nodded as Lord Ashwood replaced Essex at the table. "Welcome."

"Thank you, your Grace." Lord Ashwood surveyed the other players. "It has been some time since I last played."

Redfort noted the only one who didn't greet Lord Ashwood was his son, the young man doing a poor job of hiding a scowl. *A falling-out in the family?*

Play resumed, a fresh hand of cards dealt out. Lord Ashwood proved a shrewd player, his face inscrutable when he wished it to be. Interestingly, his presence goaded the younger Hunt to play more aggressively, even recklessly.

Lord Ashwood added chips to the pot, followed by some more. "I'll raise the bet five pounds."

"I fold." William Heron put his cards down on the table. That left Redfort, Lord Ashwood, Wilton Hunt and Lord Smith still in the game.

Redfort looked at his hand. Two queens. Perhaps enough to win if Lord Ashwood's raise was a bluff, perhaps not. "I fold."

"Fold." Lord Smith put his cards down, too.

Hunt looked at his cards and then at his father, indecision on his face. The Wilton Hunt from a few games back would have folded, and wisely so. Redfort was entirely unsurprised to see Hunt throw his chips into the pot, including the extra five pounds. Then he added more. "I'll raise you one pound."

Lord Ashwood permitted himself to drop his poker face, amusement on his face as he added chips to the pot. The cards were then turned over. "Three kings," he said unnecessarily.

Hunt didn't look happy as he laid his cards down. Two tens.

"An enjoyable game, gentlemen," Lord Ashwood said.

Hunt rose, the last of his money gone to his father. "I'll leave while I still have my shirt. Good night, gentlemen."

"My wife will be wondering where I have got to," Lord Ashwood said as he gathered up his winnings. The game looked to have run its course, the others rising too.

Redfort had a meeting with his fellow Councillors present at Dunkellen to attend in another room, *Secundus*, *Sextus*, and *Octavius* already with him at the card table.

"Bishop Redfort, a word if I may?" William Heron asked as the other three Councillors prepared to leave.

"So long as it is a brief one, Mr Heron," Redfort said. It wouldn't do to delay the meeting, or worse, miss any of it.

"Yes, yes, a brief word is all I require, your Grace," Heron said.

"Excellent. Shall we step out?" Redfort glanced at the three Councillors. "Gentlemen, I'll see you in the morning room."

"What is it, Mr Heron?" Redfort asked, not bothering to hide his impatience. If the banker wished to apologise again for the recent banking chaos, apologies didn't interest him.

"Some days ago, Mr Crowe and I were attacked separately, by two *Nephilim*. I thought you should know, given recent events."

"Attacked? By whom?" The Heron Crowe Bank was looking less and less a secure and enduring institution. Redfort made a mental note to quietly move some of his capital elsewhere.

"Foreigners, Bishop Redfort. Mr Crowe believes they were from the Carpathian Circus, as they looked and sounded Eastern European."

"You may assure Mr Crowe that the Carpathian Circus will be dealt with imminently," Redfort said. Something nagged at him. "You say you were both attacked?"

"Yes, your Grace. Had it not been for–"

Redfort's raised hand silenced him. "Had both you and Crowe been killed, who would control the bank?"

"Well, the remaining directors would. But the *Nephilim* who broke into my house was not trying to kill me. I believe he intended to abduct me."

How would the circus or Erik Keel benefit from control of the bank moving to the other directors?

"I'm relieved you will deal with the circus, your Grace," Heron added. "A great weight off my mind. It assures me Mr Crowe and I are correct in our decision for one of us to accept a seat on the Council, should one become available."

Redfort looked at him sharply. "You have been offered a Council seat?"

Heron looked guilty, as if he had betrayed a confidence. "I assumed it had been agreed by the Council."

Perhaps Regent Guillam decided not to consult us. The Elder *Nephilim* was becoming increasingly secretive, telling the Council less and less.

"We should speak later," Redfort said. Why would Erik Keel want to kill Edmund Crowe and take William Heron alive?

*

Most of the guests had moved on to the drawing room, talking of Glasgow society and other current matters of interest. Kerry was guiltily enjoying herself more as lady's companion than she had as lady's maid, and Lady MacInesker was certainly revelling in her role as lady of the house. If anyone vocally sympathised over the villagers and farmers dying elsewhere on the large estate, they did not do so within Kerry's earshot.

"Lady Delaney, I hope you enjoyed the ball?" Lady MacInesker seemed to have cooled towards Caroline.

"Most enjoyable, Lady MacInesker. I have not danced in years."

"Lady MacInesker, Lady Delaney, Miss Knox; you're acquainted, I see," said Lady Ashwood on joining them.

"I've met Lady Delaney previously, but this is the first time I've had the pleasure of meeting Miss Knox," Lady MacInesker said. She beckoned another lady to join them. "Ladies, may I introduce you to Mrs Carlton. Mrs Carlton, this is the Lady Ashwood, Lady Delaney, and Miss Knox."

Courtesies were exchanged. Mrs Carlton was maybe fifty, brown-haired and wearing a yellow evening dress. Kerry was surprised to see Mrs Carlton wore a hat; entirely expected during the day, but to wear one in the evening indoors would raise some eyebrows.

"Are you any relation to the Carltons of J. Carlton & Co.?" Lady Ashwood asked.

"Yes, the very same," Mrs Carlton said. That company owned warehouses across the city, Kerry recalled.

"I was sorry to hear about Mr Carlton's illness. Has he recovered yet?" Lady Ashwood asked.

"No, he is still confined to his bed. The doctors have yet to discover the cause." Mrs Carlton didn't sound overly upset about her husband's condition. "All they can say for sure is that it is *not* the same illness afflicting this estate."

"Who then accompanied you here?" Caroline asked.

"Lord Smith was good enough to escort me," Mrs Carlton answered.

"Very thoughtful of him," Caroline said.

"Mrs Carlton, we're due to meet some friends in the morning room," Lady MacInesker said pointedly. "Until later, ladies."

"Do not let us detain you, Lady MacInesker," Caroline said with a tilt of her head.

Chapter Thirty-Six

"Join us, Bishop," Sir Wilbur Poole said, his voice almost a wheeze. As *Secundus*, he was the seniormost Councillor present.

This old man is almost done, and not before time. "Thank you, Sir Wilbur." It was an unusual Council gathering, conducted outside the Black Wing Club. At such meetings Redfort usually thought of his fellow councillors by their title, a reminder that regardless of the position they occupied publicly, each was one of eight voices ruling the Sooty Feather Society, and through it, Glasgow and beyond.

It was also an incomplete meeting. The two undead Councillors, *Prima* Margot Guillam and *Quartus* Reginald Fredds, remained in the city. Lady MacInesker and Gwendoline Carlton were just taking a seat on one of the couches surrounding a round table, satisfying Redfort he was not unduly late.

As *Tertia*, Lady MacInesker was the secondmost senior Councillor in Dunkellen, a rather sobering state of affairs. Of the eight who sat on the Council, only three had done so six months earlier. Lady MacInesker had been *Octavia* back then, the newest member. She had fallen from the Regent's good graces after the loss of so many ghouls beneath the Imperial Mill, but her husband's family had always enjoyed special favour with the *Nephilim*.

Redfort had dreamed of joining the Council and rising through its ranks by whatever means necessary, but even he was alarmed at already being *Quintus*, the Fifth Seat, in so short a space of time. The death of a Councillor, Lord McKellen, had led to fellow High Court Judge, Lord Smith, being recruited to the Council, now *Sextus*.

Mrs Carlton – *Septima* – was a useful recent addition to the

Council. Ivan Carlton would have been the first choice, but he fell ill before he could be elevated to the Council, his wife the obvious second choice. Both were Sooty Feathers of long and good standing.

That left *Octavius*, Edwin Kenmure. Redfort would not be unhappy to see the Eighth Seat made vacant again, the police superintendent's newfound love of intrigue and disrespect earning him Redfort's disapprobation. If Kenmure did die, Redfort wondered if Regent Guillam would still elevate either Crowe or Heron to the Council as the new *Octavius*, or if she would want another senior policeman. If any suitable ranking policemen remained in the Sooty Feathers. Several had died at Dunclutha attempting to resist Rannoch's people.

"Firstly, I would like to thank Lady MacInesker for her hospitality," Sir Wilbur said.

"I hope everyone is having a good time," Lady MacInesker said. "Unfortunately, it appears Mr McKellen has so far failed to attend. A delay, perhaps."

"I should warn everyone that a Lady Delaney is here, widow of Sir Andrew Delaney, whom some of you may recall. I suspect she may have been involved in the attack on the Imperial Mill," Redfort said. He had noted Alasdair McKellen's absence, also. The young man had travelled north with McBride to visit the Hunts at Ashwood; given that the Hunts showed no signs of distress, perhaps McKellen and McBride had encountered a delay?

"A woman succeeded in destroying a Crypt of ghouls?" Sir Wilbur sounded sceptical.

Lady MacInesker's lips thinned. "Women and children who worked at the mill were questioned. They spoke of two women and a man as being responsible, their faces covered. Perhaps Lady Delaney and her young companion?"

"Perhaps. We should consider it." Sir Wilbur sounded befuddled, his flushed face suggesting he had extensively enjoyed Lady MacInesker's hospitality. *An embarrassment. Someone should do him the mercy of putting him out of his misery. An unfortunate fall down a flight of stairs, perhaps. Or maybe a tumble into the river. The countryside can be so dangerous.*

"Any other business?" Sir Wilbur asked.

Redfort sensed the opportunity to make amends for

McBride's apparent failure and burnish his own reputation. "Prior to leaving Glasgow, Regent Guillam tasked me to send Roderick McBride and Alasdair McKellen to Loch Aline to *encourage* Lord Ashwood to sell her the Browning Shipping Company. For reasons beyond my ken, they have somehow failed to impress upon Lord Ashwood that this would be beneficial for his family's continued good health. As such, I propose that we take this matter into our own hands tonight."

"It would be a novelty in these times to be able to report *success* to Regent Guillam," Lady MacInesker said. Her support came as no surprise, the lady eager to atone for her own recent disaster.

Redfort noted Smith, Kenmure and Carlton exchange looks.

"If this Lord Ashwood successfully defied a man with McBride's reputation, I'm not convinced we could quietly succeed," Lord Smith said. Redfort belatedly recalled that the Lords Smith and Ashwood were friends of a sort. But he was confident a majority of the Councillors would side with him.

"I agree," Mrs Carlton said.

"With whom?" Sir Wilbur asked.

"With Lord Smith."

Two against, two for, and two still to cast their votes. Sir Wilbur would not want to appear weak in front of his peers on the Council, and Kenmure would want to cement his recent elevation to *Octavius* with success prior to attacking the circus. *Two for me, I think.*

"I must agree with Lord Smith and Mrs Carlton," Kenmure said, Redfort's irritation towards him flaring into hatred. *Damn the man!*

"We are tasked to deal with a demon and his circus minions," Redfort said between clenched teeth. "I am satisfied we can bully a man into selling his company, given his wife and son are present and vulnerable. It may be that Ashwood left his estate prior to McBride and McKellen arriving, and the 'offer' was never made."

But Kenmure shook his head. "I think to do so risks alarming the other guests – those not part of the Society. Lord Ashwood can be dealt with later."

"I'm inclined to side with Bishop Redfort in this matter," Sir Wilbur said, not that his support mattered a damn anymore. Three for, three against. An impasse.

"Very well," Redfort muttered, slouching defeated back into his seat. *The impertinence!* How dare the three newest Councillors disagree with the three seniormost present.

Were Councillors not protected from Possession by the spell imbued onto their feather tattoo, Redfort might suspect they were demons. *It would certainly explain Kenmure's unbecoming change of character recently.*

"Is there anything else?" Sir Wilbur mumbled, fidgeting as if he needed a piss.

Redfort thought to mention that William Heron had approached him regarding the attack on him and the *Nephilim* Edmund Crowe, if for no other reason than to delay the old fool tottering off to find a water closet. *One of the bankers is next in line to join the Council, and Keel's minions did attempt to kill Crowe and take Heron...*

Take Heron... Pieces fell into place like a jigsaw, revealing an alarming picture. Redfort looked at the three Councillors who had voted against him, seeing them through fresh eyes. *Sextus*, *Septima*, and *Octavius* watched him back, their expressions opaque. *Am I right?*

"Nothing further," Redfort managed to say. Suddenly he felt the need to relieve himself too.

"Excellent, pray excuse me," Sir Wilbur said, standing as fast as his frail legs allowed, enduring no greater problem than an old man's bladder. Lady MacInesker likewise left, her chief worry being how to appease Regent Guillam. The other three Councillors remained seating.

Redfort rose quickly too, having no desire to remain alone in their company. *I must tell someone!* But whom? Whom dare he trust? Sir Wilbur Poole and Lady MacInesker had been part of the Council longer than Redfort and were almost certainly not demons. But Poole was useless and Lady MacInesker was no fighter. The loyalty of the other Sooty Feathers present was uncertain. *I can trust none of my own.* For once, he would have appreciated Jones being present, but he was with the rest of the band dispatched to protect Dunkellen House and attack the circus.

I will sleep on it.

*

The Honourable Mr Hunt was drunk in the drawing room, Kerry saw, hellbent on drinking Dunkellen's whisky collection dry, or die in the attempt. His unruly reddish hair had been slicked down and parted to one side, tamed for the evening, and his formal tails looked expensive though the trousers needed to be brought in perhaps an inch. With black shoes bulled to perfection, he looked every inch Lord Ashwood's heir.

Until one looked at his eyes. Kerry recalled how he had looked the night he killed Rannoch and rescued Steiner, how grief and anger had chilled those eyes and hardened a mouth that had smiled easily during their time in the theatre. At first, she thought he was still stricken by the deaths of the Gerrard family, but whatever haunted him now seemed raw, a wound freshly inflicted.

"Mr Hunt, have you enjoyed the evening?" she asked with a forced smile. Was it due to the attack on his family? Part of it, maybe, but she believed there was more to the story.

He tried to force a smile, but his mouth gave up after a moment, and his eyes never even tried. "Very enjoyable, Miss Knox. Has it been enjoyable for you?"

"It's been wonderful. Dunkellen is such a lovely place," she said warmly. It was, but they hadn't come for the scenery. There was evil here, black-hearted Sooty Feathers among the guests, and they'd be dealt with. *And we may need your help, damn you, so straighten your head.*

"Yes. Where is Lady Delaney?" The question owed more to politeness than genuine interest. He drank half the glass, glazed eyes already moving to the table from where a footman was pouring drinks.

"In her room. She wants a good night's rest before our long day tomorrow." Kerry emphasised that last part, hoping Hunt would take the hint and decide he'd had enough whisky.

She sat next to him on the couch. "What's the matter with you? There are Sooty Feathers here. People who want you dead for knowing what you know. What *we* know. And you're sitting here getting drunk. Do you think your father's name and title will keep you safe?"

For some reason, he found that funny, quiet laughter twisting his face. He emptied his glass, still chuckling.

Kerry gave up. "Good night, Mr Hunt. I'll see you at

breakfast. If you're in any state to attend."

"Good night, Miss Knox," he replied with a slur. "Sleep well."

On reaching the door, she turned back to see Mrs Carlton and two men join Hunt. The older man was a judge, she believed.

*

Something grabbed Redfort as he reached the top of the winding stairs, yanking him into a cramped passage used by servants to travel the house unseen. He fumbled to release his derringer from up his sleeve but froze on seeing another derringer aimed at his face.

"Off to bed, Bishop Redfort?" Lady Ashwood asked, holding the gun. Her husband had been the one who dragged him into the passage.

It seemed McBride and McKellen had met with the Hunts after all, and for some reason disclosed who had sent them to force the sale of their company. Unless, of course, the family had some other reason to accost him at gunpoint, and he found that unlikely.

"I am," he managed. "May I ask the reason for the gun?"

"Two reasons, Bishop," Lord Ashwood said. Redfort had always been slightly wary of the seemingly mild-mannered lawyer, for no reason he could ever discern. The man had always been courteous and generous with his donations. "First, there is the matter of you dispatching Roderick McBride and Alasdair McKellen to encourage us to sell our company to Margot Guillam."

"We declined her less than generous offer," Lady Ashwood said.

Denials seemed pointless. "I was merely relaying instructions, a humble messenger." *Do they know what Guillam is?*

"We're aware of that," Lady Ashwood assured him, holding the gun without a tremble.

"Secondly," and here Lord Ashwood exuded a menacing air. "Where is our son?"

Confused, it took Redfort a moment to reply. "I've not seen Wilton since the card game."

"Do not take us for fools, Redfort," Lady Ashwood hissed. "Mr McBride did. So did the late Alasdair McKellen. You or your associates have seized Wilton as leverage."

The late Alasdair McKellen. "I swear, Lady Ashwood, that I know of no intention to abduct him." The look of cold murder in the eyes of the Hunt couple made him deeply relieved that the three possible demons had vetoed his plan to move against the Hunts. "There was a proposal made to … to repeat Miss Guillam's offer for your company while here, but no agreement was reached to do so." He thought better than to mention he was the one who had proposed it.

"If any harm befalls Wilton, Redfort, be assured it will be visited upon you tenfold. I reached an agreement almost thirty years ago with Niall Fisher that his servants would leave my family alone. I expect that agreement to be honoured," Lord Ashwood said.

Who are you to make agreements with one of the most powerful beings in the world? Redfort stared at Lord Ashwood, thinking fast. "I noted discord between yourselves and Wilton. Perhaps he is simply avoiding you?"

Lady Ashwood shook her head. "He is not in his room. He was last seen in the company of Lord Smith, Mrs Carlton and another gentleman, the worse for drink."

Those three. So, the demons had voted against his proposal to pressure the Hunts only to seize the younger Hunt themselves. "They're demons loyal to Erik Keel," he said, knowing as he did so he had no proof that was the case. "You know of him?"

"We know him. You are sure?" Lord Ashwood's question lingered heavily in the air.

Redfort swallowed. "Almost certain. I have just learned of it. Councillors are protected from Possession upon their elevation, but Keel is somehow in a position to identify the likely successors for a Council Seat, and has had them Possessed beforehand."

"And he thereafter has the Councillor killed. Clever," Lord Ashwood said grudgingly. "My son is no Sooty Feather, why abduct him?"

"Perhaps they seek to leverage you into selling the company to Keel rather than Miss Guillam?" Redfort guessed.

"Then they have gravely miscalculated. Edith, remain in our rooms while Redfort and I fetch Singh and find our son. Should we fail to return, speak with Lady Delaney and take whatever punitive action you deem appropriate."

Chapter Thirty-Seven

An aching head accompanied Hunt's groggy return to consciousness. He opened his eyes, bewildered to see shadows slithering across the room. Shadows birthed, he realised, by flickering candles. The black iron range built into a wall told him he was in the kitchen, lying on top of a table in the centre, and when he tried to move, he realised he was tied to the legs. *What's going on?*

Memories of his previous captivity seared him, panic gripping his chest so hard her could barely breathe. *Oh, God.* Chagrined, he knew Kerry Knox had been right to warn him, and he had paid the price for his stupidity, for being too lost in anger and self-pity to note the danger around him. Dunkellen House was a viper's nest, and instead of being on his guard, he had been foolish enough to get drunk.

"He's awake."

"Good. Then we can proceed. The Sooty Feathers want the company owned by this one's family; instead we'll claim it for *Arakiel*."

The first speaker was a man, the second a woman.

A third voice spoke, one familiar to Hunt. "Should we not first speak with *Arakiel*? He may have something else in mind for this one." *Lord Smith, I think.* The last thing Hunt remembered was drinking with Smith and two others.

"We are *Arakiel*'s allies, not his vassals. He forgets that, sometimes. He is no longer a *Grigori*, lording it over us. He has since Fallen to Hell like the rest of us, a demon. No more, no less."

"He intends to restore his *Grigori* flesh," the woman said. Mrs Carlton, Hunt remembered. The younger man was called Kenmure.

"And that is why I, for one, am helping him, in exchange

for his continuing to Summon us into Vessels as required," Kenmure said. "Fisher does not favour us as *Arakiel* did, so I am content to restore dominion of Glasgow to *Arakiel*."

"It's *Beliel*'s fault," Mrs Carlton complained. "Fisher was always reluctant to Summon us after assassinating *Arakiel*, but more-so since *Beliel*'s insanity twenty years ago."

Hunt struggled to free himself while they talked amongst themselves, but whoever tied him up had done their job well. *I need to get out of here!*

"Ah, Mr Hunt," Lord Smith said. "Allow us to introduce ourselves."

A wave – no, three waves – of coldness washed over Hunt like icy water. All three had Unveiled. Demons…

Should I tell them who my father is? He was distantly aware of the irony that his survival may rely on his parentage. Being cast out of Heaven had not endeared Lucifer to his former followers, however, and Hunt feared disclosing his diabolical paternity might only make matters worse for him. Best to keep that card close to his chest for now.

"I know you," Lord Smith said, and for a moment Hunt hoped – and feared – the demons already knew whose son he was. Smith tapped his head. "From this Vessel's memories. I am *Asmodiel*."

"*Ifriel*," Mrs Carlton said.

"*Maridiel*." That was a relief of sorts, Hunt having dreaded that one of them was *Beliel*, the demon who had murdered Lady Delaney's children while Possessing her husband. More recently he had once again been killed by Delaney while Possessing Neil Williamson. Lady Delaney had not sent the demon back to Hell gently, instead shooting him in the gut and setting him on fire while Hunt watched. If *Beliel* held a grudge and decided to make Hunt pay for Lady Delaney's actions…

Another man entered the kitchen, and fresh anxiety left Hunt short of breath. No one would miss him until the morning.

"Mr Josiah, are you prepared?" Smith asked the new arrival.

"Yes, I'm ready." The man spoke quietly, almost cringing in deference to the three demons. "I prepared the room while he was unconscious. That cup contains the needed blood provided by Canning."

"Excellent. I've no appetite for *Beliel*'s company, but he will be enthusiastic in his opposition to Fisher and Guillam."

Smith's – *Asmodiel*'s – words left Hunt cold. They intended to Summon *Beliel*, using Hunt as the Vessel. "No! You can't!" Time to play that last desperate card. "My father is–"

A rag was wrapped tightly round his mouth, cutting off any further words.

"That's enough from you, Mr Hunt. These walls are thick, but let us take no chances," Smith said. "*Maridiel*, bring in the sacrifice."

A tied and bound kitchen maid was dragged from the pantry into the kitchen, eyes wide in terror. Hunt struggled in vain to free himself, knowing even if he succeeded, he was no match for his four captors. He had seen *Beliel*'s Possession near Loch Lomond and knew the kitchen maid's fate.

The Demonist Josiah conducted the ritual much as the late circus-man Micha had. A knife was slid across the maid's throat by Mrs Carlton, a dark river of blood spilling onto the floor as the others dutifully chanted *Beliel*'s name. She was left on the floor, her part in this bloody theatre done.

Hunt was distantly aware of a warmth in his nether regions and knew he'd pissed himself. But he had greater concerns; as Mrs Carlton sacrificed the poor woman, the candles flickered in startled disquiet. A disorientation fell over him, a sense of distance between himself and his body. And then he felt a *presence*.

A titanic force of gleeful malevolence smashed into him, darkly joyful at having escaped somewhere awful. Hunt was resolved to resist *Beliel*, holding a forlorn hope that his demonic heritage would be enough to fend it off.

That hope withered, the sheer power of the freed demon beyond Hunt's comprehension. It flooded into him, and he felt himself being torn free from his own body, knowing his evicted soul was bound for either Heaven or Hell. Recent revelations did not bode well for him in that regard, whatever Lucifer claimed.

No! Terrified and desperate, Hunt connected with that

dormant coldness he had used when facing Rannoch, feeling it rise from within, as dark and ancient as the force trying to expel him. He felt shock from *Beliel* as the demon's takeover of flesh and blood faltered.

Samiel...?

It took every ounce of Hunt's willpower to hold on, to not lose his own body. Unveiling – he now knew that was what he had done –

No ... not Samiel ... not wholly...

Beliel resumed his bid to possess Hunt, not that it had any choice in the matter. A Demonist's magic was not something a demon could resist any more than Hunt could will himself not to strike the ground should he fall off a mountain. Not that he imagined any demon would be reluctant to leave Hell.

Hunt was vaguely aware of a commotion around him, of the kitchen door opening again. He fought with every shred of willpower to resist *Beliel*'s Possession but was dismayed to realise he wasn't strong enough. Every heartbeat found him less and less *himself*, and within moments the demon would Possess his body utterly. Being the Devil's son had only bought Hunt a short reprieve, an extra few seconds of life.

Can't ... hold on ... Hunt knew he was done. He no longer felt his body...

And then he saw his father standing next to Singh and Bishop Redfort at the kitchen door.

And his father Unveiled, a tidal wave of *will* washing over the room.

Lucifer's Unveiling joined with his own, enough to halt *Beliel*'s usurpation of his body. Hunt felt *Beliel*'s rage as it was pushed slowly back. Part of Hunt was a piece of Lucifer – had always been – and as one they expelled the last of *Beliel*'s essence. There was one last echo of hate, rage and fear, and then the demon was gone, sent back to Hell.

*

Redfort took a particular pleasure at the fear and hate in Kenmure's eyes as he pointed his derringer at him, the demon having played him for a fool. He was experienced enough to recognise that multiple demons had Unveiled. Mrs

Carlton had fled out of the back door with Cornelius Josiah, neither Redfort nor Hunt wasting their single shots on the fleeing pair. Hunt's Indian valet was unarmed save for a knife that looked ceremonial, but he had the sense not to run out into the dark after the unknown. That left Kenmure and Lord Smith. And the newly Possessed Wilton Hunt was Unveiling too, uncontrollably.

Hairs rose on the back of Redfort's neck as the Unveiling got stronger, not weaker despite Mrs Carlton's flight.

Shock registered on Lord Smith's face. "*Samiel!*" He was staring at Lord Ashwood.

Redfort would have too, were he not ensuring that Kenmure refrained from mischief. *A demon! Am I the only one in this damned place not Possessed?*

"Indeed, *Asmodiel*. Care to explain this? *Arakiel* and I struck a deal in the spring; he and his minions were to leave me and mine alone."

"*Arakiel* said nothing of you," Kenmure said. *Arakiel*. At last, Redfort had gleaned Erik Keel's demonic name. *The Regent will be pleased.*

"Evidently not, *Maridiel*," Lord Ashwood said to Kenmure. *So, that is this demon's name.*

"Still you prove a curse to your own kind, Lightbringer," Kenmure said with loathing. "You overestimated your strength and brought millions of us low."

Redfort didn't think it possible to feel more frightened, overwhelmed as he was by four demons Unveiling, but on hearing Lord Ashwood identified as Satan, he managed it. *God help me*, he thought, though he had turned his face from God long ago.

"Perhaps. Or perhaps I overestimated the strength of those who followed me, *Maridiel*." Lucifer said. His valet, Singh, showed no surprise and said nothing.

"Lucifer," Redfort whispered, his derringer heavy in his hand. Poor McBride had been sent to bully a lord. Instead he had found the King of Hell waiting.

A smile quirked on the Devil's lips. "A pleasure, Bishop Redfort. Though you should know we've been acquainted for nearly thirty years."

So, he had never met the true Lord Ashwood. The Devil had sat in his congregation all those years, until Redfort had been replaced at the cathedral by Reverend Mitchell. A second realisation dawned. "But that would mean Wilton was conceived and born *after* you Possessed Lewis Hunt." *I baptised the Devil's son. The Antichrist?*

"Indeed. Ah, Wilton, I'm pleased I was in time."

"Is he not Possessed?" Redfort asked quietly, lowering his derringer.

"I assure you, Redfort, that with my aid, Wilton was successful in repelling *Beliel*."

Then just what exactly is he?

"It was damned close," Hunt managed to say. Redfort detected a whiff of urine but thought it politic to say nothing. If that was the worst indignity Hunt suffered this night, he should count his blessings.

"You're welcome, son," Lucifer said. Redfort decided to busy himself with watching Kenmure and Smith. He was acutely aware his gun held only one bullet.

"What now?" Lord Smith asked.

"A week ago, I might have killed you as a favour to Niall Fisher, however his servants have also recently vexed me. I think it would be best we all go our separate ways, *Asmodiel*." Lucifer turned to Redfort. "Do you agree?" It wasn't really a question.

Redfort would have much preferred to kill everyone present, particularly Kenmure, but he cleared his throat. "I think that would be best, Lord Ashwood." Revealing the Possession of three Councillors would still earn him the Regent's regard. Besides, with the Demonist Josiah still loose, the demons would simply be brought back in new bodies. At least for now Redfort knew their identities.

"Excellent. Singh, see to Wilton if you would be so kind."

"Yes, Lord Ashwood." The valet used his knife to cut Hunt free from the ropes binding him to the large kitchen table. Redfort caught another whiff of urine. *I hope the kitchen staff are diligent in cleaning that table in the morning before preparing breakfast.*

The two demons left, but not before Kenmure gave Redfort a mocking smile. "*Arakiel* looks forward to introducing himself to you, Bishop."

Joyous news. Something to look forward to. Maybe it was time to replace his derringer with a revolver, never mind the inconvenience of the greater size and weight. Leaving Glasgow was an option, but he had the glum feeling that for him, all roads led to Hell.

"Thank you." Hunt forced himself to stand. *I baptised the Devil's son.* Redfort fought the urge to laugh. And was almost sick as the faint sense of corruption he had sensed since arriving on the estate suddenly blossomed. And then faded. *Something happened...*

"Thank you for your aid, Redfort," Lucifer said. "The next time you're speaking with Miss Guillam, suggest to her in the strongest terms that she would be wise in leaving my family out of Sooty Feather business." He looked down at the kitchen maid's corpse. "We'll leave you to attend to the mess."

*

"Foley!" The sharp exhalation of his name yanked him to wakefulness.

"What is it?" Foley asked as he groggily sat up. Sirk had volunteered them to assist at the church acting as a makeshift hospital for the sick that night. He and maybe half of the others had lain down to get some sleep while the rest tried to make the patients comfortable.

"Something is wrong. Can you feel it?"

Sure enough, a *wrongness* pervaded the air. "Aye, what is it?"

"Something dark. Evil," Sirk said. He stood a silhouette in the vestry, two small candles giving the room a little light.

"We burned that damned horse, I thought that would end this." None of the sick had recovered, but neither had any more died, giving Foley hope that they had made a difference.

"Perhaps not soon enough."

"Doctor!" a voice cried out from the nave. Sirk turned and left without a further word, Foley getting to his feet and following.

"What is it?" Sirk asked brusquely. A chill had fallen over the church, heavy with foreboding. There were maybe fifty sick in the church, fever dreams causing them to stir restlessly. A few moaned. The church was lit by candles, a host of shadows crawling on the stone floor and walls. Over the minister's objections, the pews had been removed as the number of sick increased. Use of the village hall had been forbidden, though that restriction was probably lifted now that Lady MacInesker had held her damned ball for her damned rich friends.

One of those tending to the sick was a weaver called Ella, her daughters among the sick. Her husband had died two nights before. Hollowed eyes were wide with fear, telling Foley he and Sirk were not alone in sensing something was wrong.

And then it broke. As one the sick exhaled a final breath and went still.

"Hannah! Mercy!" Ella knelt over two girls lying side by side.

"Professor?" Foley stood at Sirk's shoulder as he crouched by the closest patient, a grim expression on his narrow face as he examined the man.

"Dead," Sirk answered. A scream from Ella told them that at least one of her daughters had likewise passed.

Foley looked around. The other patients were still, unmoving. Ella hugged her daughters, her mouth open in a now soundless scream. A silence had fallen over the church. "They're all dead." He hadn't examined the other patients, nor was he a doctor, but he knew he spoke the truth. Dead. Killed by a pestilence born of dark magic. *God help us.*

The scream had alerted the others in the church, most related to at least one of the patients. Cries of grief echoed round the church as they likewise found their kin dead.

Foley and Sirk traded a look. There was nothing to be done. He felt sick to his stomach, useless. A village was dying in sweat-soaked fever while the rich slept in the nearby Dunkellen House, maybe footsore from dancing.

"Hannah? … Hannah! Doctor, she lives!" The hope in Ella's voice cut through the noise.

"My Bert moved! He lives too!"

"She opened her eyes … Jessie!"

Mournful wails turned to hopeful shouts as everyone tending to a patient reported movement. Foley grinned at Sirk, a weight lifting from him. "Maybe we were premature in our diagnosis, Professor." The oppression that had hung over the church minutes before had gone.

Sirk looked uncertain. "Perhaps burning the pale horse was enough to weaken the sorcery." He walked over to Ella and her two stirring daughters. "Let me see one of them, miss."

Ella turned, tears of relief running down her face. "I thought they were gone, Doctor. I thought–"

Sirk put his hand to Hannah's neck. A frown creased his brow and he fumbled in his pocket for a small mirror. He held it next to her mouth, his frown deepening.

"What is it?" Foley asked. Ella was too busy hugging Mercy.

He spoke quietly. "I can feel no pulse. And no breath fogs my mirror."

Mercy jerked up and Ella screamed, thrashing wildly.

"Jesus!" Foley stared as he saw blood spill from Ella's neck, her daughter's mouth biting down hard. Other screams echoed round the church. Sirk tried to separate Ella and Mercy, but by the time he succeeded Ella's neck was a gory mess. She curled up on the floor, wailing in pain as her daughter jerked up to her feet. Mercy's face was pale and bloody, shadow and candlelight making dark pits of her unblinking eyes.

Movement caught Foley's eye. "Sirk!" he warned as the older daughter, Hannah, sat up and reached out for Sirk. Instinct made Foley shove her away, giving Sirk time to scramble to his feet.

"What the hell is this?" Foley shouted over the screams. The other patients were rising up, attacking those who nursed them. Two men and a woman were already down, howling as the afflicted bit away flesh from them, eating them alive. "Are they undead? Ghouls?"

He didn't wait for Sirk to answer, instead pulling out his revolver and cocking it. His spare ammunition had been left in his trunk at the inn, but he had six silver bullets loaded. Part of him baulked at shooting these people, but the sight of Hannah and Mercy tearing the flesh from their unmoving mother (dead, Foley prayed) killed any hesitation.

He aimed at Mercy, then noticed a stableman called Paul shuffling towards him. He shifted his aim to Paul's heart and forced himself to calmly wait until he was only three feet away before pulling the trigger.

The gunshot exploded around the church, deafening Foley. Paul showed no reaction to the sound, and Foley felt fear leap within him as the undead showed no reaction to the bullet in his heart either.

"He's not undead as we know them," Sirk shouted, his own revolver in hand. "None of them are."

Foley opened his mouth to ask what the hell they were but realised they had more pressing concerns. "How do we stop them?" he asked instead. He backed away to avoid Paul's outstretched arms.

"An excellent question, one which I cannot answer." Sirk shot Paul in the right knee, Foley shooting him in the left.

The dead stableman collapsed to the floor but showed no pain or alarm, crawling after them.

"To hell with this," Foley snarled as panic threatened to overwhelm him. He shot Paul in the head, surprised but pleased to see the corpse cease moving.

Sirk looked down at the unmoving Paul. "The head ... yes, shoot for the head. Sufficient damage to the brain should prove effective."

All well and good, but they were down to eight bullets between them, with maybe fifty rising dead in the church. "We need to get out of here!" Two corpses stood between them and the church doors, but shots to the head 'killed' them, leaving the doors uncontested.

Foley and Sirk fled into the night, the others in the church already dead or dying. Had the fifty risen corpses not been too busy killing and eating flesh, Foley knew he and Sirk would have been trapped in that horror.

He chanced a look behind him, seeing silhouettes leave the church in a shambling mob. "What are they?" he gasped out as they slowed. The dead were not pursuing. Instead they were heading for the village. *God help these people.*

"The dead, animated by sorcery," Sirk said slowly. "You recall when Miss Guillam tasked us to deal with George Rannoch, she made mention of necromancy?"

"Aye. Maybe," Foley said, not really sure and impatient for Sirk to get to the point.

"I think this is it. A magician has raised the dead. He or she is most likely responsible for the plague in the first place, using that slaughtered horse."

"What of the dead?" Foley asked. "How do we stop them? Will they just wander around killing anyone who gets in their way?"

Sirk started at the distant shapes disappearing between the cottages of Kaleshaws. "I think they're being controlled by the magician."

Foley's heart sank. "Shit. It's a fair guess that everyone sick died at the same time, aye?"

"Aside from those who died in the preceding days, yes."

"Many of the sick were being tended to at home, especially in the farms," Foley said.

"Unfortunate," Sirk said with heavy understatement. "And potentially even worse than that. Recall many died before tonight."

Foley closed his eyes briefly. The local doctor had wanted to burn all the dead, but the church minister had refused, and most of the next of kin wanted their dead buried, not burned. The compromise suggested by Dr Essex was that they all be buried in a mass grave outside the village...

"What now? We should warn Hunt and the others at Dunkellen House, but the village needs our help," Foley said.

"Our spare bullets are back at the inn. And I do not fancy the notion of blundering around in the dark, not knowing what lies out there."

Foley nodded, thinking of the dead clawing their way out of that mass grave. "We'll make our stand in the village then." He could already hear screams, knowing that those who had elected to tend to their own sick relatives were now being attacked by them. Many would die, others would escape out into the streets, only to find the dead from the church waiting for them.

Chapter Thirty-Eight

"Who are they?" Miss Knox asked.

Hunt was curious about that too. Seven large tents had been erected in a fallow field, enough for maybe twenty people. No one was visible. "Men working for either the Sooty Feathers or *Arakiel*, I suspect." *Here to protect the guests or murder us during the garden party.*

"We should find out," Lady Delaney said. The trio had borrowed horses from the stable for a morning ride around the Dunkellen estate.

Hunt felt no great enthusiasm for the notion of finding yet more people to pick a fight with, having come within a hair's breadth of being Possessed.

I was nearly gone. My body would have walked and talked, but it would have been a demon doing it, and looking through my eyes. I'd have been ... gone. Off to Heaven or Hell.

He had been helped back to his room, falling fast into an exhausted sleep, aided by the remnant of whatever drug the demons had slipped in his drink. If nightmares had twisted his dreams, he awoke with no recollection of them.

His expression must have betrayed his thoughts, because Miss Knox asked, "Are you quite recovered, Mr Hunt?"

He forced a smile. "Quite recovered, Miss Knox." So far as the two ladies were aware, the rite had been interrupted before its completion. Redfort knew, and Hunt could only hope his father had convinced the bishop to keep his mouth shut. "What now, with the demons unmasked?"

"*Arakiel*'s demons have fled, but the Sooty Feathers are very much still here," Lady Delaney said. She always seemed to be looking ahead to the next fight.

"I think running the demons off may have aided the Sooty Feathers," Miss Knox said. Hunt suspected the same; the demons had not come all the way to Dunkellen just for the ball and garden party.

"Perhaps, but now it is just us and them," Lady Delaney said.

"They will be vigilant," Miss Knox warned. "And they know we oppose them."

"Then we must be vigilant, also. They will not act openly against us, not with so many present unconnected to their society. The revelation that three of their leaders are demons will paralyse them, leaving them reluctant to trust their fellows to coordinate a move against us."

"Lady MacInesker might act against you on her own. She has a small army of servants here." Kerry gripped the reins tightly, not looking very confident as she rode side saddle. "And we did blow up her mill."

Hunt remained silent. *Arakiel*'s supporters had once again suffered a setback, failing to Summon *Beliel* and being unmasked by Bishop Redfort. That just left the Sooty Feathers, and he hoped Redfort would quietly suggest to his fellows that the Hunts were best left unmolested.

Unless, of course, Lady Delaney and Kerry Knox riled them up again. Which was looking increasingly likely. Not that Hunt could let them continue without his help, he owed them too much for that.

The camp seemed deserted, not that it should matter if any there saw Hunt and his companions. Dressed in brown tweed and wearing his straw boater hat, to all appearances he was just a gentleman out for a ride with two ladies. The ladies themselves wore tweed riding skirts and wide-brimmed hats to protect them from the morning sun.

"How do we find out what they're about?" Miss Knox asked. Away from the other guests, her accent and diction had roughened.

"I'll make enquiries with Lady MacInesker's staff. A few voiced concerns to her butler may yield results," Lady Delaney said.

"Watch your back with that bastard," Miss Knox warned. Hunt wondered at her animosity towards Mr Peel, who had been unfailingly polite to Hunt.

"Do you think Lady MacInesker and her staff know they're here?" he asked.

"I think it likely, they are on the estate and taking no pains to hide. Regardless, a lady asking about the band of ruffians camping nearby will not be out of character."

"What about us?" Miss Knox asked.

Lady Delaney looked at them. "You two should continue exploring the surrounding estate. Discover if there are any other secrets hidden in the fields and woods."

"You want us to go alone?" Hunt was taken aback. A young man and lady riding alone unchaperoned was cause for scandal.

A look of impatience crossed Lady Delaney's face. "I believe I can trust you, Mr Hunt, to be a gentleman in my absence? And I'm sure I can trust Miss Knox to answer any impertinence, should I have misjudged you."

He felt his face warm. "I can behave myself, Lady Delaney."

"Excellent. Do enjoy your picnic." Their saddlebags held blankets for them to sit on, sandwiches and a bottle of red wine. It was a good excuse for their absence, and besides, spying was hungry work.

He watched her ride back towards the house at a fast canter. Hunt didn't envy the ladies having to ride side-saddle, but Lady Delaney at least was a confident and experienced rider. "Miss Knox, do you really expect us to stumble across some great secret of the Sooty Feathers out here?"

"No."

"No?" He looked at her. "Then why are we out here?"

She looked around with a wistful smile, trying not to slide off the saddle. "Because I want to see what's out here. Because I want to enjoy a day in the sun."

"It might look like paradise, but there are people here who keep trying to kill me or put a demon in me," Hunt warned.

"Didn't they try to kill you in Largs?"

"Yes."

"And Glasgow?"

And Loch Aline. "Your point, Miss Knox?"

She grinned. "Maybe the problem is you and not the places."

*

Kerry had rarely felt so relaxed, breathing in the warm fresh air. She had spent all her life in Glasgow, used to dung-choked streets, buildings blackened by soot, and skies turned grey by endless smoke belched out by factories. In the city, the river was dirty and stinking; here the sky was blue and the river running through the estate was clean.

Conifers and broadleaf woodland carpeted this part of the estate, a riding trail allowing easy passage. They passed a field, Kerry staring in wonder at the thick, brown hides and long, curved horns of the grazing Highland cattle, most seeking shade beneath the trees. She saw farmhands in long brown smocks carrying buckets of water to fill iron troughs.

Kerry slid off her horse and leaned on a fence as one of the cows came over with a deep-throated bellow and let her scratch its head, its hide thick and coarse. Flies hovered around a large pile of shit.

"You've made a friend," Hunt said.

"I'll probably be eating one of her kin later," she said as she managed to remount her horse, waving Hunt off as he looked ready to dismount and help her up. "I can manage."

"It's a he," Hunt said.

The bull had turned, the evidence hanging on open display. "Oh? How can you be sure, Mr Hunt?" she asked breathlessly. "Do tell me."

He cleared his throat and pretended not to hear.

Onwards they rode through the large estate. "Does anyone live here?" she asked.

"There's the village that hosted the ball last night, and farms."

"The MacIneskers own all this?" Kerry asked.

"Yes. A lesser branch of the family own Dunlew Castle. Owned, perhaps. I don't know who stands to inherit the estate now Alasdair McKellen is dead."

Her family had rented a small tenement flat and counted themselves lucky. *The rich live in a world apart.* She saw a river, diminished by the long dry summer. "Where does that come from?"

Hunt considered it. "Near Eaglesham Moor, I think. It eventually terminates in the Clyde."

Kerry dismounted again and dipped her hands in the water, splashing some over her face. "Let's follow it."

"Why not?" They tied their horses to a tree, Kerry satisfied there was enough slack for them to reach the river for water. Hunt removed the saddlebags and hung them around his shoulders.

The stream led them deeper into the woods. Not much light penetrated the thickening canopy overhead, twigs and branches carpeting the earthy ground beneath their feet. Kerry was glad she wore tweed, the wool thick enough to resist the branches pulling at it. She pulled off her hat, Hunt following suit with his own.

"Not an easy wood to walk through," Kerry said between breaths as they climbed a slope.

"You should see the Lewswood near Loch Aline. Now that's a forest."

The trees opened into a small clearing, the river fed from a small waterfall, falling water churned into white foam before continuing downriver. "What's that sound?" There was a rumbling from higher up the slope, like faint thunder.

"A larger waterfall, I think," Hunt said.

Kerry had never seen one before today. "Let's go look."

"It's quite a climb."

"Then we'd better get on with it, hadn't we?"

The climb proved troublesome indeed, the dry loamy earth giving way beneath their feet, and they were both coated in sweat by the time they reached the top. *Worth it, though*, Kerry decided on getting there.

A large pool of water waited, surrounded by trees and fed by a large waterfall falling off a low cliff of rock. Kerry took a breath, inhaling air perfumed by flowers and mulch.

*

Redfort sat in a shaded part of the garden, watching a game of croquet being played, some of the ladies content to watch, hand-held parasols protecting them from the sun. William Heron dozed on a chair two along, unaware and untroubled by the previous night's excitement. A large tent had been erected on the lower lawn the day before for the garden party, the servants busy setting up tables and chairs.

A lady walked towards him, and he felt himself tense slightly on recognising Lady Delaney. He forced himself to relax, doubting she would be so brazen as to murder him on a sunny Saturday morning with witnesses present.

"Good afternoon, Bishop. A delightful day," she said on entering the shade.

"A very good afternoon, Lady Delaney. We are blessed indeed."

"Indeed. I was out for a ride earlier when I observed a sizeable number of tents elsewhere on the estate. Should I be concerned?"

She's discovered my men, and wonders if they are Erik Keel's, sent here to assault the house. "I'm quite sure these men are no cause for concern, Lady Delaney." *And you may keep your nose out of my affairs.*

Her head nodded a fraction. "So long as you're aware of them and can vouch for their … conduct."

"I can, indeed, good lady," he assured her. Killing the circus-folk was their job, though alas it now appeared that Kenmure – or rather his demon – had 'located' the circus merely to ensure he got Thatcher's vacant Council seat.

"Very good." She walked away. Redfort returned his attention to the croquet.

Chapter Thirty-Nine

"I'm going in for a swim," Miss Knox announced, entranced by the pool and waterfall. Cherry blossoms drifted in the air and waterlilies floated near the edge. Long grass grew wildly from the bank, the woods alive with birdsong and insect chatter.

Hunt blinked. "But … you've no bathing suit," he said, sounding inane even to himself.

She was already pulling off her shoes, displaying bare feet and ankles. After that she removed her hat and hairpins, shaking her chestnut hair free. She stopped and gave him a look. "Well?"

"Well what?"

She sighed impatiently. "Are you going to stand there and gape, or turn around like a gentleman?"

"Sorry, yes!" Hunt turned, feeling his face burn. He managed to direct his gaze steadfastly ahead, conducting an intent study of a tree, but he could hear her removing her clothes. A few minutes later – though it felt longer – he heard a splash of water and a gasp.

"You can turn around," she said, a shiver in her voice.

He did so, tentatively, relieved (and disappointed) to find Miss Knox fully immersed in the pool. Her pale freckled shoulders were slightly above the water, but he could make out nothing else save for a tantalising white blurry mass beneath the rippling water.

Realising he was staring, he jerked his eyes up to meet hers, and caught a look of knowing amusement on her face. He reminded himself that she had grown up in a small flat, perhaps with siblings, and that modesty was a luxury most could not afford. "How's the water?"

"Cold but refreshing. Are you coming in?"

Walking together unchaperoned was enough to ruin her reputation and see him become an object of derision, a social pariah; bathing naked together would destroy them both.

If we're caught. Hot and sticky with sweat, the cold water did look inviting. "Turn around, if you please, Miss Knox."

She did so, the ends of her chestnut hair floating in the water. He stared at her pale skin a moment and then he knelt, pulling off his shoes and stockings. His linen waistcoat, shirt, trousers and underwear joined his jacket on the ground until he stood naked, feeling the grass beneath his bare feet.

"Are you in yet?" Miss Knox asked, starting to turn.

"Not yet!" he blurted, only to realise she was teasing him. He lowered himself into the water, sucking in a breath of air as his legs touched the cold water. Knowing it would only be worse if he dragged it out, he steeled himself and went all in, ducking his head under the water. "God!" he gasped on emerging, the shock of the cold giving him a brief convulsion.

Miss Knox turned, laughing and splashing water at him. She ducked beneath the surface before he could retaliate, shaking her head as it emerged, her hair now a slick dark brown. "Glorious, aye?"

He returned her smile, feeling oddly free. "Yes, glorious, Miss Knox."

She made a face. "I think that given the circumstances, we might be less formal. You may call me Kerry."

"Wilton. Or Wil, if you prefer."

Time seemed to stop as they swam lazily in the water, enjoying one another's company and free, for once, from the weight of terrible knowledge that burdened them. There were no undead here and no demons. *Well, myself excepted.*

"Why do you do this?" Hunt asked.

"Bathe in the water?"

"Follow Lady Delaney. Fight the undead."

She took a moment to answer. "I want to do something that … matters. I was an actress before this, working penny geggies on Glasgow Green during the summer and working in bars the rest of the year. Now I'm making a difference, standing up to evil and saving lives even if they'll never know it."

Hunt remembered the Gerrards. The dead Templars Burton

and Carter. "And what of the risk?"

"Lady Delaney has survived for two decades," Kerry said.

"Yes, but at what cost? Twenty years of fear and peril have taken their toll on her. What life does she live?"

"A life I've chosen. Where no man tells me what to say, what to think, what I may do or not do. Trapped in a cage of expectation where I must take care not to voice my opinions or disagree with a man. Where I must spend my days tending to children and mopping up their piss and shit or be considered less than a woman." She took a breath. "What life have you chosen? You tried to hide in the Highlands, in the middle of nowhere. And still they found you. Here, last night, you were moments from being Possessed. Some of us choose to fight; the fight has chosen you, Wilton Hunt."

Hunt let that pass. "You know how this will end. With you dead or worse."

She met his eyes. "How many have innocents have died because they had the bad luck to cross paths with the undead one dark night? Your Amy Newfield didn't choose to die, didn't choose to become undead, but it was chosen for her. At least I know the threat and have been trained to face it. Anyway, it hasn't ended for Lady Delaney."

"Not yet. But they know who she is now. Who you are."

"They can take it up with us back in Glasgow," Kerry said, though her bravado sounded a little forced.

"Don't think they won't, and don't expect them to send you a calling card giving you notice of their intention to 'visit'," Hunt warned, remembering Richard Canning's nocturnal visit with a razor. He still bore the scars, surviving only because of Foley's intervention. "They murdered a family and a farmer to get to me. And I hadn't caused them the trouble you two have."

"The man who makes a habit of being abducted is giving me advice on being careful?" Kerry splashed him with some water, Hunt sensing restrained anger on her part at his advice, admittedly unsolicited.

"I've seen enough people hurt," he said, not wanting an argument. Not on a day like this, far from his troubles.

"We're not dead yet," Kerry said. "And we'll be careful. Or would you have us fill our days with embroidery and our nights smiling prettily at your jokes?"

"I know some funny jokes." He let out a breath. "Are you ready for luncheon?"

She widened her eyes and adopted a simpering tone. "Shall I fetch your valet to serve it? A gentleman like yourself mustn't unman himself with domesticity."

"I don't have a valet," he pointed out, trying to hide a smile. "And we can divide the chores between ourselves."

"Poor deprived fellow." She swam to the bank and climbed out, giving Hunt a heart-stopping glimpse of pale skin before he hastened to turn around, hearing her laugh as he did so.

A short time later she said, "You can look, Mr Hunt."

He did so, seeing her dressed once more though damp hair clung to her shoulders. "I'm coming out," he said.

"In your own time." She showed no inclination to look away, a smile playing on her lips. She tossed a blanket next to the bank.

"I'd be obliged if you averted your eyes, Miss Knox. Kerry."

She laughed again and did so, busying herself with the saddlebags while he hauled himself out of the water, snatching up the blanket.

*

Kerry and Wil sat on a large blanket spread out across the grass. They were alone and yet not, surrounded by singing birds and crickets, a light breeze causing the branches to whisper and the water to ripple.

She watched him wrestle with the bottle of wine and a wooden-handled corkscrew. "I thought you knew your wines."

"Drinking them, yes, this is my first time opening a bottle," he said, his voice strained. "It's more difficult that it looks."

Kerry leaned back. "I'm sure I couldn't comment, sir."

Finally, he succeeded in pulling the cork free. He frowned on seeing the tip of the corkscrew sticking out of the cork's bottom. "There may be a bit of cork in the wine. Sorry."

"If you've ruined that wine, sir, I shall insist you return to the house and fetch another bottle from the cellar."

Wil didn't reply, too busy pouring wine into two of the three packed glasses. Kerry hadn't drunk much red wine,

Caroline's cellar mostly stocked with white. She was curious how it would taste.

He handed her a glass and sat back down on the grass. "Thank you," she said, eyeing the deep purple liquid filling half the glass.

"To your good health." He raised the glass in toast. "Long may it continue."

Kerry clinked her glass off his. "And yours." She took a sip, surprised by its intensity, rough against her throat. "Jesus, that's strong."

"It's young and very tannic. A Syrah from the Rhone Valley, according to Mr Peel." He took another sip. "Not too bad."

She scowled when he named the butler before assuming a knowledgeable expression. "Yes, I can taste the Spanish pine."

Wil gave her a look. "The Rhone Valley is in France and wine is typically aged in oak. Not pine."

"Mmm." Kerry made a show of swishing some around her mouth. "Reminds me of a Chardonnay I had the pleasure of drinking while in Cannes."

"Chardonnay is white."

"Are you sure, Mr Hunt? I can taste the hops."

He opened his mouth, doubtless to tell her hops were used in beer, when he seemed to realise she was teasing him. They drank wine amidst a comfortable silence, Kerry feeling it go to her head.

"We should return to the house soon," she said. "But first I'll need your help rearranging my hair." Returning with it in disarray would encourage lewd speculation.

"Did you forget to bring your lady's maid?" A smile creased his face at the opportunity to tease her for once.

"Maybe she ran off with your valet?"

"Can we stay a little longer?" he asked.

Kerry listened to the waterfall, soothed by the sound. "Why not?"

Chapter Forty

Kerry stood in the courtyard, having been helped out of the saddle by a groom. He led her chestnut horse into the stable to be brushed down and fed. Riding through the estate had been quicker and less tiring that walking, but she suspected her legs would be no less sore afterwards, muscles unused to riding side-saddle stretched and tender.

Dismounting with rather more grace than she had managed with her traumatised legs, Wil noticed her discomfort. "A hot bath will help with your legs, or you'll struggle to walk tomorrow."

"A fine idea, Wil. Just don't expect to join me this time," she said, taking care none of the grooms or stable boys were within earshot.

To her delight, he turned crimson and struggled to think of a rejoinder. Evidently failing, he settled for brushing some dirt from his trousers as a stable boy came over to take their crops.

"Why, Mr Hunt, you seem to have caught the sun. Your cheeks are red," she said loudly. Caroline waited by the courtyard archway, having met them shortly before they returned to the stable, maintaining the pretence that she had chaperoned them the whole time. *So long as no one who saw her return to the house thinks to wonder where Wil and I were.*

Kerry and Wil followed Caroline from the stable, walking along a path leading to the main garden. The river flowed to their left, a wall and trimmed hedge to their right. "Did you both enjoy your ride?" Caroline asked. Instead of walking directly to the house, she led them up a cobbled path leading to gardens where vegetables grew and flowers flourished.

"It was very pleasant, Lady Delaney," Wil said.

"Very," agreed Kerry, neither looking at the other.

"And was it productive? Did you notice anything of note?" Caroline led them through a walled herb garden, the air smelling of lavender and chamomile.

"Nothing, Lady Delaney," Kerry said. "The estate was quiet and peaceful. And Mr Hunt was a perfect gentleman."

"Too much of a gentleman to point out that you've missed a button on your riding skirt," Caroline said.

Damn. Kerry quickly fastened it. "Thank you."

Caroline glanced back at her. "Curious that I did not notice it earlier."

"You had a lot on your mind, Lady Delaney," Kerry said. Wil thankfully succeeded in trapping a laugh from escaping.

"Hmm. A hot bath will help ease any discomfort tomorrow."

"I suggested as much to Miss Knox, Lady Delaney," Wil said, Kerry wishing he would just keep his mouth shut.

"Very thoughtful of you, Mr Hunt. However, perhaps if you had balanced your interest in Miss Knox's legs and posterior with the rest of her, you could have informed her that her hair and hat are slightly askew."

"Perhaps my attention was *wholly* elsewhere, focused on more pressing concerns than Kerry's figure?" Wil said with some asperity.

"'Kerry'?" Lady Delaney looked between them. "My, you two *have* become fast friends."

Keen to hurry past Wil's lapse, Kerry asked, "Did you learn anything about the men camping nearby, Lady Delaney?"

Mercifully, Caroline seemed content to let the subjects of Kerry's arse and mussed hair drop. "Bishop Redfort gave no reason for their presence but assured me they should occasion no cause for concern."

"That in itself is surely a cause for concern," Wil said.

"Perhaps. I suspect they are here to prevent a repeat of Dunclutha."

"Unless Redfort intends his own repeat of Dunclutha," Kerry said.

"The thought occurred, however if that were the case, I believe he would not have his men camping in plain sight."

"So, what now for our intrepid band?" Wil wanted to know.

"We wait. Watchful. Vigilant. And ready, Mr Hunt, for anything." Caroline's exasperated look included Kerry.

Kerry thought Caroline's rebuke towards *her* was unnecessary but let it pass. Despite an (almost) entirely innocent afternoon, she conceded that there was evidence to suggest otherwise.

*

Impatience almost drove Redfort to profanity. Sir Wilbur Poole – *Secundus* – was not taking well the revelation that the three newest Councillors were demons. Redfort had quietly gathered the two remaining Councillors for a meeting in the library. The continuing excellent weather and fresh lemonade being served in the garden left him little fear of being interrupted.

"That's almost half the Council," Sir Wilbur said, stating the obvious.

"Indeed, Sir Wilbur. Fortunately, they have fled, but who can say what mischief they managed here beforehand?" Redfort asked.

Lady MacInesker looked at Redfort with some suspicion. "I'm curious how you came to learn of this."

She wonders if I've had them killed and their bodies hidden. "Their behaviour made me suspicious, particularly once Mr Heron told me that he was the victim of an attempted abduction. And that he is in line for the next vacant Council seat." *Of which there are now three.* "I found them in the kitchen last night, preparing to Possess Wilton Hunt with *Beliel*."

"You stopped them – alone?" Lady MacInesker asked, her tone politely disbelieving.

"I had some help," Redfort admitted. "Lord Ashwood and his valet. We were armed and took the demons by surprise. Mrs Carlton fled with the Demonist, Josiah, so killing Kenmure and Smith would have just meant the demons being Summoned into new bodies, us being none the wiser as to their identities. Ashwood and I convinced the demons Possessing Kenmure and Smith to leave Dunkellen."

"Josiah," Sir Wilbur said for no apparent reason. *The silly old fool.*

Lady MacInesker ignored him. "I was unaware Lord Ashwood was so formidable."

"As were Messrs McKellen and McBride. We should perhaps be grateful the three demons voted against my motion to move against Lord Ashwood last night," Redfort said. He decided against revealing Ashwood's true identity. Better to tell Regent Guillam privately first.

Lady MacInesker looked at Redfort questioningly. "Cousin Alasdair was supposed to arrive yesterday, but he's sent no word. Are you telling me he was involved in McBride's mission against Lord Ashwood?"

"He was, on Regent Guillam's instructions," Redfort said. "Lady Ashwood implied he did not survive this early test of his abilities."

Lady MacInesker looked shocked to hear of McKellen's death but not overly upset. He was, after all, a distant cousin of her late husband's, and as he had no siblings, perhaps her son was now heir to Dunlew.

"At least we still know the location of the Carpathian Circus and can deal with it," Sir Wilbur said.

A profanity hovered on Redfort's tongue, but he managed to let it pass unvoiced. "I think we can assume that Kenmure lied about the location of the circus. At best going there would be a waste of our time. At worst, we would risk an ambush. Tomorrow, I will lead the men back to Glasgow and report to Regent Guillam."

Sir Wilbur's eyes widened. "The knave!"

Lady MacInesker looked at Redfort. "There may still be other demons among us."

"I agree. I can assume you two are not demons, as you were both warded prior to Rannoch's coup and Keel's return."

"We can trust no other Sooty Feathers here. I suggest we remain vigilant and keep our own counsel," Lady MacInesker said.

"Vigilant," Sir Wilbur said with a nod.

"I agree," Redfort said, ignoring him. "Upon our return to Glasgow, we can put the matter to Regent Guillam. And suggest that she avoid the more obvious choices for replacement councillors. Keel has been killing off the Council after first Possessing the next candidate for the seat with a demon loyal to him."

"At least the three demons are unmasked, and we have a score of armed loyal men nearby," Lady MacInesker said. She rose. "I have guests to attend to. Do try and enjoy yourselves, gentlemen. Summer will be done and gone soon enough, and winter upon us."

*

Servants discreetly crossed the lawn, carrying trays of food and drink to waiting tables, ensuring no one wanted for anything. Lady MacInesker's guests had gathered on the lawn, either seated on chairs, lounging on rugs spread across the mown lawn, or standing in small groups, talking. Some sat on wooden chairs set up beneath a large trio of oak trees providing shade while others congregated within the refreshment tent. Large parasols were attached to most of the chairs to ensure no guest was subjected to too much sun.

Sofas and armchairs had been carried from the house to provide comfort, interspersed with basket and garden seats. The musicians from last night's ball had remained to provide music, a wooden platform set down for dancing.

Hunt saw a few guests playing croquet. Bows, arrows and archery butts had been set up on the riverbank just outside the garden, sensibly arranged so that even the poorest of shots would endanger no one, except maybe a duck or low-flying bird.

The garden party looked to be a triumph for Lady MacInesker, honoured by the attendance of many eminent notables of Glasgow. Surrounded by sunshine and merriment, last night seemed like a fading nightmare. Hunt looked at Dunkellen House's walls, almost trembling as he recalled how close *Beliel* had come to Possessing him. Had Lucifer – his father – not arrived, he would be off to whatever afterlife awaited him while *Beliel* walked about freely in his body.

He had so far managed to avoid his parents, though found himself frequently finding Kerry Knox. She wore a white summer dress and bonnet, acting and looking the part of a well-bred young lady, a testament to her acting skills and Lady Delaney's instruction.

A fair number of Black Wing Club members were in

attendance, Hunt wondering how many were also Sooty Feathers. It was possible he and his father were the only club members present who had not been inducted into the secret society at its heart.

"Mr Hunt, I trust you're well recovered from last night?"

He turned to see Bishop Redfort standing behind him.

*

"Entirely recovered," Hunt answered, not that Redfort was fooled. Wilton Hunt was a man out of his depth. Avoiding the Hunts would be the prudent course of action, but Redfort couldn't resist. He studied the Devil's son, wondering just what he was. Sired by Satan Himself, how much was human and how much demon? Was this uncertain young man truly the Antichrist? There was little about him to inspire dread or suggest that the End of Days was any time imminent, let alone that Hunt would be its architect. *Perhaps he'll grow into it.*

"I'm pleased to hear it."

"Excuse me, your Grace," Hunt said, almost rudely as he walked away.

"Don't be offended, your Grace. I rather think it is Lord Ashwood and me he wishes to avoid, not you." Lady Ashwood had joined them, a small parasol protecting her from the sun.

Redfort made a dismissive motion. "I take no offense. Your son has a lot on his mind." *Does she know who her husband is? What he is?* He decided to be circumspect in case she didn't, not wanting to aggravate Lucifer with unwelcome revelations.

"Yes, Wilton has had a rather eventful week, learning an uncomfortable family truth." There was a knowing look in her eyes. "A truth we would rather he had learned under more managed circumstances, but Roderick McBride and Alasdair McKellen forced our hand."

Ah, so she does know. Redfort had always admired Lady Ashwood, finding her a formidable woman who was generous in her tithes to the Church. How could she marry the Devil and bear his child?

Lord Ashwood arrived, impeccably dressed as ever,

standing next to his wife. Redfort wondered if that was amusement in their eyes, if they guessed he wondered at their marriage. They had always seemed a strong couple, Lewis Hunt the London-based lawyer, and Edith Hunt, the shrewdly ruthless director of the Browning Shipping Company.

"I trust you'll explain matters to Miss Guillam, Bishop?" Lord Ashwood – it felt better to think of him by that name – asked. "It would be unfortunate if I had to trouble Lord Fisher with news that his regent and Council are failing to abide by honourably struck agreements."

Lady Ashwood nodded once, crisply. "Leave her in no doubt that the Browning Shipping Company is most assuredly not for sale."

"I will speak with Miss Guillam," Redfort promised. Did Lucifer truly have the means to contact Niall Fisher? Best to assume he did.

"And she would be well advised to leave Roderick McBride in absolutely no doubt that he is to stay away from my family," Lord Ashwood added. "Should there be a repeat of his previous behaviour, I will express my *disapprobation* to Miss Guillam in the strongest terms. Am I clear?"

A cold shard of fear tore through Redfort as he looked into Lord Ashwood's clear blue eyes, seeing the devil within. "McBride will not trouble you again."

Lucifer held Redfort's gaze, perhaps gauging his sincerity. "Excellent." And then the affable Lord Ashwood was back. He took his wife's arm. "Shall we investigate the buffet table, my dear?"

"A sound idea, Lewis."

Redfort mopped his brow with a handkerchief, feeling sweat beading beneath the rim of his top hat. *I think a brandy is called for.*

A young footman approached. "Your grace, Mr Henderson asks if he might speak with you in the smoking room?"

Redfort had little interest in speaking with his secretary, an employee he was becoming increasingly dissatisfied with, but it gave him an excuse to go indoors for a while. *He may have become increasingly insolent, but at least he is no demon.*

*

Kerry sat next to Caroline, an old oak tree shading them from the sun. The garden party, Kerry's first, was beautiful, and she marvelled at the organisation required. And the money. Men, women and children employed by Lady MacInesker were worked to exhaustion and injury for a pittance while she owned a large house and vast estate.

The refreshment tent had been filled with more food and drink than Kerry had ever seen in once place before; kettles of tea and coffee, jugs of fresh lemonade, baskets of buttered bread, bowls filled with fruit, jellies and salads, and plates overflowing with cold chicken, ham, salmon, and cakes. Delicate glasses filled with punch, champagne and wine were lined up.

Caroline seemed content to enjoy the day, sitting back with her eyes closed, seemingly oblivious to the enemies around them. She had said little but Kerry had the feeling that tonight would see them make their move against Lady MacInesker and any other Sooty Feathers who got in their way. That prospect alone allowed Kerry to eat and drink from the buffet tent with only a little guilt.

Wilton Hunt walked over, Kerry noting a hesitance. "May I fetch you anything?" he asked. "Some food or wine perhaps?"

Kerry smiled. "No, thank you, Mr Hunt. Why don't you join us?" She patted an empty seat next to her.

"Thank you, I think I will." The band was playing lively music, some younger guests dancing on the platform. Several men tested their archery skills, not that there was much skill on display.

Chapter Forty-One

Redfort entered the smoking room, its walls panelled in oak, a red rug covering the parquet flooring. The room was empty except for Henderson who Redfort was appalled to find relaxing in an armchair, smoking a cigar with a generous glass of whisky sitting on a small adjacent table. *As if he owned the place...*

Redfort cleared his throat, incensed at his man's presumption.

Henderson looked up, but rather than have the decency to jump up and stammer an apology, he merely smiled. "Bishop, excellent. Have a seat."

Redfort rarely found himself at a loss for words but this was one such occasion. His secretary had been acting above his station for a few months, but never had Redfort seen him act with such breath-taking insolence. *One word to Lady MacInesker, and her servants will horsewhip you to within an inch of your miserable life!*

"Have you taken leave of your senses?" he said, finally. "You're dismissed! Get yourself from my sight."

"Do sit down, Redfort." Henderson sounded unimpressed. There was a note of command in his voice, one Redfort had never heard him use before. "*Maridiel* did tell you I wished to introduce myself."

A tightness seized Redfort's chest as realisation dawned. *I'm a fool.* "You're Erik Keel. *Arakiel.*"

Henderson – the demon *Arakiel* – seemed to be relishing this. "I prefer Erik Keel for the time being, but yes. Consider this my resignation as your secretary." He pointed to the chair next to him. "I believe I told you to sit?"

Redfort sat, too wrongfooted to defy him.

The demon spoke. "I've been looking forward to this

meeting, Redfort." Eyes that had once always flickered to the floor when Redfort looked at them now met his, the mask of subservience Keel had worn badly since Possessing Henderson now cast aside. "I was tempted to say nothing, to leave you to your fate unaware. However, working for you was such an unpleasant experience, I decided to introduce myself first."

The demon hadn't decided to reveal himself today on a whim. *It has something set in motion.* "When did you Possess Henderson?"

The demon's eyes glinted, clearly enjoying this. Redfort was uncomfortably aware of the degrading little tasks he had given to Henderson, such as polishing shoes and needlessly doing accounts. "Wait," Redfort said, thinking back. "Henderson was taken at Dunclutha, was he not? He disappeared for some days, leading me to assume he had been killed until he – you – returned a week later." It had been around that time he had noticed the change in behaviour in his secretary.

"Well reasoned, Bishop. Yes, he was taken at Dunclutha, Rannoch keeping him alive to become my Vessel at the Necropolis. I don't believe he anticipated me being confined to it for so long, but Rannoch's death has delayed my reckoning with Niall Fisher."

Redfort decided this conversation had run its course, reaching into his pocket for his derringer but finding nothing.

Keel placed it on the table with a knowing smile. "Had you not seen fit to assign me a valet's duties while here, I would not have had the opportunity to take that."

"I see." *Is this where it ends?*

"You have a reputation among the Sooty Feathers as a man of wits and resourcefulness. I've seen little evidence of either during our time together, just a petty man scheming for scheming's sake. If you survive this day, we may talk again." He stood. "I've business elsewhere. I'd bid you a good day, Redfort, but it will be no such thing."

*

"Come on!" Foley shouted at Sirk, almost dragging him on. The past night and day had become an unending horror of death and carnage. They had retrieved guns and bullets from their trunks in the inn, the guests and innkeeper already woken by screams as the dead swarmed the once-quiet village famed for its textiles and weaving.

Maybe half the village survived the initial onslaught, most of those caring for sick relatives dying at their loved ones' hands. By the time Foley and Sirk had rallied the villagers, armed them with anything that could be used as a weapon and impressing upon them to aim for the head, their chances at holding a few large buildings like the inn and hall looked fair.

And then those killed by the afflicted rose and joined their killers, and Foley had known the fight was lost. The survivors had fled, many dying as desperation forced them to fight through the army of corpses overrunning Kaleshaws. On leaving the village, the dead in relentless pursuit, Foley had at first thought they had a clear run at Dunkellen House.

But fatigue and injury slowed the fugitives, and the dead caught up. The group had splintered, Foley and Sirk left on their own. Their bullets were spent, and their last hope was to get to Dunkellen House. Unless it too had fallen.

*

The day drew on, many of the guests withdrawing to the house. Lady MacInesker's servants had returned the couches and armchairs to their proper rooms, leaving garden chairs on the lawn for those guests remaining outside.

"What do they think they are doing?" a scandalised voice said. "Are they drunk, the rascals?"

Kerry joined Sir Wilbur Poole at the drawing room window, curious as to what was going on. So far, the guests had been well-behaved.

A mob had entered the garden, dressed like villagers and farmhands, savagely attacking those guests still relaxing on the lawn. *What the hell...?*

"What madness is this?" a man demanded as he stood next to Kerry at the window. "Has the pestilence driven them mad?"

The hairs on the back of Kerry's neck rose as she stared at the violence outside. Hapless guests tried to defend themselves but were no match for the villagers. There were gasps and small shrieks as the guests looking out the windows witnessed their fellow ladies and gentlemen being mauled, beaten and bitten to death.

Kerry shook off her shock, knowing she must act. The attackers were not crazed by fever, something else was behind this. They were not ghouls or *Nephilim* either, or the sun would have slain them. *Something else. I must find Caroline.*

Screams echoed from the front of the house, and she realised more attackers had entered the entrance hall. From there they could go down into the basement and assault the servants or go up to the ground floor and attack the guests. Kerry and Caroline had brought guns and bullets, but they were upstairs in their bedrooms. All they had now were their derringers, a few spare bullets, and a hidden blade each.

*

A cry of triumph escaped Heron's lips as he executed a perfect lunge, skewering the *thing*'s chest with a rapier he had freed from the corridor wall. *The old fencing lessons return!*

But his opponent didn't fall. The villager with the ashen face and dead eyes stepped forwards, sliding up the rapier's blade. Panicked, Heron tried to pull it free but failed. Callused hands reached out and grabbed his throat, pulled him closer.

"Help!" Heron cried out, but panic ruled the main corridor joining the front and back of the house, people fleeing or falling to the Risen dead. Desperation to live warred with the dead man trying to kill him, the latter proving the stronger.

Something exploded down the corridor, a gunshot he realised, and the corpse fell to the ground. Heron rubbed his throat and looked up to see Miss Knox striding down the corridor, a wisp of smoke leaving the barrel of the small gun she held. Flickers of fear threatened to crack the mask of determination on her face, but it held, barely trembling fingers already loading a fresh bullet into her gun.

"Thank you!" Heron gasped, his throat raw and sore.

"You're welcome. Have you seen Lady Delaney?"

"No. But we must get out of here! The dead are everywhere."

"The undead? But it's still daylight."

"Not undead. A necromancer is here, sending the dead against us."

"Jesus, there's always some new horror with you damned Sooty Feathers, isn't there?"

He didn't bother replying to that. "They're coming through the front door, we must–"

"They're in the rear garden too." She paused. "There's a side door leading out of the library. Use it and get out of here."

Heron gaped at her. "You're not coming?"

"I've friends here. Go!" A young housemaid almost frantic with terror cowered nearby. "Nell! Follow this man and get out of here." Miss Knox took off down the corridor, not waiting to see if they followed her advice.

"Miss, we must go," Heron said, taking the maid's arm. He would have fled the house in any case, but at least now he had the excuse of being this woman's protector.

They entered the library, not alone in fleeing into the garden.

*

Foley and Sirk had hoped to find sanctuary at Dunkellen House but the dead preceded them. Men and women in summer gowns, formal tails or serving livery lay dead on the lawn or on the steps leading up to the rear of the house. Muffled screams escaped open doors and windows as the *zombis* hunted within.

A small courtyard led to the kitchen door, weary legs carrying Foley and Sirk inside. Raised voices echoed up and down the servants' corridor, bouncing off white, glazed bricks.

A tall grey-haired man hurrying to the kitchen halted on seeing them, alarm crossing his face. He aimed a derringer at them.

"We're not ... whatever these people have become," Foley managed between breaths. "We escaped the village."

The man lowered his gun. "I'm relieved to hear it. They're called *zombis*."

"The result of necromancy, I surmise," Sirk said.

"You surmise correctly. We should be leaving," the man said, stepping towards them.

Foley shook his head. "Not that way, the dead are close behind us."

"Bishop!" A voice echoed down the corridor, the woman it belonged to hurrying towards them, a group of men and women behind her.

"Bishop Redfort?" Sirk queried.

"Indeed," the bishop muttered. "Lady MacInesker, a relief seeing you unharmed. And Sir Wilbur, my heart is gladdened to see you still among us. We would sorely miss your sage counsel."

Foley and the others had travelled from Loch Aline to confront this woman, kin by marriage to the late Kail'an chief, Alasdair McKellen. Now didn't seem a convenient time to gauge her involvement in Sooty Feather matters. *Maybe later.*

"I see we are of like minds, Bishop," Lady MacInesker said. "Arm ourselves from the gun room and cleanse my house of this vile intrusion."

"Of course, Lady MacInesker. Cleansed it shall be," Redfort said boldly, though Foley recalled that the bishop had been fleeing towards the kitchen when they met him. "These two gentlemen escaped Kaleshaws."

The lady regarded them. "Was it bad?"

"It was bad when the sick died and attacked the living," Foley said. "It became worse when those killed by the dead rose in turn and joined their killers in trying to get the rest of us. That was when we knew the fight was done."

Sirk tilted his chin. "I suggest in the strongest terms that you shoot these … *zombis* in the head and do likewise to any corpses you find not so dealt with. The dead do not stay so for long."

"Thank you, Mr...?"

"Professor Sirk. And my companion, Mr Foley." Sirk bowed his head slightly. Foley noted recognition in Redfort's eyes at those names. He recalled seeing the bishop briefly on the paddle steamer leaving Largs after Hunt was rescued.

Lady MacInesker turned to Redfort as she led the group the short distance to the gunroom, attached to the servants' corridor. "With my guns and your men nearby, we should quickly retake the house."

"Alas, Lady MacInesker, my men will be of no use," Redfort said heavily.

She gave him a sharp look. "Surely they will have the wits and courage to come here?"

"They are already here. I saw some killing your musicians and was obliged to put a bullet in Jack Connelly's brain when he attacked me. If any survived, they will have fled."

Lady MacInesker had no response to that. She unlocked the gun room door. "My head gamekeeper, Briggs, took ill this morning, Dr Essex giving him a tonic to purge his stomach and sending him to his cottage to rest. Fortunately, I have the spare key."

She led them into the gun room, cabinets lining the wall and filled with shotguns and rifles as well as bullets and cartridges. A man in a tweed coat stood within, facing the wall with a shotgun in his hand. "Briggs! I had not thought to find you here. Make yourself useful and assist these gentlemen in loading the guns."

Foley looked out into the corridor, near the back of the queue as Lady MacInesker's companions waited their turn to enter the room. "Best hurry, the dead are already in the kitchen." He itched to get his hands on a gun, confident he could hold the corridor long enough for the others to get ready.

Sirk frowned, watching the motionless gamekeeper. That frown turned to alarm. "He's one of them. Attend to him, somebody!"

Foley looked over Redfort's shoulder, seeing the tall gamekeeper turn. His face was white with purple blotching his cheeks. Unblinking eyes looked at them and blue lips turned up in a smile. "Good afternoon, Sooty Feathers. Mr Keel sends his regards."

"Get down!" Foley shouted as the dead gamekeeper raised his shotgun. A moment later an explosion smashed off glazed brick walls in a corridor too enclosed to hold it, Foley's ears almost rupturing. Something wet splashed over his face and he found himself falling backwards.

He lay on the ground, dizzily thinking he had been shot. On opening his eyes, he looked up to see the gamekeeper empty his second barrel into those men already in the gun room, cowering against the wall. They were hurled backwards, their blood staining the wooden walls and cabinets.

The gamekeeper picked up a second shotgun from the centre table and pulled back the hammer, looking down at Redfort. "A shame we could not meet in person, Bishop. Though I was pleased to finally learn your name."

"We may yet meet," Redfort said, raising his right hand and firing his derringer into the gamekeeper's head.

"Who was that?" Sirk asked as the few survivors capable of getting up did so, others moaning on the ground. Most were dead, ripped apart by the shotgun. *Cunning; the necromancer knew we would come here and had a pet waiting.*

"That was our necromancer speaking through the late Mr Briggs," Redfort said.

"Who is this necromancer?" Sirk asked.

"Dr Essex, I suspect. Lady MacInesker said he had treated Briggs for some complaint or other. More likely he gave Briggs a mild poison to make him ill, then gave him a stronger poison masquerading as the cure."

And then sent the dead man here to wait for us with two loaded shotguns. Bastard.

"How do we end the spell?" Sirk asked urgently.

"Kill the necromancer." Redfort looked at him. "Kill Dr Essex and pray I am right that he is the necromancer."

"If he's not?" Sirk pressed.

Redfort shrugged. "Then you've saved him from a painful end at the hands of the actual necromancer's *zombis*."

"We should arm ourselves and quickly," Sir Wilbur said. Lady MacInesker lay on the ground, either dead or stunned. There was blood everywhere and no quick way to tell if any of it was hers.

"No time," Foley said. The *zombis* were almost on them. "Just run!"

Chapter Forty-Two

Heron was part of the exodus fleeing the house, running up a grass passage flanked by long hedges. *Zombis* were at the front and rear of the house, leaving those guests and servants who managed to escape the house no choice but to flee through the gardens. The stables were in this direction, Heron hoping he might find a horse and ride away from this horror.

Screams rang out behind him but he ignored them, running on, running longer and faster than he had since he was a child, fear fuelling his legs.

There was a crashing sound and *zombis* broke through the hedge, attacking anyone in sight. Two wrestled the housemaid Nell to the grass, choking her. Heron ran past, knowing to try and help her would only see them both dead. He was a banker, not a soldier, and he knew a losing proposition when he saw one. Turning right led him into the walled garden.

Fear spiked through him as more *zombis* waited within. The old, crumbling brick wall was too high for him to climb. *What do I do?*

He recognised the closest *zombi* as Sid Jones, a man who worked for Bishop Redfort. Half his face and throat had been clawed away, his right eye missing. But that didn't impede the corpse as it closed in on Heron.

Paralysed by fear, he just stood there as the *zombis* encircled him, a noose that drew tighter and tighter.

He prayed for a quick death. It went unanswered.

*

Redfort reached the entrance hall, almost sliding on blood spilled on the marble floor. He turned and ascended the stairs leading up to the ground floor, alarmed to note he was among the slowest of those who had survived the trap in the gun room, his leg hurt on dropping to the ground in time to avoid the shotgun blasts. *Zombis* had followed them from the servants' quarters and more *zombis* came in through the main entrance, hands grabbing at him.

Sir Wilbur Poole was right behind him, terror making the old man sprightlier than his years warranted. A powerful man second only to Margot Guillam in the Sooty Feathers, he would not be long in collapsing, after which he would be *zombi* fodder. *Like me. Unless…*

Redfort turned and shoved his palm against Sir Wilbur's chest, pushing him hard. Surprise showed on the old fool's beetroot-red face, becoming panic as he fell backwards. The leading *zombis* ignored Redfort to feast on the fallen *Secundus*, his wheezy screams following the bishop up the stairs. *He proved useful after all.* Redfort didn't look back.

*

Lady Mary MacInesker held her butler's nose with one hand while her other pressed a small cushion over his mouth. Poor Peel had served the family well for years, but he had been sorely wounded when the necromancer used Briggs to gun down many of her companions. The others in the gun room were dead or as good as, but Peel wouldn't stop crying out, and so he had to be silenced.

On recovering from her fall, Mary had quickly closed and locked the gun room door. She might be trapped with the dead, but at least these corpses weren't trying to kill her. Her home had been desecrated, her guests, servants and tenants slaughtered, but she was safe for now. If she kept quiet, with luck the *zombis* would leave the door be.

And if not, she had time enough now to load some shotguns, the room filled with sufficient ammunition for her to deal with anything that smashed through the door.

Safe. I'm safe. She let out a breath.

Movement caught her eye. Had Peel's hand twitched? Surely not, he was dead. Suffocated. A mercy, really.

It twitched again, consternation filling Mary. *He'd dead! I made sure of it.* An awful realisation struck her as Peel slowly sat up, dead eyes finding her. *I should have loaded a gun immediately, should have-*

*

Hunt's palms were slick with sweat as he gripped his derringer, muscles clenched as the dead came down the corridor. Chaos engulfed the house, the only reason some still survived was that the horde of the dead had so many victims to choose from. That was no longer the case, and Hunt had seen slain guests and servants rise to attack the still-living. He recalled Margot Guillam speaking of necromancers, dark magi with the ability to raise the dead, something even the *undead* baulked at.

His revolver was hidden in his trunk in a guest bedroom upstairs, leaving him just his derringer and a basket-handled broadsword he'd found hanging over a fireplace. So far, he doubted he'd killed any with the sword, content just to clear a path. He had no idea if bullets could kill the dead and decided against experimentation unless his life depended on it. *I need to find the others.* And get out of the house.

"Wilton!" He turned to see his father fending off the dead with a cavalry sabre, his mother pushing back at them with a chair. "To us!"

"Come to me, we might be able to escape through the library."

Father grimly shook his head. "We tried, the dead own it now. We must get up the stairs."

For once, being the son of Lucifer no longer quite stung as it had. If there was ever a time for the Devil to unleash some hellfire, it was now, and Hunt would offer no complaint.

Lady Delaney and Kerry stood on the stairs, one loading a derringer, the other waiting for the best target to shoot. *Maybe these dead are similar to ghouls.*

A corpse stood between him and his parents. This one looked to have been dead for days, its eyes sunken, its flesh clinging to bone. Jellified blood clung to a gaping wound on its neck. Hunt raised his gun and shot it in the heart as it lunged at him.

To no effect. Indecision froze him just a heartbeat but one heartbeat too many, and as he was borne to the ground, he knew he might not have many remaining. Rotting fingers pressed down on his chest as that dreadful face descended towards his own.

Shit! Help me, help me, help-

That desperate prayer was answered, though at a cost. A dead youth in bloody footman's livery lurched towards Mother, her derringer aimed calmly at its forehead. Lady Delaney shot another, felling it. His parents would have a clear path to the stairs once Mother shot the dead footman.

Hunt saw his plight catch Mother's attention, indecision flickering in her eyes for the briefest of moments. Her right arm turned from the footman, shooting instead the corpse trying to kill Hunt. It fell on him, dead in truth, now nothing but a dead stinking weight. He tried to shove it off, seeing Mother taking a step back. But the dead footman was too fast and caught her, smashing her against a wall before tearing out her throat with hands and teeth.

"No!" Lucifer was there, sabre flashing left and right as he fought to get to his fallen wife. Lady Delaney's derringer fired, blood spurting from the footman's head. Hunt got the rotting body off him and struggled to reach his mother. *Oh God, no.*

Mother.

Father knelt by her side, Hunt arriving in time to see her eyes flicker up to him. Her head jerked, or perhaps it was a nod of satisfaction. *She saved me, a job well done.* Hunt stared down, the fight around him distant, a world away. He stared into her eyes, trying to think of something to say. His mouth opened just as her eyes went void.

All emotion left him. His mother was dead, his anger over his father's identity stopping him from making amends with her. And now she was dead. Killed by a dead man, a puppet on a dark magician's ethereal strings.

Lucifer looked at his son, and Hunt saw the depths of anger raging in those blue eyes that mirrored his own, barely controlled. "Move," was all Father said. "She is gone."

Lucifer channelled his anger into tightly controlled sword blows that maimed and knocked aside the dead trying to keep them from the stairs, Kerry shooting one that got too close. Hunt sensed his father's self-control dangled by a thread, frayed by the loss of a wife who, from what Hunt had seen all his life, he had genuinely cared for.

Redfort surveyed the survivors on the top landing, those who made it up the spiral staircase. Not an encouraging number, with only a handful of derringers and spare bullets between them. And a few swords.

Lord Ashwood – better to think of him by that name – stood next to his son, the latter looking lost, a cold rage issuing from the former. The absence of Lady Ashwood might explain their demeanour.

Foley and Sirk looked to be on their last legs, having escaped Kaleshaws only to face their end here. Lady Delaney and Miss Knox were still in the game, the former fuelled by a hard determination, a sick realisation on the latter's face of just what she had got herself into.

Lord Ashwood's Indian valet had left to watch the backstairs used by servants to move around the house unseen, ready to call out if any came up. It wouldn't be long, Redfort knew, before the necromancer marshalled his *zombis* and sent them upstairs to kill the last survivors.

The necromancer. "I believe Dr Essex is the necromancer behind this," Redfort said between heavy breaths. "If we kill him, it should end the sorcery animating the dead."

"You're saying if we kill the necromancer, the dead will fall?" Miss Knox said, hope sparking in her eyes.

"I believe so," Redfort said, not wanting to appear too knowledgeable on the subject. "The *zombis* are controlled by him. He cannot control each one directly, not so many, but he will issue a few instructions to the group as a whole such as where to go and to kill anyone they find."

"You are sure it is him?" Lady Delaney asked.

"He came here to treat the villagers. A doctor of his eminence should have recognised the atypical symptoms and raised the alarm. I believe he also poisoned Lady MacInesker's gamekeeper, then sending the body to the gun room in anticipation of us going there for guns to deal with the *zombis*."

*

"Dr Essex … that *bastard* killed my mother," Hunt said,

wanting nothing more than to kill the magician. "I'll rip his damned head off!"

"Control yourself," Lucifer snapped. "We must use our heads. Where will he have gone?"

"Downstairs, waiting for his *zombis* to kill the last of us," Redfort said.

"I saw him enter the library," Kerry said.

Hunt pictured the London doctor sitting in the library sipping wine amidst the wreckage and blood of today's slaughter, waiting patiently for his dead to add the last of the survivors to his fell army.

"We kill him there," Lucifer said, his affable persona stripped away.

"An excellent idea, Lord Ashwood. How do you suggest we accomplish this?" Sirk asked with a trace of sarcasm. Lucifer's answering look caused him to back off a step and swallow.

"We go down after him," Lady Delaney said.

"We cannot go down the stairs," Foley said. "The *zimbos* are now on their way up!"

"*Zombis*," Sirk corrected, raising an eyebrow at Foley's dirty look.

"They are coming up the back stairs," Singh called back. He sounded calm, but then, death only meant reincarnation for him.

"What do we do?" Foley asked. The creak of stairs heralded the coming of the dead.

Lucifer opened his mouth, but it was Lady Delaney who answered.

Chapter Forty-Three

Hunt, Lady Delaney and Kerry climbed down a drainpipe attached to the western pavilion, leaving the others to hold the bedroom against the … *zombis*. There were still dead roaming the grounds, but so far none had spied them.

He peered through a library window, taking care to make no sudden move, dreading seeing his mother among the *zombis* guarding Essex in the library. She was nowhere to be seen, one small mercy at least. His heart quickened on seeing a familiar man browse the library shelves, removing books and flicking through them as if he owned the place. *Essex, you bastard.*

He ducked back down and looked at Kerry and Lady Delaney, pointing up and mouthing, '*He's there*'.

They sneaked back to the rear door leading into the main corridor, Hunt watching as Lady Delaney worked on the lock with two small picks. There had been *zombis* standing near the now-closed library door leading to the garden, and if it was locked, alerting Essex would give him time to send more of his dead to block it.

They were each armed with a derringer, having surrendered any spare bullets to Lucifer and Bishop Redfort. If they failed to take Essex by surprise, they would not have time to reload before being overwhelmed. Hunt had insisted on bringing the basket-hilted broadsword, a legacy from the last century, its pitted blade suggesting it may have seen action in one of the Jacobite wars. He felt a smile pull at unwilling lips. The sword might even be a Kail'an blade, brought south by the McKellen who wed into the MacInesker family. *Now wielded by a Hunt against a man who can raise the dead.*

*

Redfort's throat tightened on recognising the *zombi* approaching him; Sir Wilbur Poole, looking more decisive in death than he had in the twilight years of his life. "It appears I get to kill you twice, Sir Wilbur," he said as he raised his derringer, holding one last bullet. He had left the others in the bedroom, offering to lead some of the *zombis* away, in truth an excuse to try and hide in the attic. Unfortunately, there were already *zombis* haunting the second floor, leaving him no choice but to return to the others and pray they could hold long enough for Delaney to kill Essex.

A laugh rattled in Sir Wilbur's throat. "We meet again, Bishop."

"Essex," Redfort said, realising that the necromancer was speaking through the corpse. "I commend you on your command of magic. I had not thought necromancy on such a scale possible."

"You know who I am? Impressive. The Bishop of Glasgow, a necromancer. Who would suspect it? You're a ruthless man, as this unfortunate learned when you sacrificed him."

He must have been watching through one of his pets. "Killing him was like putting an incontinent old dog out of its misery," Redfort said as he backed away. He shot Sir Wilbur in the head and retreated to the room where the others planned to make their stand.

*

Kerry tried to control her breathing as they crept through the corridor, the carpets soaked in blood and gore. The dead *zombis* remained where they had fallen, beyond the necromancer's magic, but those slain defending the house were gone, Risen to join the ranks of the dead.

Kerry had thought she was joining a grand adventure, fighting the good fight against evil. Now she had seen what that fight looks like, innocents slaughtered in a horror that would haunt her deep to her bones and for the rest of her days. What she had witnessed this day would plague her nightmares, she knew. *If I live.*

Caroline led Kerry and Hunt through the music room that led to the library. She slowed on nearing the door, carefully opening it.

Kerry's heart was in her mouth as Caroline barely hesitated before entering the library, her derringer firing. Kerry hoped she had shot Essex, but Caroline had impressed upon her and Hunt to assume she was putting down a *zombi* either by the door or blocking Essex.

Hunt was the second to enter the library, his derringer raised. He might have hoped to kill Essex with his single bullet, but Essex was not slow in sending his *zombis* to attack them, forcing Hunt to shoot the closest. *That leaves me.* One shot to end this.

Easier said than done. Kerry was left with a few heartbeats to calculate if she could shoot Essex before the dead reached them. The sums did not look promising, so she shot poor Mrs McKeen the housekeeper in the head. They were out of bullets but at least the *zombis* in the room were down. Essex had no gun though he carried a cane.

Hunt drew out his sword, letting the scabbard fall to the floor, eyes fixed on the necromancer. "I'll take care of him." He stepped over Mrs McKeen's body and lunged at Essex. Kerry feared the necromancer concealed a sword within his cane, a fashionable accessory for gentlemen, but it appeared to hold no hidden blade.

Essex thwarted Hunt's revenge with a sharp parry from his cane. Hunt swore and swung a clumsy backhanded blow at the necromancer, only to cry out as a second strike from the cane knocked the sword from his hand. A third blow struck Hunt's head, knocking him to the ground.

Dr Essex smiled. "I assure you, ladies, that I learned to defend myself many years ago. One cannot always rely on the dead for protection."

Kerry drew her stiletto and ran at Essex, dropping to the ground as his cane snapped towards her face. She tensed her right arm to stab up at him, only to cry out as his boot struck her chest.

She rolled back, her ribs on fire with every breath. *...broken?*

Essex looked at Caroline. "Disappointing. Let us hope you can do better, Lady Delaney."

*

The dead smashed through the door, trying to come through the hole like spiders scuttling between cracks in a skirting board. Redfort had shot the first one through, Foley hoping that would block the rest from getting in, but they had pulled their dead fellow back.

Foley, Sirk and Redfort had armed themselves with whatever lay to hand, Singh and Lucifer lucky enough to have brought sabres up with them from downstairs. They had obligingly stood at the forefront of the fight, *Samiel* and *Kariel*, demon and *Seraphim*. Two angels fallen from Heaven. Hell awaited Lucifer and a new life awaited Singh. *God knows what waits for me*. He had a shrewd idea what awaited Bishop Redfort, Sooty Feather and servant of the *Nephilim*.

Redfort seemed to have the same thought. "I rather suspect we will meet again shortly, Lord Ashwood."

"I'll have some tea ready, Redfort," Lucifer replied.

Foley rather doubted Hell stocked Darjeeling. The dead smashed aside the remnants of the door, crawled over the bed, and rushed at Foley and the others.

*

"You may count upon it, Dr Essex," Caroline promised as she drew her silver poniard. Kerry hoped her confidence was not misplaced as more *zombis* entered the room, bearing down on her and the stunned Hunt.

Caroline stepped forwards, her left hand flinging a small unravelling cloth at Essex even as he readied his cane. Kerry saw his arm tense to swing as black powder struck his face, his strike interrupted by a violent sneeze. Caroline stepped to her left and lunged, her poniard stabbing beneath his armpit.

Blood coughed from his lungs as his knees buckled and he fell backwards, but Caroline wasn't done. She pulled free the blade and reversed her grip on it, hammering it down into his chest.

The *zombis* collapsed as if their strings had been cut, dead in truth, as dead as their master. Kerry felt herself go limp with relief, the strength draining away from her. "Well struck, Caroline," she said, wincing as she did so.

Caroline noticed. "Does it hurt to breathe?"

Kerry managed a nod.

"Broken ribs, I suspect." Caroline carefully cleaned the

blood from her poniard. "A sharp lesson to teach you the folly of rushing against a foe you know little about."

Every day a lesson. "And to carry condiments in the future," she promised dryly.

*

"Well, gentlemen," Redfort observed as he and the other four men surveyed the corpses lying before them. "It appears we will not be going to Hell today after all."

"It can be arranged, Bishop, if you wish?" Lucifer said. A shadow had fallen over the Lightbringer with the death of his wife.

"What will happen here?" Singh asked.

"That will be for Miss Guillam to decide," Redfort said. He wouldn't normally deign to answer a servant, but this one knowingly served Lucifer. "The pestilence will be a convenient excuse for so many dead."

"Maybe claim it is still virulent?" Foley said. "Otherwise you'll have a lot of next of kin asking awkward bloody questions about why their loved ones are half-eaten, some stabbed or shot."

"A mass grave may be a prudent precaution," Redfort allowed.

"Burn the bodies first," Sirk advised.

"The Council will have a busy time of it," Lucifer said.

"Mmm." *Meaning I'll have a busy time of it. Guillam and Fredds aside, I'm the last of the Council.* Still, that meant a promotion. At the least he would be *Tertius*, maybe even *Secundus* if the Regent would rather not have Fredds too senior. She herself had been *Sexta* until the deaths of Edwards and Rannoch made her *Prima*.

*

"I'm sorry about your mother, Hunt," Foley said as the pair stood in the garden. The day was still warm as evening fell, the sun dipping to the west. It was hard to believe Lady MacInesker's garden party had been in full swing only hours before. The refreshment tent still stood, and chairs still littered the lawn.

"Thank you, Foley." Hunt wouldn't look at his friend, staring instead across the river.

"Some of the other guests and staff survived," Foley said. "Sirk's been treating them for hysteria, poor bastards. What will happen to them?"

"God knows. Maybe Margot Guillam will have them Mesmered. Or killed." He didn't sound like he cared much either way.

"Will you join Lady Delaney and Miss Knox in their fight against the undead? The Sooty Feathers have never been more vulnerable. And Margot Guillam went against her word to leave us alone."

"And see my efforts help *Arakiel*? I think not," Hunt said.

"I think they're after that demon too. His man was responsible for your mother's death."

"The necromancer is dead, my mother avenged. Killing *Arakiel* will just send him to Hell. He'll end up there in due course. Hastened, perhaps, by Lady Delaney and Miss Knox. They don't need my help." Hunt took a shuddering breath. "I look forward to leaving here and returning to Glasgow. You?"

Foley took a breath. "I'm not going."

"You can't stay here. The house stinks of blood. There are bodies everywhere, some days-old. And Sooty Feathers will be dispatched to clean up the mess."

"No. I mean, I'm not going home. I mean to learn more about my curse. I only came back to help you and your … family see an end to Sooty Feather interference in our lives. I think we can agree that, after today, those that remain will have their hands full dealing with *Arakiel*."

Hunt finally looked at him. "Where will you go and for how long? What of your pharmacy?"

"I'll ask Sirk if he can watch it for a bit longer. How much longer, I don't know."

Hunt nodded and offered his hand. Foley took it after a moment, hating himself for that hesitation. Hunt's heritage was not his fault. He saw the hurt in Hunt's eyes, a little thing against the pain of losing his mother and enduring the horror of the day's events. But it was there.

"Take care of yourself," Hunt said brusquely. He paused. "You never did say where you're going."

Foley looked north. "You know where I'm going."

Chapter Forty-Four

Foley sat at a table in the Drover's Inn taproom, a fresh pint of ale before him, his third that evening. Travelling from Glasgow to Inverarnan by horse had left him weary and saddle-sore, but he had welcomed the solitude, staying at inns when he could, sleeping rough in woods and fields when he couldn't. Mr Dale had directed him to a man willing to buy the horse from him, the price low owing to the assumption the mare was stolen. In a sense it was, but Foley doubted Lady MacInesker's heir would notice one horse missing.

He felt a nagging guilt at leaving Hunt, not least so soon after the death of his mother; no one should be held to account for their parentage, and Hunt had accepted Foley's curse with little or no qualm before learning of his own dark heritage. *But the spawn of Satan! That's a lot to accept.*

They'd reconcile, he assured himself, on his return to Glasgow. He wasn't sure when that would be, wanting to learn more of his curse. Was there a cure or a means to prevent the transformation? To quiet the beast within?

His only choice had been to return to Inverarnan at the northern end of Loch Lomond, the place where he and Hunt had been attacked by werewolves, where Foley had been bitten. If he could find the werewolves (preferably not during a full moon) he might be able to get answers.

Assuming they didn't hold a grudge for Hunt killing one of their own. But there had been no choice; the wolves attacked them. Hunt had told him that such attacks here had previously been limited to livestock, from what the locals had said. If the werewolves lived locally, likely they confined themselves during nights of the full moon, and the attack had been a mistake.

If they lived locally. Foley had been here a few days,

scouting the hills to the back of the inn and the glens surrounding it. Finding nothing. His circumspect questions met only blank looks. The innkeeper still regaled patrons with the story of the wolves surrounding his inn the full moon before last, the tale fast becoming a local legend. Foley recalled none of it, having lain feverish in bed while Hunt and the others endured a long night fearing the wolves might find a way inside.

What now? Foley stared at his ale. Money was becoming a problem. To save money (for ale and food) he had paid less to sleep in the common room rather than bother with a bedroom, but if he spent many more nights in the Drover's, he'd soon find himself sleeping outside even when there was an inn. The nights were still warm enough, especially with the blankets rolled up in his pack.

I'll leave tomorrow, he decided. Take his time following the loch southwards towards Glasgow, travelling on foot. Sirk seemed to be managing his pharmacy well enough and Foley was in no hurry to return to it. Or to Glasgow. That was McBride's turf, and he would learn soon enough that Foley lived.

News had reached Inverarnan of the terrible tragedy at Dunkellen, of so many killed by pestilence. Bishop Redfort was being hailed a hero, almost a saint, for his efforts in tending to the sick in their dying hours. Foley had shaken his head on reading that in the newspaper. *We should have killed him.* But everyone had seen their fill of death that day.

A woman sat down across from him, breaking his reverie. She was slender, dressed in dirt-stained breeches and a rough blouse too big for her. She might have been eighteen or she might have been twenty-eight, he couldn't quite tell.

"Evening, miss." He recognised her from a small estate he had visited the day before, little more than a walled hamlet supported by a farm. They kept themselves apart from the other locals, he'd heard, causing no trouble so far as could be proved.

"Is your friend with you?" she asked, her brown eyes meeting his.

"My friend? I'm travelling alone." He wondered if she meant Hunt, from his last visit. Though he didn't remember seeing her here that time.

"Good. He would not be welcome."

"Why not?"

"Because he killed Ruaridh." She spoke quietly, meeting his eyes.

They found me. Foley took a steadying breath. "Ruaridh was the one who bit me, aye? The one who made me ... like you?"

She nodded. "The only reason we let you leave our home when you came by yesterday. You didn't pull the trigger and you're one of us now. Aren't you?"

He gave a slight nod. "Aye, I am."

"Why are you here?"

Glasgow, his pharmacy and Wil Hunt seemed a thousand miles and another life away. "I want to know what I am. The thing inside me has killed, and I need to know how to stop it."

She watched him, brown hair hanging loose around her shoulders. "You can either stay here and drink the night away, and leave this place tomorrow, never to return if you value your life; or you can come with me and meet the others. The pack. Your choice."

He finished his ale in three large swallows, standing. "Lead the way, miss...?"

"Barra."

"Tam."

*

Kerry wore a black dress. Dark clouds had gathered over the Necropolis, the hilled cemetery a short walk from the cathedral where the funeral service was held. As the Hunts had been regular (and generous) attendees for years, she doubted Lord Ashwood needed to pull too many strings to convince them to host Lady Ashwood's funeral.

No small number had come to pay their respects to Lady Ashwood, the family a presence in Glasgow for many years. Employees of the Browning Shipping Company, fellow parishioners from the cathedral, friends from society, and not least her family. Standing closest to the grave were her husband and son, both dressed in mourning black.

In contrast to the still grimness that gripped Lord Ashwood, there was a restless tremble to Wil, perhaps a sense of disbelief that his mother had died and the manner of it. Kerry still found herself shaken awake at night by nightmares of that bloody day. She had been warned that even if she survived her battles against the demons and undead, part of her wouldn't, a heavy price exacted. She was beginning to understand what that meant.

She glanced at Caroline and wondered if she was looking at herself in twenty years, living only for an obsession against an enemy who was never quite within reach, maybe even losing part of her sanity in order to go out each night, risking death.

Wilton Hunt may have disappointed his mother on frequent occasions, but today he seemed intent on doing her proud. His unruly reddish hair had been waxed flat and parted exactingly to one side, his top hat held in both hands. Crisp seams ran down his black trousers, his jacket equally crisp and buttoned up.

An older and younger man stood nearby, a similar cast to their features. Kerry had gleaned that they were Lady Ashwood's brother-in-law and nephew.

Kerry and Caroline were among the few women present. Upper class female relatives were encouraged to stay away from funerals lest they get overly upset. Lady Ashwood had a sister, Kerry recalled from her obituary that took up half a page in the Glasgow Herald. A full page would ordinarily have been expected, but there had been a great deal of prominent deaths recently. A virulent fever resulting from the long summer was being blamed for the deaths at the Dunkellen estate.

Spring and summer have culled the Sooty Feathers. Winter might end them once and for all. Or maybe not.

Kerry had only previously attended pauper funerals, but the tradition of the undertakers drinking heavily beforehand seemed universal. Lord Ashwood had given them a thin-lipped stare on watching them arrive at the cathedral that morning, reeling from drink. She suspected they would find their fee paid exactly, with no gratuity offered.

Wil, his father, uncle, cousin and Professor Sirk had been among the six carrying the coffin inside to its bier. There had been a small stir on seeing Lord Ashwood's Indian valet,

Singh, acting as the sixth bearer.

The minister conducting the funeral, a Reverend Mitchell, looked old and frail, his hoarse voice barely reaching the rear pews. Kerry gave him even odds on surviving to the end. Rain started to fall, a light shower that encouraged Reverend Mitchell to keep his graveside words brief.

Lord Ashwood picked up a handful of dirt and looked down into the pit where his wife lay, letting the dirt fall from his gloved hands.

Wilton tossed in the second handful, his face hardened by grief and anger. Kerry wondered if his mother's death would push him towards or away from the war between *Arakiel* and the Sooty Feathers. Caroline had already written to Wolfgang Steiner, asking that he again raise the matter with his Templar superiors. Summer was nearing an end, autumn soon to fall upon them, and the lengthening nights would soon turn dark and bloody. *Arakiel*'s quiet war against the Sooty Feathers was turning noisy.

*

"My thoughts are with you," Lady Delaney said to Hunt as she and Kerry Knox prepared to leave the Hunt home on Windsor Terrace. Father had arranged a series of carriages to convey mourners from the Necropolis to the West End. A surprisingly thoughtful gesture; Hunt wouldn't have bothered, too lost in his own guilt and grief to care about receiving guests.

"Thank you for coming," he managed. "My father asked me to give you this. He said my mother agreed to it before…" He handed Lady Delaney a brown envelope.

Lady Delaney opened it and smiled, pulling out a faded photograph. "It was kind of your father to remember."

The photograph was of the Hunts' parlour, a familiar young woman seated on a couch holding a baby with two older children on either side. "Is that you, Lady Delaney?" Kerry asked, likewise seeing the similarity.

"Yes, Kerry. Me, Andrew and Christopher." She pointed to the baby she held and looked at Hunt. "And young Master Wilton, as he was then."

"A small world," Hunt said as Kerry laughed in surprised

delight before recalling the sombre occasion.

She looked him in the eye and offered a small nod.

"Take care, Miss Knox," he said. She knew now the perils waiting on the path she had chosen to walk. That day swimming by the waterfall and drinking wine on the grass seemed a lifetime ago.

"You know where we are, Wil," she said quietly, her hand brushing his.

He was grateful they had come, though he missed Foley. His friend would have found a way to distract him, make him laugh, and got him drunk.

"Shall I refresh your glass, sir?" Singh asked.

"No, thank you." Singh the valet might have come over to ask if his master's son wanted more wine but Hunt suspected that *Kariel* had other business to discuss with the son of *Samiel*.

Sure enough, the valet remained. "How are you faring?"

"I'm getting by," Hunt said, vague enough to mean anything. "It burns that she died before we fully reconciled. That she died to save me."

"She made her choice, you before herself. Honour her, son of *Samiel*. You are hers as much as *his*. Do not let fear and anger turn you cold and hateful." Dark eyes met his. "I like you. It would be a pity should I need to kill you."

"A pity," was all Hunt could think to say. Now his father's valet was threatening him. Singh nodded once and left to see to the other guests.

Father joined him. "Your trunk is still unpacked, Wilton. Shall I instruct Singh to see to it?"

Hunt looked at Lucifer, wondering how much he was his mother's son, and how much the Devil's. Regardless, this house had barely felt like home even when Mother lived. Now it felt even less so, his father a stranger to him. "No. I'm not staying here. I'll be returning to Foley's flat to look after it until his return."

Father didn't look pleased, but neither did he look particularly displeased. "You can't run from this, from who I am. From who *you* are. Your mother was an exceptional woman. Mourn her; I shall. But you won't find answers at the bottom of a bottle."

Hunt knew he'd have a damned good look all the same.

"I'll keep in contact," was all he said, turning to leave.

"Wilton."

Hunt stopped.

"You may not like it, but remember I *am* your father. You know where I am if you need me. I rather suspect you will before this is done. *Arakiel* knows who we are. Who *you* are. So does Bishop Redfort, which means Margot Guillam will too."

Hunt walked away.

Sirk met him at the door. "My condolences, Hunt."

He had been hearing that all day. "Thank you. It was thoughtful of you to come." Realising that was the pro forma reply he had been giving all day, he added. "How have you fared? It was thoughtless of Foley not to tell you when he'd be back, he can't expect you to run his pharmacy indefinitely."

"Oh, I've ample free time to manage it."

"What about when you're giving your lectures, Professor?" Hunt asked. He was one of Sirk's students, though the last semester felt like an age ago.

A bitter smile crinkled Sirk's gaunt face. "I received a letter from the university advising that my services are no longer required."

He knew how much Sirk enjoyed giving his lectures (moreso than the students enjoyed receiving them), managing to feel pity for the professor despite his grief. "I'm sorry, Professor. The Sooty Feathers are behind this, aren't they?"

"That does seem likely, Hunt. A rather petty revenge, I feel. But it means I can continue to manage Foley's shop for the foreseeable future, though I fear the income will be insufficient for me to maintain the shop, the flat and my home."

"Well, there I may have some good news," Hunt said. "I received a letter from a Dr Mortimer, soon to take up the post of Senior Professor of Anatomy at the university's medical school. He was rather circumspect, but it appears his predecessor, the late Angus Miller, confided in him the, uh, arrangement between himself, Foley and me. Mortimer wishes to continue this arrangement." Meaning Mortimer wanted extra corpses for his personal study and perhaps to provide extra anatomy lessons to those students willing to pay.

If Sirk thought Hunt crass to raise the subject of bodysnatching the day of his mother's funeral, he was diplomatic enough not to say so. "Oh? Do you intend to resume your previous trade? I thought you done with it."

With Foley away, Hunt had intended to write a letter to Dr Mortimer declining his offer, unable to exhume the corpses on his own. "I thought so too, but the money will help keep our heads above water. Interested?"

Sirk pondered it for several moments. "It is not a trade I ever envisaged myself doing, not even when I studied anatomy in Edinburgh. Given the circumstances, I find I've little choice. When do we start?"

"I was invited to attend the new professor's residence before the new semester starts. We'll find out then." With his savings almost gone, at least it meant he would not be dependent on his father for money. *He can keep his thirty pieces of silver.*

*

"A fine house, *Arakiel*," the demon *Maridiel* said from Kenmure's body.

"It will do for now, a modest investment," *Arakiel* said. An investment funded by money stolen from the Heron Crowe Bank. Not that Canning was minded to complain about the extravagance; he was done lurking in cellars and sewers. When the heavy rains fell, the river would flood the sewers.

"You summoned us all here for greater reason than to show off your new abode, I trust?" *Asmodiel* asked. He showed no fear at the look *Arakiel* gave him. Possessing Lord Smith meant he sat on Glasgow's High Court, a position of value to *Arakiel*.

"I summoned you all here to witness the formation of a council. *My* Council," *Arakiel* said. "Fisher's Sooty Feathers suffered many losses at Dunkellen House and are weaker than ever. With autumn soon upon us, now is the time for us to confront the Sooty Feathers as equals."

It sounded as if *Arakiel* was finally ready to go to war against his nemesis, Fisher; Canning hoped so, keen for blood and mayhem. He had felt largely overlooked this summer. The lengthening nights would provide him more opportunities. He wondered if Fisher's undead had felt equally frustrated at being confined to their Crypts during the summer.

"There are nine of us here. Will we match Fisher's Council in numbers? With you as *Primus*?" Bartholomew Ridley asked, clearly wondering but too afraid to ask who among them would *not* sit on the Council. He was the leader of a faction of magicians who had been promised *Arakiel*'s favour in exchange for their support. Canning was not being given a seat on the Council, nor did he wish one, content to attend to the bloody practicalities of the war.

"I will, until Fisher falls. He stands above his Council, as will I. It will be a Council of equals, each seat unnumbered. Those who sit on it will rise or fall by power and merit."

"An auspicious day," *Ifriel* said, her mouth curled up in a smile. "The first meeting of your Council. I wonder if Margot Guillam has enough Sooty Feathers left to reform her own?"

"Fisher's Council, not hers," *Arakiel* corrected. "Never forget he is the true enemy."

"A *Dominus Nephilim*," Bresnik said in his Eastern European accent. "How do you plan on dealing with such a one?" One who defeated *Arakiel* at the height of his power, when he was *Grigori*. Now Keel was a demon confined to a mortal body and Fisher was a *Dominus*.

"He will be attended to when the time is right," was all *Arakiel* would say on the matter. "For now, our task is to wage war on the Sooty Feathers without mercy or refrain."

"Three of us would still sit on Fisher's Council had we not been discovered by Bishop Redfort," *Maridiel* said. "We should deal with him."

"In time. For now, we have influence over the High Court. We have control over the constabulary." *Arakiel* then gestured to a man slouching by the wall. "With *Gadriel* Possessing Walter Herriot, a director of the Heron Crowe Bank, we have eyes and ears in that institution. William Heron's death means Edmund Crowe must step out from the shadows to control his bank. Mercenaries have been hired and city officials bribed. This is our time."

It might please his lord and master to present that as a success, but Canning knew that *Gadriel* had been intended for William Heron, until his *Nephilim* associate Edmund

Crowe interfered with the abduction and thus prevented the Possession. Since then, the Heron Crowe Bank had increased its security, both practical and arcane. As such, contact with *Gadriel* was done carefully and infrequently in case Crowe had employed magicians to spy on its own. Canning idly wondered how the abduction would have turned out had *Arakiel* sent him rather than the now-dead circus *Nephilim*.

"Two warehouses are being utilised as Crypts," *Ifriel* said, assets it controlled through its Vessel, Mrs Carlton.

"Good," *Arakiel* said. "The mercenaries were hired through an independent broker and should arrive soon. Khotep may have died, but for him that is but a temporary inconvenience."

Canning had been amused to hear of the necromancer's death, even if he would return in another body.

Each of the seven Councillors swore fealty to *Arakiel*: The demons *Ifriel*, *Maridiel*, *Gadriel* and *Asmodiel*; Cornelius Josiah, the Demonist, in recognition of his efforts in Summoning so many demons, *Arakiel* foremost among them. The sixth Councillor was magician Bartholomew Ridley. Bresnik, the last surviving *Nephilim* loyal to *Arakiel* from before Fisher's betrayal, was the last to speak his oath.

"What of *Samiel*?" *Asmodiel* asked.

"He and his son are to be left alone." *Arakiel*'s tone brooked no argument.

None of the other demons looked happy. "A *child*. Who would have thought one of us would conceive, *could* conceive. What game does *Samiel* play?"

"That is not your concern," *Arakiel* said. Canning hoped *Arakiel* would dispatch him when the time finally came for the Devil to return to Hell. Wilton Hunt would be a bonus. His friend Foley, too; Canning still recalling the pain of Foley shooting him months before. Murder was a meal best enjoyed slowly, the meat carved rare and bloody. He intended to savour every cut made with his knife.

Chapter Forty-Five

"Regent Guillam, this Council commands my first loyalty, be assured," Redfort lied, spreading his hands across the table.

Margot Guillam didn't precisely exude warmth towards this announcement, but neither did she kill him, which was a relief. Six Councillors had been present at Dunkellen House, two dying and three revealed as demons loyal to *Arakiel*. Part of him had been tempted to flee Glasgow lest Guillam or Fisher decide to start afresh with the Council. But perhaps unmasking Kenmure, Smith and Carlton as demons had satisfied the Regent that he was still useful. Or perhaps the Sooty Feathers could simply not afford to lose any more members in important positions.

Indeed, he had been honoured with the position of *Secundus*. He had half-expected Fredds to be made *Secundus*, but perhaps Guillam shared her predecessor Edwards' caution that to place a fellow *Nephilim* in the Second Seat might tempt them to try for the First. Fredds would have to content himself as *Tertius*, the Third Seat.

The events at Dunkellen House had decimated the Sooty Feathers and reduced the Council to just Guillam, Fredds, and Redfort. The three of them sat at the High Table, silence briefly falling. Guillam rang a bell, and a door opened, five robed men and women walking inside. *I wonder if these ones will fare better than their predecessors.*

At least this time *Arakiel* had not infiltrated the Council with demons, Regent Guillam avoiding those who would have been considered an obvious choice. Dr Essex had saved her a lot of trouble in that regard, his *zombis* killing many of the Sooty Feathers. A handful of those at Dunkellen had survived.

Edmund Crowe was the new *Quartus*, his elevation to the

Council a bid to tie him and his bank tighter to the Sooty Feathers. With William Heron dead, the bank was now solely in the *Nephilim*'s pale hands.

Magdalene Quinn, one of most respected practitioners in Glasgow's arcane community, was *Quinta*. With a score of the Society's soldiers lost at Dunkellen, the Society was in no position to ignore any means of fighting Keel, no matter how unconventional.

The new *Sextus* was Neil MacInesker, the son of the late Sir Neil and Lady MacInesker. Ordinarily Redfort would have been puzzled by the apparent favouritism the family enjoyed, especially given young MacInesker's short time as a Sooty Feather, but the secret was in the name. He had guessed that on seeing the MacInesker coat of arms, keeping that knowledge to himself.

Roddy McBride was a surprising choice for *Septimus*, not even a member of the Black Wing Club, never mind the Sooty Feather Society. With the losses endured and the losses to come, a place on the Council was his price for putting his contacts, killers and bully boys at the Society's disposal. Redfort had thought to be the one to reveal Lucifer's presence in Glasgow, but McBride had stolen his thunder, reporting to Regent Guillam upon his return to Glasgow.

Amy Newfield's rise to the Council as *Octavia* was an even greater surprise than McBride's appointment, the undead girl still a ghoul, one to three years away from her Transition to *Nephilim*. Perhaps the Regent wanted her protégé to learn power and politics quickly.

Once the oaths were given and accepted, Regent Guillam rose. "This has been a hard year for the Society, perhaps the hardest it has ever suffered. Many members have died, some have betrayed us, and be assured that more will die and betray us before this year is out. We face a demon, one who ruled this House and city for centuries before his ambition for greater prizes saw him neglect it, leading Lord Fisher to take his place.

"The demon wants his revenge and this city back. But his victories have been tainted with defeats, and now we know the enemy we fight. We know the faces worn by the demons *Arakiel, Ifriel, Maridiel* and *Asmodiel*. They are to be hunted down and sent back to Hell. There is a reward for anyone who kills them. And for anyone killing the *Nephilim* George Canning and the Demonist Cornelius Josiah."

A smattering of applause filled the Council Chamber. Redfort wondered how many in this room would still be alive by the end of the year, and which faction would prevail. *Arakiel* had done well since Rannoch had Summoned him, but Lord Fisher was still out there, among the most deadly beings in the world. Quite how the demon intended to defeat a *Dominus Nephilim* was beyond Redfort's ken, but it would be wise to assume *Arakiel* had something in mind.

Whatever the outcome, Redfort intended to be among the living, seizing every advantage presenting itself.

*

The journey had been long, the first step involving a thickly curtained carriage. On arriving at their destination, Amy and Neil MacInesker had been ordered to place a sack over their heads, and then led from the carriage, descending steps after a while.

Cloth brushed against Amy's face as the sack was removed from her head, and she found herself looking at Regent Guillam. The Regent had led them down into an old stone cellar or crypt. The only light came from a lantern Amy carried, Regent Guillam needing both hands to guide the blindfolded pair to their destination.

Guillam removed the sack from Neil MacInesker. The late Lady MacInesker's son had said nothing in the carriage, clearly fearful of his undead companions. The journey had passed in silence, the Regent keeping her thoughts to herself. The loss of so many Sooty Feathers at Dunkellen House had devasted the Society at a time when it needed to be strongest. A war had begun, or at least a war already underway was now waged openly, more fiercely.

Amy wondered what was so important it required three Councillors. Part of her marvelled that she was one of eight who ruled Glasgow from the shadows, part of her horrified at what she was becoming. But every day saw her less and less the sixteen-year old girl murdered by George Rannoch and Made undead in the spring. Still a ghoul, at least a year from Transitioning to *Nephilim*, she had been given much responsibility by Regent Guillam.

Guillam stood before an old oak door with uncharacteristic trepidation. A coat of arms had been engraved into the wood, Amy making out a fish and a castle.

"Why is my family's coat of arms on that door?" Neil MacInesker dared to ask.

Regent Guillam looked at him. "You have been privileged to inherit the wealth and land of the MacIneskers, but you have also inherited a grave responsibility. One that has been passed down your family for many centuries."

She raised her hand as if to knock on the door but decided otherwise. "The original Sir Neil MacInesker was a 13th century Scottish knight with a castle on what is now the Dunkellen estate. A man with power and influence locally, he caught the eye of Erik Keel and his *Nephilim*. Dying, he agreed to become undead, leaving everything to his son.

"Being well known, he travelled south for several decades, anglicising his name before eventually returning to Glasgow, where he revealed himself to his family. His descendants were wise enough to see the benefits of a patron who stood among Glasgow's immortal rulers, and the family increased their lands and wealth over the centuries."

Neil MacInesker listened silently, his breathing the only other sound. Amy had never met or heard of this MacInesker *Nephilim*. He must have died, perhaps one of the many casualties when Erik Keel was overthrown.

Guillam continued. "In return, the MacIneskers were appointed the guardians of Sir Neil's Crypt, acting as his mortal agents in the world beyond."

"This was his Crypt?" MacInesker asked, his words hushed.

"It *is* his Crypt," Regent Guillam corrected.

Amy frowned. "I've never heard of a *Nephilim* called Sir Neil MacInesker." Given he originated in the 13th century, surely he would be an Elder by now. But Miss Guillam was the last Elder of Fisher's House. Though it was rumoured that Edmund Crowe, now fully part of the House, was an Elder, too.

She looked at the door, at the castle and fish coat of arms … "You said he anglicised his name," she said slowly, a suspicion dawning. "What is MacInesker in English?"

Neil MacInesker stared at the door. "Fisher." He looked at Guillam for confirmation. "You're saying the original Sir Neil MacInesker is Niall Fisher?"

Margot Guillam nodded. "I am. Come, Mr MacInesker. It is time to meet your ancestor and learn what he expects of you." She knocked hard on the door.

"Enter." The voice was like dry leaves being blown by the wind, scraping off cobbles. Miss Guillam opened the door, a rotted skeletal figure seated at the far end, reading a book by lanternlight. He looked up as they approached, his yellowed skin wrinkled and dry as parchment. Strands of long hair hung lank about his head, a smell of death lingering. The clothes he wore were faded and worn, at least a century out of fashion. Spectacles hung off a gnarled nose, little more than a stub of withered skin.

"Margot, welcome." Fisher's was a hoarse whisper. Amy found it difficult to reconcile this withered corpse with the undead ruler of Glasgow, rumoured to stand among the most powerful creatures in the world.

"He needs much blood to be at his fullest strength, a drawback to his Maker being many generations removed from their *Grigori* progenitor," Miss Guillam said quietly. "But rest assured, he could still kill us all even weakened as he is right now."

"Miss Newfield, my regent speaks well of you, young though you may be. And Neil; well met, kinsman." Fisher looked at Miss Guillam. "Your report, Margot. How fare my House and city?"

*

"An interesting place to meet," *Arakiel* heard Lucifer say as he joined him in Victoria Park's Fossil Grove. He found peace in the dimly lit building, staring at the petrified forest bed and tree stumps.

"It reminds me how transient existence is. Millions of years ago, this was a swamp in the tropics, the land itself half a world away. Now? Frozen, out of time."

"I thought we had an agreement not to not interfere with one another's interests." So, Lucifer had little interest in discussing the fossil grove.

"I am sorry for the loss of your wife, your family was not intended to be among the slain. Had I known you were there, I would have warned you," *Arakiel* said honestly. Lucifer's death would have complicated matters, and the death of his wife risked awakening his wrath. At least his son survived.

"I am surprised at you, employing a necromancer. You must be desperate indeed to stoop so low. And you wonder at unintended deaths?"

"Essex is dead, your wife avenged," *Arakiel* said. Which was true enough, though the body's death had simply released the lich's soul back to his phylactery. On informing Essex's valet, Yates, of his master's death, Yates had assured him Essex had identified a suitable replacement body on arriving in Glasgow, and that arrangements had been made to transfer the lich's soul from his phylactery to his unwitting intended host.

Lucifer need know none of this. Let him believe Essex had merely been a talented necromancer rather than a lich who had Possessed many bodies over the millennia.

"And the attempt to make my son *Beliel*'s Vessel?"

"A mistake. They overstepped themselves, unaware of your identity."

"See that there are no further mistakes, or I shall make 'mistakes' of my own." The threat was as clear as a bared blade.

"I'll bear that in mind," *Arakiel* said coldly. "If you wish to protect your son, I suggest you caution him against further involvement in the conflict between myself and Fisher."

"I'll speak with him, however we are somewhat estranged at the moment."

"I'll remind my servants he is not to be harmed, however you understand I cannot speak for Fisher's undead or the Sooty Feathers," *Arakiel* said.

"Understood. It may be time for me to introduce myself to this Margot Guillam and reach an understanding," Lucifer said. He tapped the brim of his top hat. "Good day to you, *Arakiel*."

He returned the gesture. "A good day to you, *Samiel*."

After Lucifer had left, *Arakiel* returned his attention to the fossilised grove. He had been content, at first, to honour his truce with Lucifer. But then he had realised why Lucifer had accomplished the seemingly impossible and sired a child. *Your pride exiled us all to Hell, and yet you think you can cheat the banishment and return to Heaven. No, Lightbringer, it is the Darkness for you, now and forever.*

But he was not yet ready for Lucifer to be returned to Hell. Fisher was among the most powerful *Nephilim* in the world; killing him would be challenging, but to restrain him sufficiently to remove his heart and use it in the ritual to truly restore himself verged on the impossible. Fortunately, there was one who was a match for Fisher, who would likely assist *Arakiel* in exchange for news of Lucifer's escape from Hell. A letter had been sent beyond Europe, a reply awaited. Until then, Lucifer must live.

*

Hunt knocked on the door, determined to make a good impression. It felt strange to return to the medical school residence of the senior Professor of Anatomy, adjacent to the medical school itself. Months before, he had attended here late at night with Foley and whatever corpse Professor Miller had requested they exhume. Now he was here with Sirk, to meet a Professor Mortimer and see if he was truly amenable for Hunt to resume his nocturnal trade.

A man answered the door, either a butler or valet by the look of him. "Yes? How may I help you?" His accent was from London.

Hunt removed his top hat. "Good day. Kindly inform Professor Mortimer that Mr Hunt and Profess – Doctor Sirk are here to see him. He is expecting us."

"Follow me, gentlemen," the man said with a surly air.

He led them through the entrance hall to the study and chapped lightly on the door.

"Yes?" a muffled voice said from within the study.

"A Mr Hunt and Dr Sirk to see you, sir."

"Excellent. Send them in." Mortimer's accent was curious, English but not quite. Perhaps he had travelled extensively?

The servant opened the door and held it open, allowing Hunt and Sirk to enter.

A man in his sixties with thinning white hair sat behind the desk, spectacles lying on his desk. He had a thick white moustache atop his lip. "Welcome, Mr Hunt. Dr Sirk. We have much to discuss," he said with a curious familiarity. Mortimer looked at his servant, a smile half-hidden by his moustache. "That will be all, Yates."

Epilogue

Ahmed leant on his stall in Marrakesh's Jemaa el-Fnaa, the day's heat slowly leaving the clay walls surrounding the market. The night air was still a little too warm to be called pleasant, the market square busy with merchants, musicians, snake charmers and storytellers. Jemaa el-Fnaa truly came to life when the sun set, the minaret of nearby Koutoubia Mosque visible above the cramped souks of the medina.

He straightened as a small woman approached his stall, studying his wares. She wore a hijab and robe, her face sallow to the point of greyness, but she did not look like a resident of the city. Her distinctive facial features marked her as foreign, her cheekbones high. She was also foolish enough to be travelling alone, Ahmed realised.

"*Masaa' al-khayr*," he said, bidding her a good evening before switching to French. "What are you looking for?"

"*As-salaam 'alaykum*," she said. "For nothing," she continued in excellent if accented Arabic. "I am out for the air."

She walked on, and Ahmed was surprised to see her enter a darkened souk a short distance away. Consternation turned to alarm as he saw three rough-looking men in dirty djellabas follow her.

What do I do? He was no fighter, no match for three thugs haunting the medina for victims. But neither could he just stand there and let the woman be attacked. He walked over and turned into the souk, taking a breath to shout, hoping the commotion would scare them off and alert the foolish woman to her peril.

He heard a struggle inside. Fighting back fear, he ventured into the narrow street, surrounded by shadows, almost tripping over a body.

It was one of the men, lying motionless on the ground. *Is he dead?* Ahmed touched his throat, feeling a wetness on his fingers. Movement caught his eye, and he looked up to see a small silhouette throw a larger one impossibly against the far wall with bone-breaking force.

The third and last man attacked what Ahmed realised was the woman. She forced him to his knees with little effort, her head craning towards his throat. He screamed briefly, Ahmed too shocked to move or intervene. After a short time, the woman let the man fall to the ground.

What did I see? A woman small and slender had just killed three strong men with inhuman ease. And now she looked at him.

"Your concern for my safety is appreciated, if misplaced," she said. "These three will not quite quell my Thirst, so I regret I must look to you as well." He felt her will on him, his thoughts confused. "But I will not take enough to kill you, and you will leave here soon after. And you will not remember this."

Darkness swallowed Ahmed.

*

"Mistress Lily," one of her maids greeted her, eyes downward. She enjoyed the nocturnal life of Marrakesh, finding it a busy city, but she was pleased to return to the tranquillity of her riad. A small pool and fountain sat in the centre of the tiled courtyard, the four walls of the house facing inwards.

Sated after drinking the blood of her three attackers and would-be saviour, a look in a mirror showed her grey skin had turned olive, a hint of red in her lips and cheeks. The problem with feeding from scum was that their blood reflected their poor diet. Better to feed from people of quality but that had dangers of its own, the risk of discovery. Mesmering victims was all well and good, but wounds remained, as did the bodies of the slain. Not that three dead cutthroats in the medina would occasion much interest or comment.

"A letter arrived for you this afternoon, mistress," her maid said, holding out a silver tray. She took the letter and sent away the maid. She had been in reverie from dawn until dusk, hidden in a locked, windowless chamber. On night falling, sating her Thirst had been her first priority. The strength and power of being a *Domina Nephilim* was balanced with the amount of blood required to maintain it. She was fortunate in being a first generation *Nephilim*, her Maker a *Grigori*.

The more generations separating a *Nephilim* from the *Grigori* beginning the line meant more blood was required to maintain its full strength. *Domina* or *Dominus Nephilim* who were separated by many generations from a *Grigori* were faced with either having to drink so much blood as to risk discovery, or endure a weakened (relatively speaking) existence in seclusion. Or risk being attacked by an Elder *Nephilim* hungry for ascension.

Thinking of her Maker soured her good mood, millennia of hatred not something she could put aside. She read the letter, her English a little rusty. But the gist of it was clear; the demon *Arakiel* wished her assistance against the *Dominus Nephilim* Niall Fisher of Glasgow.

In return, he offered the location of her Maker, making mischief on earth once again. She considered the demon's offer; Scotland was a long way from Morocco, but that wasn't an issue for an immortal, beyond the consideration of logistics such as ensuring sufficient victims to sate her Thirst during the journey.

She was Lilith, first and eldest *Nephilim*, Made by Lucifer. She had sent it fleeing thousands of years ago, destroying its kingdom and those loyal to it, all but ending its bloodline. She had hunted it down, finding its wolf-torn body. But she hadn't killed it personally, and that had always rankled. Now she had the chance to face Lucifer again, slay its mortal shell, and send it back to Hell.

The thought pleased her. "Anya, fetch me a pen and paper."

She composed her reply to *Arakiel*, sitting back once it was done, her thoughts wandering to her nemesis.

Lucifer, my Maker. An age ago I destroyed your earthly kingdom and tore your world asunder. Now I'll do so again, with the greatest pleasure.

In Glasgow.

THE END

Acknowledgements

My name appears on the cover, but as always other people helped bring this book about.

Thanks are owed to my wife, Dana, for her unceasing love and encouragement.

Again, to Christine, Shosh and Danny for their help, not least with our daughter Sophie.

To Sophie herself for almost eighteen months of joy.

To Peter, Alison and everyone else at Elsewhen Press for not only publishing *Lord of the Hunt* (and my two previous novels) but also for their work in polishing the text and turning a Word document into a proper book. The turnaround for this novel from acceptance to publication was particularly short, and the hard work put into it is greatly appreciated.

Lastly, a number of 'Westerosi' have consistently bought my books and taken the time to review them. Their support is appreciated. Thanks also to those book reviewers who took a chance on an unknown author, and spent their valuable time reading my work and reviewing it.

David, February 2020

Elsewhen Press

delivering outstanding new talents in speculative fiction

Visit the Elsewhen Press website at elsewhen.press for the latest information on all of our titles, authors and events; to read our blog; find out where to buy our books and ebooks; or to place an order.

Sign up for the Elsewhen Press InFlight Newsletter at elsewhen.press/newsletter

Resurrection Men
The first book of the Sooty Feathers

David Craig

Glasgow 1893.

Wilton Hunt, a student, and Tam Foley, a laudanum-addicted pharmacist, are pursuing extra-curricular careers as body snatchers, or 'resurrection men', under cover of darkness. They exhume a girl's corpse, only for it to disappear while their backs are turned. Confused and in need of the money the body would have earnt them, they investigate the corpse's disappearance. They discover that bodies have started to turn up in the area with ripped-out throats and severe loss of blood, although not the one they lost. The police are being encouraged by powerful people to look the other way, and the deaths are going unreported by the press. As Hunt and Foley delve beneath the veneer of respectable society, they find themselves entangled in a dangerous underworld that is protected from scrutiny by the rich and powerful members of the elite but secretive Sooty Feathers Club.

Meanwhile, a mysterious circus arrives in the middle of the night, summoned to help avenge a betrayal two centuries old…

Resurrection Men is the first book in David Craig's *Sooty Feathers* series, a masterful gothic tale about a supernatural war for control of the Second City of the British Empire, and the struggle of flawed characters of uncertain virtue who try to avert it. It is set in a late 19th century Glasgow ruled by undead – from the private clubs, town houses and country manors of the privileged to the dung-choked wynds and overcrowded slums of the poor. Undead unrest, a fallen angel, and religious zealots intent on driving out the forces of evil, set the stage for a diabolical conflict of biblical proportions.

ISBN: 9781911409366 (epub, kindle) / ISBN: 9781911409267 (400pp paperback)
Visit bit.ly/ResurrectionMen

Thorns of a Black Rose

David Craig

Revenge and responsibility, confrontation and consequences.

A hot desert land of diverse peoples dealing with demons, mages, natural disasters ... and the Black Rose assassins.

On a quest for vengeance, Shukara arrives in the city of Mask having already endured two years of hardship and loss. Her pouch is stolen by Tamira, a young street-smart thief, who throws away some of the rarer reagents that Shukara needs for her magick. Tracking down the thief, and being unfamiliar with Mask, Shukara shows mercy to Tamira in exchange for her help in replacing what has been lost. Together they brave the intrigues of Mask, and soon discover that they have a mutual enemy in the Black Rose, an almost legendary band of merciless assassins. But this is just the start of their journeys...

Although set in an imaginary land, the scenery and peoples of *Thorns of a Black Rose* were inspired by Egypt, Morocco and the Sahara. Mask is a living, breathing city, from the prosperous Merchant Quarter whose residents struggle for wealth and power, to the Poor Quarter whose residents struggle just to survive. It is a coming of age tale for the young thief, Tamira, as well as a tale of vengeance and discovery. There is also a moral ambiguity in the story, with both the protagonists and antagonists learning that whatever their intentions or justification, actions have consequences.

ISBN: 9781911409557 (epub, kindle) / 9781911409458 (256pp paperback)
Visit bit.ly/ThornsOfABlackRose

Working Weekend

Penelope Hill

Sometimes authenticity sucks!

Marcus Holland, European Folklore expert and award-winning writer of Horror and Fantasy fiction, is guest of honour at the CoffinCon convention being held in an old gothic mansion-turned-hotel. He's looking forward to the weekend, as he's hoping for a break from the pressures of work, the enthusiasm of his agent and the demands of his ex-wife. There's to be a midnight masque, a Real Ale bar, and the convention committee have even arranged to have a 'real' vampire wandering the halls, to help add to the atmosphere.

From the moment Marcus arrives he starts to feel uneasy, but can't quite put his finger on the reason why. Although he soon comes to realise what is wrong, he knows he can't broadcast his concerns without being thought insane. Far from being a relaxing break he will be working harder than ever in order to safeguard his friends and fans.

ISBN: 9781911409717 (epub, kindle) / ISBN: 9781911409618 (240pp paperback)

Visit bit.ly/WorkingWeekend

THE MAREK SERIES BY JULIET KEMP
BOOK 1:

THE DEEP AND SHINING DARK
A Locus Recommended Read in 2018

"A rich and memorable tale of political ambition, family and magic, set in an imagined city that feels as vibrant as the characters inhabiting it."

Aliette de Bodard
Nebula-award winning author of *The Tea Master and the Detective*

You know something's wrong when the cityangel turns up at your door
Magic within the city-state of Marek works without the need for bloodletting, unlike elsewhere in Teren, thanks to an agreement three hundred years ago between an angel and the founding fathers. It also ensures that political stability is protected from magical influence. Now, though, most sophisticates no longer even believe in magic *or* the cityangel.

But magic has suddenly stopped working, discovers Reb, one of the two sorcerers who survived a plague that wiped out virtually all of the rest. Soon she is forced to acknowledge that someone has deposed the cityangel without being able to replace it. Marcia, Heir to House Fereno, and one of the few in high society who is well-aware that magic still exists, stumbles across that same truth. But it is just one part of a much more ambitious plan to seize control of Marek.

Meanwhile, city Council members connive and conspire, unaware that they are being manipulated in a dangerous political game. A game that threatens the peace and security not just of the city, but all the states around the Oval Sea, including the shipboard traders of Salina upon whom Marek relies.

To stop the impending disaster, Reb and Marcia, despite their difference in status, must work together alongside the deposed cityangel and Jonas, a messenger from Salina. But first they must discover who is behind the plot, and each of them must try to decide who they can really trust.

ISBN: 9781911409342 (epub, kindle) / ISBN: 9781911409243 (272pp paperback)
Visit bit.ly/DeepShiningDark

BOOK 2:

SHADOW AND STORM
Never trust a demon... or a Teren politician
The annual visit by the Teren Throne's representative, the Lord Lieutenant, is merely a symbolic gesture. But this year the Lieutenant has been unexpectedly replaced and Marcia, Heir to House Fereno, suspects a new agenda.

Teren magic is enabled by bloodletting. A Teren magician will invoke a demon and bind them with blood. But demons are devious and if unleashed are sure to create havoc. The Teren way to stop them involves the letting of more of the magician's blood – often terminally. But if a young magician is being sought by an unleashed demon, their only hope may be to escape to Marek where the cityangel can keep the demon at bay. Probably.

Once again Reb, Cato, Jonas and Beckett must deal with a magical problem, while Marcia must tackle a serious political challenge to Marek's future.

ISBN: 9781911409595 (epub, kindle) / ISBN: 9781911409496 (336pp paperback)
Visit bit.ly/ShadowAndStorm

CAN'T DREAM WITHOUT YOU
FROM THE DARK CHRONICLES

TANYA REIMER

Legends say that tens of thousands of years ago, Whisperers were banished from the heavens, torn in half, and dumped on a mortal realm they didn't understand. Longing for their other half, they went from being powerful immortals to lonely leeches relying on humans to survive. Over the years, they earnt magic from demons, they left themselves Notebooks with hints, and by pairing up with human souls, they eventually found their other halves. Humbled by their experiences, they discovered the true purpose of life and many were worthy of returning to the heavens. But many were not.

The Dark Chronicles are stories that share the heartache of select unworthy Whisperers on their journey to immortality after The War of 2019. *Can't Dream Without You* is one of those stories, in which we meet Steve and Julia, two such heroes.

Steve isn't a normal boy. He plays with demons, his soul travels to a dream realm at night using mystical butterflies, and soon he'll earn the power to raise the dead. Al thinks that destroying him would do the world a favour, yet he just can't kill his own son. Wanting to acquire the power that raises the dead before Steve does, Al performs a ritual on Steve's sixteenth birthday. He transfers Steve's dark magic to Julia, an innocent girl he plans to kill. But Steve is determined to save Julia and sucks her soul to Dreamland. From the dream world, he invokes the help of her brother to keep her safe.

Five years later, Steve can't tell what's real or what's a nightmare. Julia's brother wants to kill him, a strange bald eagle is erasing memories, and Steve's caught in some bizarre bullfight on another realm with a cop hot on his trail looking to be Julia's hero. All the while, Steve and Julia must fight the desperate need to make their steamy dreams a reality.

ISBN: 9781908168924 (epub, kindle) / ISBN: 9781908168825 (288pp paperback)
Visit bit.ly/CantDream

JAPANESE DAISY CHAIN

DAVE WEAVER

In *Japanese Daisy Chain*, Dave Weaver takes us on a very individualistic journey around contemporary Japan through the eyes of the participants in a series of apparently unrelated incidents. Events that, to an outsider may seem a little strange or hard to explain, but to which we are given an exclusive insight – enabling us to see the consequence of contact with the paranormal, fantastic or downright weird. As each episode unfurls and our journey progresses, we alone can see the invisible thread that connects these events, albeit tenuously. A participant on each occasion, a minor character if you will, becomes the main protagonist in the next, creating a human daisy-chain.

Just like a daisy-chain, what goes around comes around. The chain is completed and we finally understand karma.

Though born and raised in the distinctly un-exotic heartlands of Surrey, 'the land of the rising sun' has held a fascination for Dave Weaver since he first visited it with his Japanese wife. A fascination for the beautiful colours of its landscapes and the subtlety of its culture, for its contradictions and certainties, intelligence and passion, spirit and diversity. Yet beneath all these things lies another Japan; one of ghosts and shadows, unspoken secrets, demons from the past and uncertain visions of the future. It's what makes this intriguing country ultimately unknowable, unique, Nippon.

ISBN: 9781908168504 (epub, kindle) / ISBN: 9781908168405 (240pp paperback)
Visit bit.ly/JapaneseDaisyChain

REBECCA HALL's *SYMPHONY OF THE CURSED* TRILOGY

INSTRUMENT OF PEACE

Raised in the world-leading Academy of magic rather than by his absentee parents, Mitch has come to see it as his home. He's spent more time with his friends than his family and the opinion of his maths teacher matters far more than that of his parents. His peaceful life is shattered when a devastating earthquake strikes and almost claims his little brother's life. But this earthquake is no natural phenomenon, it's a result of the ongoing war between Heaven and Hell. To protect the Academy, one of the teachers makes an ill-advised contract with a fallen angel, unwittingly bringing down The Twisted Curse on staff and students.

Even as they struggle to rebuild the school, things begin to go wrong. The curse starts small, with truancy, incomplete assignments, and negligent teachers over-reacting to minor transgressions, but it isn't long before the bad behaviour escalates to vandalism, rioting and attempted murder. As they succumb to the influence of the curse, Mitch's friends drift away and his girlfriend cheats on him. When the first death comes, Mitch unites with the only other students who, like him, appear to be immune to the curse; together they are determined to find the cause of the problem and stop it.

INSTRUMENT OF WAR

"A clever update to a magical school story with a twist." – Christopher Nuttall

The Angels are coming.

The Host wants to know what the Academy was trying to hide and why the Fallen agreed to it. They want the Instrument of War, the one thing that can tip the Eternity War in their favour and put an end to the stalemate. Any impact on the Academy staff, students or buildings is just collateral damage.

Mitch would like to forget that the last year ever happened, but that doesn't seem likely with Little Red Riding Hood now teaching Teratology. The vampire isn't quite as terrifying as he first thought, but she's not the only monster at the Academy. The Fallen are spying on everyone, the new Principal is an angel and there's an enchanting exchange student with Faerie blood.

Angry and nervous of the angels surrounding him, Mitch tries to put the pieces together. He knows that Hayley is the Archangel Gabriel. He knows that she can determine the course of the Eternity War. He also knows that the Fallen will do anything to hide Gabriel from the Host – even allowing an innocent girl to be kidnapped.

INSTRUMENT OF CHAOS

The long hidden heart of the Twisted Curse had been found, concealed in a realm that no angel can enter, where magic runs wild and time is just another direction. The Twisted Curse is the key to ending the Eternity War and it can only be broken by someone willing to traverse the depths of Faerie.

Unfortunately, Mitch has other things on his mind. For reasons that currently escape him he's going to university, making regular trips to the Netherworld and hunting down a demon. The Academy might have prepared him for university but Netherworlds and demons were inexplicably left off the curriculum, not to mention curse breaking.

And then the Angels return, and this time they're hunting his best friend.

Visit bit.ly/SymphonyCursed

Now available as audiobooks from Tantor

[Re]Awakenings

AN ANTHOLOGY OF NEW SPECULATIVE FICTION
• ALISON BUCK • NEIL FAARID • GINGERLILY •
• ROBIN MORAN • PR POPE • ALEXANDER SKYE •
• PETER WOLFE •

[Re]Awakenings are the starting points for life-changing experiences; a new plane of existence, an alternate reality or cyber-reality. This genre-spanning anthology of new speculative fiction explores that theme with a spectrum of tales, from science fiction to fantasy to paranormal; in styles from clinically serious to joyfully silly. As you read through them all, and you must read all of them, you will discover along the way that stereo-typical distinctions between the genres within speculative fiction are often arbitrary and unhelpful. You will be taken on an emotional journey through a galaxy of sparkling fiction; you will laugh, you will cry; you will consider timeless truths and contemplate eternal questions.

All of life is within these pages, from birth to death (and in some cases beyond). In all of these stories, most of them specifically written for this anthology, the short story format has been used to great effect. If you haven't already heard of some of these authors, you soon will as they are undoubtedly destined to become future stars in the speculative fiction firmament. Remember, you read them here first!

[Re]Awakenings is a collection of short stories from exciting new voices in UK speculative fiction, compiled by guest editor PR Pope. It contains the following stories: Alison Buck: *Dreamers*; *Intervention*; *Mirror mirror*; *Podcast*. Neil Faarid: *The Adventures of Kit Brennan: Kidnapped!* Gingerlily: *The Dragon and the Rose*. Robin Moran: *The Merry Maiden Wails*. PR Pope: *Afterlife*; *Courtesy Bodies*, *On the Game*. Alexander Skye: *BlueWinter*, *Dreaming Mars*, *Exploring the Heavens*, *Worth it*. Peter Wolfe: *If you go into the woods today…*

ISBN: 9781908168108 (epub, kindle) / ISBN: 9781908168009 (288pp paperback)
Visit bit.ly/ReAwakenings

About David Craig

Aside from three months living on an oil tanker sailing back and forth between America and Africa, and two years living in a pub, David Craig grew up on the west coast of Scotland. He studied Software Engineering at university, but lost interest in the subject after (and admittedly prior to) graduation. He currently works as a resourcing administrator for a public service contact centre, and lives near Glasgow with his wife, daughter and two rabbits.

Being a published writer had been a life-long dream, and one that he was delighted to finally realise with his debut novel, *Resurrection Men*, the first in the *Sooty Feathers* series, published by Elsewhen Press in 2018. *Thorns of a Black Rose* was David's second novel, also published by Elsewhen Press. He returns to the *Sooty Feathers* series with *Lord of the Hunt*.